ELEANOR COURTOWN

Lucy E. M. Black

ELEANOR COURTOWN

Lucy E. M. Black

Seraphim
EDITIONS

The publisher gratefully acknowledges the financial assistance of the Canada Council for the Arts and the Ontario Arts Council.

Canada Council   Conseil des arts
for the Arts   du Canada

ONTARIO ARTS COUNCIL
CONSEIL DES ARTS DE L'ONTARIO
an Ontario government agency
un organisme du gouvernement de l'Ontario

Library and Archives Canada Cataloguing in Publication

Black, Lucy E. M., 1957-, author
    Eleanor Courtown / Lucy E.M. Black.

ISBN 978-1-927079-48-5 (softcover)

    I. Title.

PS8603.L2555E44 2017   C813'.6   C2017-905819-3

Editor: Richard Van Holst, Karen Alliston
Design and Typography: Rolf Busch
Author photograph: Jonathan van Bilsen

Published in 2017 by
Seraphim Editions
4456 Park Street
Niagara Falls, ON
L2E 2P6

Printed and bound in Canada

to the love of my life, my very own Doctor

Chapter the First
MORTIFICATION

Suffering has come upon me and my strength and senses are both dissipating. Waves of nausea and vigorous tremors shake my frame. I am troubled by all manner of violent contractions. The furnishings spin about the room. I wonder if I shall ever ride again in the park or climb the rocks on my beloved Wexford shore.

Mr. Carey has been uncommonly kind and serves me hot broth and thin gruel for nourishment. I cannot make out his character. I wonder that Lily has aligned herself with someone whose status is so inferior to her own. And yet, like a mongrel dog, he bides with her as a ferocious protector and has kept her safe during a time of desperate need. He is no match for her in beauty, fortune, or connection, and yet he has some small amount of charm and wit, and may still, perhaps, prove himself worthy of the match.

It is several days since I have been well enough to complete my small routines. For much of the day I remain above stairs, confined to this small chamber and in wretched discomfort. Fever dampens my brow and gown, and the water I pass is brackish. Lily would have Mr. Clement ride for the Doctor, but I am not eager for his ministrations. He is an impatient and proud man, so sure of his own opinions that I am often provoked. He cautioned me against this direction and I do not wish him satisfied in his low opinion of my judgment.

~ Diary, October 5, 1870

The poisoning is when my course became clear. I shall set down these remembrances so that you understand the treachery which transpired. My sweet Daughter is asleep beside me on the grassy verge as I recollect these events. My adventures having led me to this place, I intend to record, for her benefit, my entire story. The tale began in Ireland and has ended here in Orange Hill, Canada.

In June of 1870 I left my home in Wexford to join my beloved Cousin, Lilian Courtown-McDonough. She and her new husband, Rowland McDonough, had earlier set sail with their trunks packed and full of dreams. Rowland, having served with distinction as a member of the Royal Irish Rifles in India, had been offered a land grant in the Dominion of Canada. Lily convinced him that they would do well in a new country, and that they should lay claim to the land. Rowland was unwilling, but I suspect that Lily used her charms to persuade him, for as the youngest of the McDonough sons, his portion of the estate would not have afforded them a generous income. In truth, Ireland had little to offer, with so many good families struggling in reduced circumstances.

Lily was as a Sister to me, her Father and mine being brothers, and our Mothers, both of whom had passed when we were young girls, being themselves cousins. People always commented on our likeness and mistook us for true sisters. We were similar in our manner and appearance, with long dark hair, blue eyes, small frames, and clear complexions. Although we resemble the Kavanaughs, some would say that our temperaments were pure Courtown. I confess that we were both of us wilful, determined, and fond of new experiences, and no doubt it is that character which has very nearly ended my life as well as destroying Lily's.

Father and I went to the docks to say our farewells to Lily and Rowland. It was a scene of great confusion, with dogs barking, pigs squealing, and crowds of people pressing against us. The smells were putrid; I was forced to hold a perfumed handkerchief to my face. Lily, though, was a vision of bravery and beauty both. The excitement had coloured her cheeks and her eyes were shining brightly as she took in her surroundings. Her travelling costume consisted of a heavy fur-lined cloak, pinned with Rowland's large brooch, over a matching gown. She clung to me quite passionately and begged a promise of me to follow her soon after. "My true Sister," she whispered, "you must know that as I leave you my heart is rent, and will be healed only when we are once more together."

I knew that Father would not grant his consent for such a journey, but I boldly committed myself nonetheless. Father always believed that Lily's actions were impetuous; he felt that Uncle had failed in his duty to instill in her the need for caution and discretion.

I wept at our parting. I could not help but notice, however, that Lily did not shed a tear; she had become impatient with the excitement and her eagerness to get on board. It was cold and just beginning daybreak when she took Rowland by the arm and guided him up the rough boards forming a bridge to the steam tug that would take them to their ship. I thought my breath would stop I was so overcome with grief. I will never forget Lily's proud carriage as she navigated the crowds, holding on to her Husband. Although I was devastated by the parting, I determined that I would keep my promise and join them once they were established.

Rowland died of ship's fever during the crossing. Lily wrote that they sewed him shut in canvas and tipped him into the ocean, and that the Captain said a prayer. Thereafter Lily stayed mostly on the deck, keeping to the spot where Rowland went over the side. Her grieving in the open probably saved her health; that's what Robert has said.

Lily was alone, and terribly sad and frightened. She didn't eat for fully three days, but then the ladies aboard ship, learning of her delicate condition, forced her to take nourishment for the child's sake. She had Rowland's claim and all of their goods, but she was only half the way to a new land. I received her distressing brief a full month after Rowland died, and began furtive negotiations to follow her.

Mrs. Stevens, the gentlewoman employed as my companion, was easily persuaded to travel to London, where I contrived a visit with my second cousin, Charles Kavanaugh, and his daughters. I had often spent a month in their pleasant company, and so my proposal did not seem at all untoward. Mrs. Stevens, an appreciator of the fine arts, welcomed an opportunity to visit the collections at South Kensington Museum and the British Museum in Bloomsbury. She commenced immediately to order our trunks ready, and began an examination of the state of our gowns.

I did not much like deceiving her in this way, but my Father had left me no recourse. When I had confronted him about Lily's situation, he dismissed me, saying that it was "McDonough business now." Uncle had visited the McDonoughs' estate at Mourne Abbey and demanded they make arrangements for her, but that meeting had not gone well and Uncle left dissatisfied. Nonetheless, it was my Father's way to seize upon a decision and hold fast to it. He had decided that Lily's fate was now in the hands of her Husband's family, and I knew that I could not convince him otherwise.

Father would, of course, have forbidden me to go had he known, and so I conspired in secret. After making discreet enquiries, I discovered that no permission was needed to leave my homeland. Sullie, my lady's maid, was the only one I dared take into my confidence. When she understood the full direction of my plans, she begged that I take her with me. Her reasoning and affection were such that I did not question the wisdom of taking an unmarried girl as my second travelling companion. She and I planned together and made our travel arrangements quietly, as the loyalty of the staff to Father was such that I dreaded discovery, knowing with certainty that they would report all to him.

Sullie's brother, Flurry, we also took into our confidence, as his assistance was vital to our journey. My Father, I knew, would be absent from the estate for several days' duration. Therefore, on the day appointed, I breakfasted with him and then hurried to the drive where Sullie and Flurry, along with the unsuspecting Mrs. Stevens, waited in a carriage. I could not speak, for a large lump had formed in my throat that choked me completely. Flurry drove us to the train station in Wexford where we parted quickly, not wanting to linger lest we encounter acquaintances. The train took us to Dublin and from there to Belfast and on again to Londonderry.

Excited by our adventure and the many new sights, Sullie was a most agreeable companion. I had to caution her to keep close, as I did not wish for us to become separated. When we arrived in Londonderry we were accosted by a throng of beggars wanting to take charge of our baggage. Fortunately, a gentleman noticed our distress and enlisted a porter to come to our aid. Such situations were a little frightening to me but did not alter my resolve.

At four o'clock in the morning of our second day in Londonderry, we set out for the harbour by van with many other women and children. The men were expected to walk. The ship was majestic, imposing in size and with life boats suspended around the sides. Dozens of men seemed to be swarming all over it, engaged in intense labours. We watched as trunks and baggage were caught up in ropes and slung by machinery from the dock to the ship. The stench, however, was most vile and left us feeling sickened.

While we observed the final loading of the hold, steerage passengers were made to line up and were given bed rolls and cans and plates and forks. Mrs. Stevens, Sullie, and I determined that we should find the group of first-class passengers and prepare to leave dry land. I was excitable and felt stimulated by the many new sights. Sullie was hovering very near to me; she began to look tremulous and fearful. I confess that both of us were shivering a little with the cold morning air and the overwhelming sense of our daring. Mrs. Stevens, meanwhile, plagued me with questions about our passage. I assured her that this ship was far grander than the ones that sailed from Belfast and that our journey would be only the slightest bit lengthier in duration. She was a good and trusting soul and wanted to believe me, but my unwillingness to show her our tickets had aroused suspicion.

Presently a steward approached and helped us to embark, leading us to a salon aboard ship where we were served a breakfast of hot rolls and butter and tea. It was by then six o'clock, and we ate heartily of this repast. Afterwards we were directed to our cabins. Mine was the tiniest room possible; it was quite filled with two bunks, our trunks, and a compact arrangement for washing and dressing. There were closets at Rosslare Hall far grander and better appointed than this cabin, and yet, determined to enjoy myself, I laughed merrily at the diminutive proportions and assured myself that if this was the worst trial of my adventure, I would be well able to meet adversity. I could not have known how sorely I was to be tested. Mrs. Stevens was in an adjoining cabin of equally diminutive proportions, and had become pensive with worry.

We were still below deck, in our small closets, when the ship's engine began to rumble and growl. It was as though a fantastical dragon had awakened in its bowels and was now thrashing to escape. Mrs. Stevens would not leave her chamber, so Sullie and I went above stairs and saw the whirlpool of water surging at the stern. Hundreds of people crowded the deck, waving handkerchiefs, as we slowly moved away from our dear country and glided forward into the unknown sea.

The momentum of the ship accelerated gradually but mastered an even speed after only a short while. We navigated parallel to the shore, where I could see a train travelling, I thought, far faster than the ship. Parties of people drifted off together. Sullie and I were among the last passengers clinging to the rail, greedily taking in what we recognized to be our last view of Ireland.

For luncheon we were given a selection of hot fowls and beautiful pies of all kinds; champagne was served in liberality, and fine port and claret were also to be had. Among our party were a newly married couple, a gentlemanly young man, and some Americans. Captain Edwards introduced himself, and although his face was covered with unkempt whiskers, he seemed kindly.

It was during the course of our luncheon that Mrs. Stevens gleaned the truth about our travel plans. She was conversing with another passenger when I saw her become agitated and put down her cutlery. She turned in her chair, while grasping the table's edge, and demanded that her table partner repeat her words. Placing her napkin upon the table, she excused herself and came to stand by my side. "I believe, my Lady, that we have made a grave error. I request that you join me at your earliest convenience." She swept from the room in a rustle of angry black sateen, my heart sinking at her displeasure. I made my excuses and joined her below. She left me in no way unsure of her feelings. Our conversation filled me with shame, for I had an affection for Mrs. Stevens and was sorry to have deceived her. There was another whom I had also not treated well, and I was sorry to think what pangs of emotion he might feel by my hasty departure.

The first two days were very fine steaming and passed without further incident. On the third day, as we moved further from the coast, large waves and strong winds began to buffet the ship. Land disappeared from our sight and we were suddenly alone, surrounded in all directions by the wildness of an angry sea. As the ship rocked and pitched in the rough water, I fancied we were being rejected as unnatural by the forces that control all of nature. As though by design, many passengers became violently ill at the same instant. Sullie and I returned to our closet and lay still upon our bunks, hoping for our own nausea to subside. The steerage was directly beneath our cabin and we could hear the belching and retching of those below us, along with the crying of babies and children.

In the morning we were attended by a maid, who held us upright while we dressed and completed a hasty toilette. In this way our good humour was restored; we were able once again to walk on deck to enjoy the fine breeze and cool air.

The following Sunday, an English service and sermon was conducted by Captain Edwards in the grand salon. We met a vivacious Miss Julia Taylor and her sister, Miss Amelia Taylor, who were travelling to Montreal with their brother. Sullie formed an acquaintance with a young man from Donegal. I was not in favour of such associations.

Mrs. Stevens continued to be unsociable and morose, spending much time alone in her chamber. And yet many entertainments were to be had each day. A gymnastic apparatus, rigged up on the quarter-deck, provided amusement and exercise for the young men. There were diverse games for the children, which their parents closely supervised, as there was much concern lest a child fall overboard—ropes had been threaded around the decks as a precaution, but these provided some small security. Meal times too were often quite diverting.

A sudden lurch of the ship would easily dislodge the roast and send it flying to the floor, where it rolled at our feet, often followed by the sauce boats and cutlery. We learned to manage our own place settings with dexterity, but much fine china and crystal was lost in this manner. In the afternoons we gathered in the small salon for card games, and reading materials were shared amongst us. After our dinner, concerts were held in the grand salon, with passengers providing entertainment. Hymns were sung before retiring for the evening.

One afternoon, after a week at sea, we heard a great commotion, and even Mrs. Stevens condescended to join us on deck, where we saw the most magnificent sight. An iceberg floated in the sea very near to us; the sun shone upon it, making it radiant with a bright light. Sea gulls squawked and flew in all directions about us, making a welcome din. Very late that same evening, Captain Edwards invited a group of us to join him outside for what he termed "a view of the northern lights." It was a magical display, an unworldly flickering of green and purple and yellow lights that seemed to dance in the heavens. I stood in awe, attempting to feature what curtain had been lifted to show us this spectacle.

Sullie was often parted from us during the last several days aboard ship. Not being a great reader, the quiet of the small salon was not diverting for her. She had instead befriended people in steerage and spent much time in their company, an arrangement I did not much mind, as she remained considerate of my needs and was very careful not to take liberties.

Mrs. Stevens, however, continued to abuse me throughout our journey. Fearing she would be "eaten by bears," she refused to entertain the idea of travelling further with me once we reached Montreal. My Father, she was certain, would expect her to force my immediate return to Ireland. Mrs. Stevens asked that I not place her in the unforgivable dilemma of either returning without me or forfeiting her life by remaining my companion. She wrung her hands continually until I saw that the skin had become quite chafed and was beginning to crack and bleed. My offer of a salve from my toilette kit was refused. Mrs. Stevens's unhappiness left me despondent, and yet I felt certain that the menfolk had abandoned my Cousin, and that I must be the one to find and sustain her.

On the fourteenth day we arrived at the Island of Montreal. I was not sorry to leave our floating home as I felt much eagerness to continue my journey. Several first-class passengers disembarked with us, and upon their suggestion, we took a carriage to the Ottawa Hotel on Great St. James Street. The rooms were beautifully fitted in a modern style and the proprietor was most obliging. From the window in our room we could see the harbour, a market, and some very fine rapids.

Sullie had lately become morose and would wonder aloud about the well-being of her newly formed friends. Obsessed as I was with my desire to locate Lily, I confess that I was not sympathetic to her change in spirits.

The proprietor of the Hotel, a very pleasant English gentleman, had suggested to me that an advertisement in the *Gazette* would be the most expedient way to commence my enquiries. I duly wrote an advertisement, and set out to navigate my way to the newspaper office so that I might place it in the paper. Sullie accompanied me, but continued to sigh and contemplate her thoughts in poor humour.

We were not long established in our Hotel before Mrs. Stevens made enquiries about return passage to Ireland. She presented me with the details and pressed me to return with her on the next leaving. I was sorry to be the source of her distress, but I would not waver. I assured her that I would advertise for another companion at once. I did not know that this undertaking would be far more difficult than at home.

Mrs. Stevens had been retained by my Father when I returned from Mistress O'Halloran's Ladies School. She was a widowed lady whose family came from Mayo. Her Husband, she once told me, was a young Surgeon who had set sail for Australia and never returned. She believed he was killed by pestilence but had never had confirmation, and so was left both bereaved and unsatisfied.

I had assumed that an advertisement in the paper would produce a number of similarly genteel companions, with letters attesting to their character, and that I could simply select from the lot an agreeable and compliant substitute. In this, as in many other such convictions, I was sadly mistaken.

Mrs. Stevens and I parted badly at the end. Sullie, uncharacteristically distraught, wept as though at a funeral. Mrs. Stevens's own tears were intermingled with dithering and fuss-making. "What, my Lady, am I to tell your dear Father?" was the subject of her litany; I grew weary of answering her patiently. Having already bade her to take him my love, I thought at the last to send with her a letter absolving her of any wrongdoing or foreknowledge of my scheme. I hoped, in this way, to shield her from my Father's temper. A longer letter, begging his forgiveness, I delayed writing. Finally Mrs. Stevens boarded the ship, and despite her many tearful entreaties and genuine distress, I could not help but be relieved.

When Sullie and I returned to the Hotel in mid-afternoon, a Mr. Hugh O'Donnell was waiting for us in its small lobby. Sullie's face brightened when she saw him, and I understood then what it was that had so affected my companion. He had, he told us, secured lodgings for himself closer to the harbour, and had come to check on our situation; he asked Sullie whether she might step out with him for a walk about the city. Sullie did not return until it was time to retire, and she then led me to understand how it was between them.

Hugh O'Donnell called for Sullie each morning, and they each began to search for employment. Hugh, a strongly built man, intended to secure a position in labour. Sullie was searching for a position as a maid. The prospect of losing Sullie was a little oppressive to me. She was my last direct connection with Rosslare Hall, and her loyalty afforded me some small measure of security. I worried that I might become solitary and easy prey for persons of disreputable stature.

However, the Hotel proprietor, a most obliging man, assured me that a great many ladies were in need of honest work. He proposed that, for a small fee, he would assemble for my choosing a group of such, and arrange the introductions. I saw the expediency of this arrangement and sanctioned the experiment.

On the appointed afternoon, Sullie and I were established in a small parlour and the proprietor began his small parade of candidates. None were suitable. I could not imagine retaining the company of such coarsened persons, who had neither a history of good houses nor a knowledge of the rightness of things. I did not wish to be overly difficult, but it seemed then that to choose an untrained female for such a position would be to lessen my stature. Far better to wait for an appropriate companion, I reasoned, than to choose one so obviously unsuited.

Sightseeing activities and long walks became a way to fill the hours. The proprietor kindly suggested places that I might find of interest and drew me intricate little maps so that I might walk to and fro safely, and without confusion.

Several days were spent contentedly in this way. Then, at once, two significant events took place. Hugh found employment for both himself and Sullie in a great house outside of Montreal. Lodgings were provided; they were to commence their duties within the week. I gave them a small gift of coin for their wedding present, and they parted from me in great spirits. Sullie did weep a little at our last farewell, clinging to me and kissing me sweetly, but she was happy to be marrying Hugh and her tears did not last long, I think.

Then, the very day of Sullie's leaving, I was summoned to the front desk where an officer of her Majesty's Navy stood waiting; he introduced himself and said that he had information for me in response to my advertisement in the *Gazette*. On the *Lord Melbourne* crossing, he told me, there had been a Lilian McDonough, who was widowed at sea. She was now married to a rich miner by the name of Carey; they had left to claim land somewhere near Port Gibson, in the south of Ontario.

Lily remarried? Before even a few months of mourning had passed? This seemed strange to me. Yet I was overwhelmingly relieved to hear word of my Cousin, and was determined to reunite with her as soon as I could. The Hotel proprietor assured me that a train would take me directly to Port Gibson, and that several respectable establishments could be found near the station upon my arrival.

When I boarded the train, the first compartment I entered was occupied by a smartly dressed gentleman. I bade him "good day," and would have sat down across from him, but his manners seemed overfriendly and his countenance florid. I excused myself immediately and went to the next compartment, which I shared with an older lady. As the train made its way westwards, I gazed upon many views of forests and of small farms dotting the riverbeds; the river itself seemed very wide and very long.

The lady, meanwhile, had introduced herself as Mrs. Hattie Johnson. She was recently widowed, she told me, and was travelling to Port Gibson to take up residence with her son. Mrs. Johnson solicited my opinion as to how best to respond if she found that her daughter-in-law had arranged the household in a fashionable style rather than one which provided comfort and ease to its occupants. No one, she told me, could be expected to sleep in a northern room with the winter pounding a gale upon the window glass.

"I am confident," I assured her, "that your daughter-in-law will provide you with the best comforts any daughter can provide her mother, and that you will live together agreeably for a long time."

I was, in truth, not at all sure of such a thing, and yet I could not bear to see my companion fret for the rest of her journey. I hoped my words would calm and succour her.

When we arrived at Port Gibson, and after I had taken a prolonged leave of Mrs. Johnson, I was surprised by the industry of the small port and by the number of fine buildings. I settled into a large Hotel, where again I advertised in the newspaper, enquiring as to the welfare and whereabouts of my Cousin. Ten days passed, during which time I began to grow both concerned and impatient. I berated myself for the fool's errand I had set myself and thought how many better ways there might have been of securing my goal, had I only waited and consulted more carefully.

Finally, a letter arrived written in my fair Cousin's hand. I was gladdened by the sight of it and stood at the reception desk to read its contents. The letter read as follows:

> To those enquiring after Mrs. Lilian McDonough, née Courtown, formerly of Wexford, Ireland, I am Lilian Carey, being recently married to Mr. Jack Carey. I was widowed of ill-fated Rowland McDonough while crossing from Ireland on the Lord Melbourne. If you have news regarding me or my family or any business dealings so to do, I beg that you write by return mail, care of Doctor Rob't. Stewart, Esquire, Orange Hill. With sincere obligation, I am yours most truly, Lilian Carey

It was news of Lily at last, and I was overcome. I made immediate enquiries in the town, determining that a coach and driver could be hired to take me directly to Orange Hill, and that a good Inn with clean rooms could be engaged once I was located there. Staff at the Hotel were able to secure a stage coach to Orange Hill but were unable to engage a maid to accompany me. I felt the incivility of this strange place and resolved not to be downcast by it.

On the day I was to depart, a thin man, dressed in a threadbare black suit, stood waiting outside the Hotel for me, holding a grimy hat in one hand and a pipe in the other. "What ya be wanting to do with Orange Hill?" he asked me abruptly.

"To seek my dear Cousin; I have travelled this long way to see her."

"Well den, ya best be comin' wi' me," he answered. "It's a full day hard on 'ta road. Ge' yer trunks t'gether."

Shaking and bumping cruelly, the crude coach, with only a rough board seat and wool rug, drove from mid-morning to late afternoon. My frame ached terribly from the activity. We stopped mid-day at a shabby establishment, where I was nonetheless grateful for a hot bowl of soup.

Finally, I was ceremoniously deposited at the Orange Hill Inn along with my two large trunks and several bags. The proprietor and his good wife insisted on showing me to my room and brought me warm water for washing. Fatigued after my long travelling, I was grateful for such small kindnesses.

The McLenaghans, as the Innkeeper and his wife were called, informed me that Doctor Stewart also took lodgings at the Inn and would return at some point in the evening. I asked them if they had heard of Mr. and Mrs. Jack Carey, but they could not feature who I meant. I was somewhat puzzled, but thought it more politic to ask questions in the later evening of Doctor Stewart, the very man to whom Lily had directed all enquiries.

I passed an hour in my room, resting first and then exchanging my dusty travelling outfit for a clean gown. I missed having Sullie dress my hair and thought that I must soon again make enquiries for a companion and maid. When I entered the parlour a cheerful fire was burning in the grate, although none too hot, and a gentleman was seated reading the paper with a small glass of sherry. I stood for a moment at the door, waiting for him to note my presence and invite me into the common area, then cleared my throat quietly so as to further draw his attention. He looked up from his reading straightaway and said, "Miss Courtown?"

"Yes," I said, entering the room, crossing to stand before him, and dipping into a modest curtsey.

"Robert Stewart at your service, Miss Courtown," he said, standing immediately and bowing as was proper. He stopped at that and gave me a quick inspection, taking in my hair and costume and looking back to my face. "I trust the McLenaghans have made you comfortable."

"Thank you," I said simply. "They have been most kind."

"Will you take a drop with me?" he asked, indicating a cut-glass decanter of sherry and small glasses set nearby on a tray. He was a Scot; the brogue was still evident in his speech. Although he was not a very old man, he was not young either. His face was quite ugly, with an unnaturally large brow and an over-large mouth. His red hair was long and untamed. He wore a rough tweed suit and clean shirt. All of him looked rumpled and in need of a brush and a trim, yet his manners demonstrated time spent in good society.

I sat with him in the parlour, and, as soon as I deemed it polite, asked him for news of Mrs. Carey.

"I can take you there in the morning," he offered. "I have a patient to see and it would not be out of my way."

"Thank you," I said again. "But will you not tell me how she is? Is their estate prosperous?"

He gathered in these questions and then responded with careful words. "Mrs. Carey is doing well enough. This is perhaps no the life she is accustomed to."

I sensed a reluctance on his part to speak freely, and began to feel that perhaps not all was well. "Tell me true," I pressed. "I have come this long way to be united with her again."

"I think," he said slowly, "you must decide that for yourself when you see her."

"How did you first make her acquaintance?" I asked.

"I treated Mrs. Carey for an ailment when she first arrived; I am sure she will tell you. Perhaps," he added, "we might talk about your travel adventures." Thus did Doctor Stewart skillfully redirect the subject, and we conversed in a friendly way until Mrs. McLenaghan called us to dinner. As the two of us were the only guests staying at the Inn, Mr. and Mrs. McLenaghan made free to sit at table with us; they entered into the conversation as though we all held the same station. They were kindly individuals and did not mean to be so forward, I thought. It is perhaps the way here in this new country.

After dinner, a heavy meal consisting of Colcannon and a sweet plum cake, Doctor Stewart asked if I would like to take a turn with him in the village. As I had determined him to be a gentleman, I collected my stole, and we walked out together. The village was a sweet place with a long row of wooden cottages, a bank, a dry goods store, a post office within a general store, and two churches. Signs posted at some of the houses advertised a Weaver, a Tailor, and a Wagon-Maker. At the edge of town was a school built of a log construction. We walked past the churchyards to a small mill and Blacksmith's shop, and past that again to a lovely road cut through the trees. Doctor Stewart was agreeable company. While I travelled beside him I had not to look directly at his protruding brow and could enjoy his discourse without being distracted by his disagreeable appearance.

He told me that he had trained in Edinburgh, and to quickly make his fortune, had taken the job of ship's Doctor on a convict ship to Australia. He had not enjoyed the experience, and therefore, upon returning to England several years later, had taken a position on an immigrant ship bound for the Canadas. Deciding to establish his own practice, he had come to Orange Hill and was now working to build a Surgery of his own. I, in turn, continued the recital of my small travel adventures and spoke to him of my beloved Father from whom I had hidden all details of my journey, knowing that he would not permit me to leave.

The light had long since faded and we were required to return to the Inn with the dark surrounding us. We had walked several miles, with Doctor Stewart congratulating me several times on my ability to keep up. It was fortunate that I had worn my laced boots with their thick soles, and so did not feel so much the stones and uneven ground. Although he had resisted giving me any information about Mrs. Carey's well-being, I otherwise found him most obliging.

The next morning I wakened early and made haste to fasten my trunks and put together my bags. After I dressed carefully, choosing my smartest blue day gown, I went downstairs to breakfast; I saw that the McLenaghans and the Doctor were partaking of an early meal together. The room grew quiet when I entered, and I surmised that either I or the Careys had been the subject of their discourse. Mrs. McLenaghan jumped up guiltily to pour me tea while Mr. McLenaghan passed me a plate heavy with sausages and potatoes. The informality of their arrangements seemed indecorous, but after hesitating only a moment, I sat down and prepared to fortify myself.

Mrs. McLenaghan asked Doctor Stewart if she should expect us both back for dinner that evening. She looked at him with affection, I thought, and remarked that a leg of lamb was at the ready. He had only to say the word and she would commit it to the pot.

"Oh, no," I interjected, "I won't be returning to the Inn." All three turned to look at me with surprise. "I intend to stay with Mrs. Carey and her husband," I continued. "It wouldn't be proper for me to remain here when I have family close by. They will insist upon it."

The three were silent again, exchanging quick glances. Doctor Stewart spoke first. "Perhaps, Miss Courtown, it might be best if you made your visit first and returned another day when you have had the lay of things."

"Oh tosh," I responded impatiently, "I've travelled this long way to see my dear Cousin, and I don't expect other than that she will be quite overcome to greet me."

"Begging your pardon, Miss Courtown," said Mr. McLenaghan, "but maybe the Doctor speaks good sense. Leave your things here and prepare to come back for one night at least."

"And when you're sure you wish to stay with your Cousin, Dear," added Mrs. McLenaghan, "Mr. McLenaghan will drive your trunks over in the evening, once Doctor Stewart brings us word."

This seemed to me to be a reasonable although unnecessary compromise, and I reluctantly agreed. The McLenaghans and Doctor Stewart were kindly but had no understanding of the bond between me and my Cousin or of what was proper with single ladies travelling on their own. I noted to myself that I must include this in an aside to Lily. Their solicitude was touching even as it was ludicrous.

I gathered a few things in my smaller carpet bag, including for Lily a small present of good Irish linen, enough for a large table covering and napkins. There were other things besides—a new lace stole

I had spied in Montreal and a small handful of Irish pebbles from the beach at home. I had nothing prepared for her new Husband, however, and so I begged leave of the Doctor for a moment in order to purchase some tobacco.

Doctor Stewart accompanied me into the general store, and engaged in conversation with a couple of gentlemen there before us. I saw that he was well thought of by these men and that he, in turn, made easy with them. He was a strange man, I thought. Mannered and educated, but not uncomfortable with those beneath his station. He seemed rather to relish a lack of propriety.

After I made my modest purchase, Doctor Stewart gave me his hand and helped me into his buggy. It was a comfortable equipage, with wind shields at the sides which he carefully fastened. He, or Mrs. McLenaghan, had thought to add warm wool spreads, and these he carefully laid out around my skirt as we set off. I was so very excited that I chattered on about nothing in particular. Doctor Stewart was, by contrast, quite morose.

"Are you thinking of your day's work, Doctor, while I am just prattling?" I asked.

"No precisely, Miss Courtown. I am thinking that Mrs. Carey might have wished warning of your visit. I should have ridden over to give her notice."

"Oh, no. I should never have allowed that!" I exclaimed. "The surprise of it all will be half the pleasure."

"I am no much for surprises, Miss Courtown. I hope this one goes as you have planned."

I did not trouble to answer him. He could be most disagreeable, I thought. No wonder he was yet an unmarried gentleman. Despite his friendly manner, his countenance had not improved upon acquaintance and I still thought him quite grotesque.

"I hope that I have not offended you, Miss Courtown. I am concerned about both you and Mrs. Carey. I am not sure that you will find everything as it may have been at home."

"Thank you for your concern, Doctor Stewart," I responded stiffly. "But I am certain my Cousin's Husband will bid me welcome and that my Cousin will see me looked after. There cannot be any cause for worry."

Shortly thereafter we turned down a grassy lane and began driving towards a small compound of roughly built buildings. I believed that the Doctor had decided to make his patient call before going on to the Careys', and so I remained in the buggy when we stopped. The Doctor sprang from his seat. "We're here, Miss Courtown," he said quietly. He reached for the spread and began to fold it. "Give me your hand." Very gently he helped me down and I looked around in wonder.

"Are we stopping first on a medical visit?" I asked.

"No, we are now at the Careys."

"But where is the house?"

I saw two men making their way towards us and moved closer to the Doctor, not sure what I was hearing or seeing. My heart began to beat rapidly and I became quickly frightened.

"Jack," he called. "I've brought someone to meet your Wife. This is Miss Courtown. She is your Wife's Cousin and has come from Ireland." One of the farm hands came towards me.

"Well, is that so?" he said, peering at my face. "Well then. Welcome, Cousin." He bowed deeply. I had not forgotten my manners, and although feeling wary, curtseyed in response.

"Imagine my joy," he said, grinning broadly at the Doctor. "Mrs. Carey will be deeply gratified and have no end of pleasure."

Jack Carey was very tall and quite elegant, with fine features. He radiated confidence and continued to smile and grin at us in a show of goodwill that was most obliging. His overall presentation was that of studied charm. Yet there was something I discerned in his posturing that seemed unnatural. Although he was dressed as a gentleman, he had recently been engaged in manual labour; his hands and shirt front and cuffs demonstrated the marks of his work. His long, tapered fingers wore several ornate rings, and this also struck me. I could not make him out.

Doctor Stewart came close behind me and put his hand on my arm, steadying me. I felt him there but did not mind the forwardness just then. "Will you oblige me," said my Cousin's Husband, "and give us great joy, by joining us for refreshments?"

Doctor Stewart guided me towards the middle-sized building. It was the farthest away and did not improve upon scrutiny. It seemed to me to be a large wooden box, with rough planks lining the outside and only two windows set on either side of the door. It was not half the size of the cottages in the village and not nearly as tidy or well put together. I began to feel myself grow more frightened and hesitated in my steps, sure that these folk were somehow making merry with me. As Doctor Stewart continued to hold my arm I found that we were soon entered into a tiny dark parlour, overfilled with fine furniture and carpets.

"Mrs. Carey, Doctor Stewart has brought someone to call."

A woman then entered the room, her hair fallen down about her shoulders in a most slovenly way, her dress and apron visibly soiled. I looked at her face and saw at once that there had been a misunderstanding. This woman was tanned dark like a walnut and did not bear resemblance to my Cousin with her clear Irish complexion and striking countenance.

Pressing her hands against her stomach, she cried, "Eleanor! Eleanor! Can it really be you?!" She stood still for a moment and then ran towards me in a furious blur. I held my hands out to hold her away.

"Lily?"

"Oh, Eleanor, don't you recognize me?" she cried.

"Lily?" I repeated. And that's what I remember. I, who am never given to fits of emotion and nerves, felt the room misting around me and fainted dead away.

Someone must have carried me to the settle, for I was lying there, disbelieving the sequence of things, when the objectionable smell of salts were wafted under my nostrils. I opened my eyes to see a hideous face and let out a faint scream at the sight of it so close to mine own.

"It is only me, Miss Courtown," sounded the soft, comforting words. "It is only your friend, Robert Stewart. Come now, rouse yourself." I saw that he had moved away from my face and was standing near the end of the settle. The woman who claimed to be Lily was kneeling on the floor beside me, sobbing. Two men were standing at the doorway staring intently. Remembering where I was and what had transpired, I struggled to sit up.

The Doctor supported my back while I righted myself. The woman claiming to be Lily looked up at me and said, between small sobs, "Are you well, Ellie?" No one but family had ever called me that, and only those close to us would have known this. I stared hard at this woman, trying to make her out.

"Lily?" I asked again.

"Yes, my love," she replied, reaching for my hand, "it is Lily." I looked down with disgust at the rough, hardened hand that held mine own. But on the middle finger shone a red-gold claddagh—the ring that Rowland McDonough had slipped on Lily's finger the day of their betrothal. I carried the hand to my lips and kissed the ring, turning the palm over and wondering at the strangeness of this scene. Tears slipped from my eyes and we wept together.

Fingering her apron, I asked, "Lily, have you been pressed into service?"

"No, Eleanor, no," she soothed. "It is only that help is hard to hire here." She reached behind her to untie the apron and remove the offending item. I saw at once that she was far with child and that the apron had helped to conceal her condition.

"Oh Lily, what has happened to you?"

Mr. Carey stepped forward at this and approached me with chill rancour. Bowing stiffly, he said, "Mrs. Carey and I are homesteading. It is the way things are done in this country. We have no inherited estate to rely on for our comfort and are honourably engaged in bettering our situation."

Doctor Stewart then intervened. "The ladies have both had a shock and tea might be just the thing." He asked Mr. Carey if that were possible. The men stepped from the room and left Lily and me alone.

"Lily," I said, "you knew I would follow after you. How is it that you have married again? Is Mr. Carey a gentleman? Has he means?"

Lily looked away and hesitated, ever so briefly, before responding. "Yes, of course. He is a mine owner. Did you really think that I would marry beneath me?" Lily looked hurt and pulled back from me, smoothing out her gown.

"I didn't mean that," I began.

"Oh, I know," she said, coming close and kissing my cheeks. "Of course, I know." She embraced me tightly and whispered, "I never thought to see you again, my faithful Sister. God is good." I held her to me, the smell of her hair unpleasantly close.

Doctor Stewart soon returned with a tray, and poured us each a cup of clear tea. He drew out a small silver flask from his inside jacket and, without asking, added a splash of something coloured to mine. I sipped it gratefully. Then, after a few minutes of polite conversation, he put his index finger on my wrist while looking at the gold watch he now held in his hand. "Your pulse is still quite elevated," he said. "I'd best take you back. Mrs. McLenaghan will be happy to look after you."

I began to protest, as did Lily, but he dismissed our entreaties and directed me to put my arm around his neck while he bent over me. As I did so, he lifted me easily and held me against his chest. Lily kissed me and held my hand whilst he carried me to the buggy and tucked me in carefully with the spreads. Mr. Carey hovered behind Lily, shadowing her with his tall presence.

The infused tea must have done its work, for I dozed immediately and woke only when I felt myself once more being lifted. My head ached terribly and I closed my eyes again, resting against the rough tweed. I was laid down upon my bed in the Inn. Mrs. McLenaghan undid my gown and underpinnings; then I heard her begin to rummage through my trunk for a night dress. I was worried about so many things and thoughts were so swirling round my head that I felt quite overcome. Once she had finished pulling my night dress on, Mrs. McLenaghan called for the Doctor, who dosed me with a teaspoon of a bitter draught. I coughed and sputtered at the taste of it, but he assured me that I would feel better before long. I was in a state of mortification: embarrassed to be seen by him in such compromising undress and ashamed to have made such a display. I tried to apologize for causing him such inconvenience but he shushed me abruptly and quit the room.

I slept for fully two days. My travels had finally taken their toll, and I found myself greatly weakened. Mrs. McLenaghan, however, proved an efficient nursemaid, wakening me to take some clear broth, or to dose me with a teaspoon of bitter medicine, or to bathe my temples with rosewater. From time to time I heard Doctor Stewart speaking with her, after which he took my wrist or put a tube to my chest. Although I have a vague remembrance of crying out for my Cousin, Lily did not appear, and I wondered if I had misremembered the strange situation I had found us in.

On the third day, Mrs. McLenaghan entered my room to find me sitting upright in bed. "You have been so kind," I said.

"It is nothing, Lass, you've had quite an ordeal for one so young."

"Tell me, did you know what I would discover?"

"Well, Doctor Stewart did let on that the Carey place was a bit rough and that he thought you were accustomed to a more refined way of things."

"And why, then, did he not think to caution me?" I countered.

"Why, I don't rightly know, but he's a good Doctor and he knows what he's about."

"He should have told me."

"Well, Lass, you need to be talking to him about that then." She picked up a tray with empty cups and glasses.

"I should have told you what?" asked Doctor Stewart, entering the room just as Mrs. McLenaghan was leaving it.

"You should have forewarned me about Mrs. Carey's situation," I answered whilst arranging the bedcovers and adjusting them for modesty's sake.

"Ah, I see." He sat down and smiled at me from a wooden chair in the corner. "And the headstrong girl who defied her own Father and left the protection of her family to cross the ocean and drive into the bush would take a caution from a man she scarcely knew?"

"I am not a girl any longer," I responded angrily. "I am twenty this winter." I felt tears in my eyes and blinked hard to work them away. His words had stung me, as my own Father had often remarked that I needed to take more care when making decisions that affected people other than myself.

The Doctor's large hideous mouth formed into an amused smile. Tears were now leaking down my face; I wiped them hastily with my handkerchief. "I'm sure, Doctor Stewart, that while I am most grateful for your attentions, I am no longer in need of your services." I intended thus to dismiss him, but he was not so easily rid of.

He began to question me, crossing the room to feel my forehead for signs of fever. "If you're feeling stronger, Miss Courtown, might I suggest fresh air before dinner? I could send Mrs. McLenaghan to help you dress, and will accompany you on a short walk in the village if you feel so inclined."

"And if I do," I countered, "will you explain to me all that you know about my Cousin's situation?"

He bowed and quit my company without responding. Mrs. McLenaghan was shortly knocking at the door, and although she was not familiar with the lacings and hooks of my things, I was grateful for her assistance and began to ready myself to go below. Doctor Stewart was waiting for me at the bottom of the stairs. Mrs. McLenaghan stood watching us with a curious smile as he offered me his arm.

We started in the direction opposite to our previous walk. I was delighted when we came upon yet another row of houses in the village; unlike the wooden cottages we had seen, these were more respectable brick establishments of a substantial and imposing size. A new house was being added to the row, with the makings of a magnificent structure. Over the front door rose a tower that reached well above the roof line of its neighbours.

"How lovely," I exclaimed to my companion. "Can you imagine how pretty the view must be from that window?" I pointed at the tower window and Doctor Stewart followed the direction of my gloved hand.

"Yes," he answered, "it would be very attractive to anyone who appreciated the wilderness of this place."

"Whom do you suppose is building it?"

"Oh, someone with too much money, likely; I think it needs a fence. Do you really think it a nice house?"

"Why, yes, of course I do," I responded pertly. "There were homes as nice in Port Gibson and Montreal, but I never supposed to see anything quite so fine in Orange Hill. Mrs. Carey should live in a house such as this." I grew quiet, reflecting that my cousin's dire circumstances were ones I might not readily alter. The Doctor turned us around then and we headed back to the Inn.

Mr. and Mrs. McLenaghan were waiting for us in the dining room. The table, I noted, was set for only two places. "We've already eaten," said Mrs. McLenaghan. "We did na' wait on your walk, not knowing how long you'd be. You haven't overwrought yourself, I hope." Mr. McLenaghan held my chair out and then left to follow his Wife to the kitchen. Doctor Stewart sat down across from me, looking slightly flushed and uncomfortable.

We had a dinner of roast pork, tiny potatoes, and turnip mash. Doctor Stewart focused on his dinner with intensity, making little attempt to be conversational. I was surprised and not a little affronted with his sudden lack of sociability.

"Is something troubling you?" I asked him upon rising. "I wonder at your lack of speech this evening." He rose quickly to pull away my chair, opening his mouth to speak but closing it again without having uttered a word. Finally he bowed to me, said "Good evening," and quitted the room. His was a changeable and unpleasant nature.

The next morning I joined Mr. and Mrs. McLenaghan at the dining room table, where one place setting had already been cleared away. Mrs. McLenaghan saw me looking at it. "Doctor Stewart was up early this morning, Miss. He's ridden over to the Carey place to report on your health. I expect he'll be back by dinner and you will have news then."

I was grateful that he had made this small mission a priority. Doctor Stewart continued to be a most awkward gentleman, with much that was accommodating and, by turns, much that was disagreeable.

I spent much of the day writing my Father a letter. It were a difficult task. I kept picturing him comfortably seated in his study while in receipt of it. And his dear face came to me, filling me with remorse for the wound I had caused. I could not bear to think of the pain and disbelief my departure must have engendered. Mrs. Stevens would no doubt have reported to him long since, but there was still much that I needed to say. Affections must be expressed, and forgiveness asked for.

After posting the letter, I turned in the direction of the brick houses and walked a little way on my own. To my great astonishment, I saw that a crew of men working at the new house were putting up an impressive iron fence. How odd, I thought, since Doctor Stewart had said only the night before that a fence would enhance the look of the place. Somebody else, I reckoned, must have thought so also.

Believing that Lily and Mr. Carey might appear at the Inn with Dr. Stewart for dinner, I went to my room and began my evening toilette. I had brought with me a tightly fitted grey silk, and I struggled into it without assistance. As the hour was yet early, I dressed my hair carefully, weaving in a string of seed pearls and fastening on pearl ear drops. The glass in my room was only a partial one, but by bending carefully I could see that I looked presentable. I had last worn this gown at a dinner party following a shoot at Rosslare Hall, and had been much admired. Lord Driscoll had been my dinner partner; we had spent the first of many pleasant evenings in each other's close company. Wexford seemed so far away just then, and the letter to my Father had made me homesick. A tear or two escaped before I could descend the stairs.

Entering the parlour, I saw only Doctor Stewart at his liberty there. I had spent much of the day in anticipation of his return, thinking that Lily and Mr. Carey would rightly follow after him; to see him reading his paper quite alone in the room made me despondent. I must have sighed, for he looked up at once and got quickly to his feet. "Miss Courtown," he said, bowing. I curtseyed in return but then turned around and made to go back up the stairs.

"Wait," he called after me, "you have not yet had your meal." He stretched his hand out. "Please join me; I have news of your Cousin. The baby will soon be born."

"Yes?" I entered the room and was seated.

"She asked after you. She is not in the way of riding now, Miss Courtown. I would not recommend it."

His words struck my heart and I looked at him with water-filled eyes. "Have they no carriage?"

"Mrs. Carey is a fine horsewoman, Miss Courtown. She was often seen riding when they first arrived." Again he had chosen to answer with tact.

He was correct, of course. Lily and I had both ridden since we were girls. Her Father was known to be an excellent judge of horses: his Arabians often won the races at Curragh. My Father would buy those horses which Uncle recommended and we, too, kept splendid animals. I had a lovely black mare at home called Mariah. Lily particularly liked a spirited jumper, as she often rode with her Father in the hunt at Powyss Hall and Lowry Castle.

"Are there stables about with horses for hire, Doctor Stewart?"

"Why, yes, Murty O'Brien at the Smithy hires horses. Do you ride, Miss Courtown?"

"Of course. My Father thought it good exercise."

"Were you thinking of riding to see your Cousin, perhaps?"

"Perhaps," I replied obscurely. I was irked and did not want to prolong our discourse.

"Well," he replied, "I agree with your Father. The fresh air is wonderfully good for many ailments."

I softened to him then. His deference to my Father was appreciated and I recognized that he was trying, once more, to be kind.

"Have you made any plans?" he asked me.

"What manner of plans do you mean?"

"Plans for your future. Will you be returning to Ireland?"

"Why, that depends on Mrs. Carey," I replied. "I am not prepared to leave her in her current situation. I could never look at her Father again if I did."

"But she is married and about to become a Mother. Surely you do no intend to take her away?"

He seemed incredulous at the thought, and although I had not carefully formulated my course of action, I felt defensive and abused by his tone. "I am sure that I don't know how this is any concern of yours, Doctor Stewart." I gathered myself up with dignity and faced him squarely. He stood also and looked at me boldly until I coloured.

"May I say that you look particularly well, Miss Courtown. Good evening." Doctor Stewart bowed, then abruptly left the room. I heard the front door shutting a moment later.

I slept poorly that night. My emotions were in turmoil, as I was both vexed by the Doctor's overly familiar questioning and utterly distraught about my Cousin's situation. Mrs. McLenaghan heard me descend the stairs in the morning, and appeared straightaway with a merry face. I smiled to see her so obliging and friendly.

"Good morning, Miss. Let me fix you some tea."

I had ready, folded in a piece of paper, a week's lodgings, and I passed this to her with a quiet and sincere "Thank you." I had taken stock of my resources and knew that I would soon need to visit a bank. I wondered how long it would take for funds to be given clearance. My allowance was generous, as Father believed I should manage my own accounts for "ribbonds and frippery." He did not presume to take a deep interest in my wardrobe or entertainments and simply expected that I would be provident. Before I left Wexford my Father had given me a cheque for my expenses, believing me, of course, to be travelling only to London. Yet I had knowledge of the household accounts, and the ready monies that were kept in a drawer in his study for immediate expenses; unbeknownst to his man, Mr. Meagher, I had taken a liberal sum from this drawer, leaving a small note saying what I had done lest the staff be blamed for the shortfall. That liberal sum was now depleted, and I needed once more to draw upon my allowance.

While I was at my tea, Doctor Stewart entered the dining room and approached me. "I wonder," he began, bowing briefly, "if you would permit me to escort you to the Careys'? The Smithy has a horse for hire, but I thought you might have trouble finding your way."

I looked at him with some astonishment. I wanted not to be dependent upon his goodness, but as I considered his offer I realized that I had no other means of getting to Lily. "Thank you," I replied in a cool tone, "you are most kind."

He bowed once more. "To be at your service will be my pleasure."

We arranged that I would put on my riding outfit while he went to secure the horses. I dressed quickly, not wanting to take the time to smooth out the creases in my skirt. It was cut in the Irish fashion, with the left side tapered and the right side full and long so that it would hang properly when I was mounted. I did not like to wear a petticoat when I rode, as the bulk of it made my seating less secure.

Hastily I buttoned my neat vest and jacket and then located my crop.
My hat was crushed, and in haste I abandoned it, removing the long
black veil and tying it loosely around my hair and face instead. Rushing downstairs, I nearly collided with Mrs. McLenaghan.

"Why, Lass, where are you off to?" she enquired, taking in my
costume.

"Doctor Stewart has offered to ride with me to the Careys', and I
do not wish to keep him waiting."

"Well then," she smiled, "be off with you."

Doctor Stewart had the horses at the front, and had carefully positioned a small mounting block for my ease. I looked at the saddle in
dismay, however, for it had only one pommel and would be uncomfortable to ride side-saddle.

"Murty has only these saddles for hire, I'm afraid."

Taking his hand, I stepped upon the block and then settled myself
on the horse, adjusting the fall of my skirts and clutching tightly to
the reins. "I will be fine," I said, attempting to smile for his sake, "as
long as there are not too many high fences." I would not have him
think me a nervous rider. I had ridden horses since before I could
walk. My own saddle was double-pommelled and especially certain
for female equestrians, but I was a Courtown and would ride as such.

Our trip was breathtaking. Doctor Stewart had a good seat and
rode well. I turned to look at him once or twice and allowed that,
from a distance, some might consider he looked distinguished. We
cantered briefly, and then, once outside the village, I nudged my
lovely mare and broke into a full-out run. I had not felt so free since
arriving in Canada and enjoyed the exercise. The panoramic views
of unspoiled hills and valleys were quite impressive, and I began to
formulate an appreciation for the rugged beauty of this place.

We arrived at the Careys' in short order; I waited on my horse while the Doctor dismounted. Mr. Carey appeared from within the barn and approached us at once, bowing deeply and welcoming us formally. I had prepared for him a few pretty words of greeting, pledging my fealty to him as my new Cousin, but found that I could not speak them. There was something about his manner, and his studied simpering, that alarmed me. He invited us into the house, assuring us again that it would bring him great joy if we condescended to accompany him indoors. We followed him to the parlour, where my Cousin drew her arms about me in a tight and uncomfortable embrace, her heavy form pressing against me.

Lily brought us a tea tray with ample portions of buttered bread cut in squares. I noticed that her Husband did not take the laden tray from her and that he sat at his leisure, long legs outstretched before him, waiting to be served. As she looked to him from time to time, darting quick glances of apprehension in his direction, I continued to take his measure carefully. He was, by nature formed, an attractive specimen, but although his words were carefully spoken, his manner appeared uneasy, as though he were distracted by heavy thoughts. He continually drew the Doctor's attention to one thing or another and framed many of his statements in a staid, emotionless way.

After a time, Doctor Stewart asked Mr. Carey how the wheat was progressing. He feigned great interest in Mr. Carey's response and then asked if he might be shown. Mr. Carey stood quickly and walked to the door. I noticed that he was deferential with the Doctor and treated him with exaggerated attention. Doctor Stewart excused himself, and both men bowed and left the room. Grateful to have time alone with my Cousin, I turned to her eagerly.

"Tell me, Cousin," I said, "how it is that you have married again quickly and without a period of mourning?"

Sighing, Lily looked at me and began quietly. "Rowland had

invested all of our resources in several pieces of valuable jewellery. He believed that they would be transferable wealth and provide us an income while we became established. After he died, I waited to speak with the Captain to enlist his assistance in selling one of the large pieces. The Captain was not available, but Mr. Carey, whose acquaintance we made on board, seemed willing to assist me.

"Mr. Carey had several times spoken to Rowland about his interests in a copper mine. He had attempted to entice Rowland into sharing in the investment. Rowland found him quite amiable. His manners were charming and Rowland believed him to be genuine. And so I gave him Rowland's Tara brooch, and he went to trade it for me. Several days later he returned without the brooch and told me that such things were not especially valuable here and that he had only realized a small sum for it.

"I wept at this, for I knew that it was solid gold and embedded with small rubies and a diamond. The sum earned would not pay return passage nor keep me long in Montreal, and I had no assurance that help from family would be immediately forthcoming. I was utterly friendless and wretched. As the McDonoughs had many sons, I was not certain they would reach out to his widow. My Father, as you well know, would be loath to take action without first carefully consulting their feelings in the matter. I needed to quickly establish myself in a situation that would allow me to provide for Rowland's child. I thought that to remarry quickly would ensure me a respectable position and liberate the McDonoughs from any obligation. Without independent means, it seemed to be my only choice."

"Mr. Carey assured me that any gentleman would be honoured to marry a lady, and that I must not grow despondent. His kindness bolstered my courage and gave me a glimmer of confidence. Throughout that terrible time I was inconsolable with grief, unable

to eat anything but the plainest of foods. Despite my unhealthy countenance, Mr. Carey began to take a kindly interest in me and made
it evident that our union would be propitious for us both. He would
benefit by claiming Rowland's land, and would delay his journey to
Arizona to offer me protection. There was no subterfuge. It was a
pact consciously entered into, on both our parts. I did not believe,
having loved Rowland so entirely, that any other gentleman would
ever transplant his memory. Other men could only ever be but poor
substitutes. And by this measure, Jack Carey was as likely a candidate
as any other. He is not wholly unattractive or without charm."

I embraced her at the end of this narrative and told myself that I
must accept her choice even if I could not readily recognize its merits.
We talked quickly, interrupting each other and finishing each other's
sentences. She assured me that she was well and was growing accustomed to being a farmer's wife. On the subject of household help, she
informed me that Mr. Carey had hired several maids but that each
had run off by turn, leaving her to manage things on her own.

Rowland's baby was strong and healthy, I was told, and that while
early on it had kicked, she could now scarcely feel it, as it had moved
into position and was getting ready for the ordeal. Before many minutes
had lapsed, Mr. Carey and Doctor Stewart returned and I knew that
it was time to go.

I kissed Lily on the cheek before taking my leave of Mr. Carey, who
bowed stiffly and thanked me for bringing his Wife such inestimable
joy. Although he smiled when he said this, I discerned that he was likewise studying me, and that his words lacked genuine affection.

Doctor Stewart led my horse to a mounting block and extended his
hand to me while I mounted and settled onto my saddle. The ride back
to the Inn was not quite so pleasant: I had much to reflect upon and was
feeling troubled. Doctor Stewart practised a rare economy of speech.

When we arrived back at the Inn, Mrs. McLenaghan stood waiting. "Jack Burridge has just been," she began. "His Wife's time has come. The water broke this morning, just."

Doctor Stewart nodded his head, then mounted the stairs two and three at a time. Calling down to her, he asked if she was available to ride with him. I gathered from this that Mrs. McLenaghan sometimes assisted him with birthing. He returned carrying his medical bag and larger carpet bag, bowed in passing, and begged my pardon for leaving so abruptly. I stood in amazement at the sudden flurry while he and Mrs. McLenaghan set off together.

They did not return that evening, and for supper Mr. McLenaghan put before the guests a cold plate of bread and cheese. We ate together morosely. I spent my evening alone in the little parlour, reading a small book of poetry I had with me and conjuring up pictures of Wexford, where now everything seemed to have been so secure and happy.

It was late afternoon of the next day before Mrs. McLenaghan and Doctor Stewart returned. Mrs. McLenaghan reported that it was a "bonny wee boy" and that the Mother was worn out.

"Well, let's hope this is the last. A woman her age should no still be having babies," said the Doctor.

"Don't be telling me what I already know," said Mrs. McLenaghan. "You should be telling that to Jack Burridge so that he will stop his pestering of her."

I coloured to hear them talking so indecently and would have slipped away, but instead I astonished myself by offering to make tea. Mrs. McLenaghan looked at me with a pleased expression. "Why Lass, that would be most welcome. Can you manage?"

I curtseyed by way of response, and walked down the small hallway to the kitchen. A kettle filled with water was already on the hob; I had only to search out the china and set the tray. I opened the larder, found the leftover cheese we had eaten for our dinner, and thought to myself that rarebit would be easy enough to manage. I had sometimes made this for Father when the staff were given their half holiday, and I smiled at the recollection. I seized a loaf of bread and cut generous chunks of it, setting it by the fire to toast. Looking around the kitchen, I found some eggs and a bottle of ale, and mixed these together with some scraped cheese and a bit of pepper. Then I spread the mixture on the toasted bread and let it roast awhile by the fire whilst the tea steeped. Placing the lot on a large tray set for four, I proudly made my way to the parlour, where I found the McLenaghans and the Doctor at their leisure. Doctor Stewart jumped up directly to take the tray from me as Mrs. McLenaghan exclaimed with delight at all that I had wrought. I never in my life enjoyed a cup of tea or a taste of Welsh rarebit so much as I did that afternoon.

After our tea I felt the need of further occupation, and went for a walk. I was curious to see if the iron fence at the new house was near completion. It would be good fun, I thought, to show Doctor Stewart the finished fence and tease him about his ability to predict building enhancements. I returned to the Inn and dressed quickly for dinner, exchanging my plain wool gown for a violet satin, which I wore with a lace stole across my bare shoulders. Supper was once more set for simply the two of us. The Doctor looked as though he had only recently woken from his rest; his hair and shirt collar were damp from a hasty washing up. "I have a surprise for you," I announced, joining him in the dining room. "After your dinner I should like to show it to you."

"As you wish."

We did not luxuriate at our meal. He was yet fatigued and I was anxious to show him the fence. I hastened upstairs for my outdoor cloak and came down quickly to where he stood waiting for me at the newel post, smiling broadly as I drew near. His mouth presented the least offensively when he was smiling or laughing, but I thought again, uncharitably, how unfortunate it was that nature had ruined his countenance with such an ungainly brow. I took his arm and led him out towards the row of brick houses.

"Don't say a word," I directed, "until we stand before your surprise." Tugging gently on his arm, I made way to stand directly in front of the new house. "Do you see it?" I exclaimed. "You have predicted an enhancement on this house and someone has done the very thing you declared." I looked at him, waiting for a word of merriment in return, but instead he coloured and looked uncomfortable.

"What is it?" I said, placing my hand on his arm. "Have I teased you overmuch?"

He shook his head and reached into his jacket from which he drew a key. "Would you like to go inside?" he asked me, moving a few steps towards the front walkway.

"Do you know the people then who have built this place?"

"Yes," he replied. "And I should perhaps have told you before. When it is complete, this is to be my home and Surgery."

I was all astonishment and saw quickly how foolish I must appear. "No, I think not. It is late."

"Very well," he said, turning back to me. "Another time perhaps."

We were quiet on our return walk to the Inn and parted from one another immediately upon entering. I curtseyed and went directly to my room, yet again experiencing a deep sense of mortification.

Chapter the Second
DESPAIR

Homesick for the rocky Irish coast and for Rosslare Hall, I wondered, not for the first time, if Father was grieving my absence. I had left forwarding addresses at all my stops in the event that a letter from home might soon make its way to me. It occurred to me that Father might entrust an associate to travel here so as to escort me back to Ireland. I also considered that he might, perchance, follow himself, determined to castigate me in person and secure my obedience. The McDonoughs had several sons, I knew, and one of them might also be commissioned to bring home Rowland's widow.

The following morning was the Sabbath; I had already enquired of Mrs. McLenaghan the time for divine service. Leaving the Inn without stopping for refreshment, I walked out in the direction of the church and mingled with the small crowd assembled for morning prayer. They wore country fashions and only a few of the ladies had hoops. Feeling that my costume was the subject of some notice, I rather wished I had worn something less fine. My Cousin and her Husband, I noted, were not among the devoted.

The words of the liturgy brought tears to my eyes: it had been many weeks since I had knelt in prayer. The closing hymn was "I Bind Unto Myself Today," and I sang it joyfully, as it deserved to be so sung. It was shaming to think that I had not made time to practise the devotions I'd had instilled in me as a child. At the conclusion of service, the Minister mounted his horse and made for another church some miles to the east. The congregants bade me "Good morning," and likewise dispersed.

When I arrived back at the Inn I saw at once that something was amiss. The Doctor's buggy stood out front with Murty O'Brien holding the reins of the two horses. The door opened and, while I stood there, Mrs. McLenaghan came bustling out carrying a large basket, followed by Doctor Stewart with two bags.

The Doctor walked forward, bowed, and then addressed me. "Mrs. Carey is in labour," he said, "and we are just on our way. We will send word when we have news."

"No," I cried, "I must come with you."

"Have you ever attended a birthing?"

"Why no," I said, chastened somewhat, "but she is my Cousin and it will give her comfort to have me there."

He hesitated only briefly. "Very well, you may sit up front with Mrs. McLenaghan, and I will ride.

"Get me a horse, Murty!" he shouted at Mr. O'Brien.

After Mr. McLenaghan helped me enter the buggy, Mrs. McLenaghan twitched the whip, setting the horses at a trot. I kept looking behind me and, in very few minutes, saw that Doctor Stewart was mounted and galloping towards us.

Lily was half standing, half leaning against her Husband when we arrived. Doctor Stewart took immediate charge. Mr. Carey hovered nervously, but he also looked strangely excited, his Wife's discomfort not seeming particularly to distress him; he even attempted to converse with the Doctor about the changeable weather. Mrs. McLenaghan was told to ready the room, whilst I was given the job of bathing Lily's temples and keeping her soothed.

An attack grabbed her in the middle and she bent double, groaning like an animal in pain. I was frightened, but Doctor Stewart looked in and said only that she was "doing well."

Mrs. McLenaghan came to lead us to the primitive bedchamber. When Lily allowed her to remove all but her shift, I was ashamed to see the state of her linens and wished Mrs. McLenaghan had not glimpsed them. We both of us put Lily down on the bed. Mrs. McLenaghan drew from her bag a thick twist of white cotton, which she fastened to the underside of the bed and brought the ends up for Lily to grasp.

"Pull on these hard," she admonished, "the next time you feel a pain coming."

It were not long before Lily had occasion to pull. She struggled against the pain, crying out loudly and straining herself against the ropes, her legs kicking over the two chairs placed at the foot of the bed.

"How long must this go on?" I asked Mrs. McLenaghan tearfully.

"Bless you, Lass, she's just at the beginning. This will take all the night, I expect."

I could not imagine seeing my beloved Cousin suffer for so many long hours yet. "Is there nothing the Doctor can do? Surely this isn't customary."

"The Doctor knows what he's about, Lass. You cannot pluck them out before they are ready to come."

I despaired at Lily's great discomfort. I had seen horses foaling at home and they did not experience this same agony, I thought. "But surely there is something we can do."

"We can bide with her and do the Doctor's bidding, Lass, and that is all." Mrs. McLenaghan was infuriatingly calm and I felt a fit of pique coming upon me.

Doctor Stewart opened the door then. "Is everyone managing?"

"Yes, Doctor," responded Mrs. McLenaghan before I could speak. "We're all set and ready."

I saw him looking at me, taking my measure. "You might want to remove your jacket, Miss Courtown, before the sleeves become ruined."

Mrs. McLenaghan nodded at his words, then reached into her bag and passed me a large, clean apron. Yet with only a fine shirtwaist under my jacket, I was not willing to bare my arms.

"I cannot" I said primly. "I would not be suitably covered."

Lily sobbed at this, laughing and crying both with pain. I rushed to her side and put my arms around her shoulders. "Look at me, Ellie," she whispered, "I've naught left of my dignity."

Doctor Stewart excused himself and returned a minute later with his carpet bag. He opened this and passed me a man's shirt without the collar or cuffs. "I always carry a change," he said. "Perhaps this will be of assistance." Mrs. McLenaghan unbuttoned and removed my jacket, then guided my arms into the shirt and used the long, white linen apron to truss me like a Christmas goose. Lily, for all her discomfort, looked amused to see me swathed so, and I myself entered into the ludicrousness with better grace than I had earlier felt.

Then another series of attacks savaged my Cousin. She was all over covered in perspiration, her hair had become slick, and she shrieked when the pains came. I was horrified, not only by her distress but by her lack of composure.

Mr. Carey had absented himself from the birthing room. I was gladdened to be spared his company, for I had begun to suspect the genuineness of his affection for Lily and had questions about his breeding and fortune. Leaving her with Mrs. McLenaghan, I strode through the house and out into the yard, where I stormed about in a tight circle, clenching my fists and thinking dark thoughts. I must have looked a curious sight because Doctor Stewart shortly approached and asked if I was well.

"It's not me you should be tending to," I retorted. "My Cousin is dying and no one is doing anything to help her."

I saw the corners of his mouth form into a smile, but he swallowed it back and said, "The head has no crowned yet, Miss Courtown. There is naught we can safely do for your Cousin until the baby has moved further down. It is best to wait things out and let the Almighty have a hand."

When we returned to the bedchamber I saw Mr. Carey bending over his Wife, whispering something to her; she looked anxious and unsettled. He left off when he saw me glowering at him, and quit the room. Doctor Stewart gestured something to Mrs. McLenaghan and together they approached the foot of the bed. She held the sheet up for him while he stood between the chairs, reached in, and bent my Cousin's legs up and apart. My face burned hot with the shame of it.

"Is this the way it is always done?" I finally asked Mrs. McLenaghan. "Is there no better way?"

"Bless you, Lass," she laughed, "it's the way God intended it from the time of Adam and Eve."

The labouring seemed interminable. I did not think it possible that a human body could hold so much pain and for so long. Lily was covered all over in damp, and although we wanted to change her shift, we could not find a clean one. I was dismayed to see that she had let her wardrobe fall to such a state—our friends in Dublin and London would disown the acquaintance of any lady who appeared in such a shameful way.

Doctor Stewart and Mrs. McLenaghan took rests through the night, each by turn, in the parlour. Although I insisted on staying with Lily throughout, I was not much in the way of being useful. I saw Doctor Stewart remove his shirt cuffs and roll up his sleeves past the elbow. He continued to look between her legs, first washing his hands in boiling water so that they came out looking all red and swollen, and then touching her, apparently feeling for the baby's head. I was so mortified by this that I could not look at his face or speak with him. Early in the morning he said he thought it was nearly time. Lily was overmuch worn out by this point. And although both the Doctor and Mrs. McLenaghan were on at her to bear down, she seemed capable only of panting and weeping; she did not have the strength to do as they asked.

Doctor Stewart, looking grim, went to fetch Lily's Husband. As Mr. Carey was made to hold one leg to the side while Mrs. McLenaghan held the other, all the while I was by Lily's face, whispering sweet words to her and bathing her temples. The Doctor washed his hands in the boiling water once more and then dropped two long metal spoons in the pot. He then asked Mrs. McLenaghan and Mr. Carey if they were ready.

"I'm reaching in to help the baby now, Mrs. Carey," he said. "I need you to be brave."

Lily made no response at all and I believed that she were now dead. I saw Doctor Stewart bend over her and insert the metal spoons between her legs. Lily let out one long piercing shriek, a sound that terrified me, but gladdened me also that she were yet living. I looked at Doctor Stewart and saw him hand a grey and bloody infant to Mrs. McLenaghan.

It were not breathing, and I thought to myself that all our waiting and all our suffering were for naught. Doctor Stewart was busy cutting and tying the cord that connected the dead child to my Cousin. He turned when he was done, held the babe upside down by its feet, and proceeded to whack it fiercely on the back. I let out a cry at his cruelty but my voice was not heard. The baby was wailing and alive now; Mrs. McLenaghan took it from him and began to wipe at it with soft white towelling.

"It's a girl, Mr. Carey," said Doctor Stewart, "a beautiful Irish Canadian girl." Mr. Carey grinned and looked fully satisfied, as if it were he who had accomplished something of merit. He approached Lily, about to kiss her cheek, but she turned from him and he, colouring, stormed from the room.

Doctor Stewart also left the room, and Mrs. McLenaghan now told me to pull off Lily's wet shift. I did so not knowing what clean thing we had to robe her in. Mrs. McLenaghan bent over her with the baby and helped it to suckle on Lily's small white breasts. "You lay there quiet and let the baby feed," said Mrs. McLenaghan. "The wee thing needs to hear your heart."

It was by now mid-morning and I was overcome with disgust and repulsion for all of it. Mr. Carey had not secured a wet nurse; it was obvious that Lily was expected to feed and care for this infant entirely herself. Nothing in our shared upbringing had prepared us for this task. The child's prospects were not likely to be good. Mrs. McLenaghan was busy putting the room to rights, bundling up the bloodied sheets with the mess in the enamel bowl and setting it aside, she told me, for Mr. Carey to burn.

Taking the sleepy baby now from Lily's breast, Mrs. McLenaghan left the room to put her down somewhere. I rushed to Lily to pull the sheet over her nakedness just as Doctor Stewart returned with his black medical bag and once more scrubbed at his poor boiled hands. He took a large needle and threaded it with a thick black thread.

Mrs. McLenaghan had come back now and was positioned by Lily's head, holding her shoulders and whispering something soothing as Doctor Stewart lifted the sheet and removed the bloodied towel from between her legs. He wiped her nether parts and then made as if he were going to stitch together the rip the baby had made. Feeling quite faint at this, I made my way out to the carriage, throwing my arms around the horse's neck and beginning to weep. Sometime later Doctor Stewart approached, loosened my arms from the animal, and suggested that I be seated.

I looked down and saw that the blood had mostly soaked through the apron. "I've ruined your fine shirt," I said.

"No matter," he replied. "It was well worth a shirt. She's a lovely bairn." The Doctor looked deeply happy. Yet I felt devastated by his words, for they made me realize that I had not welcomed this child of my Cousin's, nor asked her name, nor kissed her nor blessed her.

Doctor Stewart said naught as the tears began to drop again from my eyes; he simply helped me into the carriage. I sat down, despondent and exhausted, and tried not to look at the bloodied costume I was still wearing over my shirtwaist. The Doctor went back into the house and returned shortly carrying my good jacket, which he passed to me silently. Shortly thereafter Mrs. McLenaghan appeared, whereupon Doctor Stewart hitched the horses and we commenced driving back to the Inn. The Doctor rode merrily alongside us on his horse, passing the occasional lively exchange and banter with Mrs. McLenaghan.

They were both of them sensitive to my trauma and fortunately did not expect much in the way of conversation from me. Still, I was fearful of returning to the Inn, not knowing how to conduct myself with a gentleman who had witnessed my Cousin's complete disgrace. I had never thought before about what it was he did and this new awareness made me quite discomforted.

Mrs. McLenaghan drove the carriage to the Smithy, where we dismounted and then walked to the Inn. We saw at once that the place was astir. Mr. McLenaghan greeted us with, "Well, Mother, we've six travellers just come late for their supper. I've taken them to their rooms but there is naught to eat." Despite what must have been a great weariness, Mrs. McLenaghan went bustling off towards the kitchen while I slipped upstairs to change out of my soiled garments. I washed as best I could using the bowl in my room and discarded my ruined clothes. Drawing on my plainest gown, I tidied my hair and determined that I was just scarcely presentable.

I made my way to the kitchen to see how Mrs. McLenaghan was managing. Entering the cheerful room, I saw that she was instructing Mr. McLenaghan in the correct way to scrape a potato, while at the same time trying to cook some chops in the large black pan. The McLenaghans, despite their hurry, were quite merry with one another; I marvelled at their good humour. Mr. McLenaghan turned to me and said, "I hear that the birthing got a bit messy."

I nodded, not knowing how to respond to such a comment in mixed company.

"It gets that way sometimes," he continued. "I've seen the gore a time or two."

"Yes, thank you." I hoped he might change the subject of his discourse.

"Yep," he said. "Before Doctor Stewart came, I used to drive Mother to birthings and give her a hand when she needed one. Why, I remember a birthing in Tinkertown. This woman, she had two babies come out, one a couple of minutes after the other, and she was ripped so wide open you'd never believe it were possible to heal. The blood and gore that came out of her was an unforgettable mess, near enough to fill a bushel basket, I'd say. What was it, a year later maybe, she had another? Was it a year, Mother, or shorter than that?"

"No, t'were about that," replied Mrs. McLenaghan.

This was not my opinion of a civilized conversation, but I was not confident of a way to be quit of it without giving offence. I excused myself at the earliest opportunity and retired early, feeling unable to sustain a sociable manner.

In the morning, I rummaged through my trunk and selected a fawn-coloured gown that had not been much worn. I folded this into a small carpet bag and changed into my riding costume. I took with me the bag and went back down the stairs. Mrs. McLenaghan met me in the hallway. "I think I shall ride to the Careys' this day," I said to her, "to see how things progress."

"That's what I thought, Lass," she said, looking at my bag. "Is there room in there for a nice meat pie? I have one spare." I followed her to the kitchen and waited while she wrapped it in several cloths, both of us tucking it carefully underneath my gown. I saw Mrs. McLenaghan eyeing the fabric and puzzling it out but she said naught about it.

Next I went to the dry goods store and quietly asked Mrs. Nesbitt, the proprietor's wife, if she had any ready-made personals. Taking me behind a curtained alcove, she showed me her small stock. I selected from these two night dresses, two petticoats, two shirtwaists, one corset, six pantaloons, and three pairs of hose. She wrapped these in brown paper for me and I placed them also in my bag. Moving towards the baby items, I purchased a wool shawl, one dozen flannel nappies, pins and pilchers, several soft cambric gowns, and four binders. "Is there anything else a baby would need?" I asked Mrs. Nesbitt.

"Only this, perhaps, Miss," she said, showing me a glass bottle. "If the milk has trouble flowing, a bottle is sometimes of use."

"Yes," I agreed, "it may prove needful."

My carpet bag was now filled and I had two large paper parcels besides. After paying for my purchases, I walked to the Smithy where I commissioned a horse. It was a quick ride, only three quarters of an hour, and I felt confident of my route. The closer I drew to the farm, however, the less sure I became of my duty; it were only my great love for Lily that spurred me to continue.

The farmyard was empty when I arrived. I tied the horse to a post near the trough and patted her side, wishing I had thought to bring with me an apple or a carrot. Then, laden with my many parcels, I approached the house slowly and awkwardly. I knocked at the door and waited several minutes before it were opened. There Lily stood, holding the babe in her arms and looking ghastly.

"Oh Ellie," she cried to me, "I'm so glad it's you."

I followed her into the dark parlour and offered to hold the baby while she unpackaged the items I had brought. After I'd sat upon the settle, Lily deposited the baby in my lap. I tried to support it as I had seen Lily do, but the baby's head tipped perilously backwards and the child woke up and began to scream. I became greatly disturbed by this and Lily rushed to my side, took the child back into her arms, and sat down beside me. Then she reached into the front of her gown and disclosed a swollen breast which she offered to the baby to suckle. It stopped its screaming directly and clung to her—sucking and making soft sighing sounds. I was horrified by this display. Lily merely smiled at me over the baby's head, presently disconnecting it from her one breast only to switch sides, presenting the other distended one to the child. It was an unseemly sight.

"Is there no wet nurse?" I finally asked.

"None that we can afford."

"Could I secure one?"

"You would have to ask Mr. Carey, but he would likely not want to expend funds on something we could manage without. What little we have must be invested in our farm until the copper mine begins to produce."

"But you will ruin your figure!" I cried.

"I think it's too late to worry about such things as that."

I moved close to her, embracing her shoulders. We sat there like that: the baby half asleep on her breast, and we, reconnected Cousins, silent and miserable.

"I'm calling her Kathleen," said Lily, "after our Gran. I think she has the look of a Kavanaugh about her. What do you think?"

"It's early, perhaps, to say," I responded, "but Kathleen is a fine name."

"Kathleen Rowland McDonough," said Lily. "I believe it suits.

"Do you think," Lily continued, "do you think Father would send me a portion of my inheritance if he knew my circumstances?"

"Your Father would want you home, Lily," I answered smartly, "as you very well know. He would not be happy to see you in this situation."

"Mr. Carey thinks I should write to him."

"I think not. You will only make him worry."

"Mr. Carey is of the opinion that my Father, who has so much, would be pained to know that I was in need. It would be only a small loan until the mining dividends are received."

"Uncle will be pained to know that you have remarried without his blessing," I replied, "and he would question the integrity of any man who could not adequately provide for his family."

There was a long silence.

"There are times, Ellie, when it is best to be pliable in order to survive. I can no longer seek my own pleasure in such matters as I must now always think what is best for Kathleen. If Mr. Carey is unhappy then I cannot safely provide for her."

"Lily, be clear with me," I begged. "I do not understand what you are saying. Are you unsafe here?" I was much frightened by her tone and her countenance both.

"I only meant to say, Ellie, that things are not always what they seem. We are no longer protected by our families and our wealth and position. We must rise to the challenge of this new world, and bide our time before we can do as we see fit."

"Lily, I do not know of what you are speaking. Tell me at once. Has Mr. Carey abused you in some way?"

"Your language is emotional, Cousin, and not helpful to the situation. I know what I am about and am resolved to follow my course." She spoke this proudly, with her chin tipped upwards, and I saw that she was determined upon something I could not comprehend. I was troubled by her words but did not wish to provoke her; I understood that some secret thing had now come between us, one that she was clearly intending to keep from me.

"Mr. Carey will shortly come in for his mid-day meal. I should prepare things."

"Let me," I said. "Tell me what it is you would do and direct me."

"Very well. Put on an apron first so that you do not spoil your gown. There are potatoes ready to be fried—can you manage that? The stove is tricky."

She stood up, and with the baby adhered to her front, made her way to the kitchen to light the stove for me. There was a bowl of eggs on the table and she pointed at these. Following her directions, I cracked them open and fried them together with the potatoes. While I managed the fry pan, Lily wiped the table and set one place at it. Then, moving to the small larder, she returned with a plate containing the remains of some cold fowl which she set by the place for Mr. Carey.

"And what of your meal?" I asked her.

"I will eat after he has done," Lily said quietly.

I wondered at this strange order of things but had no wish to estrange her with my criticisms. I heard Mr. Carey's approach. "Who's here?" he shouted. "There's a horse tied up outside."

"It is only I," I responded, walking up to him and curtseying. "I have brought gifts for the baby."

"Miss Courtown," he said, staring at me boldly before bowing, "a pleasure and a very great joy, I'm sure. Will you join us for luncheon?" He sat down at the small table, unfolding his table napkin with a flourish before laying it across his legs with much ceremony. His hands, I noted, were yet unwashed; nor had he acknowledged my Cousin. I was disgusted by the oversight and excused myself, taking my leave and quickly returning to my horse. Mr. Carey half stood from the table when I bade them both farewell, but he did not trouble to set aside his cutlery.

I rode hard back to town, where Mr. O'Brien took the horse from me and led her to the stable. Impulsively, I told him that I would require her again the next morning, at the same hour.

I walked the short piece to the Inn, calling out "Hello" upon entering. Mrs. McLenaghan appeared in the hallway and took my coat from me.

"How are the sweet ones?" she asked me by way of a greeting. "Is the wee one latching on and feeding?"

"Yes," I said with contempt, "that does not seem to be a trouble."

Mrs. McLenaghan looked at me curiously but did not ask for an explanation. I went directly upstairs to my room and freshened my toilette. The vulgarity of the entire scene broke my heart. The scullery maids in Rosslare Hall were not sunk so low as Lily. I wished that I could consult my Uncle or my Father as to what best to do.

I could not force Lily's leave from Mr. Carey if she did not choose it, and I could not readily improve her situation with a man so wanting in refinement. Even should I give her half of my available resources, I had no belief that it would improve her circumstances. Mr. Carey's attempt to access her Father's fortune was troubling to me. I knew that a dowry had been paid to Rowland, and that it was a large sum. Surely an amount that substantial had not already been squandered. I wondered what Mr. Carey's mining interests were and if they had already consumed Rowland's wealth.

It were better, I reasoned, that I maintain control of my funds while I continued to appeal to Lily's sensibility. If I waited for the spring sailings, I could perhaps book our passage and make arrangements to steal her away prior to setting out. We could then return to Ireland, she called a widow, and retire to Rosslare Hall. My Uncle would provide her a modest allowance, and with my allowance together, we would be amply supported. We could leave Kathleen with a nursemaid and the two of us could travel and enjoy the delights of good society.

I could not puzzle out what it was about Mr. Carey that inspired Lily's loyalty. She could not be blinded to his many deficiencies, and surely there was no possibility of an affection between them. It must be some moral obligation that kept her at his side, or perhaps a mental affliction caused by great sorrow. Her silence on this matter was distressing.

We had a quiet dinner at the Inn that night. No other guests were present, and again the McLenaghans sat at table with Doctor Stewart and myself. Mrs. McLenaghan had made a steak and kidney pie along with some cooked cabbage and apple, altogether a tasty dish, and we enjoyed our meal. After dinner, the party taught me how to play a card game that is quite popular with the locals here. I had not played cards for a long while and found it quite diverting; we had an agreeable time together in the parlour. Mr. McLenaghan mixed some punch with the tiniest drop of rum, which warmed me pleasantly. Doctor Stewart proved himself a terrible cheat at cards and we laughed at his outrageous frivolity. Mr. McLenaghan was his partner and he also entered into the game with great sport. With the group of them such merry company, I was sorry when the hour grew late.

Come morning, I rode out again to see my Cousin. The ride was growing familiar and, despite my concerns regarding Lily's situation, I cantered at a leisurely pace, enjoying the exercise and the changing reds and oranges of the leaves. Mrs. McLenaghan had presented me with a fresh basket of biscuits, which I had wrapped in my saddle bag. As usual, however, I found myself growing anxious as I drew near the house. It was hard for me to reconcile my history of Lily with her current state. Each day I told myself to avoid judgment, but this was very difficult to do when confronted with her harshly reduced circumstances.

Mr. Clement, the hired man, greeted me when I arrived. He took the reins and helped me to dismount, bidding me "Good morning" in the most respectful of fashions. I thanked him but moved directly to the front door and rapped smartly.

My Cousin opened the door and welcomed me dispiritedly. "How are things this morning?" I enquired. "Is the baby well?"

"She is well," said Lily quietly. "We are all well."

"Well then," I replied gaily, "shall we have some tea? I've brought fresh biscuits from the Inn."

"Eleanor, I've no time for tea," said Lily crossly. "I can't sit down for half the day and pretend there is no work to do. I've laundry to wash, and food to prepare, and beds to make, and no end of things to do for Kathleen. I'm not at my leisure to visit for the morning."

I was mortified to hear her speak thus to me but felt at once the overwhelming burden of which she spoke. "Well, you must give me some instruction so that I can make myself of use."

"No!" she said, colouring. "I didn't mean that you should labour, only that I needed to keep at my work."

"Nonsense, if you can do these things, then so can I. We are made the self-same and I am as capable as you."

Lily wept at this. She sat down and sobbed for some minutes, her shoulders heaving and her tears steady. I paced the kitchen, unwilling to allow myself the luxury of tears, knowing that if we began to weep together no work would be done that morning. Mr. Carey, I sensed, would not be entirely pleased.

Lily calmed herself after a few minutes, using her apron to wipe her face dry. I was appalled to see such a vulgar act, and bit my lower lip deliberately to distract myself with a little pain. Lily began to move about the kitchen, filling a large kettle with water for washing and readying a soap mixture of lye and ash to use for boiling the diapers. I was able to help her lift the heavy kettle and was enlisted to assist with several other small chores, but mostly I watched her closely, amazed at her strength and fortitude. When I sensed that such scrutiny was making Lily feel awkward, I made my excuses and left. It was clear that social calls were not only inconvenient but created additional anxiety for her. This saddened me and I allowed myself a few tears as I rode back to O'Brien's.

A few days later, Doctor Stewart enquired after my Cousin. "I shall be on calls in the east side of the Township today," he said. "Shall I look in on Mrs. Carey?"

"I am sure she would be most grateful."

"Very well then, I shall perhaps meet with you again this day." He lingered a moment before quitting the room, and I wondered if I had been uncivil or if he had waited for a softer parting. I was not, I knew, particularly good company that morning. I had not been to the Careys for four days and was dreading a further visit. Still, I resolved to do my duty. Before walking to the Smithy I begged a bruised apple of Mrs. McLenaghan, which I placed in my pocket for the horse.

The sounds of Kathleen's wailing met me as I approached the house. My knock could not be heard over the noise and so I tentatively opened the door and stepped inside. I soon discovered Lily seated upon the settle, her top half unclothed, with Kathleen on her lap screaming and waving clenched little fists. Mr. Carey seemed to be absent.

"What is it, Cousin?" I asked, rushing over. "What is the matter?"

"She cannot eat for some reason," said Lily, "and my breasts feel as though they are on fire. I have been up with her all the night long and she has not ceased crying and fretting."

"We must feed her somehow," I said. "Have you no idea what has happened?"

"No, my breasts are swollen but somehow they have become choked and nothing comes from them."

"There is a bottle," I said. "Have you tried the bottle?"

Lily shook her head at me. I went to the kitchen and found the bottle and the calf's nipple that came with it. Moving to the larder, I seized a pitcher of milk and poured some in the bottle. I added a teaspoon of honey which I had also spied. Shaking it gently, I fastened the nipple tightly with the little piece of string and brought it to Lily. Kathleen's lips soon closed greedily upon the nipple and she began to suck at the mixture with vigour. It was drunk quickly and we both watched her relax in Lily's arms. Lily stood up and placed her in the small bassinette, rubbing her back gently for a moment until she slept. Both of us were silent, fearful of waking her. Lily began to cover herself and to adjust her clothing. She motioned to me and I followed her to the kitchen.

"It has been a terrible night," she said. "I began to wonder if the little folk had switched her for a changeling as she has not yet been christened."

"Doctor Stewart is coming today. You must tell him. There may be a way to rectify this."

"Are you often in Doctor Stewart's confidence?" she asked with sudden interest.

I looked at her carefully, trying to discern the meaning of her enquiry.

"What is it you suppose?" I finally asked her.

"I only ask if you are much together with the Doctor. You speak of him often and I wondered if you were forming an attachment."

"Of course not!" I retorted indignantly. "He is far too old and disagreeable. We are constantly quarrelling. He is very set in his opinions and can be bad tempered."

"I think him amiable."

"He is old and ugly!" I said crossly.

"Not so old, and certainly not so ugly," Lily responded gently.

"But his brow is deformed. How can you ignore such a thing?"

"His heart is loving and good, I think, Ellie. He is a true gentleman, and is refined. And I have not much noticed the small bump you speak of. Any lady should consider herself fortunate to be the object of his affections. He cannot be more than fifteen years your senior. There was almost as much difference between Rowland and me."

Again I looked at her wonderingly. "What is it you are saying,

Lily? Surely you do not believe that I have captivated him?"

"I had rather hoped so," she said sadly. "I would desire one of us, at least, to be happily situated. What of Lord Driscoll? How did you part with him? I was led to believe that you had formed an understanding."

A pang of remorse struck me then. My Father would not be alone in thinking me foolish and untrue.

"Lily, come home with me to Rosslare Hall! I have sufficient resources and can make the arrangements. We will take Kathleen. Uncle and Father will be delighted to see us both home again."

"Mr. Carey would never allow it," she said simply. "I am ruined now, Ellie, and utterly ensnared. I cannot escape the obligation."

"Lily," I countered, "do not continue with this madness. We do not belong here. This is a bad dream and I would have you waken to realize it. We must return home to our proper places. We have positions to uphold, and a family name to honour. Why should you labour here like a scullery maid? It would break my Uncle's heart to know of it."

"Eleanor, you must try to understand that I have no choice."

"And so you choose to raise Rowland McDonough's only child in a shelter fit for stable boys? Is that how you honour his memory?"

Lily looked stricken at this, remorseful even. I continued. "Lily, we will say only that you are widowed. No one need ever know about the second marriage. Mr. Carey will not object, I think. You could allow him to retain this holding in exchange for his silence."

Lily shook her head at this. "It is not so simple, Ellie."

There was a knock upon the door, and when I went to the window I saw a horse tied beside my own. I curtseyed while the Doctor entered and bowed.

"I am glad you have come," I said. "Mrs. Carey is unwell."

He nodded and walked over to my cousin. "Let us go upstairs," he said, "so that I can examine you."

I followed them up the narrow stairs to the Careys' bedchamber. Lily sat down and once more unfastened her bodice and chemise. Doctor Stewart touched each of her swollen breasts by turn, tracing the angry red streaks that marked her pale skin. I coloured deeply to see him again so intimate with my relation.

"These show me that there is milk fever present," he said. "The channel is inflamed and the milk is blocked. You must apply hot compresses regularly. Despite the discomfort, you must continue to have the baby suck; it will pull on the nipple and perhaps draw the milk out.

"Mrs. Carey," he added quietly, "are all manner of things here well? Is there naught I can do to assist you?"

Lily spoke softly in turn. "Doctor Stewart, I thank you for your attentions, but I am well. I know what course I must follow."

"There are friends close by, willing to be of service."

She nodded at him but did not speak further. I wondered at the strangeness of this exchange.

The Doctor excused himself while Lily adjusted her clothing. I went downstairs and rejoined him in the kitchen.

"What do we feed the baby?" I asked him.

"What has been tried thus far?"

"Only some milk with honey in a bottle."

"Try some bread mashed in milk with sweetener. Molasses or honey will do. She will need to be fed with a small spoon. Also some water in a bottle to keep her from becoming too dry. The compresses for Mrs. Carey should be applied every hour."

I simply nodded at him, mortified anew. Lily, fortunately, was descending the stairs, and remembering her manners in a most untimely fashion, determined that we should have tea.

"I shall come, Cousin," I said to her, "and stay with you a while. I will try to help with the baby while you treat your affliction. Mr. Carey will have no objection, will he?"

"It is not necessary for you to do so, Dear. I shall manage."

"No. I think not. I will return to the Inn for some things and will come again in the morning."

"As you wish. I will be grateful for some small relief."

I stood to embrace her carefully and began to take my leave. The Doctor stood also.

"Miss Courtown," he began, "I have now completed my visitations. May I impose upon you for the pleasure of your company? There is a small glen but a short ride from here that you may find to your liking. I should be happy to show it you."

"Thank you, Sir, but no," I said haughtily. "I have much to prepare and should soon begin."

"Nonsense!" said Lily. "A good ride is just the thing! I only wish that I could join you."

"Is it settled then?" enquired Doctor Stewart, smiling at us both. "Have you been persuaded?"

Not wishing to be ungracious, I acquiesced while glaring at my Cousin, who wrinkled her nose at me playfully. She was pleased at least, and I was gladdened, in some small part, to see her, briefly, a little light-hearted.

Moving to my horse, I prepared to mount awkwardly without a block, but the Doctor came to my ready assistance. Grinning like a naughty schoolboy, he lifted me and swung me high before placing me upon my saddle. I gasped at his forwardness but he only laughed at my displeasure. His face relaxed when he was laughing, I noticed, and his mouth did not then seem so over-large. I considered this critically, remembering my Cousin's recent remarks, and found myself colouring deeply. He had touched her bosom with these very same hands, I thought, and performed goodness knew what other such indignities this day.

Doctor Stewart swung himself up easily onto his horse and led the way down the grassy lane and across country further eastward. Once I had caught up with him, we rode alongside one another without conversation. I glanced at him from time to time and saw that, despite his years, he was fit and strong. If it were not for his disfigurement, he would look quite presentable overall, and perhaps, as Lily had suggested, not entirely unattractive. He was genteel enough and had never behaved indecently towards me in any way, save for his bold conversations. If he would only abandon his heavy tweeds for finer wool suiting he might look very much improved.

"You seem quite serious, Miss Courtown," he began. "What are you contemplating so intently?"

"Only something foolish my Cousin has said to me. Nothing of consequence."

"We are almost there, just beyond the next rise." He pointed to a hill a mile or two in the distance and then kicked at his horse, setting off at a fast gallop. I did likewise, laughing at our sudden flight. We rode hard for several minutes and gradually eased up as we neared the glen, where our horses picked their way slowly down the steep embankment. Shortly we found ourselves in a lovely spot next to a small river. Dismounting, Doctor Stewart allowed his horse to drink and wander freely. He came next to my horse and reached his arms up to my waist, pulling me down beside him quickly and easily. He did not at once release his hold of me and I stiffened my carriage, becoming quite rigid.

"You are as light as a child," he said, stepping away. "You ride well.

I can imagine that you and Mrs. Carey have had much pleasure riding together."

I softened at this, and felt relieved that he was once more attempting to be agreeable.

"Yes," I said. "But my Cousin was always the better rider. She was bolder and not nervous of jumping walls or hedgerows. She was, at a young age, permitted to join the hunt. Father would not allow me to accompany them, as I once tumbled while attempting to jump a stone fence near home, and damaged my wrist."

"Was it much hurt?" he asked, reaching for my hands and scrutinizing the gloved wrists.

"No," I said, "it was only a sprain. You could not now tell which one it was."

To my astonishment, he turned over my left wrist and carefully unbuttoned the glove. Pulling at the leather tips, he slowly slid the glove from my hand and began to feel each of the fingers by turn, caressing them softly and stroking the bones. Circling my wrist with his middle finger and thumb, he pushed gently at the bone. His bent head was close to my face and I studied his thick, wavy red hair and saw how clean it was, and glossy. His collar was fresh and the scent of clean soap came from him. I found his touch strangely soothing.

I wondered if he was about to make love to me and thought quickly how to respond. Lily considered him an appropriate suitor, but I was determined upon returning to Ireland and had no plan to become attached. Besides which, there was yet a gentleman there who was owed the courtesy of a full explanation.

"It is this one, I think," he said, retaining my left hand in both of his own. "I have noticed that you favour it sometimes."

"Yes, you are correct. But I am right-handed and you have only made a lucky guess."

He chuckled at this. "That may be, but I have had the pleasure of studying it nonetheless."

I removed my hand from within his clasp, colouring deeply, and said, "You are very bold, Sir." Even as I did so, I thought how strange it was to be so much alone with this man and to feel comforted by his company and the sense that he would gladly share in my small cares and worries. Removing his jacket, he spread it on the ground and encouraged me to be seated. We had a pleasant time there in the still glen as we listened quietly to the bird calls and the river sounds. I was relaxed, and unbuttoned my jacket in the hot sun, feeling a deep sense of contentment and peace.

"I am happy here," I said, reclining upon the grass. "I can almost imagine that I am but a short ride from home and that Mrs. Finnigan, our housekeeper, will have a lovely dinner ready for us upon our return. Father will be late back, and his man, Mr. Meagher, will be impatient to dress him for the evening. If no one joins us for dinner, we will retreat together to the library where he will enjoy a glass of whiskey and I will read to him." I sighed at this. "I miss him," I said. "He will be so alone with me abroad. I can only hope that he is much in company."

Doctor Stewart had stretched out upon the grass and was entirely close to me. I could imagine that I almost felt his long legs nearly touching my skirt.

"I have something of a familiar nature to ask of you," he said.

I felt a panic, suspecting, as Lily had indicated, that he might now ruin this interlude with clumsy love-making and an unwelcome declaration.

"Please do not speak," I said, leaning over him and placing my fingers lightly upon his lips. "Do not spoil our time together in this beautiful place."

His eyes caught mine and we looked at each other intently.

"Miss Courtown," he began, "you must know by now that I am intending to be your friend, and as your friend, I must say that I am unhappy about your decision to reside with the Careys, however briefly. You are not suited to such a place, and I have a strong foreboding of ill."

"Is that all?" I asked him quietly.

"No!" he replied, standing up and becoming quite animated. "That is not all! You are headstrong and determined but also vulnerable and in need of protection. I am driven half mad with worry about you some days. It is miraculous to me that you have come this far and are yet unharmed."

I was taken aback by the direction of this outburst. "Why should I not be safe?" I enquired, standing up also and facing him. "I travel mostly in good company and conduct myself as any lady would do. I am very capable of managing and can look after myself."

"You are not!" he said gruffly. "You underestimate danger. Here you are, for instance, at Perry's Glen in the middle of a wilderness, and in the company of a man you have known but a month. What would you do if I acted improperly? How would you correct me? You are but a slip of a woman, trusting too readily as I suspect your Cousin has also done."

I was incensed by the comparison to Lily and tears of anger filled my eyes. "You are a gentleman," I said, moving close to him, "and I am not afraid of you!" I looked up angrily into his face. "You would not dare to insult me," I continued fiercely, "not even in this uncivilized place. I am your equal in rank and station, and I will not be cowed!"

He looked down at me, his face conflicted with much emotion. I saw tenderness there, but also arrogance.

"And what," said he, "would you do to stop me from making improper advances? Any man could overpower you." He placed his hands on my arms and held them firmly to demonstrate his point. Both of us were angry and breathing fast, but also perhaps aware of something else besides.

I placed my hands upon his arms and grasped them tightly. "I would fight you," I said evenly, "to the death." He released me at this and began to laugh. I was furious with him and stood with clenched fists ready to prove myself, but he moved apart from me and sat down once more, laughing each time he looked at me. I was insulted and stood over him, ready to abuse him for his lack of civility.

"You are quite correct," he said, becoming sober, "and I am mistaken. Please forgive me. I will not broach this subject with you again." Despite his recent merriment he looked contrite, and so I stiffly offered him my hand. He stood and bowed then, kissing the back of it and releasing it quickly.

"We should return to the Inn," he said. "May I assist you in mounting?"

I nodded and he cupped his hands for me. I mounted quickly and began to ride up the embankment without waiting for him. We rode in silence. I was brooding. Our visit to the glen had been mostly pleasant, but he had ruined that pleasantness with his clumsy manner. I had much to prepare for morning and could not indulge myself with thoughts of suitors and courtships. Besides which, there were those at home who might consider that I was already engaged. There had by no means been a public announcement, but he had already received my Father's consent and encouragement enough from me to make everyone think the negotiation was soon to be completed.

I dismounted at the Smithy. "I shall ride further yet," the Doctor said. "Good day." I curtseyed but did not speak. It was an awkward parting. Walking the short distance to the Inn, I rubbed my arms where he had pressed them and coloured at the remembrance of our uncomfortable intimacy.

Chapter the Third
DESOLATION

Returning to the Inn, I found Mrs. McLenaghan in the kitchen. After I explained my plans she offered to prepare foodstuffs for my visit and agreed to keep my trunks until I returned for them. I went upstairs to pack some things into a large carpet bag and set aside some money to settle my account. This I would give the McLenaghans in the morning. My remaining coin I transferred to a leather wallet which I placed at the bottom of my bag, underneath the gowns I had packed. The bills that remained I put between the pages of my prayer book, tying it fast with a ribbond for that especial purpose. I had travelled that way quite safely, carrying my prayer book always with me and in plain sight. My bank book I sewed back into its special pocket, in the lining of my heaviest petticoat.

Come morning, I was ill rested and saw in the glass that my eyes were rimmed with dark shadows. Leaving my bags in my room, I went down to the kitchen where I found the McLenaghans seated at their breakfast. "The Doctor is in the dining room, Lass," said Mrs. McLenaghan, "with the other guests."

"I can only stop a moment. I have much to attend to this morning." I placed my envelope with the sum for several weeks' lodgings in it upon the table.

Mr. McLenaghan thanked me, taking it up at once and placing it in his vest. "Can I drive you there?" he asked. "We can take a buggy from O'Brien's and not deprive him of a horse."

I saw the logic of this and agreed.

"The Doctor will be by to visit you, I suppose," added Mrs. McLenaghan, "and will bring us news."

"Thank you," I said, rising. "You have been most kind." Surprisingly, I felt tears welling in my eyes, but managed to control my emotions and maintain my composure.

Mr. McLenaghan went outside to ready the horses and buggy. I stood waiting for him by the front door, my bags having been carried downstairs, and the two small wooden crates filled with the baking and preserves that Mrs. McLenaghan had readied nearby.

Mr. McLenaghan had just joined me in the front hall when the Doctor emerged from the dining room. We greeted one another coldly, I curtseying and he bowing, without exchanging pleasantries. I saw him assessing the situation. When Mr. McLenaghan opened the door, he silently reached down for the larger of the two crates and carried it to the buggy. Returning to the Inn, he carried out the second crate and placed this also within the buggy.

Drawing close and speaking softly so that no one could overhear, he said to me, "Please know that I am your friend and will remain always at your service." His face was much flushed and he bowed abruptly, leaving me no opportunity to respond.

Mr. McLenaghan helped me into the buggy then and we drove to the Carey farm directly. Lily stood at the open door when we arrived; I saw that her hair was pinned up and her apron removed. These were good signs, I thought, and so I stepped lightly from the buggy and moved towards the house.

"Mr. Carey has not yet risen," said my Cousin, "so we need to remain quiet and not disturb his rest."

"But it is near mid-morning!" I exclaimed. "Has he no work to do?"

"It is best," said Lily, looking much worried, "if we do not much speak while he is resting."

I grimaced at this but obliged her, motioning for Mr. McLenaghan to carry the two crates into the kitchen.

"How are you?" I whispered. "Is there any improvement?"

She shook her head and looked uncomfortably about.

"Is there something more amiss?"

"No," she said, "the mash is keeping Kathleen satisfied."

Mr. McLenaghan interjected to wish us both farewell. He clasped me warmly by the hand and pumped it vigorously. He was a simple man, but I had grown accustomed to his genuine manner. As I watched him drive off I felt a pang of sorrow.

Lily and I then emptied the crates together, stowing things in her larder and pantry. When Kathleen began to rouse and fuss I went to the kitchen and easily prepared her mash. Holding her on my lap, I fed her tiny teaspoons, followed by sips of water. She ate greedily; I confess that I found her a bit ferocious in her need. As she rested there in my arms I looked at her wonderingly, asking her quietly if she knew who I was and if she had heard of Ireland.

Lily then began her preparations for the hot compresses. She sat beside me with a shawl covering her discreetly. I was gratified by this and believed that she was after remembering how to conduct herself.

Late in the afternoon Mr. Carey wakened and went directly outdoors. The hired man, John Clement, had been in to check on him several times, and had finally gone off on his own to work in the fields. I believed Mr. Clement had much to recommend him by way of his concern for Mrs. Carey and the deferential manner in which he spoke to us both.

Nightfall came early, it seemed. Lily had prepared a simple dinner and laid it out on the kitchen table; Mr. Carey and Mr. Clement came in at dark and sat down with us to eat. Mr. Carey crossed himself and muttered a quick grace before attacking the meal set before him. I sat there in disbelief: he had crossed himself as the Catholics did. Surely this was not possible. I picked at my meal but did not much eat. I caught Lily staring from time to time, her eyes pleading with me.

"Are you far from home?" I finally asked Mr. Clement.

"Not so far, Miss," he answered. "I came from Kirby with my Brothers a couple of years back and we found work in Port Whitby. Winter came and I took a job farming and have been working on farms ever since. Learning about local practice. My Brothers and me, we will all get together to buy our own place."

"Well, it is good to have family near," I replied meekly. "Family is a great comfort."

We finished our dinner in silence. I could not look at my Cousin. The men left after their meal and Lily and I began to clear the table together.

"Tell me it's not true," I said to her. "Tell me he's not a Papist!"

"What possible difference would that make now, Ellie?" she replied. "The deed is done."

"Did you know?" I pressed her. "Did you know this when you married him?"

"It matters not," she said. "Things in this country are very much different. We're not in Ireland now."

"Not that different! Did you or did you not know that he was a Catholic?"

"Ellie, this will not improve things. For the love of all that's holy, leave off," she rejoined.

Lily and I commenced the dish-washing, each of us lost in our thoughts. "Do not judge me, Cousin," she said after much silence, "or you will break my heart."

Later, as I lay in bed, I heard Lily speaking to her husband in quiet tones before they came upstairs. I could not make out the words, but she seemed to be answering questions and attempting to soothe him. I wondered if, for her sake, I should offer a gift of some sort. A wedding gift to purchase something needful for the farm, perhaps.

I heard them come upstairs, then their door shutting and the sounds of them pacing around their room. Presently I heard the bedstead creaking and, for a moment, all was quiet. To my great shame, I soon heard other sounds. The bedstead was screeching as though something unnatural was causing it stress. Groaning and panting came through the thin walls until I could almost feel the surging of violence that was taking place. I was mortified to think that Mr. Clement, asleep below in the kitchen, was also witness to my Cousin's humiliation. I lay there, fearful and angry, throughout the long night. Kathleen was scarcely two weeks of age and Lily's wounds could not yet have healed.

My resolve to free her from this domination was reinforced. I knew that I must ingratiate myself with Mr. Carey to remove any suspicion he might have about my intentions. At first light, I descended the stairs and set the kettle to boil, attempting to put together a breakfast. Mr. Carey was surprised to see me dressed and cheerful when he came downstairs. He sat down and ate the meal without complaining.

"I have been thinking," I said, when the others had joined us, "that I have been remiss in providing a wedding gift. I wonder, Mr.

Carey, if you would allow me to purchase something for your farming operation. It would gratify me to feel that I had been able to provide something of use."

Lily looked up at me, smiled tentatively, and put her hand on Mr. Carey's arm. "How generous," she said. "Eleanor, thank you."

Mr. Carey stared at me boldly. I could see him measuring and evaluating my offer, calculating his response. "Your presence, Cousin, has already brought us much joy, but I would by no means risk offending you by refusing an offer so generous."

"I would be happy to finance any one thing you thought needful, Mr. Carey. The gift is intended to be liberal. You need only say what it is you require, and I will draw you a cheque."

I stood at that point and busied myself with the making of tea. Lily eyed me guardedly. She suspected that I was up to something, but she would not, I knew, betray me.

"I will happily consider your offer," said Mr. Carey. "I do not suppose there is an urgency in the matter."

"No, of course not. I am delighted that you will allow me the privilege."

At that he and Mr. Clement left the kitchen, and I worked hard to stifle a little laugh.

"Ellie, what are you about?" asked Lily.

"Simply trying to ease things," I said. "Mr. Carey is family now and I thought to make him a suitable gift. Every man likes an expensive horse. I shall let him choose his pleasure."

"You must be careful," Lily cautioned. "Jack is not a man to be trifled with."

"I simply intend to make him a gift for the betterment of your family. How could that be taken amiss?"

"Please be careful, Ellie," she said again. There was a warning in her words, and a fear, and this made me quiet and sober.

Late in the morning, Mr. Carey appeared unexpectedly in the kitchen. "I have been thinking, Cousin," he said, smiling at me and bowing, "that it would give me great satisfaction to purchase stock before winter. About eighty head. We would also need a shelter for them and a fence. The gift would need to be sufficiently ..." He paused for a moment, searching for a word. "Liberal. Sufficiently liberal to facilitate this."

"A wonderful idea," I enthused.

"It would cost you a sum," he added, studying my face. "Seven hundred dollars would suffice."

"As much as that?" I said, feigning surprise.

"That would cover all the requisites as I am sure you intended."

"Of course. It is rather more than I expected, and will exhaust my wealth, but you are most welcome to it. I shall write a cheque this afternoon." Although it was outrageous, it was no more than antici-pated. I intended to let him think that I would be destitute now, with no means to purchase passage for Lily and Kathleen and me. I hoped by this ruse to disarm him of any suspicion.

When the men returned to the outdoors, Lily reproached me. "Do not give us all your fortune, Cousin," she said. "Half that amount is over-generous. Set aside enough so that you can return home."

I patted her arm and told her that I could always write my Father and request further funds. Then I went upstairs, unpacked my small secretary, and wrote a cheque. I also wrote a direction to the bank. I placed the cheque and this letter in an envelope which I further fastened with my seal pressed in a small dollop of wax.

It was my intention to hand over the envelope to Mr. Carey at dinner that evening, but he was not so patient as that; he returned to the house mid-afternoon to see if I had it ready. I placed it in his hands, thanking him for the privilege of being allowed to do so. He took it from me, bowing deeply. "Much obliged," he muttered, and then jammed the envelope into his waistcoat pocket and left the house forthwith. Mr. Carey took the horse and rode off in the direction of town. I assumed that he was riding straight to the bank.

He did not return for several days, which provided a pleasant respite. Mr. Clement, who suggested that he had gone further east to purchase the cattle, busied himself with setting fence posts and readying an enclosure of sorts for the stock.

Mr. and Mrs. McLenaghan paid us a call on my third day with the Careys. Mrs. McLenaghan embraced me tightly and wept a little. Lily made us tea and we sat in the parlour while Kathleen slept nearby in her little crib. Mr. McLenaghan went outside to visit with Mr. Clement and left his wife and me alone in the parlour for a private conversation.

"We have been missing you at the Inn," began Mrs. McLenaghan. "Doctor Stewart has moved out also, you know. His house is all finely finished. He still comes for meals, so we are not all that often without his company. He asked after you last evening, as a matter of fact. He wondered whether we had heard news of you. And I said to Harry, 'Harry,' I said, 'I think we should just take a little drive out tomorrow and make certain that our Miss Courtown is being well looked after.' And then Harry said, 'Well, Mother, if it would make you feel better, I reckon that's just the thing.' And so here we are now. Checking to make certain you are not in need."

"I am quite well," I said cheerfully. "You can see that my Cousin and I are dear to one another, no matter the situation."

"But is the situation to your liking, Lass?" probed Mrs. McLenaghan, looking about the room pointedly. "Is it as it should be?"

"Of course," I lied. "We are becoming established in our

routines and Kathleen grows stronger and healthier each day."

"Is Mr. Carey away from home?" she enquired.

I coloured at this, and responded carefully, "He is travelling just now, in search of some stock to purchase."

"Yes, we had heard as much," nodded Mrs. McLenaghan. He was at the Hotel yesterday and made free to tell the men that he had come into money. Apparently dividends from a copper mine were paid to him. He was quite animated, as I understand. Stood half the village to drinks."

Mrs. McLenaghan studied my face. "Are you sure now that things are as they ought to be? Your room is ready at the Inn and we can take you with us."

I shook my head. "Thank you," I answered, "but I am yet needed here."

Mr. McLenaghan and Lily soon rejoined us in the parlour and the McLenaghans made ready to leave. I was sorry to see them go and sorrier still to have heard the news about Mr. Carey.

I turned to Lily after their departure. "Mrs. McLenaghan has told me that Mr. Carey was at the Hotel in the village, buying drinks and making free to celebrate his good fortune. What do you know about his copper mine?"

"Oh, Ellie," she said, "do not be so harsh. He intends well. He will return home soon, I'm sure, with the stock purchased."

"I am not so certain. It may be that I have bought your liberty."

"Eleanor, enough!" she burst out. "No more of this! I beg that you would stop. I know that it is not so fine a place as one might wish. But it is a start. And Jack has striven hard for it. He has done it for me. He could be in Arizona tending to his mining investments. This is the best that I can hope for. There is nothing for me in Ireland. With Rowland gone, I was quite adrift. Father has the boys and the estate must be portioned to support them. The McDonoughs have several sons and they could not be expected to support me for long even though they be generous. I knew when Rowland died that I would have to remarry."

"But Lily," I interjected, "why did you act so quickly? Why did you not wait for me? You knew that I would come."

"Ellie, please ..." Lily left off speaking and began to weep. "You cannot know," she sobbed, "you cannot know what I have endured. What I continue to endure. You do not understand the cruelty of a man without scruples or conscience. I am not at liberty to decide these things."

I saw how deeply distressed she was, and felt that this was as true an accounting as any she had given. Each day of Mr. Carey's absence had filled me with a greater sense of hope.

We were readying the house for bed when we heard a great clattering outside. There was much shouting and the sound of several voices. Mr. Clement reached for the rifle behind the door, and took a lantern with him outdoors.

"Be careful, John," whispered my Cousin. "It could be anyone."

"Secure the door behind me," he replied, "and get upstairs with the baby." I ran to the parlour, lifted Kathleen out of her crib, and passed her to Lily. We went upstairs together and crowded into my room, waiting silently.

"Perhaps it is Jack returned," whispered Lily.

"Let us hope not," I muttered. But sadly she was correct. Mr. Clement knocked loudly upon the door and said that Mr. Carey and some friends had returned home. I remained with the baby whilst Lily went down to remove the bar from the door. I heard several men enter the kitchen and then much roaring and carrying on. Mr. Clement's voice could also be heard from time to time, trying to calm the group.

Presently Mr. Carey bade his friends to the table and offered them the hospitality of his house. There was much bustling and scraping of furniture; I realized that Lily and Mr. Clement had prepared a late evening meal for them. At length Mr. Carey, having discovered that no whiskey was in the house, shouted at Mr. Clement to produce some or die. He accused him of drinking it in his absence. It were a nasty accusation, and despite Mr. Clement's reasonable tones, it escalated into violence. There was a thumping and some crashing sounds, and then I heard Mr. Carey ordering Mr. Clement from the house. Lily came upstairs and tapped quietly upon the door. I moved the chair to let her enter.

"What is happening, Cousin?" I asked her. "No good will come of this night."

"No," she said, "Jack has fought with John."

The three of us slept together on my small cot. Kathleen snuggled happily between us, and was, fortunately, mostly quiet through the night. I woke early and lay still, trying to discern if there was movement below stairs. Lily woke also and we looked at each other, wondering if it were safe to go down.

"You stay here with Kathleen," she said, "and I will see what has transpired."

A few minutes later, she returned upstairs. "It is fine," she said. "The men have all left. Jack is the only one I can see."

"And what of Mr. Clement?"

She shook her head sadly. "I can't see him."

I followed her downstairs, where Mr. Carey was sprawled on the settle in the parlour. The front door stood ajar and a mess of broken crockery lay scattered on the floor. Furniture had been knocked over and the house looked worse than its usual terrible state.

I collected my wrap, told Lily that I needed some fresh air, and went for a long walk out of doors, knowing that I needed to mind my tongue and not give way to temper. Somehow I must book passage, and must make these arrangements in haste and secrecy. I wondered if I could engage the bank manager's services in these matters. He might, if appealed to, be prevailed upon to assist me. I would need to visit him in person to solicit his assistance, and to do so, I would need to borrow Mr. Carey's horse. This must be my first step, I reasoned. Pleased to once more have a plan, I turned and began my walk back to the house.

Upon entering, I saw that my Cousin had prepared luncheon, and that Mr. Carey was at the table, eating. "Good afternoon," I greeted them. "I have been for a most lovely walk. The air is crisp and fresh this day."

"Sit down, Cousin, and join us," invited Mr. Carey.

Smiling, I sat with them, remembering my early training in charm, and began to eat. Mr. Carey said little, but Lily bravely attempted to carry a conversation.

"Was your business venture a successful one?" I finally asked of Mr. Carey. He had the grace to look slightly abashed, but answered me.

"I bought stock," he said, "but was cheated on the price. They will be driven over in a week's time. There is fencing to finish first."

"Perhaps Mr. Clement can assist you in your labours," I suggested.

"Mr. Clement has left our service," replied Mr. Carey rather grandly. "I found him to be dishonest and have dismissed him." I glanced at Lily and saw that she looked frightened.

"I'm sorry to hear it," I said. "But hired help is often fickle. I'm sure it is nothing you have done."

He looked at me suspiciously and stood abruptly from the table, scraping his chair back and striding directly to the door without his usual effort at courtesy. "I've work," he said curtly, and left the house.

Lily and I spoke not. Both of us were worried. Mr. Carey worked outside until late in the evening; I saw from the window that he was attempting to fasten wire to the posts Mr. Clement had set. He was having great difficulty managing this on his own, and the effect looked skewed and haphazard.

The next morning at breakfast, I approached Mr. Carey to ask the loan of his horse for the day. I told him that I was anxious to see if I had mail from home and wondered if I could perform any errands for the household. I claimed to have need of a warmer jacket and said that I had left one in my trunk.

"It would be my joy to accommodate you," he said, "but allow me to go in your stead. I will gladly get what is required." Although I protested, it was clear that Mr. Carey now intended to go to the village and that I was to remain imprisoned in the house. I had no choice in the matter but to graciously thank him for his trouble. I felt thwarted and angry. He rode off shortly.

Although I was frustrated in my plans, there was a small measure of relief in knowing that we were to be without him for a few hours. We stood by the front door and watched him leave. Lily put her arm about my waist and said, "I'm sorry, Eleanor, I know that you must be craving some varied society."

"Not at all," I assured her. "You are the only society I require."

Both of us sighed and we stood there, each with an arm about the other's waist and our heads resting together. It were an intimate moment of great sadness and mutual despair.

Mr. Carey did not return at dusk and Lily began to fret at the length of time away. Although I allowed myself the happy thought that he had fallen from his horse and was killed, I saw that my Cousin was increasingly anxious. "What is it that worries you?" I finally asked her.

"Only that he has stopped at the Hotel for a game of chance," she replied quietly, "and that he will return home in a foul temper."

"Does that much happen?"

She did not answer directly, but I saw fear in her expression.

"You must stand up to him," I said, "and not let him dominate you."

"No," she said, "I must do no such thing. He is not a man to take such from a woman. That is why we have no maids to help us. His demands were not reasonable and they fled when they experienced the force of his temper."

"Has he hurt you?"

She busied herself then, pretending not to hear my repeated question. I went to bed early, determined not to aggravate the situation should he arrive home in a bad state.

I must have dozed off, for it was soon morning; I heard Kathleen rousing. I went over to her and saw that she was kicking her chubby little legs, and that her bedding was sodden and unpleasant. I picked her up and changed her, cuddling her close and kissing her a little. Her fair hair had a copper tinge to it and her bright blue eyes seemed very alert. I studied her to assure myself that she was entirely Rowland McDonough's daughter. She seemed not unhappy to see me and I held her by my side while I went downstairs to prepare her mash.

Mr. Carey was in the kitchen, asleep with his head upon the table. I tried not to disturb him and tiptoed about my business. He sat up shortly, rubbed his eyes, and then reached for Kathleen. He held her high in the air and said all manner of foolish things to her, but I was able to finish preparing her meal and did not snatch her back. When the mash was prepared, I sat down at the table across from him with the small bowl and spoon.

"Shall you hold her while I feed her?" I enquired politely.

"No," he said, passing her to me. "You take her. My wife is sleeping still. I will make the porridge."

This astonished me as I had never before seen him at such a domestic task. I watched him critically between my feeding Kathleen small mouthfuls. He seemed to know what he was about and promptly pronounced that the porridge was done. He poured one bowl of it ready for me, topping it with some cream and sugar. This he placed before me before readying his own bowl. I waited until Kathleen was fed before tasting my breakfast. It was hot and overly sweet, but I thanked him for his trouble and began to eat.

He seemed well pleased with my compliments and in very fine humour. "There are letters for you," he said, shoving two envelopes towards me. I recognized the hand on the one, and saw at once that it were from my Father.

I took it from him and clasped it to my chest. "Thank you," I said. "This is welcome indeed."

"Do you have much family?"

"Not really, we lived quietly by the sea. Father was much in Dublin and Lily and I were often together."

"Do you have brothers?"

"No, Lily has brothers. And they will inherit both her Father's house and mine." His interest in these things had aroused my suspicions.

"Is that common?" he pressed. "It seems unusual."

I answered carefully. "Our families are close and it has always been understood. I expect that Lily's youngest brother, Denis, will visit in the spring to ensure that we are both well situated."

"She has never said so to me. We will be vastly overjoyed to receive him."

"Yes, I am sure you will be quite taken with Denis. He has been educated at Trinity for the law. People always find his manners charming."

I made myself busy with Kathleen while Mr. Carey prepared to go outside. I saw him take a saffron-coloured jacket from a chest by the door and slip it on. This caught at my heart, and I took in my breath sharply. He turned and looked at me, grinning at my discomfort. "Is there something the matter?"

He was wearing a piece of Rowland's uniform for his out-door labours. It was the saffron coat of the Royal Irish Rifles: I had recognized it immediately. "I am only a little surprised," I replied. I had last seen the coat in Ireland when Rowland wore it to his wedding. Many of the regiment were there, clad in their coats and kilts. I felt my face flush hot. Mr. Carey laughed meanly at my obvious distress and left the house.

With Mr. Carey gone, I made free to slit open my letters and begin to read them. My Father had written a long letter filled with the entire spectrum of his emotional state: anger and disappointment that I had disobeyed him; relief that I was yet safe; fear that I would not continue to remain so; pride that I had braved the journey on Lily's behalf. There was much pleading that I would quickly return to Rosslare Hall and also some news about the servants and neighbours. He had enclosed a bank draft for further funds, lest we be in need of them. There was no indication that anyone had been dispatched to return us safely home.

The second letter I enclose here, lest in my pride I minimize its contents and do a further disservice to its writer.

Miss Courtown,

My hope is that my missive finds you in health and happiness. I beg that you would pardon the forwardness of this communication.

I have been led to understand that overwhelming concern for your Cousin created the necessity of a hasty departure, without affording you time to bid farewell to those who might wish you to do so. You are in no doubt as to my own intentions and desires. Given your abrupt leave-taking, I can only assume that your affections are not, as I believed, engaged, and that the match which I had believed to be of mutual satisfaction has in some way now become undesirable. If I have given offence, or in any way been the source of displeasure, please know that I would be deeply grieved by the knowledge and would not hesitate to make amends, with the intention that all would once more be restored. If, however, you are established in the direction that I believe your leave-taking indicates, then I release you with my blessing and my every wish for your continued well-being and happiness.

Robert J. Driscoll, Esquire

I was yet at the table rereading these words when Lily came downstairs. She looked haggard and I rose to greet her, extending my Father's letter. She took this from me and smiled weakly. "How are things at home, Ellie? What news is there?"

I began to recount some small domestic details when I noticed that she was rubbing at her left arm. "What has happened, Lily?" I asked her. "You favour your arm."

"It is nothing," she said, colouring. "I have only slept on it in a peculiar way and it is stiff."

I watched her as she went to pour some tea and saw that her wrist looked reddened. "Are you sure that is all?" I asked again.

"Yes, of course," she said, looking down at the letter. I watched her reading the brief and saw different expressions flit quickly across her face.

"Put that away carefully," she said, passing me the bank draft. You must use it to go home."

I took it from her and secured it neatly under a garter. "It will do here for a while," I said. "There is enough for passage for all three of us, Lily. I can make the arrangements."

She looked at me slowly and shook her head. "Do not think so, Ellie. I am not in your situation. I will not be allowed to leave."

"Oh Lord, Lily! I can extricate you from this mess! We can return to our former life. Kathleen can be raised in privilege."

"Eleanor," she sighed, "do you not think that I know whereof I speak? I cannot do other than what I am doing. Do not make this harder for me, please God."

The day passed slowly and in much silence. I would not broach the subject again and was not much interested in anything else. The next morning, I went downstairs to discover that Mr. Carey was again risen before us to prepare the morning porridge. Unaware of my presence, he held a bowl of it to his mouth and supped noisily, like a dog. I was taken aback by this and coughed discreetly to signal my presence. He put the bowl down at once and stood to greet me, his face a smiling mask, his manner disarming and convivial.

While I fed Kathleen, he served me a bowl of porridge carefully treated with fresh cream and too much sugar. Lily joined us and took Kathleen from me. As she did so, I saw the sleeve of her gown fall away from her wrist. Where it had been reddened the day before was a bruise growing purple in a complete circle around her wrist. I eyed it quickly and then looked away. Mr. Carey excused himself after we ate, and I stood to clear the table. As I did so, a sharp pain drew my breath away and caused me to lean on the back of the chair.

"What is it, Cousin?" asked Lily.

"I don't rightly know," I said. "I had the strangest of pains."

"Is it your monthly course?"

"No, and that never troubles as this has done. I don't know what it was."

"You should rest today, Ellie," she said. "It may be that you are over-exerted."

"Yes," I agreed, "we are both doing more than we are accustomed."

The balance of the day was uneventful save for the arrival of the drovers with the cattle. I had several more stabbing pains and a very troubled constitution. I drank a glass of cream, hoping to settle it, but this did not help at all, and I continued to feel compromised.

To my great relief, Doctor Stewart paid us a call in the evening. I was eager to speak to him in private and attempt to press for assistance in rescuing Lily, but Mr. Carey was in an unusually good humour and did not leave us alone for a moment.

"The McLenaghans have been missing you, Miss Courtown," said the Doctor. "They have engaged me to bring you their greetings and affection. I know that they would have gladly accompanied me here this evening, but there are guests at the Inn and they could no leave."

"Thank you," I replied, "the McLenaghans have been very kind. Please tell them how grateful I am for their attentions."

Mr. Carey interjected then, insisting that Doctor Stewart accompany him to admire the cattle.

"Will you join us, Miss Courtown?" enquired the Doctor.

"Thank you, but I have no marked interest in cattle and am not feeling entirely well."

He stood and bowed before taking his leave with Mr. Carey. I could have wept with disappointment. Lily looked at me strangely as I threw myself upon the settle.

"What is it, Ellie? Are you upset by the call? Shall we join the men outside?"

"No," I said petulantly. "No, that will not do at all." I felt devastated to have lost my opportunity to plead for help from the only friendly face I had seen for some days. I sat fretting quietly. Then came a knock upon the door, and the Doctor re-entered.

"You said you were not entirely well," he remarked. "Is this a matter in which I might provide you some comfort?"

My eyes filled with tears at this but I shook my head, for Mr. Carey had followed him inside and was standing also in the parlour, listening carefully to our exchange. "Thank you, Sir," I replied. "I am well enough, only tired perhaps from an eventful day."

"Very well, then," he said, "I should leave you to retire." I saw him scrutinizing my face while he bowed. I was sure that he had read my unhappiness and would know that something was amiss.

"Well, well," said Mr. Carey, turning to me brightly. "It seems the Doctor has taken an interest in someone."

"It was good of him to call," I responded. "He is a busy man."

"Do you know him well, Cousin?"

"I am certain I have no idea what you mean. Doctor Stewart is the most casual of acquaintances." I stiffened my carriage at this, and swept out of the parlour and up the stairs to my room.

Much later, Lily brought Kathleen in and settled her in the crib. I looked over at her and found myself thinking that, for all her wasted beauty and talent, she was a fool who had once more got us into trouble. We were often, as girls, disciplined for her daring schemes and misadventures. Lily lingered for a moment, kissing the baby and adjusting her blankets.

"Are you very unhappy, Cousin?" she asked me softly.

"Yes, deeply unhappy."

"Have you formed an attachment?"

"I have not! I long only for us to return safely home."

"Then you must do so," she said quietly, "but understand that you go alone. I will not attempt it."

I slept but poorly and was sick in the night. The pains afflicted me greatly. It seemed that I had contracted some sort of influenza and it was working hard upon me. I had chills and fever and loosened bowels, in addition to retching many times. I knocked upon Lily's door and suggested that she take Kathleen from my room so as not to expose her to my illness. She came at once, pausing only to bring me some water and some peppermint tea to ease my upset. She asked if I wanted Mr. Clement to ride for the Doctor but I declined the offer, needing not his scorn and reprimands but wanting only some assistance with Lily's liberation from this place.

Two days later, waking early, I went downstairs to the small parlour and was seated there when I heard the sound of a buggy outside on the gravel. Mr. Carey opened the front door to see who it was.

"Well," he said, "it is the Doctor again." Mr. Carey went outside and shut the door behind him.

I stood up and tried to tidy my hair, wishing that I had taken more time with my morning toilette.

Chapter the Fourth
PROVIDENCE

To my great relief, Mr. Carey ushered Doctor Stewart into the house. The Doctor was bearing a small basket with a berry pie. "I beg your pardon for this early call," he began, "but Mrs. McLenaghan bade me bring you this pie last evening during my rounds, and I left it behind. She begged of me to drop it off, and as I was the one at fault, there was no avoiding it."

Lily had come downstairs by now and she greeted him graciously, bidding him join us for a cup of tea. "I have breakfasted," the Doctor said, but would no like to keep you from yours. Miss Courtown," he added, bowing in my direction, "will you grant me the favour of your company?"

I stood and curtseyed at this, and took my leave of Lily. Walking to the door, I took my wrap down from the peg and went outside with him. He offered me his arm and I took it gratefully. We walked slowly down the dirt drive towards the main road.

"You do not look well; your eyes are darkly shadowed and you are pale. I hope that I am your friend as well as your Doctor, and that you will tell me what ails you."

I hesitated before replying, choosing my words carefully. "I have felt very oddly," I said. "There is something here that does not agree with me. For five days now I have risen, eaten breakfast, and then been taken with intense pain. It grows worse each morning. There has been cramping and …" I hesitated, unwilling to continue.

"And?" he probed.

"And I have also been sick at my stomach. Several times each day." I would not look at him, ashamed as I was to be speaking so openly about my bodily functions.

"Does this only happen in the mornings?" he asked.

"Yes," I responded, "shortly after breakfast it is the worst."

"Is there no one else in the house who has been taken ill?"

"No. I am alone afflicted."

"And is this pain and sickness unlike others you have experienced? Is it your monthly discomfort perhaps?"

"No," I answered sharply, chagrined that he would think so, "it is more intense and violent than I have known. Clots of blood come up with the sickness."

"What do you eat each morning?"

"Only a bowl of porridge. Mr. Carey makes it of late. He has undertaken just recently the making of our morning meal."

"Would you," he asked, "consider returning to the Inn with me? Mrs. McLenaghan would be delighted to see you and you could rest more comfortably there from this affliction."

"No," I said, "I cannot leave. Lily cannot manage all of the household and the baby as well. It is an unhappy situation."

I looked at the Doctor to gauge his mood. He seemed deeply perturbed by my condition. "Miss Courtown," he said, "I will return to visit you early tomorrow morning. You must give me your word that no food or drink, save a sip of water you pump yourself, will you take until I come back. It will do your body much good to rest from its recent trouble and I wish to see you myself should you become ill in the morning."

"Is this an ulcer perhaps, or influenza?"

"It is likely something quite serious," he said. "You must give me your word to do as I ask."

I agreed, of course, but then asked, "Will Lily likely be taken with this or the baby?"

"No, they are in no immediate danger," said my friend.

He turned us around and we walked slowly back to the house, I leaning heavily upon his arm. We parted quietly, he bowing and I curtseying. I saw Mr. Carey smirking at us. I spent the balance of the day in solitude in my room, resting uncomfortably. Lily checked on me several times; my Cousin was worried deeply by my malaise, I could tell, but she was also much preoccupied. She did not linger with me above stairs but the once.

"Ellie," she began, entering my small chamber and sitting upon the bed. "Ellie, I am in need of a small loan. Mr. Carey has it in his mind that a small supplement to our household income would recompense us for your board." She looked mortified at the asking and I was shocked by the meanness of it.

"Can you tell me," I responded in a serious tone, "that an increase of wealth would improve your circumstances?"

"Ellie, I can only tell you that without it, my circumstances may worsen."

I was stricken by her words and looked at her sharply. "What has happened here?" I asked. "I insist upon a full account from you."

"Only that," she began, "only that Mr. Carey is unprepared to labour for a child not his own and that he makes daily demands upon me to write my Father for compensation." She looked miserable with this communication and deeply ashamed.

For my own part, despite my wretched constitution, I felt uneasy; the fine down on my arms stood straight. "Very well," I answered her, "you will have all that I have when I am recovered. You must not write Uncle. He will be overcome by the worry of it."

She reached across and squeezed my hand tightly, but acknowledged not my generosity.

"That blackguard ..." I began.

"Ellie," she interjected, "Ellie, it is not all as it seems. He can be charming and act the part of a gentleman when he chooses. I am not wholly unobservant and know whereof I speak. He is also a violent man capable of great cunning and deceit, but I believe him to be overall concerned for my well-being."

"If he expresses concern," I countered, "it is for your wealth and connections alone. You have made a rash decision in aligning yourself with him."

"Ellie, I beg you, let us not quarrel. You are not well and I am fatigued by it all. We have talked of this many times."

In the early evening we heard a knock upon the door. Mr. Carey ushered in our callers. Mrs. McLenaghan entered the room smiling and made straight for the baby, holding her up and kissing her doll-like face. Doctor Stewart followed behind looking fierce and foul-tempered. He had for some reason removed his coat and stood there in his vest and shirt sleeves toying with a horse whip. Mrs. McLenaghan asked after my health and I began to converse with her while listening also to a conversation between the men.

"I have heard from Donald Nesbitt that you have rats, Mr. Carey. I understand that you have bought some arsenic of late. It is very dangerous stuff. I wonder at your risking the use of it. Will you show me to your barn?"

Mr. Carey looked most discomforted at this. He was flushed and stared at the Doctor before answering. "I only thought it were rats," he said. "I did not want them after my corn."

"Well then," said Doctor Stewart, "perhaps you will oblige me by stepping outside a minute."

Mrs. McLenaghan again drew my attention. "The Doctor says that you're to come home with me. He said you was unwell. Your room is waiting at the Inn."

I shook my head at her to decline, but to my surprise, Lily interjected.

"Yes," she said, "I agree. That would be best. You need a rest, Ellie. I would like you to take your leave."

I coloured at her ungracious speech and might have protested with her further but we all of us heard a noise outside. Moving in unison to the window, I was horrified to see Doctor Stewart brandishing his whip and lashing violently at Mr. Carey. Mr. Carey lay in the dirt and twisted and writhed to avoid the snapping leather. His shirt was torn and we could clearly see that he was already covered with blood.

Lily drew back from this sight and sat down away from the window. Her face was still. I discerned from this that she had not been wholly unprepared for something of the sort. Yet the brutality of the assault was alarming to me. Mrs. McLenaghan drew me away and assisted me in the collection of my things. I made bold to ask her if she knew what had precipitated such cruelty, but she shushed me and said, "It was a man's business and something that needed doing."

I went with her quietly to the front door, stopping first to kiss my Cousin. "I do not know what iniquity has happened here," I said, "but you are dearer to me than life and I will always be faithful to you. You have only ever to ask anything of me and I will oblige." She said not a word in response and looked away without kissing me in parting. I shivered with the coldness of her demeanour and featured then that something evil had transpired.

I saw Doctor Stewart enter the house and then return outside with Lily. She was shaking her head and he appeared to be remonstrating with her. I could not discern the meaning in this strange scene and thought only that she was castigating him for the act of violence we had witnessed.

I sat in the buggy and spoke not a word. Mrs. McLenaghan placed my bag at my feet and heaved herself in beside me. "Doctor Stewart will ride apart," she said. She picked up the whip and I noted quickly that it was not the one that had been used so brutally upon Mr. Carey; Doctor Stewart, I saw, held that one yet in his hands. He walked near the barn, over to Mr. Carey, and I heard him say, "And if anything amiss should happen to your Wife or Child, I will take great pleasure in personally seeing that you are hanged!"

We had driven only a short distance when the cramps attacked me again. Mrs. McLenaghan stopped the buggy while I retched violently on the side of the road. Perspiration broke out upon me; I was shaking and trembling from both the illness and the scene I had just witnessed. Mrs. McLenaghan had to assist me into the buggy as I could scarcely pull myself up.

"The Doctor is not much given to anger," said Mrs. McLenaghan. "That man deserved worse than he received."

"What is it?" I asked. "What has Mr. Carey done?"

"The Doctor will tell you in good time, Lass. Do not be fretting now."

"I have never seen such a vulgar act," I said. "No gentleman would behave so. I shall *not* speak to the Doctor about this."

Mrs. McLenaghan straightened herself and rose to his defence, addressing me sharply. "That good man could have called in the constables and had him imprisoned for what he done, but he handled things himself to spare both you and Mrs. Carey. It were all done on your account. He acted as he always does and is as true a gentleman as there ever was. And he has been a good friend to you though you may not know it."

"On my account?" I queried.

"That Jack Carey's heart is as black as the Earl of Hell's waistcoat," she remarked cryptically. By then we were arriving at the Inn and she did not respond further to me. I knew that she was in a huff but I was too ill to care. Mr. McLenaghan met the buggy and helped me down. Seeing how weakened I was, he gave me his arm and escorted me to my old room. I lay down upon the bed feeling miserable. I must have slept for an hour or more, and was wakened by a knocking at the door.

"Come in," I called, rising awkwardly. Doctor Stewart and Mrs. McLenaghan both stood there.

"I have come to examine you," said the Doctor, "and Mrs. McLenaghan will stay."

"Thank you, no," I replied stiffly and with as much dignity as I could muster. "Some sleep is all that I require and I will not trouble you further."

I saw that he intended to withdraw, but he stopped himself. "You are disgusted with me, I think," he said, "for the display you witnessed. I did no intend for the ladies to be traumatized. Mr. Carey would no retire to the barn and I had no choice in the matter."

"There is always choice, Doctor Stewart, when it comes to doing what is proper," I replied primly.

"He has acted like a criminal and needed to be treated as such!" he flared.

"He is my Cousin's husband!" I responded in equal measure.

"He is a murderer!" cried Mrs. McLenaghan. "Tell her, Doctor. He tried to kill you with poison, Miss Courtown. We all knows it."

I gasped at this and clutched my stomach. Another wave of cramps beset me and I turned quickly to the wash basin. I was violently sick. The Doctor took the bowl from me when I was done and looked at it. "There is much blood here," he said to Mrs. McLenaghan. "She needs to be in bed."

Mrs. McLenaghan came to me and offered her assistance. I heard the door close and knew that the Doctor had stepped outside. I could not speak I was so overcome.

I'm told that I was bedridden and out of my head for nearly two full weeks. Mrs. McLenaghan stayed with me throughout, as faithful a nursemaid as one could ever wish for. In my delirium, I heard a voice calling for Lily, and repeatedly tried to raise myself from the bed so that I could cling to her. The poison took a devastating toll on my appearance. My hair grew to feel like straw, coarse and dry, and it came out each morning in small dull handfuls. My nails became thin with small ridges upon them and they split and peeled easily, shaling in fine layers. My complexion was likewise ghastly. Large purple shadows circled my eyes, marking me as an invalid. I was shamed by my looks and embarrassed to see the McLenaghans and Doctor Stewart taking in my reduced measure. Their pity cut me and made me feel the more depressed. My own Father would not have recognized me in this state.

One morning there was a sharp rap at the door and Doctor Stewart appeared with a bouquet of fresh yellow chrysanthemums. Someone had arranged these in a small vase and he placed this on the small bedside table after encouraging me to inhale their fragrance.

"Where did they come from?" asked Mrs. McLenaghan.

"I have ways and means," replied the Doctor mischievously. "A traveller, on his way through from Oshawa, brought them from a small greenhouse there and wondered if I knew a lady who might appreciate them."

"You are too kind," I replied. "I have not seen such lovely flowers for a long time." And then, unfortunately, my eyes began to tear up, and soon I found that I was weeping again.

"Miss Courtown," the Doctor said, "it is very hard on a gentleman come to call, if all the lady does is weep at the sight of him." He meant by this to make me merry, but I wept again at his kindness. Mrs. McLenaghan came to sit by me and hold me to her bosom.

"It's not you," she said to him quietly. "She's never very far from tears."

"Yes, that is to be expected. She has had a terrible shock. She'll come along, I ken."

"Miss Courtown," he said, addressing me, "I wonder if you would allow me to write to your family. I think they should know that you have been ill and should perhaps hear it from a friend. I will send the letter for you. Your family will know how to respond."

"No, Sir, thank you. I will write myself when I am well. They will worry to see a stranger's hand and I must think carefully what to say." Although I was trying to compose myself, the tears continued to come. I wiped them away but they would not stop.

"I think that you are ready for some diversion. You have spent time enough in this room and must now begin to exercise your limbs and move around. You must join us for afternoon tea, perhaps dinner as well. We have missed your company and it will be good for you also." He left the room then, closing the door softly behind him.

"Well Lass," said Mrs. McLenaghan, "them's Doctor's orders."

I nodded at her and tentatively swung my legs to the floor. She strode over and gave me her hands while I stood. Slowly I moved to the small dressing table and began to brush at my coarse hair. I pulled it back tightly into a large plait and then pinned this to the top of my head. The effort of lifting my arms and dressing my hair very nearly exhausted me. I rested for several minutes before washing and powdering my body. Mrs. McLenaghan rummaged through my trunk and pulled out a plain grey wool gown.

"It looks warm," she said, "and you can liven it with a pretty shawl."

I went to the bed and sat down while she helped me with my stockings and under-garments. The corset we left loosely done up as I felt short of breath and was not much worried about my appearance. She helped me slip the dress on and fastened it.

Tea was welcome. Doctor Stewart was all silliness and Mr. McLenaghan was full of fun. Together they entertained us with their light-hearted banter. Mr. McLenaghan told us about Mousey Findley and his recent shenanigans. Two months previous, a Catholic family, the Donnegals, had moved into the township, and everyone had turned out to help them with a barn raising. Mousey was there too, swinging a hammer and working on the top ridge. By sundown the frame of the barn was set and the assembled gathering left for home, fully satisfied with their day's contributions and merry with a pint or more of good ale. Then, by the dark of night, Mr. McLenaghan confided, didn't Mousey and a couple of other Orangemen sneak back to the Donnegals' and burn the whole thing down again. "T'weren't personal," insisted Mr. McLenaghan while we laughed, "'twas just the thing an Orangeman had to do."

At length I grew weary, and the Doctor, who had been watching me, noticed at once. "We must return you to your room, Miss Courtown," he announced. "Perhaps if you have a little rest, you can join us again this evening."

In the days following, no one spoke to me of Lily or Mr. Carey or of my niece, Kathleen. I was too abashed to make a direct enquiry and was not confident that they would answer me regardless. Mrs. McLenaghan made it her especial mission to fatten me with rice puddings and custards and heavy sweets. A day did not pass without her turning out an apricot cake or a jam tart, laden with fresh cream or accompanied by a side dish of pudding. Although my appetite had not fully returned, I dutifully sampled these dishes for fear of hurting her feelings. Doctor Stewart had instructed that I was to be up and exercising an hour each morning, afternoon, and evening, and that I should try to shorten the time each day between my rests. My regimen was to include stair climbing. He intended thus to help build up my muscle. Knowing that he practised his own extensive fitness exercises, and wanting to demonstrate that I was no malingerer, I was determined to become once more strong and able.

Although Mrs. McLenaghan was a protective force, she mostly left me to my own pleasure during the day, allowing me to do as much as I felt able. When it was time for me to rest, she rushed to cover me and to ensure that I did not want for anything. Her tender care often brought grateful tears to my eyes. I knew, but did not tell her, that I was resolved upon returning to Ireland. I could not take Lily with me, and it was unlikely that Lily would let me take Kathleen, but I must and would return home to Rosslare Hall. I would speak in person with my Uncle, and let him determine who should be dispatched to force Lily's return.

One afternoon I found myself comfortably established in the parlour, a cheery fire blazing, my legs covered with a warm wool spread, my sewing laid beside me for an occupation. Mrs. McLenaghan had left to make a pot of tea and I was content to pick away at my fine handiwork. I heard the front door open and shut;

Mr. McLenaghan soon popped his head into the parlour.

"Now don't I have a letter for you, Miss," he said. "I was passing by the general store and didn't Mrs. Nesbitt call out to me and give me this for you. And I made straight back to the Inn, forgetting my small errands, knowing how pleased you would be to have it."

Smiling at me broadly, he passed me the much travelled brief; I saw by the return address that it was from my Uncle at Lowry Castle, Wexport, Ireland. I clasped it to my bosom and thanked Mr. McLenaghan for his trouble. He left me there to savour it and I did so joyfully, kissing it twice before slitting it open with my embroidery scissors. I read the brief quickly, letting out a small cry, and then I read it once more to be sure. It fell to the floor as I began to shudder and weep, and finally I gave in to my grief utterly, sobbing without control. So much had happened in the few months since I had left my home, and now this news was more than I could bear.

I heard someone approach and try to comfort me but I could not rouse myself from my grieving to recognize them. I thought vaguely that it was Mrs. McLenaghan come with the tea and I tried to look at her but could not see. Presently, I felt two strong arms reach around me and lift me from my now prostrate position on the floor. Whoever it was carried me comfortably and I felt secure in this embrace, weeping the harder to feel such an evidence of caring.

"Let her cry it out," I heard. "She must have distressing news from home. The shock will be too much for her after her recent illness." I recognized the Doctor's voice and realized that it was he who had taken me up and was now holding me as a child upon his lap. I turned my face against his chest and wept without restraint. My emotions confused me. My poor father had often sat with me so when I was a child, and that recollection made his loss feel the more real. And I was ashamed to be seen weeping anew and in distress by the Doctor and the McLenaghans. It seemed they were always discovering me in a disadvantaged and weakened state.

I heard the McLenaghans also in the room, and the Doctor speaking to them in a quiet whisper. Smiling at me kindly, he pulled from his pocket a generous plaid handkerchief and began to mop at my nose and wipe at my face. I knew that I must look frightful but found that I did not much care. His kindness precipitated another outburst of tears, and I sobbed against him until I was fatigued. Resting finally, my tears spent, I tried to extricate myself.

"Sssh, lass, sit awhile, and tell us your sad news."

I pointed at the letter and he reached down for it. "Should I read it for myself?"

I nodded, not yet trusting my voice. He read the letter slowly and then passed it silently to the McLenaghans.

My beloved Niece,

I pray that this letter finds you in good health and in a situation of God's providence, and pray also that you will have found and been reunited with my beloved Daughter. It grieves me to send you unwelcome and shocking news. Your Father, my loving Brother, has left this world and is now returned to your Mother's side in Dunstan's Chapel at Rosslare Hall. It was the seventh of August that he took a spell and the Almighty caused his heart to cease in its beating. He was not long ill and suffered only for want of you.

Not knowing of your future plans, I have leased Rosslare Hall and its contents and grounds to your Cousin Henry and his new wife Margaret. They were newly married in August. Her people are wool merchants and Henry has now taken to sheep farming. The terms are handsome and I enclose a cheque for rents in the event that you may make use of it abroad.

Please write to me with haste and relieve my misery with word of you both. Lord Driscoll has informed me of his interest and presses me for news of you.

I remain your most affectionate Uncle.

"This is tragic indeed," the Doctor said. "I am sorry."

My fever returned and I succumbed to a depression filled with longing and dreams of home. My only desire for so long had been to return to Ireland with my Cousin, and now I found the thought repulsive. I could not bear the thought of entering the Hall knowing that my Father would not be there in his rooms. It was too much.

Mrs. McLenaghan encouraged me to return to my stair-climbing routine, and to walk the short corridors of the Inn. I ate my meals with the McLenaghans and the Doctor each day, but excused myself from their evening social time in the parlour. I had not the heart for merriment, nor did I wish to dampen their spirits.

Mrs. McLenaghan, in a less than delicate exchange, asked me pointedly one day if I had lately experienced my course of bleeding. I coloured at the intimacy of this but was curious to know the reason for her inquiry. "Well, I only asks," she said, "as the Doctor asked it of me."

I was mortified to know that my bodily functions had been the subject of their joint discourse. When I began to protest, she came and took my hands and sat beside me on the bedstead. "Sssh, Lass, do not trouble yourself with such things. He's a Doctor and is only interested in your recovery. A poisoning, he says, might leave a young woman damaged for things such as childbirth. He was only wanting the information for your own good." Her words chilled me. Was there no end, I wondered, to the damage wrought by Mr. Carey?

A quiet period of mourning followed. I remained much on my own and did not attempt to write my Cousin. She was now lost to me. One morning as I passed by the dining room, I saw Mr. John Clement seated and partaking of a hearty stew. He rose at once when he spied me, and reached out his hand to shake mine own.

I was pleased to see him. "Mr. Clement," I exclaimed, shaking his hand. "How wonderful to see you! Have you been well?"

"Yes, Miss, I went visiting with my Brother over in Whitby and got the lay of the land there for a while and then I thought that maybe I'd just come back here to see if there was work for an honest man in the winter months. If I find work, I'll stay, and if not, I'll move towards Peterborough before the heavy snow sets in. I am glad to see that you are well."

"Mrs. Carey and I were both worried about you, Mr. Clement."

"Well, Miss," he answered, "things didn't work out so well with Mr. Carey."

"Yes, but through no fault of yours. I hope you find work."

"Work!" chimed in Mrs. McLenaghan. "There's always work. No shortage of work here, I'd say. I'm sure Harry can find a couple of days for you, Mr. Clement, and he will know who else is looking for a man. I think Doctor Stewart may even be in need."

"Thank you, Ma'am."

I was a little surprised by their familiar rapport. "Please, sit down," I said, "and finish your meal while it is hot. I must excuse myself." I left him there to eat, knowing that he would not feel free to do so while I stood by. The Inn was a strange place where social order was skewed, and it was difficult, at times, to maintain one's place.

Mrs. McLenaghan approached me one afternoon and asked if I had made any immediate travel plans. "The reason I was asking," she continued, "is that Mrs. Thomas, that's the one lady school trustee, well Mrs. Thomas was in at the post office yesterday and she and I fell to talking and she said to me that if you was going to stay awhile, you might perhaps think of helping out at the school. Mr. Dickie, the schoolmaster, is doing a fine job, but there's no one to teach the girls fancywork and you might have the occupation of doing so, if you were inclined." Mrs. McLenaghan finished her prepared little speech in a rush as if she were frightened that I might interrupt her before she had finished her message.

"My goodness," I said, "what an unusual request. I never thought of *my* giving tuition. Is there really an interest in such a thing?"

"Why certainly there is," affirmed Mrs. McLenaghan. "I told Mrs. Thomas that I'd seen some of the fine stitching you can do and how your fingers fly across the linen, and she said to me, 'Janet,' she said, 'that sounds like just the sort of thing we should be teaching our girls at the school. They won't have much need of sums and history but knowing how to use a needle is a skill that girls can use all their lives.' That's what she said."

"Well, it seems then as if things are settled. Does Mr. Dickie know of these arrangements?"

"Likely not yet," said Mrs. McLenaghan, pondering. "But I made bold to suggest to Mrs. Thomas that *if* you were interested, then you might just as well walk over to the school yourself and see to arranging things directly with Mr. Dickie."

"Why, that was very thoughtful of you."

"No trouble at all, lass," she said, "and I know that the Doctor will be mighty pleased. He said to us only last week that it was such a pity there was no ladies for you to spend time with, as he felt you were in need of some company or a suitable occupation."

"Well then," I said, "if the Doctor approves, it seems that things really are decided." I couldn't help but be amused at her evident delight in having made these arrangements. She stood there beaming at me, rocking back and forth on her feet as she sometimes did when she was happy, her clasped hands resting on the mound of her generous stomach. She was the most delightful woman I had ever encountered.

Nothing would do but that I should put on my outdoor wraps and march down to the little schoolhouse. I rapped smartly on the door and was ushered into the room by a small boy of about eight. He had the most impish face and I was utterly charmed by his polite manner. I took a seat at the back while Mr. Dickie finished conducting his lesson on cursive writing. He stood before the room at a large slate board and demonstrated with rapidity the correct shaping of the letter R. Each of the students had before them a smaller slate and they too were busy shaping R's in tidy succession. Mr. Dickie surveyed his pupils, and then stepped down from the small dais and began to march up and down, inspecting their work and correcting them.

I nodded at him when he passed me by and he responded with a curt bow. Returning to the front of the room, he assigned further work to the various groups of students and then strode directly towards me. "Good morning, I am Mr. Dickie. How may I be of service?"

I rose and offered him my hand. "Good morning," I said. "I am sent by Mrs. Thomas. She has suggested that some of the girls might benefit by weekly tuition in fancywork and I am here to offer my services."

He looked at me quizzically, taking in my deportment and ensemble. "And have you experience with such a thing?" he enquired somewhat haughtily.

"None at all," I said, smiling. "But I am deft with a needle and believe that I might perhaps be able to teach the girls."

"Well then," he replied slowly, considering, "well then, perhaps we should set up a little trial. Will you come to the school or shall I send the girls to you?"

"By all means, send them to me at the Inn," I replied. "Tell them to ask for Miss Courtown."

"Very well," he said skeptically. "How many shall you want?"

I was surprised by this question and looked around the schoolroom quickly; it was filled mostly with young girls, many of them quite small. "Perhaps," I answered, "perhaps I should begin with a few of the older girls. Those that seem most interested."

He nodded curtly. "Yes, shall we say Wednesday at four o'clock?"

"That would be fine," I agreed. We shook hands briefly and he opened the door for me to leave. I felt rather breathless after the exchange. Mr. Dickie, a very young man of no more than twenty-eight, had made it very clear by his manner that he thought me unequal to the task. I found that I felt wounded by his reserve.

I walked from the schoolhouse directly to the dry goods store, and secured from Mrs. Nesbitt a paper card with needles, two pairs of embroidery scissors, several twists of cotton thread, and a length of plain white cotton. I would teach hemming first, I thought. Hemming was the most basic of skills and would come in most handy for any one of the girls. "Are you about to set up shop as seamstress?" enquired Mrs. Nesbitt.

"No," I replied patiently, bristling just a little at her intrusive question. "I am going to help a few girls at the school learn some fancywork."

"Why that's wonderful!" she enthused. "I am sure Mr. Dickie will be most pleased. He is a single gentleman, you know," she added in a conspiratorial tone. "I am sure he will very much appreciate your interest."

"Thank you," I replied coldly. "I am looking forward to the endeavour."

When I returned to the Inn, I sought out Mrs. McLenaghan in the kitchen and told her of my arrangements. "I think perhaps," I suggested, "that we should start with tea. What do you think?"

"Why I thinks that's a splendid idea, that's what I thinks," she responded merrily. "With biscuits and jam. Them girls won't mind a light biscuit before their suppers. Just leave that to me."

"How wonderful. Thank you. Might I use the parlour for their lessons?"

"Of course, my dear," she said, "you are most welcome to use what you like for your project."

"Thank you," I said again, smiling warmly at her. "You are most kind."

I spent my evening cutting the white cotton into large squares. As I did so, I remembered the look of my Mother picking away at her own fine handiwork. She embroidered on the finest silk and was able somehow to make the back of the work look as fine as the front, so that any piece she finished could be worn on either side. My dear Father proudly wore a waistcoat for many years that she had embroidered. The front of it was covered in trailing vines and leaves with clusters of grapes, but when you opened the waistcoat and looked on the other side, you saw that the reverse of the very same embroidery was transformed into a mass of roses fully opened and in bud. Much as it was studied, no one could ever find a knot or a loose thread, Mother had woven the silk threads together so carefully. Father always claimed that she had enlisted the help of fairies. Looking at the finished project, it was not hard to believe.

I had not her facility with the needle but I was handy enough, I knew, to teach these girls enough of the practical skills to get them well started. I found myself looking forward to the tuition and went several times to the kitchen the next afternoon to ensure that Mrs. McLenaghan had remembered the engagement. I arranged the chairs in the parlour so that they formed a tight circle and I laid upon the table all the materials that I determined we would need.

When the door knocker sounded, I found myself breathing quickly, nervous a little but also excited. Mrs. McLenaghan greeted the girls at the door, instructing them to remove their outer wraps. She ushered them into the parlour and I stood to greet them, curtseying and tipping my head gently. There were seven of them; they bobbed down at me in response, looking awkward and unaccustomed to such things.

"Please sit down," I welcomed them, "and then perhaps you can tell me your names."

The girls sat down quickly on the chairs and looked down at the floor, none of them offering their name to me. "My name is Miss Courtown," I began, "and I am so pleased to meet you. Now, who will be next?"

The tallest girl, dressed in a heavy woollen dress of dark green, looked up at me and said, "My name is Mary Shaw and I am pleased to meet you, Miss."

The girl next to her, a sweet-faced little one with tightly plaited hair, went next. "My name is Alice Moore and I am pleased to meet you, Miss."

Next went the tiniest girl. She had on a thin cotton dress and a cardigan that was done up tightly but was over-small on her. She stood up to speak, sliding off her chair to do so. "My name is Iris Mewhinney, Miss, and I am pleased too." She smiled at me, and even though a couple of the other girls giggled at how she had misspoken, Iris continued to smile delightedly. She climbed back on her chair and swung her legs down happily, looking around the parlour with great interest.

The other girls finished the introductions quickly: Harriet McCaffrey and Jane Findley and Louise O'Donaghue and Anne Neary. Mrs. McLenaghan entered the parlour with the tea trolley then and I saw the girls eyeing it with great interest. "Mary," I said, addressing the first girl, "would you be so kind as to assist me in serving tea?" She stood up at once and came over to me, bobbing. I poured the first cup of tea and asked Alice how she took it.

"Sugar please, Miss," she responded, "if there is." I added two tiny spoonfuls of sugar to the cup and passed it to Mary who carried it to Alice. We continued in this manner until all eight of us had our tea. I then indicated the tea biscuits and suggested that they might like to help themselves. Little Iris was on her feet and beside me in an instant. "Please, Miss," she said, "may I assist you?"

"Yes, of course you may."

"Would you like jam on yours?" she asked me. "Or butter?"

"A little jam, please."

Iris selected a tea biscuit which she placed on a china plate and then delicately spooned some strawberry jam beside it. She passed this to me with a small butter knife and napkin. Spreading the napkin carefully on my lap, I broke off a morsel of biscuit and placed a touch of jam upon it before eating. I was conscious of the girls' steady interest in this process. Iris proceeded to pass all the girls plates with tea biscuits and jam, and they likewise spread their napkins out and broke off delicate morsels of biscuit before consuming them. In this way, we made short work of Mrs. McLenaghan's tea biscuits.

I set aside the tea things and dusted my fingers lightly with the napkin. The older girls followed my lead immediately. Iris and Harriet seemed more reluctant to do so, but they also followed suit. "First," I said, "we need to thread our needles. Is there anyone here who will need help with their needle?" No one responded. "Well, then," I continued, "I shall need someone to pass out the needles. Who would like to do that for me?"

Iris jumped off her chair and stood by my side before any of the other girls could indicate their desire. I smiled at her, and passed her one needle at a time. "Be careful," I whispered to her, "I don't want you to prick yourself." Iris rushed around the circle handing out the needles carefully to the other girls, who held them gingerly pinched between their thumb and forefinger.

"Next, you will need a length of thread," I said. "The thread must be as long as the space from your hand to your shoulder, and then back again to your elbow. If it is any longer it will tangle. Each of you will have to line up beside me so that I can cut you the right length."

Dutifully the girls lined up beside my chair, extending their arms so that I could measure for them a length of thread. This they carried back to their chairs and began the process of threading it through their needles. I stood up and walked around the parlour to ensure that each of them was able to thread their needle. Iris insisted on bringing the needle towards the thread, as opposed to pushing the thread through the needle eye. This made me laugh, but when I saw that her feelings were hurt, I stopped and patted her shoulder and told her what a good job she was doing. I caught her eye and she looked down at once, seeming shy and not so ebullient as before.

After I had returned to my seat, I turned once more to the smallest girl. "Iris, will you come here while I show you something I have done?" She slipped from her chair and crossed the room at once, coming to stand close by my chair. I pulled out my small sample of silk which I had been working and showed her the raised strawberry on one side with the perfectly matching rose bud on the other. It was not so fine as my Mother's handiwork, but it was fine enough to show. Iris looked at it carefully and reached out with one small finger to pat the berry's silken mound.

"It looks good enough to eat, Miss," she said, finally looking up at me. "How did you come by such a thing?"

"I worked it myself, and someday I may show you how to do so as well."

At this, a couple of other girls, curious to see, left their chairs and stood near, reaching out and stroking the work. Anne's response was the most disarming to me. "It looks the work of fairies, Miss," she said earnestly.

I smiled at her. "Thank you, Anne. That is a very great compliment." Her words lodged in my heart. I wondered after she spoke if I would ever have the opportunity to show my own daughter how to do such things. Mrs. McLenaghan's earlier question about my course of bleeding had made me aware that the poisoning might well have made such a thing an impossibility.

I showed the girls how to make a delicate knot, and from there we folded the cotton and I demonstrated a simple hemming stitch. Some of the girls had an easy time of it, with good tension and tiny, delicate stitches. Others had more difficulty, pulling so hard that the fabric bunched and rucked and the thread came out of the needle. Little Harriet fastened her cotton to her skirt and I had to unpick it for her carefully. An hour passed quickly in this way, and I was sorry to tell them that they needed to tidy up for the afternoon. They folded their work into neat squares and returned their things to my basket. I escorted them to the front hall where they wrapped up for the damp, chill weather and prepared to take their leave. The girls thanked me one by one and bobbed sweetly before slipping out the door. Little Iris threw her arms around my waist and gave me a giant hug. "I love you, Miss," she said. I stood at the door and watched with amusement as she ran to catch up with the rest of the group.

When I returned to the parlour, I saw that Mrs. McLenaghan had arrived before me and was straightening up. "Well, how did it go now?" she asked.

"It was delightful," I enthused. "They are lovely girls. I had such fun with them."

"That Alice Moore is a looker," said Mrs. McLenaghan. "Did you ever see such bright blue eyes? Her mother was a beauty too. They live on the edge of town. Miles Moore is a wagon-maker. They come from Kilkenny way."

"Yes, she is pretty, but I am quite enchanted by Iris Mewhinney. She is as cute as a button."

"Now she's one I don't know," responded Mrs. McLenaghan. "That's not a name I've heard before. Her parents must likely be among them tinkers."

"Perhaps. She wasn't very warmly dressed. But she's awfully sweet."

"Well, let's hope she stays that way," said Mrs. McLenaghan. "Tinkers don't have much in the way of an easy life."

At dinner that night, Mrs. McLenaghan announced to our small group that my first day as a sewing teacher had met with great success. Mr. McLenaghan expressed his pleasure, saying, "Well, isn't that fine now," in his typically good-natured way. Mr. Clement was among our group, the Doctor having provided him with board in exchange for his part-time labours, and he too beamed his pleasure. Doctor Stewart was especially interested in the girls and asked me to name those whom had attended. I rhymed off their names with Mrs. McLenaghan beside me counting them on her fingers.

"That Alice Moore is a looker," repeated Mrs. McLenaghan when I finished. "Do you remember what a beauty her Mother was, Harry? I can't say as I've seen her for a while, but I knows she sure was a pretty thing when she was young."

"Yep," agreed Mr. McLenaghan, "she was so, Mother, she was so."

Doctor Stewart smiled at me and asked after Iris Mewhinney. "Oh, she was my favourite," I exclaimed. "When I was teaching them to thread their needles, she insisted on bringing the needle towards the thread instead of the other way around. She was so eager to help and to try everything."

"Her Mother died last winter of pneumonia," said the Doctor, "and her Father and Grandfather are combers. They go from place to place, finishing wood to make it look more fine than it is. They do good work, but it's a dying trade."

"I don't know that there's much call for it around here these days," put in Mr. McLenaghan.

"Why, Harry," exclaimed Mrs. McLenaghan, "we could use a comber here at the Inn, couldn't we?"

"Well I don't know about that," he said. "I hadn't much thought about it, to tell the truth."

"I think some combing would be just the thing." Mrs. McLenaghan bobbed her chin at him. "It would fancy up the front hall and stairs and parlour and make the Inn look like a first-rate establishment."

"Now, Mother, that combing could cost a lot of money. Are you certain we need so much?"

"Why, Harry McLenaghan, I never know'd you to be cheap in all my life! If a thing is worth doing, it's worth doing right, is what I say. Now here we have a chance to get some nice work done by a couple of local men and all you're worried about is the cost. Winter is coming on and it would be honest work to hire out and you should just be grateful that you've got the wherewithal to pay for it being done."

And so, just like that, it was settled: Iris's Father and Grandfather would comb the Inn. Dr. Stewart and I ate our meal quietly, sneaking peeks at one another and smiling at the nonsense between the couple. It was clear at the outset that as soon as Mrs. McLenaghan got a notion in her head, nothing would do but for her to have her way.

Mr. McLenaghan could protest all he wanted, but the Inn would be combed if he wanted any peace.

After the McLenaghans cleared the table, Doctor Stewart proposed a game of whist. Mr. Clement excused himself and we retired to the parlour and began to set the card table in place. Then the Doctor leaned down to pick up one of the squares of cotton from the sewing basket. "Now, I wonder, Miss Courtown, if you can teach anyone to hem a seam. I think I would be willing to try if you would be my teacher."

Mr. McLenaghan chuckled, but I found myself colouring. I went over to the Doctor and took the cotton from his hands. "This is Harriet's work; she is the girl who stitched it to her skirt at first."

"I must admit," he replied, "that I didn't understand what was wrong with Iris's method of threading a needle. I thread a needle from time to time and I thought there was only the one way of doing it. Perhaps I really do need you to give me a lesson." He was standing very close to me at this; I could feel his breath upon my face and neck while he was speaking. I stepped back from him and replaced Harriet's work in the basket.

"You are mocking me, Doctor Stewart, and I shall have to put you in your place when we sit down to cards."

"I look forward to your attentions," he responded with what sounded to be a hint of flirtation. He caught my gaze and held it until I looked away.

I felt slightly disconcerted but was soon engaged in our game of cards and the lively interplay between the McLenaghans and the Doctor. It was an enjoyable game, and yet it ended early when Doctor Stewart rose from the table and excused himself. He thanked Mrs. McLenaghan for dinner and bade me a good evening's rest, taking my hand and kissing it before taking his leave.

"Oh my!" exclaimed Mrs. McLenaghan, chuckling loudly, "aren't we fancy tonight."

I coloured instantly and saw, to my surprise, that Doctor Stewart was likewise flushed. He reacted immediately, sweeping Mrs. McLenaghan up in a bear hug and kissing her rosy face repeatedly. "Go away, you silly boy!" she laughed, "and save your kisses for someone who wants them."

Doctor Stewart grabbed her hand and kissed it also, and next went to Mr. McLenaghan in an attempt to kiss his hand as well. "That's all right, Lad," said Mr. McLenaghan, tucking his hand under his arm, "that's all right now."

"Isn't he a saucy one!" said Mrs. McLenaghan after he left the room. "Such a scoundrel. But mark my words, he'll make someone a fine Husband someday. Maybe even someone we know," she added. I wasn't entirely sure but I thought I saw her wink at her Husband. Feeling compromised by this insinuation, I withdrew, seeking the quiet solitude of my small room.

In the morning, I determined upon a short walk before breakfast. It was early yet and I did not expect to encounter very many people out and about. A tall, rather frail-looking man was walking delicately before me. The boarded walk was icy with morning frost and he was stepping carefully so as not to slip. I, however, was in a hurry and quickly overcame him, passing him by just as I approached the general store.

"Miss Courtown!" he exclaimed. "I did not expect to see you out this early."

I was startled to see that Mr. Dickie was my morning companion, and was obviously making his way to the schoolhouse.

"Mr. Dickie," I greeted him, curtseying. "Good morning."

"I was wondering," he said, "whether you might be at home this evening about seven. I believe that I should pay you a call to discuss our mutual interests."

Astonished by his overture, I hesitated before responding. "Yes, thank you, Mr. Dickie," I replied slowly. "I will be at the Inn this evening. You are most welcome to call."

He doffed his hat and bowed woodenly before continuing along the boarded footpath. He looked a ridiculous figure, thin and stiff, taking tiny baby steps like an old woman.

Returning thoughtfully to the Inn, I brooded about the purpose of his forthcoming call. I was of two minds regarding the McLenaghans. While I desired telling them that I was expecting Mr. Dickie that evening, I did not intend to provide them with opportunities for merriment. The McLenaghans mostly ate their mid-day meal in the kitchen and I had taken, of late, to joining them. It seemed foolish to dine alone in the dining room and to cause them the extra trouble of serving me there. Sometimes the Doctor would drop by for a bowl of soup but more often than not he was on calls and didn't join us. I determined during the course of the morning that I would tell them over luncheon about my caller. At least, in this way, they would not be taken unawares in the evening.

Mrs. McLenaghan poked her head in the parlour at mid-day. "Soup's ready, Miss," she said.

"It smells good," I replied. "I have been trying to guess what kind it is."

"Barley and vegetable, with beef scraps thrown in. I don't know when our guests are arriving and I thought a pot of soup would be a good thing to have on hand."

"I'm sure they will be delighted," I said. "It smells wonderful."

I followed her to the kitchen, where Mr. McLenaghan and Doctor Stewart and Mr. Clement were already seated. Mr. Clement recounted a story of his sheer panic in the night when he was wakened by the sound of a horse ru of the Doctor's house. Doctor Stewart laughed loudly and admitted that the weather had been so cold of late that he had taken to exercising indoors and had forgotten that John was yet asleep upstairs.

"I thought as we were being attacked in our beds by rebels," continued Mr. Clement, "and all the while, there's the good Doctor in his drawers just tramping around doing his exercising, while I was having the fright of my life and couldn't get into my boots fast enough to save our souls. And when I gets to his part of the house, there he is running up the stairs half naked and I'm looking around trying to see who's after him, and there's nobody there. Well, you can just imagine my state while I was trying to get the lay of things."

"Oh my, John!" laughed Mrs. McLenaghan, wiping at her eyes. "I can just see it all!"

Mr. McLenaghan was laughing also and the Doctor looked much amused by poor Mr. Clement's tale. I joined in the fun and smiled, imagining the well-intentioned Mr. Clement endeavouring to save the Doctor's life.

Despite the presence of the others, I felt that I must speak up. "I have some news," I interjected in a moment of silence. "This morning when I went for a walk, I encountered Mr. Dickie. He said that he was going to call upon us this evening at seven."

"Call upon *us*?" enquired Mrs. McLenaghan. "That young man has lived here for two years and he has not once called upon us. Mark my words, it's you he's coming to see."

Mr. McLenaghan chortled in response and I made a point of looking down and studying my soup. "No," I replied evenly, "I'm certain that it is all of us whom he intends to favour with his company."

"Well, imagine that then!" huffed Mrs. McLenaghan. "He's never paid us any never mind before. I wonder at his sudden interest."

"Well," said Doctor Stewart, "I'm sure we'll all look forward to finding out. John and I have no plans this evening, do we John?"

"No, Doctor, no plans to speak of."

"Well then," continued the Doctor, "it should prove to be a very interesting evening."

I continued to study my soup carefully and would not allow myself to look up. The Doctor was evidently taking delight in my situation, but I would not give him the satisfaction of seeing me in a state of discomposure. Fortunately Mr. Clement and he finished their meal quickly and excused themselves before I was subjected to any further questioning.

I went downstairs late to dinner, hoping to avoid excessive socializing with the Inn's new guests. As I entered the dining room I saw that a place had been left for me across from Doctor Stewart and beside Mr. Clement. The other guests, four gentlemen respectably attired, were sitting at a smaller table by themselves. Both Doctor Stewart and Mr. Clement stood; Mr. Clement pulled out my chair. I was conscious of the men at the other table who had noticed my entrance and were commenting among themselves upon my appearance. I had dressed my hair differently for the evening, loosening the tight bun and folding it into a softer chignon.

"May I say that you look well this evening, Miss Courtown," said the Doctor.

"Thank you."

"I am sure that Mr. Dickie will be charmed," he added.

"Doctor Stewart," I admonished him, "is it not enough that I have to endure Mrs. McLenaghan's jests? That you should add to them seems most unjust."

"I beg your pardon. I simply meant to pay a compliment."

Mr. Clement was silent and seemed particularly intent on examining his chop. By the time we stood from the table it was past seven o'clock; I saw the Doctor checking his pocket watch deliberately and with exaggerated gestures.

"Time for our caller," he grinned, walking round to pull out my chair and offer me his arm. We moved to the parlour, where we discovered that Mr. Dickie had arrived before us and was comfortably ensconced in an armchair by the fire. He stood directly upon our entrance and rushed over to bow and greet us with great enthusiasm.

"Miss Courtown," he said, "I have just been reading at my Ovid, and thought you might enjoy hearing my own translation. Shall I read it to you?"

"Yes, please do, Mr. Dickie, I'm sure it will be a delight for all of us." Doctor Stewart led me to a chair nearest the one where Mr. Dickie had been seated and left me with no recourse but to accept the arrangement. I adjusted my skirt as comfortably as I could but felt quite self-conscious. Doctor Stewart and Mr. Clement were both watching me with great interest while the other guests followed us into the parlour and arranged themselves upon other chairs and settles.

Mr. Dickie picked up his Ovid and drew out a sheaf of papers which he had folded up inside the front cover. He positioned himself before the fire, one foot resting upon the fender in a greatly affected pose, and began to read loudly and in the most sonorous of tones. There would be no opportunity for quiet discourse in the room that evening. Mr. Dickie's voice resonated with a steady throb and we were all of us subjected first to his rendering of Latin, followed by his exegesis:

> *"In nova fert animus mutatas dicere formas corpora; di, coeptis,*
> *nam vos mutastis et illas, adspirate meis primaque ab orgigine*
> *mundi ad mea perpetuum deducite tempora carmen!*
> *"To tell you of bodies changed into different shapes is my purpose.*
> *The gods, who were responsible, will help me with verse that will*
> *spin from the beginning of the world to our time!"*

Mr. Dickie would insist upon interrupting his own reading to congratulate himself on a fine point of translation or Latin grammar. We were told repeatedly that, "in the light of all good translators, no liberty can be too great in the pursuit of a flowing narrative."

The schoolmaster read for a full hour without once stopping for breath. I was at pains to remain focused on the text but was all too conscious of the other guests who had fled at their earliest opportunity, leaving only the McLenaghans, Doctor Stewart, and myself. Mr. McLenaghan was sleeping in the corner, his feet extended on a gout stool, his hands across his chest, snoring lightly. Mrs. McLenaghan was trying to remain alert but kept yawning and nodding off and sitting bolt upright by turns. I, for my part, was conscious of Doctor Stewart's steady gaze. Whenever I looked up at the small assemblage, I found his eyes were upon me and did not waver when he saw that I was looking at him.

Mr. McLenaghan finally roused and rescued us all. "Well, Lad," he said, "I think as I've had enough Latin for tonight. Would anyone like to join me in a wee dram before bed?"

Mr. Dickie stopped reading mid-sentence and stared at him with his mouth open. It was hard to tell whether he was more shocked by the interruption, by a fill of Latin, or by the concept of a dram before bed. I almost allowed myself to laugh at his astonishment but quickly remembered myself and stifled my amusement.

"Thank you, Mr. Dickie," I said graciously. "Your reading this evening was most enlightening. I'm sure that we all benefited by the experience."

Mr. Dickie bowed at this and looked somewhat mollified by my flattery.

"Yes," continued Doctor Stewart, "I don't know when I've had a more enjoyable evening. I thank you, Sir."

"Why," replied Mr. Dickie, "I flatter myself that I am making rather good progress for an amateur."

"Absolutely so," said Doctor Stewart. "No one hearing you would think otherwise."

I looked at the Doctor and tried to make a study of his expression. I suspected him of mocking poor Mr. Dickie. I could find no trace of mockery in his expression, however, and decided that I had been too rash to judge my friend.

Mrs. McLenaghan unlocked the drinks cabinet and began to pass around tumblers. There was whiskey to be had for the gentlemen and claret or sherry for the ladies. I chose a drop of claret but saw, at once, that this was a mistake. Mr. Dickie, having himself declined anything, seemed quite taken aback by my accepting the proffered spirits.

"I am a temperance supporter, Miss Courtown," he began as he sidled up to me. "And while I don't discourage the taking of spirits by others, I must say that I am rather surprised by a lady in your position accepting a drink."

I placed the glass upon the nearby table and turned to my companion. "I would by no means offend anyone who offered me such hospitality, Mr. Dickie. I find it easier to accept such an offering and to neglect it rather than risk offending the host." I hoped by such quiet words to avoid an exchange uncomfortable to us both, but he was not keen to let things stand as they were.

"Well, Miss Courtown," continued the now simpering Mr. Dickie, "while I am always at pains to oblige those around me, I must say in such matters as these, I find it best to be direct about one's most deeply held convictions. I find that I must ask whether you absolutely refute the abuses of alcohol and spirits and embrace the temperance view?"

Doctor Stewart stepped close at this point, and placed his arm around Mr. Dickie's shoulders in a most convivial manner. "Yes, Miss

Courtown," encouraged the Doctor while nursing the whiskey in his free hand, "do tell us your position on temperance. We would all of us be interested to know."

I glared at him and found myself colouring dreadfully. "I find that the hour has grown late, and I must excuse myself." I stood up, straightened the ruching on my skirt, and swept from the room without so much as a nod or a good night to any of them. Once in my chamber, I decried the disobliging scene, ranting to myself at the awkwardness of the situation. How ludicrous Lily would have found it, and how we might once have laughed together at Mr. Dickie's expense. It made me despondent to think, yet again, of her betrayal and to wonder what force was at work to sever our connection.

The next morning I arrived downstairs to find the front hall floor filled with mounds of freshly cut evergreen boughs and the lovely scent of fresh pine. Mr. Clement was busily stripping leaves from what I learned were mountain ash branches, leaving the little berries extant. Mountain ash grew in abundance near the marsh, and he had helped himself to generous amounts of the berried branches. Mrs. McLenaghan, apron-clad, was rushing from the front hall to the parlour and back again, directing both Mr. Clement and her husband in their activities. I peeped into the parlour and saw the good-natured Mr. McLenaghan working desperately to weave garlands from the greenery while trying to fasten it to the mantel piece. I stepped in at once to offer my assistance.

"Bless ye, Lass," he puffed at me, "you will know better than me what it is I'm supposed to be about. The Missus is determined to decorate the Inn this morning and I've not had my morning tea yet and she's near wore me out."

Mrs. McLenaghan walked in just then and clucked away at him in her scolding, affectionate manner. "Miss Courtown," she began, "you've not had your morning meal yet. You should not be so hard at work without a small bite of toast and an egg to nourish you. Let me bring you a tray while you watch this clumsy man for me." At this she rushed off, and I smiled at my companion.

"That's enough of that, then," said Mr. McLenaghan, dropping into the nearest chair. "It will take her a minute to fix your tray and I can catch my breath while she does so." He stretched his legs out before him and leaned his head back.

"You will catch it, Sir," I protested. "If she finds you at rest, we will both be held accountable."

"All right then," he said, huffing slightly as he pulled himself upright and stood once again, "we'd best be starting with them berries, and me with my stomach half falling out of me. Come on with me, Miss; if I'm to decorate with berries, you can be helping."

Amused, I followed him to the front hall where he filled my arms with several boughs of mountain ash. We returned to the parlour and I stood before the garland while he broke off small sprays of berries and tucked them into the evergreen. The effect was quite charming.

"I take it," I began, "that there is no holly available and we are making a substitution."

"Exactly," replied Mrs. McLenaghan, walking into the parlour brandishing my breakfast tray. "Exactly, Dear. Now sit ye down and have your breakfast while the rest of us get back to work."

"I've not had any nourishment this day, either," suggested Mr. McLenaghan. "Do you think I might just stop a minute and have a wee bowl of porridge?"

"I do not!" his Wife answered. "You know full well that as soon as you've ate, you will find an excuse to escape me and I'll be left with all the work myself. You can eat when you've done and not a minute before."

I was seated by now on the settle with my tray beside me. I took the plate with toast over to Mr. McLenaghan and quietly offered it to him.

"Bless ye' Dear," he said, "I'd be half over starvin' to death were it not for you." He munched away happily on my toast while continuing to force sprigs of berries into the garland until at last it looked well and truly decorated.

Mrs. McLenaghan returned and said what a good job he had done, and that he could now eat before starting upon the dining room. With great protestations, he followed her to the kitchen where I could hear them teasing each other. I left my tray where it was and ventured into the dining room where Mr. Clement was hard at work fastening evergreen garlands together in much the same fashion as Mr. McLenaghan had done. I reached out my hands silently, taking from him the cumbersome arrangement and fastening it quickly together. "Here," I said after several minutes of work, "let us try this now."

Mr. Clement took from me one end of the green rope and he and I together fastened it in large swags around the generous fireplace mantel and down each side. Together we began the tedious process of bending in place the small sprays of berries. We worked quietly at our task for some long time. My mind wandered to Rosslare Hall and I wondered to myself whether Christmas would be there this year. Henry's wife might be eager to have it at the Hall, but Henry might be just as happy to return to Lowry Castle and celebrate it there with the rest of his kin.

The servants would be sorry, I thought, not to have Christmas, and would miss my Father and his liberal ways. I hoped that Henry would know to give them all a Christmas favour. Father always made sure that they had bowls of punch and extra tea and sugar at the season.

All of this I was thinking of when Mr Clement interrupted me: "Miss Courtown, are you feeling poorly? Can I get you a chair? Miss Courtown?" I realized that tears had begun to run down my face. Mr.

Clement was standing near and looked troubled.

"I'm sorry, Mr. Clement. Please excuse me."

I went upstairs to my small room and bathed my face with rose-water. I did not feel much ready to be in company, and yet I knew that solitude was not the remedy. I lay down upon my bed and composed myself, waiting for a small while before once more joining those below stairs.

Thoughts of liberality and Christmas at home made me realize with some little panic that I had made no preparations for it here. We were but three weeks away and I had no gifts made and no engagements. It would be a bleak season away from family and from my home, but I could at least, I reasoned, be generous with those who had nurtured me. I would busy myself readying small gifts, I thought, for the McLenaghans and Mr. Clement, and Doctor Stewart. Each of them, by turn, had been extraordinarily kind to me and this would be a fitting way to acknowledge their many acts of service.

The dry goods store, I reasoned, would likely have some ready-made handkerchiefs for gentlemen. I could neatly embroider these with their initials and have them pressed and ready in time. Mr. Clement seemed in need of some warm outdoor clothing but I must not embarrass him by choosing a gift so personal. A wrapped gift of coin might accompany the handkerchiefs and allow him to select anything he chose as needful. Mrs. McLenaghan would be the easiest to please; she would take great joy in anything that seemed fancy and out of the ordinary. I would ask Mrs. Nesbitt to help me select some new caps or anything in that line. Mr. McLenaghan enjoyed a pipe of an evening, I had observed, and a tin of good tobacco might be easily procured for him.

Doctor Stewart alone posed a difficulty for me. Since he was a single gentleman I must not choose something too intimate, but neither could I slight him with something unthoughtful. A book would be best, I thought, but a suitable one would likely not be easily procured in Orange Hill.

Collecting my outdoor things, I went downstairs and prepared for the short walk to the Nesbitts' store. "I will be back shortly," I called to Mrs. McLenaghan. "I'm off to the dry goods for some shopping." Mrs. McLenaghan popped her head out of the kitchen, saw me, and came out into the front hall.

"Are you well enough, my Lamb?"

"Yes, thank you, I have a small bit of shopping to tend to."

"All right then, Lass, goodbye."

I slipped outside and felt the effects of a cold, bracing wind almost immediately. The weather was clearly changed and winter seemed to be near. My gloves and cloak did not protect me from the bitter chill. I was glad to step inside the shop after only a short walk.

Mrs. Nesbitt greeted me formally and retreated to her place behind the counter to wait upon me. "Good morning, Mrs. Nesbitt," I said, "I am looking for gentlemen's handkerchiefs and wonder if you have a stock of them ready made?"

"Right over here, Miss Courtown," she directed, indicating a tall wooden chest filled with small drawers. Each of these was carefully labelled with a card, and I spied her opening a small drawer that read "Gentlemen's Handkerchiefs." It was a neat system, I thought, marvelling a little at the organization. She reached inside the drawer and lifted out a small stack of starched white linen squares. They were large and without adornment but of good quality and nicely finished. I selected twelve of these, thinking to make six for Mr. McLenaghan and to give six unmarked to Mr. Clement. I deliberated on the purchase of six more for the Doctor but then thought better of it.

Thanking Mrs. Nesbitt for her assistance, I next enquired about lace caps. There was, I discovered, a wide array to choose from, and I carefully chose two of the most elaborate with the finest of lace and ribbond trimming. They would please dear Mrs. McLenaghan mightily, I thought, as they were clearly superior to the unadorned cotton ones she mostly wore.

Although I did not wish to seem lavish, I noticed a fine cambric apron with a generously sized bib and skirt, and this I selected also, thinking that such an apron would not go amiss in Mrs. McLenaghan's routine. A large amount of fine pipe tobacco was also easily located.

It was a little exciting to have done some Christmas shopping, but it was also, I thought, a little strange. This was very unlike previous years, when Father and Uncle would accompany Lily and me to Dublin, where we would stay in a Hotel overnight. We would shop for an entire day before taking the train home again with our parcels. And all the while, Father and Uncle would complain good-naturedly about our expenditures and chivy us gently about financial ruin.

I made my way back to the Inn and rushed upstairs with my parcels. It would not do to have the others suspect me, I thought. I hid my purchases in one of my trunks and, after a few moments to tidy my hair and straighten my gown, I went downstairs and joined Mrs. McLenaghan in the kitchen. She was busily chopping some dried fruit but greeted me and made me welcome. I seated myself at the large kitchen table and watched her at work.

"Mrs. McLenaghan?" I began after a few moments or so. "If I were wanting to send my Cousin and her baby a gift at Christmas but didn't know what would be suitable, what items would be considered useful and not out of the way?" I tapped my fingers lightly on the table whilst framing my delicate question. I was a little frightened that Mrs. McLenaghan's dislike of the Careys might flavour her response and that I would be captive to one of her bitter tirades.

"Well," she said thoughtfully, setting aside the knife for a minute, "if someone was so inclined, Miss, I would think that a filled basket might be appreciated, and maybe something for the baby. You could ask Nellie if her man would deliver it to the Carey place and save you the trouble. Something like that would be best, I'm thinking." At this she nodded her head, seeming to agree with her own advice, and resumed her chopping with vigour.

"Thank you. That's a splendid thought. With maybe some tea and sugar and soap?"

"Yes, and ready-made things for the baby."

"That sounds well; no one could take such a thing amiss, could they?"

"Well, Miss, people is as likely to take it well as not, I'm thinking. If they're inclined to take offence, they will, and if they're inclined to be grateful, they will. There's just no telling how some people is going to respond to things."

"Yes, I'm sure you are correct, but I shall feel the better for trying to do the right thing."

"Well now, that's 'cause you're a good girl, and you just never encountered a devil like that Jack Carey afore."

I rose from my seat. "No, I have never before encountered the likes of that disreputable man, and it is my passionate desire that I never see him again."

"That's the spirit," she responded. "It is better to be right cross with a brute like him than it is to be all Christian."

I left the kitchen at that sombre thought and made my way back upstairs to begin embroidering *HM* on the handkerchiefs. I chose a heavy black silk and made the letters quite ornate by design. I amused myself with this small handiwork for some hours, anticipating the delight with which I believed the gift would be received.

Our supper that evening was a light-hearted affair. Mrs. McLenaghan had begun her Christmas baking and we were treated to rich raisin pudding with warm cream afterwards. While we were settling ourselves in the parlour for a quiet evening together, a knocking came at the door, and Mr. McLenaghan invited in a large group of carollers. We enjoyed their performance hugely; Doctor Stewart gave them some pennies by way of thanks. It was a comfort to see that Christmas was come to Orange Hill and that, despite the sad outcome of my own adventure, rejoicing was to be had by those around me.

Mr. Clement informed us that he would be taking several days' holiday, riding first to Port Gibson and from there to Port Whitby, to spend Christmas with his Brothers. Before his return, he would also be travelling to Toronto. At this, Mrs. McLenaghan was certain that he would know a confectionary store on King Street that carried a particular kind of taffy to which she was partial. Despite disavowing any knowledge of such a shop, or the taffy in question, he committed himself to locating this particular sweet for her.

"No," she interrupted at one point, "it's not King Street, it's the one *near* King Street that has the shop. It is a grocer's shop but they carry biscuits and confectionery. Near Yonge Street. Harry, you know the one. We was there together once." She looked at her husband accusingly, as though he were being willfully unhelpful. "Harry, think what it's called, can't you? You don't want poor John walking around Toronto lost because you can't trouble yourself to remember such a thing, now do you?" And by this means Mr. McLenaghan found himself once more in a great deal of difficulty without having actively done anything to deserve such distinction.

I was amused, as I often was, by their exchange, but poor Mr. Clement looked quite agitated at the prospect. He had been charged with securing the taffy and I knew that the good man would walk every street until he located it.

"Mrs. McLenaghan? Is there any chance that the shop advertises in the *Almanac* or the paper, do you think?"

She hesitated at this, and seemed to ponder my question before springing into action. "Well, aren't you the cleverest?" she clucked. "Harry, where's the *Almanac* and where did you put the last of the papers?" Both she and Harry jumped to their feet and left the room to begin their search for the advertisement.

Mr. Clement rose from his chair and bade Doctor Stewart and me a good evening, expressing his desire to rise early in the morning and begin his travels. He assured us that he would stop by the Inn before leaving to gather further taffy instructions.

Doctor Stewart and I remained in the parlour. He was at his leisure, with his legs spread comfortably out before the fire, and I was seated nearby, picking at some fancywork.

"She won't rest this evening," began the Doctor, "until poor Harry has examined every sheet of newspaper and every *Almanac* in the Inn. It is a cruel task you have set him to!"

"Me!" I exclaimed. "I am in no way responsible for his misery. I meant simply to prevent Mr. Clement from searching all of Toronto for taffy." I saw that the Doctor was laughing a little and had intended no affront.

"You tease me cruelly," I said, rebuking him.

"No, Miss Courtown," he replied, "it is evening, and Christmas approaches, and we are both of us far from home, and I in no way intend to alienate the one Lady whose company I most desire." He gazed at me steadily while he spoke thus, and I coloured deeply under his gaze, grateful that the dim lighting did not reveal the extent of my discomfort.

Mrs. McLenaghan came bursting into the parlour, waving *The Canadian Almanac.* "It's in here," she said triumphantly. "I found it. It's on Temperance Street, just like I remembered. Dodgson Shields & Morton, it's called. Grocers & Provision Merchants, and Manufacturers of Biscuits & Confectioneries. But where is John? Has he left already?" She began looking around the parlour carefully, as though Mr. Clement had deliberately concealed himself from her.

"Yes," I said. "He has retired for the evening with the assurance that he would stop by in the morning."

"Well, that's good then," she said, sounding gratified. "I thought perhaps I had missed him entirely."

I smiled at her and then remembered my gift for Mr. Clement. "I have something small for him upstairs," I said, "a remembrance for his Christmas. If I collected it now, would you be so good as to give it to him in the morning?"

"Of course we will," she said, smiling at me. "I'm sure he will be honoured by your kindness."

"The kindness is all on one side," I replied. "Excuse me."

I went upstairs and wrapped quickly the half dozen handkerchiefs that I had purchased for him. Selecting an envelope and paper from my small secretary, I wrote him a note, wishing him a joyous Christmas. Inside the letter I carefully folded some bank notes, sealing the envelope with a drop of wax and my small signet ring. Rushing downstairs again, I handed the small parcel to Mrs. McLenaghan and thanked her for being my messenger.

In the morning, I discovered Doctor Stewart had been called away to Peterborough to act as Coroner. Despite the McLenaghans' good-natured banter, the Inn seemed a little desolate without his company. I kept to my room and the parlour most days, wishing to avoid a

collision with Mrs. McLenaghan and feeling, in truth, rather despondent. I visited Nesbitt's Dry Goods one further time and arranged for
a delivery to be made to the Careys' establishment.

"Mrs. Nesbitt," I enquired, "do you happen perhaps to know if
Doctor Stewart orders his shirts from you?" I coloured at this, sure
that I would be misunderstood. "I ask," I continued, "because I was
the cause of his ruining one, and I feel obliged to replace it." I was
entirely mortified by this explanation and was well aware of Mrs.
Nesbitt's increased scrutiny.

"As luck would have it, I can tell you, Miss Courtown, that we order in the Doctor's shirts for him, as he is most particular about the
fastenings on the collar and cuffs."

"Would you happen to have any such suitable shirts in stock now,
as it were?" I knew that my countenance was flaming scarlet and I
could not meet Mrs. Nesbitt's gaze.

"Well, let me look a minute." She retreated behind a curtained
enclosure and I heard her rifling through a stack of boxes. I stood
entirely still, conscious of my discomfort but unwilling to abandon
my errand.

"Here we are," she said, returning through the curtained partition. "We have two such shirts in stock. Shall I show them to you?"

"No," I responded abruptly, "that is not necessary. Would you
wrap them please?"

"Collars and cuffs?" she enquired.

"I don't think so; it is only the shirt that was ruined." The entire transaction took perhaps less than five minutes, but it seemed as
though it had taken hours, and I felt indecorous and severely compromised by the exchange.

Returning to the Inn, I took my contraband directly upstairs.
Downstairs was all astir; I sought out Mr. McLenaghan, who informed

me that unexpected guests had arrived, and that "Mother was all jumpy and overwrought." Taking my direction from this, I slipped quietly into the parlour where I sat working a small piece of embroidery. I was engaged in this work when the door opened some hours later and I looked up to see Doctor Stewart.

"I thought I might find you hiding in here," he laughed. "I expected that you would have found a quiet place and retreated like a little mouse." He walked to the drinks cabinet, and turning the small key, opened it and poured himself a small glass of brandy. This he placed by the fender of the fire, allowing it to warm.

"We have missed you these past few days," I said by way of greeting. "You were a long time in Peterborough."

"Yes," he said quietly, "it was an unwelcome business. I was called to an inquest. A young man was employed as a stationer and printer and was thought by all to have very good prospects. Working the press, he had a pain in his right side and passed some terrible gas, according to those who were there. The next morning he returned to work looking poorly and with a fever. A well-meaning friend secured the services of a chemist, who insisted that he be bled and have leeches applied to the swelling. In addition to this, the young man was fed Anti-Bilious Pills to cure Dyspepsia and Liver Complaints. He screamed violently, they say, and writhed in a great deal of pain, until he died later that night. Doctor Whittemore sent for me to do the autopsy as he did no wish to alienate the locals who believe in their cures and tonics. It were a clear case of ruptured appendix. Any medical man would have known."

The Doctor walked over to the fender and picked up his brandy, swirling the warmed liquid in the glass and inhaling its fragrance before tasting it. I could see that he was deeply troubled, but I did not know how to respond. Instead, I redirected my attentions to my handiwork and continued to work at the small pattern.

"You are very quiet this evening, Miss Courtown," he said. "Have I upset you with my tale?" The Doctor crossed the room at this and sat beside me on the small settle. Instinctively I pulled my work basket closer to my side, creating rather more space for him but ensuring a barrier remained that was proper.

We sat silent for a few minutes, and then Doctor Stewart rose and excused himself, leaving his unfinished drink on a small table. "Ach, I am no fit company this night, Miss Courtown. Forgive me," he said, and quitted the room.

Chapter the Fifth
FIDELITY

I rose early the next morning, and looked out my window to see that a hard frost had touched the ground, edging things in a stark white line. The dining room was empty when I looked in, and so I headed towards the kitchen where I was sure I would find both company and a hot fire. I was not mistaken, and was happy to see the others and to feel the warmth of the room.

"Good morning, Miss," greeted Mr. McLenaghan as he rushed over to pull out a chair for me. "It's a quare fine day, if it ever is so."

"Good morning, Dear," chimed Mrs. McLenaghan.

"Miss Courtown," completed the Doctor, standing until I sat down.

"Good morning, all," I replied. "It seems a frosty morning, I think."

"That it is," said Mrs. McLenaghan.

Mr. McLenaghan bustled about after his wife, passing her those things that she called for and standing at the ready for further instructions. I watched them together, amused by the scene, and relaxed in the familiar setting. Mrs. McLenaghan came by me to pour the tea and I smiled my thanks at her.

"I was wondering, Miss Courtown," began the Doctor in a voice so low I could scarcely hear him, "if you would be at liberty to join me for a small ride. We have only a few more days of fine weather left, I think."

Surprised by his amiable tone after his ill-mannered behaviour the night before, I agreed. "How lovely! I should enjoy a ride."

"Very well then; let us say eleven o'clock. I will meet you with the horses."

I noticed then that the McLenaghans had stopped their activity and were listening attentively. I sipped at my tea and did not speak further. The Doctor, following my lead, finished his oatmeal and stood to take his leave, bowing first and thanking the McLenaghans for their hospitality.

As soon as the Doctor left, Mrs. McLenaghan presented me with a hearty breakfast of eggs and sausage and toast. "Eat up, Lass," she said. "If you're going out riding with the Doctor, you'll need all your strength, God love you." She nodded her head at this, as though confirming her own words, and beamed at me. I returned to my room and changed into my riding costume, discarding my petticoat. There were many women of my acquaintance who wore chamois breeches under their riding skirts, but my Father had disparaged such a lack of propriety and railed about the need to preserve decorum between ladies and gentlemen.

At eleven o'clock I went downstairs and saw that the Doctor was out front with two horses. I noted that he had troubled to dress in a proper riding costume; I had only ever before seen him in ill-fitting tweeds. Today he wore a snug green riding jacket and vest, with tight ivory pantaloons and polished boots high over his knees. He looked smarter than his usual self and I could not help but notice, with some embarrassment, his heavily muscled physique.

Off we rode in the direction of Browne's Lookout, racing one another by turn and enjoying the exercise. We were well matched riders; I was energized and invigorated by the run. "Look there," the Doctor said, pointing. I followed his direction and saw a large number of deer emerge from a bush and cross into a field. They moved with such stillness that they seemed entirely fluid, blending with the surrounding tones so naturally you could scarcely tell they were living creatures. There had been a break in the onset of our winter weather, and the day had become warm and sunny despite the early morning frost. The Doctor dismounted first, then took the reins from me and fastened them to a tree branch while I slipped off and stood to the ground.

"You are a very good rider!" he exclaimed. "I always forget how well you ride until I see you upon a horse, and then I think you should ride always, you look so at ease."

I laughed at his nonsense and took from him a woollen blanket which I spread upon the ground. He then removed from his satchel a small packet with two hearty rolls and some wedges of cheese. He had also managed to stow two small, crushed jam tarts and we ate these with our fingers, licking them clean when we were done. It was a simple refreshment but much appreciated after our long ride in the fresh outdoors.

"I have been pondering our respective situations," began Doctor Stewart once we had eaten. I looked at him expectantly, waiting for him to continue.

"I am a miserable Bachelor living in an unfurnished house and eating all my meals with the McLenaghans. I never remember to order coal and I suspect I pay far too much for things, although people will never directly say. And I find the house hollow and empty; it needs a lady's hand in the decorating and running of it."

I felt my pulse quickening as he spoke, frightened that he was now about to make a declaration of love. He continued, "You, on the other hand, are in need of protection. You seem unwilling to return to Ireland without your Cousin, and it is clearly not provident for you to live with the Careys. Neither can you continue infinitely abiding at the Inn. The company is no always suitable for a lady, and there is no respectable occupation for you. It is clear to me that if you are to remain here, you had best marry." He stopped for a moment and then reached across the blanket and took my hand in his own. "I am asking you to become my Wife."

Smiling, he looked at me full in the face and waited silently, his eyes happy and bright. I knew that I needed to reply but was struck silent. I looked at his hands: they were clean scrubbed and soft to the touch, the nails buffed. They were a gentleman's hands, despite the filthy work I had seen them perform.

"But what of love, Doctor Stewart? If I should agree to this arrangement we will both of us be committing to a marriage without love."

"Will we then?" he asked softly. "Do you no think that love might follow? Our manners and habits are no dissimilar, and we have often enjoyed each other's company."

"We are but mere acquaintances; it is only circumstance that has brought us so often together."

"Yes, that is true," he replied in a gentle tone, "but I believe our short history together indicates those things requisite to a favourable domestic arrangement, well suited to us both."

"Am I merely engaged then to become the manager of your domestic arrangements?" I asked pointedly. His face went dark at this, as if a cloud had suddenly passed overhead. I had spoken something which gave deep offence.

"Let me assure you, Miss Courtown, I would never importune

you with a Husband's demands. I am no a man like Jack Burridge or Jack Carey. I propose an arrangement that provides affinity and security for us both, but that is all." He put my hand down and stood up. "I have asked you to be my Wife. You would be the mistress of my home and would carry my name. I offer you my shelter and my worldly goods and my devotion. I expect only that you would conduct yourself in all things as my Wife and that you would take comfort in having a respectable position. Unless you choose otherwise, we would each of us keep to our suite of private rooms. I have no further expectations."

I heard much emotion in his tone and looked at him in wonder. My questioning and reticence he had clearly found offensive.

"You may of course think about this offer, Miss Courtown. I am in no rush. If you are in doubt as to my character or my intentions or my small wealth you must speak it and I will allow for you to correspond with those who may give you honest assessments."

He walked towards the horses at this and began to lead them to me.

"You misunderstand me. I am grateful for your offer and acknowledge the great kindness you intend. However, in my small experience of such things, love must surely play a role." I spoke to him openly, aware that he was a gentleman and a man of honour, but remembering also Lord Driscoll and my shameful treatment of him.

"Yes, of course. I had no taken you for a romantic, Miss Courtown. You are correct. Let us speak no further of this." I saw that his pride was wounded but I did not know how to repair the awkwardness that had arisen. "I had hoped that you would see the practical merits of this proposition. Forgive me if I have been too forward." His manner was now chill and brusque. With that he held out his hands and assisted me in mounting. He mounted after and sat for several seconds before pressing his legs to the horse and setting off. We rode to Orange Hill in silence. Doctor Stewart stopped in front of the Inn and assisted me in dismounting.

"Thank you for your company, Miss Courtown," he said, again with a brittle formality that stung me with its coldness.

Before I could answer, he mounted his horse and set off at a fast trot. I wished to call after him but could not bring myself to be so bold.

I saw no sign of him the next day, at either luncheon or supper. Needlework kept me occupied, but the hours seemed long without the diversion of his good-natured visits. On the following day he remained absent, with no mention made of him by either of the McLenaghans. Since the weather was now stormy and cold, with light gusts of snow falling, I remained indoors and kept to my sewing. Two more days passed with only more cold weather and more snow. It was piling in drifts six inches deep outside and looked treacherous for walking. The Inn being empty of all travellers, I was feeling confined and solitary. Mrs. McLenaghan popped her head into the parlour on the fourth afternoon to ask if I would like some tea. I accepted gratefully and followed her to the kitchen, glad of some company and a diversion.

"It has been a while since we have last seen Doctor Stewart," I ventured.

Mrs. McLenaghan smiled and nodded her head vigorously. "Yes," she said, "he has gone to Port Gibson. The Doctor travels there regular to pick up his medicine order and visit with old friends."

"Does he stay away long then?" I asked, feigning only slight interest.

"No, not this long usually, but I think there is a lady there that has caught his interest."

"Oh," I said, a little startled, "what makes you think so?"

"Well," she began, lowering her voice to a whisper, "he said just the other morning when he left that when he returned he hoped he might be well on the way to changing his bachelor circumstances. I can't think what else this might mean lass, can you?"

"No," I said, reddening terribly. "I'm sure you must be correct, and have guessed his meaning."

Mrs. McLenaghan was staring at me openly, looking strangely smug and pleased with herself. I felt as though I had received a blow, but she was obviously taking great pleasure in this tidbit of gossip. She cared for the Doctor, I knew, and would be glad to see him respectably attached. Yet I could not reconcile his sudden courting of a Port Gibson lady with his recent offer to me. He had not seemed disingenuous, but this news demonstrated just that. I finished my tea and removed to my room, where I sat thoughtfully before the fire.

Much of what Doctor Stewart had spoken to me was, upon reflection, considered and sensible. It was not seemly that I continue for long living in a public house as an unmarried woman. I should seek a house to let, and hire staff. I should advertise for a companion at once to keep my reputation intact. Orange Hill was perhaps not the most suitable location for such an arrangement; Montreal or Port Gibson would afford a more varied society with diverse entertainments. I would not, then, be so far from Lily as to be beyond ready assistance when she had need of me, but I would be spared further exposure to her vile Husband. In relocating to such a place, however, I would lose contact with the McLenaghans, Mr. Clement, and my sewing group, and also, admittedly, with the Doctor. They were the sum of my new-found friends in this wild and beautiful place, and each had been true to me. I felt morose to think of parting from them.

Yet it was clearly necessary for me to leave and try to establish a new existence somewhere afresh. I had left Ireland without responding to Lord Driscoll's offer and I was now deeply ashamed of my treatment of him. We were well matched in family and fortune and political sensibilities. My father had encouraged me to accept him and had chastised me for dallying in my decision. It was no way to treat a man of such respectability and influence, I knew. I could not hope to believe that he was yet waiting upon my response. If I wrote to him, would he be willing yet to wait upon my return? And after my travels, would I be content to return to the prescribed life he offered me? Mistress of his estates and mother to his sons? But would I be able to bear sons, or had the arsenic left me barren? Would any man of fortune choose to marry me if he knew there could be no heir?

My head began to ache with the worry of my deliberations, and I decided to brave the cold for a short walk. I would feel better, I knew, if I could only engage in some activity. Wrapping myself as warmly as I could, I stepped out the door and pulled my muffler up over my nose and mouth. The air was so vicious that it burned at my cheeks. I directed my steps towards the school but found that the wind battled me backwards. The ground was slippery beneath my feet and my walking boots, though thick-soled, were no match for the hard-packed ice. I felt myself falling down but could grab at nothing to stop myself.

Defeated by the elements, I returned to the Inn, choosing my steps carefully and slowly. Once inside the door I removed my cloak and jacket and shook off the snow. Mrs. McLenaghan came rushing to greet me, exclaiming mightily at my foolishness for venturing out in such a storm.

"Yes, you are altogether correct. I have had a slip and landed in a pile of snow."

"Oh, you poor Lamb," she cried, "go take off those boots while I set the sookey to boil."

I made my way to do as she suggested but found that my right ankle pained me when I stood. By climbing slowly, and with a firm grasp of the railing, I was able to reach my room. I sat down upon a chair and unlaced my boots. Rubbing both feet to warm them, I felt again a shock of fire when I moved my right foot. Cautiously I placed it upon the floor and stood upon it. It produced a searing sensation.

I put on my patent shoes and made my way gingerly down the stairs. The parlour was empty and so I went directly to the kitchen. Much to my dismay, I discovered that the McLenaghans, Mr. Clement, and Doctor Stewart were there before me enjoying tea and some of Mrs. McLenaghan's fine scones. I made to curtsey and excuse myself but the curtsey was too much pressure on my poor ankle and my leg gave way. I caught myself on a chair but not before the others noticed.

Doctor Stewart, who had stood upon my entering, came quickly towards me and directed me to sit. "What has happened to you?" he asked.

I had reddened terribly and felt too discomforted to speak. I shook my head at him and said, "It is nothing."

"She had a fall this afternoon, out walking in the storm," interjected Mrs. McLenaghan.

I shook my head again. "Please, do not trouble yourselves. It is only my ankle that feels tender."

"May I?" Doctor Stewart bent down before me and reached for my right foot, slipped off my small shoe, and touched the ankle with his thumbs. "It is swelling. We will need to put ice on it and wrap it tightly, by turns. I shall get some cloths," said he, "and will return shortly. Mrs. McLenaghan, will you help her with the stocking?"

I was miserable with this attention but no one consulted my feelings. The men left us and Mrs. McLenaghan helped me remove my stocking, slipping it into her apron pocket. Doctor Stewart returned shortly with some nicely cut flannel strips, which he wrapped tightly about my foot and ankle.

"These must remain until you retire," he said, "and then we must put ice upon it to calm the swelling. We will bandage it again in the morning."

"Thank you …" I began, but he bowed abruptly and left the kitchen. A moment later I heard the front door open and close.

"Well, bless me," said Mrs. McLenaghan. "I wonder what scared him off in such a hurry. It's not like him to leave so sudden."

I said nothing to her in return but stood up slowly and made my way carefully to the door.

"I think I shall retire early. I feel weary from my walk."

Mrs. McLenaghan looked at me strangely, "Well," she said, "we'll bring you up a tray of supper and a bowl of ice for your ankle."

I thanked her for her trouble and hobbled my way awkwardly up the stairs.

The ankle was not much improved in the morning. I limped downstairs, where the McLenaghans both rushed after me, making tea and serving me a scrambled egg with a warm biscuit.

"Doctor Stewart was in this morning already," said Mrs. McLenaghan. "He said if you was not up to walking, Mr. McLenaghan should fetch him from his Surgery and he would wrap it again snug for you."

"That was very kind," I said, "but I do not need to trouble him. I can manage very well without his attentions." I did not mean to sound so haughty or ungrateful, but my ankle pained me and thoughts of Lord Driscoll had vexed me.

Mrs. McLenaghan looked at me strangely. "I'm sure he only meant to be kind," she said, leaping to her favourite's defence.

"Of course, he is always kind. But he is also a busy man with his practice and whatever plans he is now making for his nuptials."

"Oh, I see," said Mrs. McLenaghan, her face averted. "You're troubled about that now, are you?"

"I am not troubled," I said petulantly. "I am not even interested. It just seems to me that he must have many things to occupy him, and my ankle can be of no real concern."

"Oh, but it is, Lass. He is most concerned. He was here for breakfast and enquired after you and then once again while he was on his way back from his morning exercise."

Not knowing how best to respond, I bit my bottom lip and was still. Mrs. McLenaghan and her husband exchanged glances.

The day passed quietly. I watched the snow falling, large fluffy white flakes that drifted down lazily. I was not altogether sad, but not happy either. I felt quite alone and friendless and wondered at my own willfulness which had driven me from my beloved Ireland, determined upon this journey that had ended so badly. It would have been better not to have seen Lily again than to be parted from her while yet so near, I thought. Since Uncle had leased the estate I could not easily return to my rooms at Rosslare Hall and pretend that naught had happened. My Uncle would have me at Lowry Castle, I knew, at least until I married. All of this put me in mind to write him. I had been remiss and not written deliberately, thinking it best to let Lily write first with what fabrications she thought suitable. I would not let him know we were estranged but would simply direct him with regard to my business affairs and let him know my plans.

I folded up my completed handiwork and prepared to climb the stairs for my small secretary. Mrs. McLenaghan intercepted me in the hall and offered to go in my stead. I accepted her offer and returned to the parlour to wait. She returned shortly, and declining her offer of tea or luncheon, I took out my pen and began to write.

> *My dear Uncle,*
>
> *The news of my beloved Father's passing was most grievous to me.*
> *I cannot think but that if I had been at home I might have been the*
> *one to give him comfort in his last hours.*

My hand stopped at this and I sat back in my chair to compose myself. I did not intend to ruin the brief with my tears, but they continued to drop upon the paper. While I was meditating upon what next to write, I heard heavy footsteps approach behind me. Wiping my face with my handkerchief, I turned to see the Doctor entering the parlour.

"Miss Courtown," he said, bowing, "you look distressed. Is your ankle paining you?" Kneeling on the floor, he reached for my foot and began to tenderly unwrap the cloths. "It needs more ice for the swelling," he remarked. "Let me get you some."

"No, please, I beg of you," I cried, "leave me be. I am well enough."

Standing erect, he stepped back and said, "Of course, as you wish. I intend no offence." His manner and voice were cold and I knew that I had insulted him anew.

"Forgive me," I said, "it is only that I write this distressing letter and it has made me emotional."

"And what is it you write that is troubling?"

"I have resolved to leave this place. I will make my future in London, where I have some family. I am writing to direct my Uncle in some business affairs."

Doctor Stewart paused for a moment, considering my words. "Are these close connections, Miss Courtown? People whose company you find yourself desolate without? Are you perhaps already committed to one who has declared himself?"

It were a strange question and I looked at him, wondering at it.

"I only ask," he continued, "because you left them once already to follow Mrs. Carey and now I find that you are abandoning her to return to them."

"I am in no way abandoning Mrs. Carey!" I snapped. My voice was louder than I had intended and we were both startled by it. Doctor Stewart turned abruptly and shut the parlour door firmly. He returned to stand facing me directly, waiting for me to continue, but I saw that his face was very deeply flushed.

"I beg your pardon; forgive me."

"Go on," he said, speaking quietly but with an undertone that I did not recognize.

"I only meant that Mrs. Carey has forgot who she is and how she was brought up. She has sunk low and will not take steps to elevate herself. I cannot help her if she will not be helped and I cannot bear to see her so reduced."

"And so, because she has taken a different course from your own, you reject her?" he asked angrily.

I looked down at my hands, crossed demurely in my lap. "You make me quite ashamed, Doctor Stewart. I cannot speak further." I was miserable for having once again argued with him, and that, in addition to the rest of my dire circumstances, made me begin to weep.

Doctor Stewart pulled a chair up next to mine. Sitting down close beside me, he took my hands in his. "And have you thought no more of my offer, Miss Courtown? Do you reject me outright?"

"Your offer?" I exclaimed in astonishment. "That cannot be! Mrs. McLenaghan has said that you went to Port Gibson to court a lady there."

"Ah, Mrs. McLenaghan said, did she?" He chuckled at this, patting his leg and enjoying some private humour. I sat there, not knowing what had caused his sudden mirth. He stopped forthwith and looked at me soberly, taking again my hands.

"Mrs. McLenaghan was mistaken, Miss Courtown. I went to Port Gibson on business only."

We were interrupted by a fierce knocking at the front door. We stood at the commotion, and shortly heard an anxious voice calling for the Doctor. He let loose of my hand and bowed briefly before striding out of the room. I followed in wonderment, curious to know what the matter was. Mrs. McLenaghan was there before me, her apron pulled up over her face and sobbing loudly. I went to her at once and placed my arm around her shoulders.

"Mrs. McLenaghan, Dear," I soothed, "tell me, what is the matter? Can I assist you in any way?"

"Oh, Dearie," she began, lowering her apron to look at me, "oh, my dear Lamb, there has been a chimmbley fire in Tinkertown and one of your girls is in a bad way."

I felt a sensation of ice forming in my veins at almost the very instant she spoke. "Tell me," I said sharply, clasping her arm, "tell me what has happened."

"The men have come for Doctor Stewart," she said, "but there is little left for him to be doing. She is in a bad way and will soon be called to heaven with her mother."

"Who?" I shrieked at her. "Who is in a bad way?"

"Iris," she sobbed. "Little Iris Mewhinney, she who was here in your group. She was home alone when the chimmbley caught fire and instead of running outside, she tried, the brave heart, to douse it herself. The house is a pile of ash, and she was without breath when they found her."

I gasped at this, and was immediately caught up in the pillowy embrace of my companion. We stood together, rocking, while both of us wept. Yet I could not easily comprehend how a simple chimney fire could burn down a house. "How could this be?" I began. "Why was no one about to water the roof and the attics?"

"Bless ye," she said. "The men were at their work. They are poor buildings with no attics at all. They burn like tinder when there's a spark. It has happened afore in the winter months." At that, she began to mop at her face with a corner of her apron, and took my hand in hers. "I should get t' my kitchen," she said. "There will be a need of something hot."

I felt spare, and paced the short corridor of the upstairs hall, unwilling to visit the parlour and continue my correspondence, as it had been there where I had last seen my little favourite, picking at her sewing. I was also unprepared to visit my chamber, where the basket of work stood at the side of the room, in preparation for our next lesson. Both of these things filled me with sadness, and tears wet my face.

Finally resolving upon an occupation, I entered my room, moving directly to my own workbasket and the strawberry sampler I had been embroidering. I traced the name of my pupil on the cotton and began, in black silk, to stitch her name. When it was done I imagined her small fingers stroking the work, telling me again that it looked good enough to eat. I wept anew at this recollection of Iris.

I slept but poorly and heard doors opening and shutting in the night; the Inn and all its occupants seemed to be without rest. In the morning I dressed soberly, and descended to the kitchen clutching my handiwork. Mrs. McLenaghan was in full spate with Mary Ryan, the Inn's maid, hard at work beside her. Together they had turned out a small mountain of pies and baked goods and were hard occupied in their labours. Taking the liberty to pour my own cup of tea, I selected a tea biscuit from the pile cooling on the sideboard. Mrs.

McLenaghan smiled at me from across the kitchen and said that the funeral was set for the next morning. The body had been laid out in Tinkertown, she said, but I would not be expected there. I nodded at her politely and slipped out of the kitchen to the quiet remove of the dining room. I sat there alone, drinking my tea and chewing small morsels of biscuit.

Resolved to pay my respects to the little girl who had so easily captured my affections, I dressed for the outdoors and began the long walk to Tinkertown. My ankle was still paining me but I had laced it tightly in my thick-soled boots. It was not difficult to determine which house had been selected for the wake. The door was open to a small cottage near the end of the row; the keening and crying had already started. I approached tentatively, but sure that my attendance there was fitting under the circumstances.

I was welcomed inside immediately, and recognized many of the girls from my group, along with others from Orange Hill whom I had encountered without having been introduced. Little Harriet, from my sewing group, came to me and took my hand, leading me to a chair next to the open casket where Iris's tiny hands were crossed over her chest, her eyes closed as if in sleep. By her side stood a man I took to be her Father, as he was lamenting in the most pitiable and heart-wrenching way. I went to him to express my condolences, and he made free to clasp me to him and pat my back. Stepping away from him, slightly abashed, I held out my small offering. He took it, examined it carefully, and then looked at me. "She much admired my work," I said. "I thought perhaps she might have it."

Nodding, he bent over her and tenderly placed the handkerchief under her clasped hands so that her name and the little strawberry were visible beneath them. "Thanking you," he said gruffly, "it looks well. I'm sure she would be obliged." I sobbed at this, and seated myself on the chair while struggling to regain my composure. The melancholy of the occasion was such that I could not stem my sorrow. I sat weeping softly for perhaps an hour and then excused myself and began my solitary walk back to the Inn.

I spent the afternoon and evening alone, feeling morose. My ankle was quite swelled again and I bathed it in a bowl of ice. I ate my dinner on a tray in my room as I did not feel able to comport myself in society. In my grieving for Iris, I also wept for the loss of my Father, the wretched mess I had left at home, and my detachment from Lily and Kathleen. All of my recent sadnesses seemed to converge upon me and I found that I was overcome by my despair.

Reverend Carr led the funeral service in the small English church. Despite the fact that he and his wife often seemed imbued with their own self-importance, he was as moved by the tragedy as the rest, and provided comfort. The church was filled with the residents of all of Orange Hill and Tinkertown; many of those in attendance greeted me warmly. I sat at the side, pressed tightly by Mr. and Mrs. McLenaghan, Doctor Stewart, Mr. Clement, and Mr. Dickie, who were all of us sharing one pew. I could not help but think what a diverse grouping we presented.

There was only one hymn, and of the Reverend's choosing, presumably. He had recently acquired a set of leaflets with the words to a new hymn and was eager for the congregation to learn it. The piece was written by the Reverend John Monsell, who had just published another of his Hymnals. The melody was already a familiar one. Doctor Stewart on the one side, and Mr. Dickie on my other, shared with me the small leaflet when we stood to sing. Mr. Dickie had a rather unmusical voice, but this did not moderate his enthusiasm for the singing. *Worship the Lord in the beauty of holiness.* I would have found it quite moving, had it not been for the distraction of Mr. Dickie singing loudly to my left and Doctor Stewart gently tugging the leaflet to my right.

The congregation, however, was united in heart-rending grief. Mr. Mewhinney was mostly propped up by two gentlemen of his acquaintance, who steadied him while he sobbed, and many of the women were wailing and crying most piteously. I observed that the vast majority of the children looked over-awed by the proceedings, and although sad, were also frightened.

I wept a little at the words of one prayer:

O FATHER of all, we pray to thee for those whom we love but see no longer. Grant them thy peace; and in thy loving wisdom and almighty power, work in them the good purpose of thy perfect will; through Jesus Christ our Lord. Amen.

but was able soon to regain my composure. Doctor Stewart handed me one of his oversized handkerchiefs, and Mr. Dickie patted my arm stiffly in a gesture of condolence. The congregation dispersed after the service and went to the small English cemetery. I chose to return to the Inn, not wishing to see the small pine casket committed to the grave. A luncheon was served at the Hotel, and the McLenaghans were engaged in ferrying prepared foodstuffs there. Since I was not in the way of feeling sociable, I retreated instead to the quiet of the parlour.

It was soon Christmas. The morning began quite sombrely, with all of us rising early to attend the English church for service. Doctor Stewart came in after we did, slipping into the pew beside Mr. McLenaghan. We slid sideways along to make room for him. Mrs. McLenaghan was not content with the seating arrangements, however, so she clambered over me to my left and signalled, by way of a vicious pinch to the arm, that Mr. McLenaghan was to do the same. Doctor Stewart looked down at the floor to disguise his mirth but acquiesced to sidle more closely to me just the same. We shared a hymnary and the small *Book of Common Prayer.* I observed that his voice was rich and full when he sang; he seemed to do so joyfully on this day. The tower bell was rung quite loudly at the end of service, and we walked back to the Inn for our morning meal. There was a rich Barmbrack for our breakfast, filled with raisins and currants and dusted generously with sugar. We ate heartily of it and then adjourned to the small parlour with a pot of tea.

On a small table, we had each of us placed our gifts the night before. Mrs. McLenaghan was the first to approach the table and closed her eyes tightly before selecting the first present to be opened. By a happy chance, she had managed to choose one of the gifts I had wrapped for her. She opened the fancy caps, being careful to fold the plain paper and string I had used to wrap them, and exclaimed mightily. Each cap, in turn, she held up for us to admire. She was in raptures deciding which of the two was quite the finest and should be saved as her "best." Closing her eyes, she again selected a gift, this time carrying it to me.

The small inscription read: "To Miss Courtown, with affection, Harry and Janet." I was much moved. After unfolding the wrapping, I saw that they had purchased for me a fur-lined pair of gloves. They were not as finely made as my leather gloves, but when I slipped them on my hands I saw their many merits: they were strong, comfortable, and ever so soft, and would keep my hands warm in the cold winter days. Delighted, I went to Mr. McLenaghan first and kissed him on the top of his dear head, and next embraced Mrs. McLenaghan. I was touched by their thoughtfulness and generosity.

Then, smiling broadly at us all, Doctor Stewart walked over to the table and selected a parcel for the McLenaghans. "Scots do no make much of Christmas," he said, "but I hoped you would find a place for this." He lifted a small carton and placed it carefully on the floor in front of them. Mr. McLenaghan went in search of a knife so that he could cut the heavy twine it was fastened with. He was not quite fast enough for Mrs. McLenaghan, however, for she began to pluck at the twine with her fingers, calling to him to "hurry up or the day would be half over."

Upon his return, Mr. McLenaghan knelt to the floor and cut the twine easily with his knife. Mrs. McLenaghan peeked in the box and removed some straw packing. "Oh, my," she exclaimed, "it must be breakable, if they have packed it in straw." She was clearly a woman who enjoyed the suspense of a present. Meanwhile, Mr. McLenaghan reached inside the small carton and withdrew a crystal decanter. "Be careful," she scolded him, snatching it from his hands. "You'll likely drop it before we can even have a look." Mr. McLenaghan withdrew his hands hastily, and returned to his chair to observe from a safe distance. We watched while Mrs. McLenaghan placed the decanter on the fireplace mantel, and next unpacked the stopper and a set of twelve glasses. It was a lovely set and was much admired. Both of the McLenaghans thanked the Doctor and said how special it was.

I gave Mr. McLenaghan his handkerchiefs and pipe tobacco next. He was quite taken with my embroidery; he and Mrs. McLenaghan admired my handiwork and were most complimentary. The McLenaghans had a gift for the Doctor also. I watched him closely while he unwrapped a very fine cashmere muffler in a dark green—a practical gift that would be much appreciated, I thought. The Doctor seemed delighted with his present, wrapping it around and around his neck before standing to shake hands with Mr. McLenaghan and kiss Mrs. McLenaghan on her cheek.

"Away with ye, Boy," she said, laughing. "It's not me that wants your kisses." This was not the first reference she had made regarding the Doctor's affections, and I felt the indelicacy of it.

The next present to be opened was also the Doctor's. Mrs. McLenaghan passed him my gift of the shirts. I was discomforted and a little anxious. He seemed delighted with the choice, however and thanked me from across the room. "They are meant to replace the one I ruined," I said by way of explanation.

"They are most welcome," he replied, "and will be useful." He stood then and came over to me with a smallish package. I opened it, with Mrs. McLenaghan leaning over my right shoulder, peering carefully. Inside was a lovely leather ledger, with fine gold on the edges of the lined pages. The front cover had a pattern stamped in gold, of delicate fleur de lis. It was exquisite.

I looked at the Doctor and smiled my thanks. "It is for you to write down your adventures in," he said. "I have heard that ladies like to do such things."

"Yes," said Mrs. McLenaghan, nodding her head, "I've heard that a time or two myself."

"Thank you," I said simply. "It was most thoughtful and I will enjoy to use it."

We finished our gift exchanges and sat leisurely for a moment in the parlour.

"Now I just wonder," said Mrs. McLenaghan abruptly, "I just wonder what them Careys are doing today."

"Janet!" interjected Mr. McLenaghan quite suddenly, "I would like some tea."

"Well," she said, "it's not like we haven't all been a-wondering about it."

"Let me help you with the tea," said Mr. McLenaghan, standing quickly and guiding her out of the room.

I was astonished by the turn her conversation had taken and did not know how best to respond.

"Tell me," said the Doctor kindly, "how would you be spending your day if you were in Ireland?"

"Well," I began, "much the same as we have done. Service in the chapel. Gifts after breakfast. Visitors and family. And a feast for the mid-day meal. Usually fowl. As a child, the first thing I did when I awakened was to run to the crib to see if the baby Jesus had arrived."

"What do you mean?"

"The crib," I said, "was part of a crèche, a beautifully carved tableau of figures. Ours had Mary and Joseph, and the donkey, and the baby Jesus, and the Three Wise Men, and a number of sheep and cows, and three camels. As soon as Advent came, Mother would have the servants bring out the crib and we would place the pieces around the parlour. The closer we came to Christmas, the closer we would move the Wise Men to the stable on their journey. Mother always hid the baby until Christmas morning. It was magical."

"Like playing with dolls then, was it?"

"No," I laughed, "not like playing with dolls at all. These were small carvings and they were sacred. I would not dare to play with them."

"Well," he said, "it sounds a bit like doll playing."

"What about your home?" I asked. "What traditions did you have?"

"Hogmanay!" he exclaimed. "We celebrated Hogmanay. We gave out our presents on the thirty-first. That was when the fun began."

"Hogmanay," echoed Mr. McLenaghan, returning to join us. "I've heard of that. Last year, didn't young Thomas Conroy get a tongue-lashing from Mrs. Hislop for being first over the door with his blond hair? He'll not do that again, I wager. She was right cross with him.

Scolded him like there was no tomorrow and him standing there not knowing his right foot from his left."

"Yes," laughed Doctor Stewart, "and he did no bring her a black bun or a gift of salt neither."

I did not know what they were talking about it, and so I excused myself and went in search of Mrs. McLenaghan. I found her in the front hall, in her new apron and one of the new lacy caps, admiring herself in the bevelled glass. She reached for my hand and gave it a squeeze and we walked together to the kitchen where she had, the day before, mostly prepared our dinner. The rest of our Christmas passed in an uneventful way. There were no other guests at the Inn and we ate our meal as a small intimate group.

The days of Christmas slipped quietly by and we settled into gentle routines.

One morning in early January, I went down the stairs quickly, eager to join my companions and enjoy a cup of tea with them. Entering the kitchen, I was startled to see Mr. McLenaghan and Mr. O'Brien from the Smithy standing and speaking with Doctor Stewart in solemn tones.

"What is it?" I asked. "What has happened?"

"Please sit down, Miss Courtown," said the Doctor somewhat abruptly. I did so but looked at him expectantly, waiting for further explanation.

"I must go out immediately on a call," he announced. "Mrs. McLenaghan, will you assist me? Murty, will you prepare the horse and buggy?" At this, Mr. O'Brien and Mr. McLenaghan bowed and excused themselves, leaving hastily by the kitchen door.

"Is it a baby then?" I asked of Mrs. McLenaghan.

"I must go," she said, "and cannot delay."

I coloured at this abrupt dismissal and felt bewildered. Doctor

Stewart approached and stood before me awkwardly. "I must ask, are you able to provide resources that would assist in your Cousin's well-being? I cannot tell you for what, only that I think it needful."

I felt a pall come over me and looked at him steadily, trying to feature what it was he communicated. "Are the Careys in harm's way?" I asked him finally.

He placed his hands upon my shoulders and looked at me earnestly. "I cannot say for certain, Miss Courtown. There may be a need of funds. Can you assist?"

"Of course," I answered. "What is required?"

"Three hundred dollars would be ample."

"As much as that?"

"Rather too much than not enough," he countered.

I was taken aback at the sum but nodded in agreement, and stood so as to retrieve my small writing desk. I was not a little frightened by the Doctor's countenance. He waited for me in the hallway while I went upstairs and wrote a cheque for the requested sum. When I returned, he took it from me and bowed. "Goodbye, Miss Courtown," he said quietly. "I will manage things as best I can and return as quickly as I am able, God willing."

His words, intended to reassure me, served instead to fill me with confusion and worry. With Mr. and Mrs. McLenaghan both absent from the Inn there was no one to share with me my troubles. I brooded about the turn of events and wondered what it signified. It could only be that Mr. Carey had incurred debts, I reasoned, and that his creditors were pressing him for payment. And so it was that I reconciled the upset of the morning and prepared to go outside for a walk to clear my head.

Mrs. Nesbitt was standing in front of her shop as I approached. When I greeted her she nodded back at me importantly and said, "It's a great pity about your Cousin's Husband." I was abashed by her words, and my face must well have portrayed my chagrin. She leaned towards me slightly. "I do hope, for her sake, that this does not become a regular happening."

"I know not to what you are referring," I finally said. "Is there some trouble with the Careys?"

"Well," she began, moving away from the front door and coming to stand close by my side, "only that he was forcibly removed from the Hotel last night, as drunk as a lord, shouting and carrying on. He fell down drunk in the alleyway between the Hotel and the Inn and the men found him there after some time, half frozen to death."

I gasped at this, and put my hand to my mouth.

"Did the McLenaghans not tell you about it? We heard as Doctor Stewart was called to assist."

Colouring, I said, "I do not know the particulars of the Doctor's business." I nodded at her and turned on my heel, burning with the desire to know what had transpired.

I walked directly back to the Inn and waited for the return of the McLenaghans or the Doctor. After several hours had passed, I heard steps outside and drew open the front door. The Doctor stood there, looking distressed. He reached for me and clasped me to him in an embrace. I felt his arms tight about my person, and he pressed my head against his shoulder. After a moment of such, I stiffened and pulled back from him so that I might study his countenance. I was now deeply frightened. We took in each other's expressions without speaking, he trying to deduce what I knew and I trying to discern all that he would tell me.

"Mr. Carey has left Orange Hill," he began. "He will no return."

I understood now for what purpose the funds had been required.

"I see. And what has become of my Cousin and her Child?"

"They will move to town, in good time, and we will assist her as we can," answered the Doctor softly.

"How is she? Tell me what has happened."

"She will mend; she is young and strong and should recover."

I felt myself grow cold at these words. "What has happened to her? I pray that you will be forthcoming." I moved backwards a few steps and sat down upon the stairs. Taking my hand in his own, the Doctor drew near to me and knelt upon the floor. Our faces were nearly parallel at this.

"I do no know what you have knowledge of already, but I will tell you all that I know. Carey was at the Hotel last evening and was merry company, buying drinks and being generous, until he had drunk too much and lost at a game of chance. He began to make himself unwelcome and was asked to leave. He repeatedly announced that he had tamed his Wife proper. He denigrated both you and Mrs. Carey in unflattering terms."

I shuddered at this and the Doctor held my hand tighter. "Those present were certain that he had ill used Mrs. Carey, and one of them, Murty O'Brien, drove over early this morning to check on her situation. Harry McLenaghan, meanwhile, had discovered that Jack had lain drunk for some time in the small alley by the Inn, and forced him into the warmth of the Smithy. Both men came to me to report their discoveries. Murty and Harry had bound and secured Jack fast."

"But where are Lily and Kathleen?"

"I have been to see your Cousin and she will recover. Although I cannot understand how a man could abuse a woman in that way. I wish that I had first killed him when I had the chance."

His anger was frightening to me. Although he held my hand tightly, I began to tremble. I asked again after my Cousin.

"He has broken most of her ribs, and smashed at her face." He hesitated for a minute but then continued. "He has forced himself on

Mrs. Carey and ripped her, in delicate places. Mrs. McLenaghan has agreed to stay with her."

"Oh dear God!" I cried, "how can this have happened?" I began to sob, and Doctor Stewart attempted to comfort me.

"He is a brute, no fit to live in society; we were none of us gentle with him this day. Murty has placed him in the back of his wagon and is driving him towards Peterborough. He will deposit him there with the clothes on his back and the cheque. We will no see him again. He is lucky to escape so easily."

"Oh dear God, I must go to her. Rowland cherished her, and you must believe me, she was once so beautiful and talented. How could this have happened to her? I must go."

"No," said the Doctor, "you must no. She has especially asked that you remain here until she can travel. She does no want you to see her in this condition."

I stood at this and began to pace the front hall, my fists clenched tightly, my heart about to break. Finally I determined that I would ride to the farm only to have speech with Mrs. McLenaghan, but the Doctor prevented me, insisting that my presence there would only heighten Mrs. Carey's distress. I agreed, with some reluctance, but everything in me wanted to fly to her and soothe whatever hurts she had sustained.

I was yet pacing in the front hall, unsettled and in great turmoil, when we both of us heard an equipage out front. We rushed out of doors and saw that Mr. and Mrs. McLenaghan were in their small buggy, and that Mrs. McLenaghan was holding Kathleen.

"Mrs. Carey has asked," she began, "if you would care for her daughter while she mends. She will remove to the Inn when she is fit to ride. In the meanwhile, she has given us Kathleen to care for."

"But how is she?" I cried. "Will she not see me?"

I fell silent then, devastated by all that was unfolding. Seeing Kathleen in Mrs. McLenaghan's arms made real somehow the critical aspects of the situation. I was also remembering the nursemaids and nannies who had paraded through my life until I was old enough for a lady's maid and a companion. I had no real experience of babies and didn't rightly know where to begin.

Doctor Stewart reached up to Mrs. McLenaghan and relieved her of Kathleen. "Of course we'll manage," he said. "A lovely bairn like this will be a joy." He looked genuinely delighted with her and I smiled with relief at his confidence and surety. Walking over to me, he passed me the bundle, adjusting my arms so that I was holding her just so. She was asleep, fortunately, and lay there breathing quietly, a small smile on her wee lips.

"Well," said the Doctor, "we should be taking her inside and arranging a place for her. Did Mrs. Carey send any of her things?"

"Over there," said Mrs. McLenaghan, rising and pointing at a stuffed carpet bag. "There's bottles and nappies and wraps."

Doctor Stewart was utterly practical about the situation. He immediately set about making preparations. I sat in the parlour, guarding Kathleen, while he and the McLenaghans arranged things as they knew would be needful. When I was called upstairs I saw that a metal crib had been placed in my room, a small table beside it with all of Kathleen's belongings laid out.

"Where has this come from?" I asked Mr. McLenaghan. "I have not seen it before."

He looked abashed by my question, and replied soberly, "The Missus and I had need of it once but not for as long as we might have wanted." With this simple response he communicated much, and I was sorry to have pained him with my question. It was a day of uncommonly sorrowful revelations.

Doctor Stewart took Kathleen from me and placed her in the crib. It had been lined with a soft woollen blanket and he unwrapped her outer layers gently, leaving her at rest. Then he put his hand lightly upon my shoulder and we stood together a moment watching her sleep. "This will be hardest upon Mrs. Carey," he said. "She must be missing the child already. I will ride out in the morning to check upon her."

His solicitousness brought tears to my eyes. Once more he had demonstrated his ability to rise above the immediate situation to concentrate on the more pressing issue. I turned to him, about to confess my selfish thoughts, but found myself entangled in his arms instead. I was surprised by this embrace but not displeased. He sought only to comfort me in this way and it was not a romantic gesture.

Kathleen awoke then, and began to gurgle and make soft, sweet sounds as she waved her little fists in the air and looked around to see who was near. The Doctor went over at once and bent to pick her up. "She will be hungry soon, I expect," he said. "Let me give her to you while I warm some milk."

I sat upon the coverlet of the bed while Doctor Stewart passed her to me. Taking the pillows, he formed a soft wall at the edge of the bed and penned her in beside me. She seemed not at all troubled by this arrangement, kicking her legs free of the lacy child's blanket and seeming to enjoy the change in her position. I heard the Doctor descend the stairs while I continued to watch over Kathleen and whisper softly to her. Then I waved my fingers above her and, to my amazement, she seemed to reach for them. I lowered my hand and did it again, and this time she grasped one of my fingers and held it tightly in her fist. I was overcome by this, feeling a sense of deep attachment to her.

Presently Doctor Stewart entered the room again with a bottle of warm milk. He sat upon the small chair by the dressing table, settling Kathleen into the crook of his arm so that he could feed her.

Life continued in this way for several days. Mrs. McLenaghan proved to be a source of mothering expertise, tutoring me in the correct way to bathe Kathleen and pat her dry. Bath time became an extensive morning ritual. The McLenaghans would enter my chamber and stand at the ready to assist me, for which I was grateful, as mine own confidence was not strong. I was frightened of hurting Kathleen, or having her little body slip down in the small wash tub. Mr. McLenaghan took it upon himself to take her from me when she was wet, and swathe her in a large flannel while I dried my hands and readied her wraps. Mrs. McLenaghan stood over me while I patted dry the small folds in her chubby legs and arms, passing me the talc and pins as I had need of them.

I was utterly indulgent in any small attentions that I could render Kathleen; believing as I did so that I was, by extension, also offering solace to my beloved Lily who remained distant and apart from me. As a result, Kathleen was well and truly kissed. She became my sole occupation while I waited for news of my Cousin.

Doctor Stewart and Mrs. McLenaghan rode out daily to check on Lily; upon their return they would assure me that she was healing nicely and would soon be able to travel. Rose-Marie, from the village, took on the extra laundering that was required and Mary Ryan assisted me with some of the small housekeeping chores the baby necessitated.

My small room soon felt over-filled with the accoutrements required for Kathleen, but I reasoned that our stay at the Inn would not be of long duration. I began to make enquiries, through Mr. McLenaghan, for a house to let. It would be important, I thought, for Lily and I to take a house together and become resident until she was strong enough for the return voyage to Ireland come spring. I was in no doubt that this now was the correct course of action, and I began to speak to Kathleen about our impending journey.

"You are Irish," I would say to her, "and you will soon meet your family. The McDonoughs and the Courtowns and the Kavanaughs will.be overjoyed to meet you. There will be parties and festivities upon our arrival home. We shall first visit Rosslare Hall, where I am sure my Cousin Henry will welcome us. And then we will travel to see your Grandfather at Lowry Castle, and I know that he will be delighted with you."

I had just laid Kathleen in her crib one evening and descended the stairs, intending to ready a warm bottle for her should she waken, when I heard her cry out. I ran back at once and was puzzled to see that she slept soundly. I returned to the upstairs hallway and was no sooner down the stairs when I heard her crying once more. "Doctor Stewart," I called into the parlour, "there is something the matter."

The Doctor joined me quickly, but we both of us found Kathleen sleeping soundly, her cheeks flushed a delicate pink and her breathing soft and even. "I was certain that I heard her cry out," I said by way of explanation.

"She sleeps well. No cause for worry." He returned across the gallery and descended the stairs to the parlour. I stood by her silently, watching her small stomach lift slightly as she drew her delicate breaths, then left her side once more to go downstairs. The wailing began as soon as I left the room and I turned around quickly, frightened by the sheer despair in the cries. But I saw her sleeping yet, even as the wailing grew into a fevered pitch.

"Doctor Stewart," I once more called out, "there is someone crying nearby, and it is not Kathleen." The Doctor came upstairs at once and stood by me, but the wailing had stopped and did not begin again while he was near.

"It is perhaps an owl," he offered, "or a wild cat. There are such round about and the sound they make is similar." He stood quietly by, holding his glass of whiskey and listening attentively. "I hear her no," he said. "I think it safe to retire."

He bade me good evening and left me to my evening ablutions. Having checked once more on Kathleen before climbing into my bed, I lay there stiffly, not wanting to disturb her rest, but feeling uneasy and distressed.

I was not long in bed when I heard the crying commence once more. I listened carefully and discerned that the noise was coming from outside the house and was in the garden. I went downstairs, and standing by the curtained window, I could hear the crying of a woman's voice, wailing and keening in the deepest of grief. I was moving to open the front door and invite her inside for comfort, but something eerie about her tone made me pull aside the curtain slightly to look at her first. I saw crouched on the front lawn a beautiful young woman of about twenty, with long white hair hanging wildly about her shoulders and down her back. She was dressed in a white gown; there was something unworldly about her appearance overall. She seemed inconsolable in her grief, and her distress terrified me: I felt cold, sick, and frightened. I wondered who she was and why she was visiting here.

Finally, after several minutes of discomfort, I willed myself away and fled upstairs to waken Mr. McLenaghan. He roused at once and followed me to the parlour. He parted the curtains but did not see her. I rushed to the front door and opened it, but there was no longer any sign of her.

"You were maybe anxious," he said, "and likely dreamt her. I wouldna worry. Let us go back upstairs."

I returned to my chamber, and climbed again into bed. I lay there unmoving, listening for further sounds and trying to puzzle out the strangeness of our evening visitor.

When I woke the next morning, after only scant hours of fitful sleep, I remembered immediately the haunting cries of the previous night. Kathleen was awake and kicking at her sodden covers when I went to check her. Kissing her all over, I changed her quickly and brought her downstairs.

With Kathleen balanced on my hip, I pulled open the parlour draperies and looked for traces of our evening visitor. There was nothing to be seen. Moving to the kitchen, I laid Kathleen down upon a blanket and began to fix her morning oatmeal and molasses with a little cream. Mary Ryan came in while I was thus at work and offered her assistance.

"Begging your pardon, Miss," she began after studying me for some time, "but you look as though you are feeling poorly. Is there something I can get you?"

I was moved by her concern for me and felt the tears well unbidden in my eyes. "I am uneasy this morning, Mary," I said finally. "We had a visitor in the night who cried in the garden and went away before I could rouse Mr. McLenaghan. I am disturbed by not knowing why she came and why she went away without assistance."

"It is unusual, from the sound of it," replied Mary. "Was she someone you recognized?"

"No," I said. "She was a pretty young woman with long white hair, and appeared to be wearing an old night dress. She cried terribly."

Mary was still for a long while, taking in my words. "A young woman, with white hair, did you say?"

"Why, yes," I continued, "and she cried and wailed something terrible. She was very distressed. And I went for Mr. McLenaghan but she was gone before he could come."

"In a night dress?" pressed Mary. She had stopped moving about the kitchen and was standing stock still, looking at me intently.

"Yes, in a tattered-looking night dress. She must have been cold besides being so upset."

"Miss Courtown, begging your pardon, I think maybe it's the Banshee you have seen. She comes to those who are going to lose a loved one. Have you not heard of her before? It is surely someone you are bound to that will die."

"Lily ..." I gasped, "is it Lily?"

"Let me get the Doctor," said Mary, fleeing the kitchen. "He is in the dining room and will know best what to do."

Doctor Stewart came to the kitchen with Mary in several minutes' time, and while Mary looked pale and stricken, he looked amused and jovial. "Is it the Banshee you saw in your dreams, then?" he asked me. "And was she keening in our garden for someone you know? Miss Courtown, you fret too much. There is no such a thing. It is the nonsense folk make up to account for the wind or the sound of an owl. We are all fine and safe. There is nothing to worry about. I will visit Mrs. Carey this morning, if it will give you ease. Before my other calls," he added.

"Thank you, Doctor Stewart," I said. "That will put me at peace."

He turned to the maid then. "Now, Mary, you must be a good girl and put such ideas as brownies and fairies out of your head. There are no little people about and you shouldn't upset Miss Courtown with such nonsense."

Mary looked chastened by his speech, nodding meekly and curtsey-ing by way of agreement. Feeling her discomfort, I patted her arm softly when I walked past her to the stairs. I left her to mind Kathleen whilst I went up to dress and tidy my hair for the day.

My morning was quickly filled with the care of Kathleen. I had discovered that she enjoyed it when I laid her upon the carpet and let her kick and exercise her fine wee limbs. I would sit beside her, shaking a small silver rattle and watching her try to focus on it, and sometimes reaching for it or for me. I would amuse myself by carrying her around the Inn, telling her the names of things and pointing out the windows to show her the trees and the clouds and people passing by.

Mary Ryan summoned me to luncheon and fed Kathleen while I supped at a bowl of soup. We were at ease there when Mr. Clement came to the kitchen door. I saw at once that he was distraught and very ill at ease. "What is it, Mr. Clement?" I asked. "Tell me at once. Is someone hurt?"

"No, Miss. But you are yourself needed at the Surgery."

"The Surgery? Why the Surgery?"

"Please, Miss Courtown," said John, "the Doctor said as you were to come."

Mary stepped beside me and put her hand on my arm. "I will stay with the baby."

I nodded by way of reply, went to collect my outdoor cape, and followed Mr. Clement to the Surgery. We did not speak the short distance there. I had to hurry my pace to keep even with him, and he did not attempt to explain to me the urgency of our mission.

The Surgery, I saw at once, was astir. Many of the locals were standing by, looking grim and anxious. A small number of them parted to allow me passage through, and tipped their hats in a quiet show of respect. I hurried inside, anxious to see Doctor Stewart. A strong sense of foreboding had presented itself and I was feeling not a little tremulous.

I determined to retain my composure and began to navigate the short hallway with a proud and erect carriage. Upon entering the Surgery, I encountered the worst of my fears. Lily was laid out on a table in the centre of the room, and Doctor Stewart and Reverend

Carr stood over her. It was evident at once that she had passed, but I ran to her, anxious that the touch of kin might restore her.

After that my recollections are not so clear. I have a remembrance of the Doctor's stricken face as he looked at me, and a vague sense of strong arms holding and comforting me. There was someone crying, I know. But it is not clear who I heard sobbing with such sorrow and passion. It may have been my own grieving. At some point Kathleen was brought to me, and I remember taking her in my arms and carrying her from the room. I held her tightly to my heart and rocked with her in a chair in the hallway.

How I was returned to the Inn I do not remember. Nor is it clear to me how the next days disappeared in a blur of sorrow and despair. Mary Ryan stayed close by my side, and cared for Kathleen with gentleness. Doctor Stewart brought me a letter that had been left at the Carey establishment. It was difficult to read through until its end but I enclose it here so that the entirety of the story should be recorded.

My dear Cousin,

You, who have been always a Sister to me, once said that you would always remain faithful. Despite my share in the treachery against you, I am dependent upon you for one final service. It is my prayer that you will embrace Kathleen and raise her as your own Daughter, knowing as we both do the desolation of being raised motherless.

When she asks about me in years to follow, tell her stories of Ireland and our happy times in school and at balls and festivities and riding. It is my fervent desire that you teach her to ride confident and bold so that she, like all Courtown women, can take pleasure in horses. If she asks of her Father, speak to her only of Rowland McDonough and how he cherished me. I desire that the name of Carey shall not ever be known to her.

My stone, please God, should only read Courtown-McDonough, as they are my only true names. I was never married to Jack Carey. I believed, after Rowland's untimely demise, that no other man would ever truly suit me. In my illness and despair, I clung to the only person who was near. Mr. Carey endeavoured to be charming, and although I knew he was not high born, I believed that I could assist in the refinement of his ways. But he was disingenuous, and his studied attempts at social graces were only short-lived exercises. I later discovered that his manner was, in entirety, a studied act, and that his real interest lay in my small wealth.

He proposed that I would join his family, as a guest, and that he would assist me in establishing my own small household. This seemed a respectable plan and I entered into it freely. I travelled with him from Montreal in search of Rowland's holding, and we maintained separate rooms and all manner of appropriate courtesies. His own family I was not introduced to, however, and when we arrived in Orange Hill, he insisted that we appear as husband and wife. He was unwilling to continue as my man-servant and became violent, nearly killing me in a cruel rage.

To my horror, he entered my chamber one evening and forced himself upon me, securing my silence and my obedience. His savagery was infrequent at first, and I was depressed, and so thought that I could endure his violence until the baby was born and would then make a plan. But he grew to hate me and I lived in terror of him. I had no resources left; he had taken everything. I had no claim left to my respectability, and so I succumbed to his control.

When he attempted the treachery against you, I suspected him but did not know his methods. He believed that you had access to family fortune and was desperate to seize from you what he could. He acted clumsily and in haste, as he wished to secure your wealth

*before another could make a claim upon it. I did not know to whom
I could turn without compromising us both. It was for these reasons
that I rushed you from the house. That was the blackest time for me,
and I will not burden you with the details of my suffering.*

*I cannot look at my Daughter without sadness, for she has been
deprived of her Father and now I fear that both his life, and our
great love, were for naught. I am too ashamed to continue in this
life. I constantly pray for God's forgiveness and His mercy. Spare my
Father and my Daughter all that you can.*

*I remain,
your loving Lily*

*If there is an afterlife, Cousin, I will see you once more in
Ireland, and we will ride together across the park and taste the sea
air upon our lips and feel the fresh wind upon our faces, and you
will love me again, and we will be once more happy and at peace in
our hearts.*

We buried Lily in the small English cemetery at the edge of town. It
was cold and damp and I left Kathleen indoors with several ladies who
had offered to prepare tea. I did not want her getting chilled as we
all else did, and I did not want her, small babe that she was, to watch
the lowering of her Mother into the maw of earth made freshly open.
I would take her back someday when the stone was in its place, and
we would plant flowers and visit, but the cruelty of this day I needed
to shield her from.

There were not many in the church or at the graveside. There were
no hymns and there was no weeping. My own sadness had already
ebbed out of me in the several days of preparation. The grief swept
over me in waves, sometimes doubling me over and taking my breath

away. The tears leaked from my eyes and ran down my face unbidden until I felt there was not a drop of water left inside of me.

Doctor Stewart obliged me by arranging a stone for the grave, but it was not yet ready. It was to read: *Lily McDonough née Courtown. Beloved. Born 1845 — Wexford, Ireland. Died 1870 — Orange Hill, Dominion of Canada.* The simplicity of it was befitting, I thought. I did not fret lest anyone remark upon the omission of Carey's name. I had wondered about returning her remains to Ireland for burial in the family crypt, but I knew it would be some long months before I could arrange such a thing.

Also, in a way that I cannot easily explain, I wanted Lily here, in this soil, and in this place. I had followed after her to this strange country and now was gradually becoming accustomed to its rhythms and shifts. Although I still closed my eyes and willed the brilliant green of Ireland to my mind's eye, it was not done with the same desperation and longing that I once felt. It seemed fitting to me that Lily rested here, while I attempted to raise her Daughter.

Reverend Carr, in an unusual moment of enlightenment, chose a scripture verse from the book of Ruth to read at the funeral. He read it intending to refer, I think, to the sad story of Lily and Rowland, but his words resonated in a way that he could never have anticipated:

Ruth 1:16: Intreat me not to leave thee, or to return from following after thee: for whither thou goest, I will go; and where thou lodgest, I will lodge: thy people shall be my people, and thy God my God: Where thou diest, will I die and there will I be buried.

I found myself thinking of my journey and how I had followed after my cousin, driven by a bond that could not readily be explained.

The days following the burial were quickly filled. Many people stopped at the Inn to pay their respects, and in a local custom, left us with baking and cooked hams so that our meals were easily prepared. I received these callers in the parlour with Kathleen close by. Mercifully, the visitors did not tarry and I was given some respite between calls. Doctor Stewart returned each day, equally laden with preserves and cheese and cured meats. All of our shared acquaintances were endeavouring to succour us in our despair.

Mrs. McLenaghan had stopped the clocks and draped the Inn in black crepe. She had also tied a swath of it to the front door knocker, signifying to all that we were suffering a loss. Although I was dressed once more in black, I did not alter Kathleen's appearance in any way. I could not bear to see her without a lightly coloured cambric gown, festooned with ribbond trimming. She was yet a baby and I felt to preserve her innocence.

After the first week of mourning, our visitors trailed off and I was once more at liberty to structure my day as I chose. Mrs. McLenaghan had been especially nurturing of me, and abandoning all sense of decorum, had taken to simply grabbing me and pulling me to her ample bosom for long, comforting embraces.

I had, for some days, known that I would need to write my Uncle and family. The task of doing so was dreadful to me and I delayed, not knowing how to start. Doctor Stewart very gently suggested that he was willing to undertake the writing of such sad narratives and that I had only to command him and he would do so. I considered his offer, wanting selfishly to avoid the pain I would subject myself to with the task itself, but also to distance myself from the pain that I knew I would cause to those who read the news.

I had not taken much opportunity to consider the Doctor's offer of marriage. He had twice now mentioned it. Iris's death, and dear

Lily's, and the care of Kathleen, had much preoccupied me. His offer to be of such service was proof of his considerate and tender nature. But I had also seen his bad temper, his pride, and occasionally his scorn. He was not often arrogant, but he was very much a man of science and very decided in his opinions. I was not sure that the companionship of such a scientific gentleman might not become tiresome. I was also unwilling to settle in life with a partner who was not in love with me. Lord Driscoll had showered upon me many fine compliments and small favours attesting to his affections and desires. I had seen the way my Father admired my Mother and I had yet a deep-seated and foolish desire to be also so admired.

In the end, I could not avoid my familial obligation, and so I readied myself for the unwelcome endeavour. Collecting my small secretary, I withdrew to the dining room where there was no distraction. Kathleen I left in Mary Ryan's care.

There was no propitious way to begin my brief, and so I simply, in the end, began.

Dear Uncle,

Winter has come to Orange Hill and with it a sense of loss for what has been and is now no more. I write you this sad letter knowing that your heart will break to read it. Your beloved Daughter, and my cherished Cousin, Lily, has passed from this world and now lies buried in a churchyard nearby. Her Daughter, Kathleen, I have taken to my heart as my own, and she resides safely with me.

The cause of Lily's suffering must be attributed to a weakened constitution. The crossing from Ireland and the loss of her Husband while she was in a delicate condition was not something from which she entirely recovered. The birth of Kathleen took a further toll on her as she laboured strenuously for many hours. Despite excellent medical attention, she continued to weaken and seems to have succumbed to the travails of her complete ordeal.

I am, for the moment, happily situated and Kathleen is a welcome and beloved Daughter to me. I love her as well for her sweet disposition and merry wee face as I do for the cord which binds me to Lily and Rowland. She will want for nothing in my care, Uncle, you may rest easy upon that score.

Kathleen shows signs already of a keen intelligence and healthy strong limbs. To see the look of her when she is composed and at her sleep is to see a small angel with Rowland's impossible curls and Lily's features. Her eyes, when opened, are vivid blue and they light up like the sky on a fine day over the Irish sea.

Life in the Canadas is nothing like home. The society is wanting and there are few distinctions in class or rank. And yet there is something invigorating and bold to be found here, with ample opportunity for adventure and commerce. I find that I am contented. It is not clear to me how quickly I will be able to return to Ireland with Kathleen. I do not wish to alter too readily the small routines we have established.

I am gratified to know that Courtowns are yet in residence at the Hall and continue to preserve and maintain all of the estate. It is my intention to let these arrangements remain until Kathleen's sixteenth birthday. When she is of age, the estate will pass to her as her birthright. When you next have occasion to see Harris, the Solicitor, I would be obliged if you would instruct him to draw up these directions and forward them to me for signature and notary. In the interim, half of the rents should be deposited into an account in Kathleen's name, and the other half to be used by Henry as he sees fit. In this way, Kathleen will be assured of a comfortable fortune. If, for some reason, she is not able to claim her inheritance, then it shall pass to Henry's first-born child. In this manner I intend to safeguard both the future of the Hall and also Kathleen's security.

I hope, Uncle, that when you have had time to reflect upon these business arrangements, you will conclude that I have been generous and sensible with my resources. I do not anticipate any opposition with these matters and therefore draw to a close the business portion of this brief.

Uncle, I hope, by the nature of the arrangements outlined, to have communicated to you the desperation of my grief over the loss of your dear daughter Lily.

I am moreover also pleased to be the cause of Henry's improved prospects. I have always loved Henry, as you well know, as a brother, and it gladdens me to think of him in my Father's study, meeting the tenants and depositing their monies in the pie-shaped drawers of the rent table. Henry has always been kindly by nature and I know that he will be lenient and fair in all his dealings.

In closing, I ask only that you write me by return post to give me your assurances that I have acted wisely and that you do not hesitate to entrust me with your Granddaughter. I am grieved to be the messenger of the bitter and unwelcome news concerning our beloved Lily.

I remain your loving Niece,
Eleanor Courtown (Ellie)

When I finished this missive, I realized that I was fatigued. The information I had found necessary to document was all of it distressing. I could not bear to think what emotions my dear Uncle would undergo when he first took in my words. Collecting my writing things and the unsealed letter, I checked on Kathleen first and saw that she was fast asleep in the kitchen while Mary Ryan scrubbed at some carrots. I retreated to the parlour and sat there in solitude, calming my emotions and ordering my thoughts.

My letter writing was not yet completed and I began to compose the sentiments I would need to express to the McDonoughs. Kathleen was as much their blood as she was mine own, I reasoned, and they would expect to hear that one of their own was now motherless but by no means cast upon the world without family. Had she been a son, I speculated, they might reach across the ocean to claim him, but they would be less likely to do so for a daughter. They would readily accept my proposal to claim her as my own, I reasoned, with the promise especially of a generous dowry and inheritance, and the preservation of her McDonough surname. Besides these arrangements, I would pledge to return her to Ireland before her sixteenth birthday. These measures, I determined, would satisfy the proud McDonough clan.

Also, I knew that, at last, I must write to Lord Driscoll, releasing him and begging his forgiveness. I could not now, after having already so insulted him, impose upon him a barren bride.

Mrs. McLenaghan found me in the parlour, and brought with her a generous slice of warm bread and a glass of milk. She sat with me while I partook of this refreshment and seemed to take no end of pleasure in watching me.

"Mrs. McLenaghan, I have wondered about the pretty crib that Kathleen uses. Will it sadden you to tell me its history?" I knew this were a deeply private matter and did not wish to inflict pain, but I had come to care for her and believed that she might think me unfeeling if I did not pursue the subject.

"Ah, Dearie, 'twas a long time ago now. Harry and I were married young and I worked as a cook in a great house for the Stanton family in Toronto. On the Davenport Hill, it was. Harry worked at the docks and kept hisself busy with all manner of jobs. And one day he said as he'd heard the land was to be had cheap if you went north and east, and he said as we had some coin saved, we should try our fortune. I gave notice and sadly took my leave, for the Stantons were generous and kind. Mr. Stanton was a great man of business and he said as how we were both deserving, he would like to make a small investment in our endeavours. And we found ourselves here and Harry went to logging, and we bought a building in disrepair and put it to rights and made it this Inn. We hadn't a stick of furniture to begin it with, nor a pot to cook in, but the folk were kind to us and lent us those things. Harry kept at the logging and I managed the Inn and over the years we built up our establishment. From time to time, we thought that a wee one would be a welcome blessing, but we were na' worried about it for we were working so hard at all other things.

"And then, thirteen years ago, the Lord blessed us. James, we called him. He was a smart gaffer. The apple of Harry's eye, he was. A right lovely Lad, but sickly. I was maybe too old when I birthed him. He was always coming down with a cold or a cough or a fever. He was but four when he drew his last breath." She began to cry at this, and rocked herself in the chair, wiping at her eyes and face. I waited quietly for her to continue.

"Doctor Stewart, he had just come to Orange Hill and was only just biding with us at the Inn until he could get settled. He tended James as though he was his very own child. Always checking him for fever and listening with the tube at his chest. I never saw a more careful man as him." She looked over at me and nodded vehemently, reinforcing her proclamation lest I not understand how highly she esteemed him.

"He's the very best of men, and he wouldn't take a coin for the medicines or for his trouble. He saw that we didn't have much to offer in the way of such. And he insisted on paying his board full, besides, saying that one had naught to do with the other."

When Mrs. McLenaghan had finished her narrative, she became once more all efficiency, standing up from her chair and crossing the room to kiss me on my forehead. "Bless ye, Lass," she said, "for asking. It is good to remember them that we loved." She patted my shoulder at this and went off to another part of the house, leaving me at my letter writing.

I was seated there some while later, not having progressed very far with my brief, when Mary Ryan brought in Kathleen. She was freshly changed and fed, and ready for some attention. I took her and saw, almost at once, that her cheeks were unusually flushed and her little face over-warm. "Mary," I said, "does Kathleen seem feverish to you?"

Mary came and stood close by and answered, "Well, Miss, now that you mention it, I did think as she was fussy. It may be that she has a small cold."

"What should we do? Do we need to call the Doctor?"

"Well, Miss," she smiled at me, "the Doctor usually visits every day for his supper. But I could call Mrs. McLenaghan, if you wish."

I nodded at her, and she slipped away quickly. Mrs. McLenaghan soon stood with me in the parlour, taking Kathleen from my arms. "Ah, wee Kathy," she crooned, "have ye caught a bit of a cold?"

"What do you think?" I asked, slightly panicked. "Is it something I have done wrong?"

"Ah, Lass, not to worry. The Doctor will be here this evening and he will say. In the meanwhile, we should keep her warm and well fed."

She passed me back my little Daughter and I hugged her to me, feeling very unsure of myself. I spent the afternoon in my room watching her lie listless in her crib. The rattle did not long hold her attention, and she seemed not to be listening when I read to her. All of this served to heighten my anxiety about her well-being. My family would not understand if I returned home to Ireland without Lily or Kathleen. It would seem that I had utterly failed in my familial duty. I prayed fervently that the Doctor would soon come, and that my little one would be spared ill health.

I was never more glad to see a person than I was when Doctor Stewart rapped upon my door that evening. Without greeting him or any such pleasantries, I pulled him to the crib and made him examine Kathleen directly. He had brought with him his medical bag, alerted, I reasoned, by someone in the household, and he first put the listening tube to her small chest, and then tapped at her small body, front and back. He also felt her pulse and examined her diaper, before reaching into his medical bag and drawing out a small, black leather case.

"I will take her temperature with this, but will need to do so under her arm. I need you to hold her and unwrap her so that I can place it firmly without giving her a chill."

I did as bidden whilst he took a long, thin glass tube from the case and shook it gently, holding it to the light and scrutinizing it before approaching me and gently tucking it under Kathleen's arm. I was beside myself with worry by the end of these endeavours.

"She has some congestion in her chest," he said to me grimly. "She is very small and delicate and we will need to watch over her carefully. I wanted to measure her body temperature to see if she is fighting an infection. Her temperature is only slightly elevated."

I began to cry at this. "What is to be done? I will do anything."

"We must keep her warm, and hydrated. Make sure she drinks a great deal. I will continue to check on her in the night."

At this, he excused himself, and left me there holding Kathleen. I paced the floor with her, but was not long alone when Mrs. McLenaghan and Mary Ryan entered. Mary was carrying a bottle filled with warm milk and Mrs. McLenaghan had come to encourage me in my travail.

"She's well watched over," said Mrs. McLenaghan. "Her mother in Heaven will send the angels to help her and she will come through this ordeal as healthy and beautiful a little girl as ever was."

Although I wanted to believe her, and had already begun to pray, the story of James McLenaghan was still fresh in my memory and I knew how readily small children took ill and succumbed to their illnesses. I retired early but lay upon my bed fully clothed, lest the McLenaghans or the Doctor look in on the baby in the night. Mary Ryan was seated on a chair outside my room so that she would be readily available should I have need of her.

I was wakened from my uneasy rest by the hoarse sound of a little cough. I picked up Kathleen and patted her smartly on her small back, thinking to loosen any congestion that may be lodged there. She continued to make small coughing sounds and they seemed, to my ear, to grow rather more desperate. "Mary," I called, "come at once."

Mary entered the room while Kathleen was engaged upon a coughing spasm. Her breathing seemed laboured with high-pitched gasps. Her little lips, I noticed, had lost their pink colour and seemed to be turning pale. "There is something the matter!" I shrieked. "Get the McLenaghans!"

Mrs. McLenaghan joined me at once, and took Kathleen from me. "Harry has gone for the Doctor," she said. "Rest awhile, dear, while I take over."

"I can't rest," I protested, "when Kathleen is fighting for her breath."

"The Doctor will be here for certain, so try to wait patient."

Soon I heard his footsteps in the hall, and ran to him, frantic with worry. He nodded at me, went straight to Mrs. McLenaghan, and began to re-examine Kathleen. "It is the croup," he pronounced. "It has set in fast."

I did not know what the croup was, but his tone was grave.

"What is to be done? What can be done?"

The Doctor stood silent for a moment. Then he looked at Mr. McLenaghan, who had recently joined our party. "Have you large blocks of ice?" he asked.

"Why, yes, we have a number of 'em covered with straw in the cellar."

"Get one of them at once, and some canvas. Do you have any canvas tarps?"

Again Mr. McLenaghan answered in the affirmative, and then rushed out.

"He's a good Doctor," said Mrs. McLenaghan, nodding towards Doctor Stewart, who had begun to rearrange the furniture in the room. "You have naught to worry about, Lass. He knows what he's about." Mary nodded her head silently in agreement.

The Doctor had moved a small table to the window and was now pushing the crib up against it. "Stoke the fire as hot as you can," he directed Mary. He left the room and returned carrying another table which he placed at the foot of the crib. Then he took a chair and set it upon the table. When Mr. McLenaghan came back, carrying a bundle of canvas, the Doctor took it from him and began to unfold it and arrange it over the crib and chair and across to the window.

"Now for the ice," he said. Mr. McLenaghan nodded, and the two of them ran out and returned again carrying between them large iron tongs with a block of ice. This he placed in a wash tub on the table by the window, tucking the canvas in around it so that it was likewise contained in the tent. Next he opened the window and checked to ensure that the entire crib was encased in canvas. I shivered at the cold, and went to stand nearer to the fire with Kathleen.

"The hospitals make mist tents for cases such as these," he said, looking at me. "We have no time to get to a hospital, so you must trust me. When the cold ice air touches the hot fire air, we may create a little steam mist for her. This should help to open her airways. They are swelling closed now with the effort of coughing and she is struggling. Do you trust me?"

I could not—it was altogether too much. I shook my head at him and withdrew further into the corner, clutching my Daughter tightly. He approached me.

"Eleanor," he said, taking the liberty of using my Christian name. "Eleanor, you *must* listen. I do not know if this will work, but I am certain that we should try. See her lips and nails," he said. "They are turning blue. She cannot fight long if we do not try to assist her."

He reached for her and I reluctantly surrendered my charge. I saw him take her and slip through an opening in the tented canvas. I sobbed and stood still, waiting for something to happen. The room was silent. The Doctor did not reappear from under the tent. I looked to Mrs. McLenaghan. She was crying and had her apron pulled up over her face. Mr. McLenaghan had his arms around her shoulders and was trying to comfort her.

After perhaps an hour, the Doctor withdrew from the tent. "She is sleeping," he said. "Come and see her." I took his extended hand and followed after him under the folds of canvas. My eyes adjusted to the dim light after a moment, and I saw Kathleen sleeping soundly, carefully tucked into her crib. The air was moist and beads of water were upon the canvas. I watched her breathing and uttered a small prayer of thanksgiving. I felt sure that she would be well if she could only continue to breathe so freely.

"We will rest outside the tent," said the Doctor, "and stay close by."

Mr. McLenaghan was bidden to collect armchairs from the parlour, and he struggled up the stairs with these good-naturedly. All of us stayed in the room through the night, resting comfortably in the stuffed chairs.

The next morning, the Doctor pronounced Kathleen out of harm's way but recommended leaving the tent in place a while longer.

When Kathleen woke, she cried to see the unfamiliar surroundings and I went to her immediately.

The McLenaghans and Mary Ryan and the Doctor were my faithful companions during this bleak time. Word spread that Kathleen was unwell, and we had a flurry of visitors bearing small gifts of baking and good wishes. Mrs. McLenaghan in particular was delighted by these attentions, and took to inventorying on her fingers all of those acquaintances who had visited or dropped something off.

One afternoon several days later, Doctor Stewart had once more stopped by the Inn to check on his small invalid; he then joined me in the parlour to make his satisfactory report. I attempted to thank him for his kind attentions. He seemed distracted, though, and paced about the room while I was speaking.

"I have heard," he said, "that you have enjoyed many callers these last few days."

"Yes," I replied, "many people have been sympathetic. Harriet McCaffrey and her mother were here earlier today to pay their respects. It was very kind."

"You have become quite attached, I think, to some of the girls in your group."

"Oh indeed, they are sweet children."

"And you have also," he continued, "become attached to the McLenaghans, if I am no mistaken."

"Yes, I have."

"I mention this to you to demonstrate that there are those here, among your acquaintances, who would be sorry to part company with you and Kathleen."

He crossed the room to kneel beside my chair and took my hands in his. I felt a fluttering of anticipation, and waited for him to continue.

"Eleanor, I am no a romantic man, but I am a steady one. We were all much distressed about Kathleen, or I would have addressed you long since. I wish to be your comforter and to be beside you always, in times of trouble such as you have already experienced, and in happier times to come, God willing. I have before offered myself to you as your husband and protector and I do so again now. Will you reconsider your plans and remain in Orange Hill as my Wife?"

I was only a little astonished by this and felt, to my surprise, a sense of tremendous relief. The emotional stirring of the past fortnight had taken a toll on me, and I burst into tears. Suddenly I realized that I was tired of plotting my own way without a guide or companion. The merits of his proposal appeared now to outweigh my previous reservations. I considered only a moment.

"Yes," I nodded. "Yes, I will agree to be your Wife." He raised both of my hands to his lips and kissed them. I saw that he was mightily pleased.

Standing, my hands still in his, he said to me, "Let us tell the McLenaghans together, shall we? They will be glad to hear it."

I smiled my assent and made to stand also, but letting go of my hands, Doctor Stewart opened the door and turned to quickly scoop me in his arms. He carried me to the kitchen where the McLenaghans were resting. Looking at us curiously, they began to rise. Doctor Stewart put me down upon a chair and signalled to them to remain seated.

Ceremoniously, he bowed and began: "You are the first to know. Miss Courtown has agreed to pay me the honour of becoming my Wife."

Mrs. McLenaghan shrieked loudly and came rushing over to assault me with kisses. "I know'd it," she kept repeating. "I know'd it, Harry. Didn't I tell you the way it was?" Mr. McLenaghan pumped my hand and wished me well. But Mrs. McLenaghan continued to laugh and kiss me by turns, her pleasure seemingly without bounds.

After several minutes of this, Doctor Stewart consulted his watch and said that he needed to return to his Surgery. Kissing my hand, he bowed again and excused himself, promising to return for a late supper.

"We shall have a dinner party, this very night," declared Mrs. McLenaghan. "I will put on a roast of beef and make some puddings." Looking at me, she smiled and said, "You shall have a nice rest, followed by a warm bath, and can then spend your time making yourself ready."

I accepted her suggestion gladly, and left Kathleen under Mary Ryan's watchful care so that I might prepare myself for the evening. I had brought only one ball gown with me from Ireland, and this I resurrected from my trunk and hung upon a peg. It was shot silk taffeta, both blue and black at the same time. I knew that it looked well against my white skin. I had also packed in my small jewel case a pair of jet earrings.

I did as Mrs. McLenaghan had instructed and rested upon my bed. I found that I slept peacefully and wakened only to hear the O'Brien boy at my door with many jugs of hot water. After letting him fill the bath, I removed my things and soaked myself, luxuriating in the uncommon treat. When the water cooled, I stepped out and dried myself by the fire.

I was determined upon making a stunning impression at dinner, and so prepared carefully. It were still difficult to dress without a maid, but Mary Ryan pulled my corset strings as tightly as she could manage, and made my waist tiny. Some talc remained in my dressing case, and I used this to dust my bosom and shoulders. It would help the skin to shimmer in the light, I knew. It were important to look the part, I thought, even if this were just a marriage of convenience. Or was it? He had not spoken to me of love. Was I correct to assume that we would continue, as he had once suggested, to live separately but together? I dabbed on some scent, and then moved to the mirror to dress my hair. This evening I brushed it out, and finding some black ribbonds, secured these in a large bow at the back so that my hair looped down from them softly in a long elegant twist. The effect was good, I thought, although not so fine as it might have been if I'd had some skilled assistance.

Slipping into my dress, I saw that my bosom had become more rounded since the last occasion I had worn it. The gown had been made for a ball at Dublin Castle only a year ago, and the décolletage was prescribed as high dress, which meant the neckline was cut as low on the bosom as could be managed. As a young woman of nearly nineteen I had thought the fashion daring and had enjoyed the sensation my gown created within our set of acquaintances. Tonight I saw that my breasts were straining the neckline and looked full but not, I hoped, scandalous.

The clock was chiming nine hours as I shut my door. I had not realized how slowly my preparations had progressed. Grasping the railing with my right hand, and my skirts with my left, I prepared to descend the staircase. Doctor Stewart and the McLenaghans had heard my door shut and they all three rushed from the dining room to watch me. Mrs. McLenaghan exclaimed at my appearance and clapped her hands delightedly, and Mr. McLenaghan bowed. Doctor Stewart, I observed, had also dressed formally for dinner; he was wearing a handsome coat and kilt. He stared at me without bowing and seemed, I thought, struck dumb by my appearance. Remembering himself, he rushed to the stairs and took my arm, offering his assistance and steadying me carefully.

That dinner was the most pleasant evening I had spent since leaving Ireland. Mr. McLenaghan had found some fine claret in his cellar and Mrs. McLenaghan had assembled a very tasty meal. We all of us lingered at the table, enjoying one another's company and making pleasant conversation. I was conscious upon several instances of the Doctor's scrutiny. He often gazed at me, making me colour when I found his eyes upon me.

At the stroke of midnight, the McLenaghans rose and went upstairs. Doctor Stewart offered me his arm and we removed to the parlour, where he first shut the door and then busied himself setting the fire. I sat quietly, not knowing what direction our newly formed relations would take. At long last, satisfied with the fire, Doctor Stewart sat down in a chair. "This has been a fortunate day," he began. "I count myself blessed to be among such good company."

"Yes," I agreed, "the McLenaghans are very dear."

"In this place, so far away from both our homes," he continued, "you make family with those whom the Almighty sends to you."

"Yes, I suppose that is so," I said, pondering his words.

"My own family is far from here," he remarked. "I am the youngest of six Brothers and three Sisters. Although my parents were well enough situated, and provided me with a fine education and a generous allowance, their wealth was not sufficiently great to provide for us all. I made my own way in the world and have scarcely seen or heard from them since leaving Scotland as a young surgeon at age twenty-two. I could not marry as a young man, not having established myself in my profession."

This explained much, I thought, and I found myself interested in his story.

"I have had one or two experiences with women, Miss Courtown, where I did not act as honourably as I might have done. There was a woman once, from Mayo, a long time ago, whom I treated poorly, and alliances with some women aboard ship were often advantageous to both parties. Services, of particular kinds, were often exchanged for small comforts such as sugar or tea. It was the method used by men for procuring washing and sewing and other such favours. But this was a long time ago and in another land."

I was discomforted by this new knowledge of him but did not know how to respond. I, too, had a small history that shamed me. I sat silently with my hands folded upon my lap.

"I give you my word, that I will never once give you cause to regret this contract. I am committed to undertaking everything in my power to ensure your safety and care." He rose and stood behind my chair at this, and rested his hands lightly upon my bare shoulders. I shivered at his touch, and he removed his hands quickly as if I had suddenly repulsed him. I felt a strange current move through me, warming me more than the claret had done.

"Excuse me, I was carried away."

I felt stimulated, and nodded at him, trying to make out what had just happened between us.

"May I see you up the stairs?"

"Thank you," I replied, rising and giving him my hand. He walked up with me, and on the small landing nearest my room, he wished me a good evening and stiffly took his leave.

The following days provided a flurry of activity and decision-making. Doctor Stewart was of the opinion that we should marry as soon as the banns could be read. Since neither of us had family that needed to give consent or travel to join us, and since neither of us felt particularly concerned about the arrangements, it was convenient to us both that we should marry quickly. My reputation as a woman alone with a child provided incentive enough.

He was eager that I should inspect his house and provide direction as to its further finishing. We toured it together one afternoon and he showed me which of the adjoined rooms were to be mine and Kathleen's. At the end of the small gallery on the second floor, I spied a tiny ladder that led to the belvedere. I climbed this carefully, my skirts giving me no end of trouble on the small rungs. I was rewarded for my discomfort by the view which greeted me. Doctor Stewart joined me in the tiny space, and together we stood by the windows, admiring the vastness of the surrounding country. It had rained early in the morning and then frozen cold again. Ice sparkled in the trees, coating the branches and hanging in places like long, festive spikes of glass. Even in the waning afternoon light it was a brilliant sight and filled me with a kind of awe.

Doctor Stewart stood with his arms crossed awkwardly in front of him. The small room ensured that we stood very close to one another. I was uneasy with such proximity but wanted not to disturb the calm we were sharing. When I moved forward, I found that I had to rest against him slightly; otherwise I would lose my footing near the open floor. I felt then how solid he was. With his arm, he steadied me. I smiled my gratitude and he beamed back at me happily.

Presently I stole a sideways glance at him and saw that he looked utterly reposed and contented. I felt strangely glad to be beside him in this small, window-filled room. Mr. Carey and his vileness seemed very far removed from this shining little hideaway. I sighed a little.

Doctor Stewart's arm tightened slightly, and he looked down at me somewhat protectively. "Will you be happy here?" he asked.

"Yes, Doctor Stewart," I replied, "I shall be as happy here as any-where outside of Ireland. Thank you."

He coloured at this and took his arm away, motioning to the opening in the floor. "We should go below," he said. "Allow me to go first, lest you lose your footing."

I followed him downstairs, somewhat alarmed by the indecorous view he had of my skirt and petticoats, but he laughed at my discom-posure and assured me that such things were unimportant to him.

The house had been whitewashed throughout and the many emp-ty rooms stood clean and sterile. His suite of rooms I did not see. A second set of tiny stairs led from the kitchen to an upstairs apart-ment. It contained a small bedchamber and a tiny sitting room. Mr. Clement was using this suite, and evidence of his stay prevented me from lingering. As no access was provided from the apartment to the second floor, it was entirely self-contained.

The kitchen was sparsely furnished while the front hall, parlour, and dining room all stood entirely empty. "We must order furnish-ings and draperies," began Doctor Stewart.

"Perhaps we might borrow a few things from the McLenaghans in the interim. I would happily accompany you to select some other pieces when the roads are fit for travelling, and then we can wait upon my cousin to send us further."

"That sounds like our plan then. Shall we to the Inn for our supper?"

I nodded and he gave me his arm, and as we walked together to the Inn I marvelled inwardly at the risk I was taking in marrying a man I had known but a few months. I wondered what my Uncle would think of this brash move and whether he would approve of my choice. Guiltily, I wondered too if Lord Driscoll had received my short correspondence and if it had relieved him or added to his wounds. The Doctor was a gentleman in a place where such were not common, and he was highly thought of by everyone in his acquaintance. I was in no way ready yet to return to Rosslare Hall with so many changes having taken place, and this marriage seemed as prudent a prospect as any other. I could remain near Lily's grave and keep watch over it. And also, for some reason I could not readily explain, I felt entirely safe when I was with him and found that I enjoyed his attentions.

We wanted the wedding arrangements themselves to be kept to the utmost simplicity. We would marry in the local English church, inviting only the most intimate of our acquaintances. Mrs. McLenaghan was of the opinion that I needed something new to wear. I was quite prepared to wear my grey wool. I did not see the point of trying to order a new outfit and rushing some unknown seamstress of questionable ability to get an outfit ready. Also, I was still in mourning and did not think it seemly to abandon my drab colours.

"But you're going to be the Bride," she admonished me, "and everyone knows the bride has to wear something new. Why not let Harry take you to town and you can see if there is something ready-made that will do if you don't want the trouble of a seamstress measuring you up?"

"Truly, no," I said. "I am not particular about my wedding outfit and I know that the Doctor will not care. Clothing needs to be well cut and well made, but I am not particular about having the latest fashions or colours. I am happy to wear something of my own." I put my hand on her arm to show that I meant my words kindly.

"But you are the Bride," she repeated. "People will expect it."

The thought of driving all the way to Port Gibson through whatever winter weather was on hand, all for the slight hope of finding a ready-made hat or outfit for the wedding, seemed overwhelming to me. I could not reconcile the time and inconvenience for such an item, but I was not to be listened to. Mrs. McLenaghan appealed to the Doctor at dinner that evening and insisted that all of Orange Hill would be scandalized if I didn't have something bridal to wear for the occasion.

I saw him looking at me amusedly while she made her case. "Very well," he finally said, "if Miss Courtown doesn't object to the shopping excursion, perhaps I could prevail upon her to pick up a list of medicines that I am in need of. Our household will require some carpets and small pieces of furniture; why no make one trip to purchase these items? I would be loath to have all of Orange Hill scandalized."

Before I could utter a word in reply, Mr. and Mrs. McLenaghan entered into the conversation and began to discuss having Mr. Clement run the Inn while they escorted me to Port Gibson. It became quickly clear that Mrs. McLenaghan was looking forward to a shopping adventure and that the wedding had merely provided her with a plausible excuse for such an outing. Doctor Stewart told me, in a quiet aside, that he would provide me with a list of medicines and funds for any purchases that I made on our behalf. I was uncomfortable having to discuss such an item of business with him. The intimacy of such discussions was entirely new to me. My Father had always provided a liberal allowance and had encouraged me to use it as I wished. Beyond that, I was not accustomed to having anyone take an interest in my financial matters.

The building of such a fine house must have cost Doctor Stewart a large amount of capital. I assumed that his resources were depleted and that we would need to live simply. It was not my intention to tell him of mine own fortune for some time. I did not want to be seen as an indulged woman who could not function without such resources.

The McLenaghans and I set off early in the morning. We left Mary Ryan in charge of Kathleen. Mrs. McLenaghan was excited by the adventure and talked, I'm certain, the entire way without stopping once to draw a deep breath. I was wrapped up snugly in several rugs and I dozed from time to time, only to find that she had continued her narrative and was still happily chatting. The roads were frozen hard and the cutter seemed to make good time travelling upon them.

We arrived in Port Gibson in time for afternoon tea at the Parliament Hotel, where we engaged rooms for the night. I thought to myself, with some amusement, that just a few months prior, when I had last been here, had anyone told me that I would return with an Innkeeper and his Wife to choose a wedding outfit, I would have thought them crazed. But here I was, ensconced in their company and having accepted an entirely new social order.

When we were done our tea, Mrs. McLenaghan and I removed to the Millinery. It was a large, pleasant shop, and contained several dressmaker forms outfitted in a variety of costumes with matching hats. Mrs. McLenaghan was enchanted. I browsed the shop while she engaged the Milliner in conversation. Presently I looked over at her talking animatedly and saw that she stood before the glass wearing a rather large and astonishing hat with a small dead bird of some sort and long trailing feathers and netting. "What do you think?" she asked of me. "Shall I wear it to your wedding? It will look ever so smart with my fur collar."

"Yes," I laughed, agreeing, for it did indeed seem to suit her. "You look very stylish."

The Milliner nodded and took the hat from her, wrapping it carefully in paper and placing it within a large box. She approached me then, and deferentially asked if there were anything I wished to try on.

"Only this, perhaps," I said, pointing to a small pink hat with a largish brim and charming pink braid.

"Yes," she said, "it will look lovely against your black hair." Moving to the glass, I removed my grey hat and replaced it with the lively pink one. It brought an immediate flush of colour to my face and looked and felt as though it had been made especially for me.

I was pleased by the Milliner's genteel manners and refinement. She drew my attention to a very dark grey satin dress that was too deeply cut for a morning wedding. I shook my head and said that I needed something more modest. She removed to the back of the shop and then returned carrying a soft grey wool jacket. In her hand she held a spool of the delicate pink braid that had been used on the hat. "It can be worn done up over the satin dress," she said. I smiled at her and agreed to try on the ensemble. The young woman who was helping me drew me out to Mrs. McLenaghan's admiring eye. She clapped delightedly and enthused that I now looked like a bride. I pointed out to her that the gown was over-large and the jacket sleeves over-long.

"No matter, Miss," said the Milliner, "I can have it right for you by early morning. It can be easily done." I nodded my acquiescence, and in a matter of minutes, the gown was tucked and pinned tightly and showed my figure to good advantage.

Mrs. McLenaghan had drifted off to a corner of the store where she was admiring ladies' personals. "Look here," she beckoned, "there's the most beautiful wrappers." I walked over to where she stood.

"Where have these come from? The lace looks very fine."

"Yes, Miss, the plain linen ones are from Ireland, and the lace ones imported directly from France." The Milliner went to the rack, selected a white lace wrapper from the assortment, and held it out for me to feel. "It is the softest lace you can imagine."

I touched it and saw that she was quite right. The lace was finely woven and as soft as a good cashmere. She held it open and I slipped it on over my dress. It was exquisitely made. Mrs. McLeñaghan was enthusing about the need for a good wrapper when one was a new bride, and clearly had her heart set upon my purchasing it.

"It is all but transparent," I said. "One can't cover up in something so sheer."

"Now lass," she said, shaking her head at me, "there's some things you must just trust me on and this is one of them. I know that you will make good use of that wrapper and not be sorry. But if you leave it here there will be a time when you says to yourself, 'I should have listened to my old friend, Janet McLenaghan, and bought me that wrapper when she said to.'"

I laughed at her foolishness, but nodded at the Milliner.

Having paid for our purchases, and made arrangements to collect them in the morning, we next proceeded to the Cabinet Maker's. Mr. McLenaghan had gone there before us and stood waiting by the door. The shop was very large and filled with every item of household furniture one could imagine; there were rows of chairs and tables and settles and bed frames and wardrobes and dish dressers and curtain fabric and rolls of carpets and flooring. These items looked to me to be insubstantial, but Mr. McLenaghan assured me that they were of the finest quality. In the end, I chose only the kitchen table, four chairs, a large dish dresser, a deep copper bath, a changing screen, a small dressing table and stool, and several small Turkish carpets.

We next visited the Chemist, where I presented a letter of introduction from Doctor Stewart and a list of his requirements. The Chemist asked us to return in an hour's time, promising to package up the required items for us. While we waited we went for supper, and enjoyed a delightful meal at the Hotel. Mrs. McLenaghan was thoroughly enjoying her outing, and finding great delight in having people wait upon her. I could not help but find pleasure in her great enjoyment.

I passed the evening in my small chamber, writing to Cousin Henry and wishing him great joy in his new state. I then proceeded to my matter of business, telling him first of my engagement to the kindly and well respected Doctor Stewart, and then requesting of him those things which I would find comforting and of solace in my new home. I finished my letter before retiring and went downstairs to the small foyer to arrange for it to be placed with the next overseas post.

I met the McLenaghans again for the morning meal and we hastened our leave-taking. Mrs. McLenaghan was full of the delights of the city and recounted for us, several times, just how fine the food had been, how comfortable the bed, how talented the Milliner, and so forth. She was not unlike a happy child, delighted with a party. I smiled to myself, content that I had played some small part in her pleasure.

When we arrived back at the Inn, Mr. Clement greeted us and helped to bring in our parcels. As Mrs. McLenaghan bustled off to the kitchen to check on the state of things, I went in search of Kathleen, hugging and kissing her repeatedly.

Doctor Stewart was at dinner later that night and greeted me warmly as I entered the dining room. "Did you have a good journey? I have heard much about it from Mrs. McLenaghan. I hope you had as pleasant a time."

"Yes, thank you. We were very busy and spent a great deal of money in a very short time. I hope you were satisfied with the Chemist's order."

"Thank you," he answered. "Everything was as I requested. Were you able to select some furnishings?"

"Only some. The prices seemed to me to be very steep and I was reluctant to choose too many things without your direction. I wrote to my Cousin while I was away, and have asked him also to send some things from home."

"I appreciate your care with our resources, Miss Courtown, but I am anxious that you would have those things necessary for your comfort."

I smiled my gratitude at him but did not answer. It would be hard to explain to him that very few things would give me as much comfort as some belongings from Rosslare Hall. I was content to wait for them and to do without in the interim.

After our meal we walked to the Rectory, where the Reverend and Mrs. Carr waited upon us. Doctor Stewart had arranged for this meeting, as there were some details to review before the wedding. Among these was the music: Mrs. Carr would be playing the organ and wanted to confirm with us the selection of songs. Clearly displeased with our preferences, she was trying earnestly to convince us to choose something other than *Auld Lang Syne* for the recessional. I didn't mind the changes particularly, but Doctor Stewart was a little musical and wanted Robbie Burns for reasons of his own; he would not be swayed. The Doctor had also chosen *Ye Gates, lift Up Your Heads,* and this was somehow cause for particular affront. It was an amusing exchange, as I could clearly see the high regard in which Mrs. Carr held her own opinions.

The Reverend Carr wanted only to ensure that we were contented and at peace about the wedding, and to ask if we would be exchanging rings. I had not thought of this small matter and felt panicked by it. But Doctor Stewart answered the question directly, telling the Reverend that he had selected a ring for me but that a ring of his own would interfere with his work. He looked at me to gauge my reaction, and I nodded in agreement, thankful for his foresight.

I was grateful, too, when Doctor Stewart excused us and led me back outside into the cold, crisp air. "You look rather stricken," he remarked. "Is there something amiss?"

"Not at all," I replied. "It's just that talk of rings and music makes everything seem very real. I didn't realize how quickly things were changing and that I am soon to become someone different."

"Someone different?" he enquired. "Why do you say that?"

"Well, only that I will soon become Mrs. Doctor Stewart while you remain as you have always been. You will continue to live and work as you did before, but my life will be substantially changed."

"And are you unhappy with this change?" he asked gently. "Are you frightened, perhaps?"

"No, not unhappy certainly, and not frightened. Worried, perhaps. About the finality of it. I had always assumed that I would be married in Dunstan's Chapel at home, as have all the Courtowns, with my Father and Uncle and Cousins surrounding me. Afterwards there would be a ball with the staff, and our tenants, and all our acquaintances. This will be very different."

He tucked my arm snugly in his. "I understand. You have had much to endure these last several months and much sadness in your life. It is my intention to see that you and Kathy are well looked after, and as happily situated as I can manage."

"I know that," I said, smiling up at him. "I believe you." We had returned to the Inn by this point and he bade me good night without coming inside. I thought it entirely correct, of course, but felt not a little disappointed at the reserve of it all nonetheless. He had conducted himself always as a gentleman, save for an instant during our visit to the glen. I found myself wondering what it might be like to be a little courted by him, and to have him attempt to favour me as Lord Driscoll had done.

The following day I spent at the Inn, playing with Kathleen, tidying my few belongings in my trunk, and readying my outfit for the wedding. Mrs. McLenaghan prepared a simple evening meal which we were bidden to eat in the kitchen. The parlour and dining room had been cleaned and polished and set with lace tablecloths and linens ready for our small wedding reception the following day. Doctor Stewart excused himself early, kissing my hand and thanking the McLenaghans for all their trouble.

I retired then, and had a long, luxurious bath in my room. Shortly thereafter, I was within my small chamber when I heard a gentle tap on the door. "It's me, Lass," said Mrs. McLenaghan. I opened the door to her and she came and sat down on one of the two chairs. "I have thought," she began, "that as your poor mother is not here this night, I should help to prepare you for tomorrow's events."

I looked at her wonderingly.

"That's right," she said, nodding at me and crossing her arms over her rounded stomach. "There's many things that you likely have no knowledge of and I'm here to give you forewarning."

Despite myself, I was interested in her words but also mortified. I had heard Jack Carey panting and moaning in the night, and had some sense of what transpired between a couple. Mrs. McLenaghan was not to know that Doctor Stewart had already proposed a celibate marriage. This was a private detail.

"Really, Mrs. McLenaghan," I said, "you need not worry. Doctor Stewart is a kind man and I am not troubled."

She smiled at me. "Bless you, lass, I know better than most what a good man he is, of course. It's not him I was worrying about. You need to know how to enjoy things, you see. A man takes more pleasure when his Lady is not frigid. There are things somebody needs to tell you in preparation, you see."

"Truly, Mrs. McLenaghan," I interrupted, "I am unconcerned. Doctor Stewart will tell me aught I need to know if the occasion merits it."

"No Lass, I insist." She settled into her chair, nodding at me defini-tively. "Boldness is not a thing that a Lady like yourself is accustomed to. But in the way of making your Husband feel desired, you must set aside your reserve once in bed, and do what comes most natural."

I tried to silence her but she continued.

"Now the first thing you need to know is that there isn't a man alive who doesn't enjoy a peep of a woman's nakedness. You must learn to linger in the bath, and let your wrap fall open loosely from time to time." Nodding at her own wisdom, she went on. "You must in the eve-ning put your hair down your back and brush it hard so that it shines in the firelight. A man likes the feel of a woman's hair on his chest and face and it will turn him soft if ever he is cross with you."

By now I had begun listening carefully to Mrs. McLenaghan. I knew that I would not need such tricks, but the topic was alluring.

"You must take his hands, Lass, and place them where it thrills you. You will find these places soon enough. Every woman likes to be held close, and a gentle caressing in certain areas can give you great enjoyment. You must discover what you enjoy, Lass, and then let him see that he is pleasing you."

I was hot and quite reddened by her speech. She was, however, undaunted. "You will also find that there is a lot of wetness. It is best to keep a flannel near to the bed to wipe things up with. And an-other thing," continued my teacher, "you must never let him know if it hurts when he puts his shaft in you. It would make any decent man feel terrible to know this." She wagged her finger at me to reinforce her point.

"Brave it quietly at first and pretend as hard as ever that you are simply glad he has taken some pleasure in you. It goes in easier, in time, and will stop hurting before long." She stopped to catch her breath. "Ah, and also, Lass, once you are accustomed to lying with him, you must make free to gently stroke him, and you will see that his shaft thickens with very little encouragement. This is something that all men like. It is a powerful thing to give your man such a pleasure."

"Stop, I beg of you," I interrupted. "No more, truly."

"Don't be so stricken, Lass, there isn't a married woman alive who hasn't had to learn these things."

"Please," I implored, "I am weary and would like to turn in. Thank you for your many kindnesses." I stood up and indicated by my posture that I was firmly resolved.

"Well, good night then, Lass. Don't you fret. All will be well."

Mrs. McLenaghan took her leave and walked heavily down the stairs to her domain below. Grateful to be alone, I shut and latched the door carefully.

The wedding itself was a hurried blur. I remember poor Mr. McLenaghan squeezed into his good black suit and looking as though he might choke with his tightly done shirt collar. Mrs. McLenaghan's hat proved quite the sensation. She would not remove it, and I have distinct recollections of the dead bird eyeing me skeptically throughout the morning.

Mrs. Carr was a dour organist. Her playing of the hymns sounded rather more like a funeral dirge than a wedding. I wondered if she played so deliberately to prove to Doctor Stewart that her choice of music would have been preferable to his. Somehow she sucked all the joy out of the notes.

The girls from my little sewing group were there. Harriet stood upon a pew and waved at me violently.

Doctor Stewart, once again dressed finely in his kilt, stepped towards me as I neared the front of the sanctuary and clasped my arm tightly in his. I felt comforted by this friendly gesture, and although my knees were knocking together with a case of nerves, I was able to smile at him and repeat my vows. The service was a brief one, with the driest of homilies on *Love* spoken by the Reverend Carr. He made *Love* sound like rather a frightful thing and I wondered how it were possible to understand it in such a light. But soon after, Doctor Stewart slipped a ring on my finger and we were pronounced Man and Wife. The Doctor kissed me on my forehead and I coloured deeply in front of all those people. But the guests only laughed and clapped loudly.

Mrs. Carr began to play the organ again, and someone rang the church bell. We walked back down the aisle side by side, receiving many good wishes from those who had come. Doctor Stewart held my arm tightly in his throughout and I felt that he was proud and well pleased with our arrangement. We walked together to the Inn and spent several happy hours with our friends and well-wishers.

Chapter the Sixth
DEVOTION

When the last guest had left, Doctor Stewart and I thanked the McLenaghans and made preparations to leave. I ran upstairs first, to kiss Kathleen good night, as it had already been arranged to leave her at the Inn for the evening. Mr. McLenaghan helped me with my coat while Mrs. McLenaghan clung to the Doctor and whispered some manner of foolishness. She kissed me next, and called me Mrs. Stewart, and whispered to me to heed her advice. I coloured at this and was very pleased to step out into the cold winter air.

Doctor Stewart gave me his arm and we walked stiffly together to my new home. I had several times now visited in preparation for this day, and so the house did not feel at all strange when we entered it. Doctor Stewart took my coat and laid it on the stair railing. "We will need to order a hall stand and some furniture, Mrs. Stewart," he laughed. "The rooms are yet empty."

"I shall be happy to oblige, Doctor Stewart. It will give me much pleasure to plan the purchases." I smiled at him warmly.

"I have had John carry your trunk upstairs," he replied. "You may wish to check that all things are as you desire them."

"Thank you, I will do that just now, if I may. Shall I join you again in the parlour?"

"Certainly! That would be pleasant."

He bowed and quit the room, heading towards the Surgery. I thought it likely that he, like myself, was feeling awkward with our new circumstances and desired a diversion of sorts. I hurried up the stairs and shut myself in the upper sitting room. This room was adjoined to my dressing room and it, in turn, was now adjoined to my bedchamber. Doctor Stewart had had the carpenters insert interior doors between these rooms so that I would have a spacious private suite to myself. The nursery, a bright, southern-facing room, was at the end of the hall. The arrangements were generous and, compared to my chamber at the Inn, seemed commodious. The Doctor's rooms were across the small gallery.

Although I was alone among my few possessions, I did not feel at ease. I moved about the room, hanging a few of my gowns on the pegs and unpacking my sewing box and jewel case. As I did so, I looked at the lovely band set with diamonds and emeralds that now sparkled on my left hand. "Green for Ireland," Doctor Stewart had whispered when he slid it on my finger that morning. It were a thoughtful gift and I winced to think that I had made no similar gesture. Rummaging through my small jewel case, I at last spied a pearl stick pin. I fingered it carefully. This had been my father's pin; he had worn it often. Once, when I was a girl, I had begged it of him, wearing it to fasten my cloak, and later my shawls. This was not the fashion for it, of course, and we had often laughed at the indecorous use to which I put it.

I selected from my writing desk a piece of stationery, and began a brief note to my Husband.

Dear Doctor Stewart,

Please accept this small token from your Friend and Wife. The pearl was my Father's and is valuable to me for that especial reason.

~ Eleanor

I folded the paper quickly, placing both it and the pin in a tidy envelope. Then I removed my little wool jacket. The seamstress had done a superior job of altering the satin gown; it fit tightly, revealing my waist and bosom to good advantage. I went downstairs after this to join the Doctor in the parlour. He had, I saw, taken two chairs from the Surgery and placed them in the empty room. A fire was banked nicely, and two cups of steaming milk sat upon a tray on the floor. I smiled to see this welcome and entered the room quickly, approaching him eagerly with my small gift. He stood to bow when I approached but then stopped himself. We smiled each of us at this new awkwardness. I handed him the envelope and retreated a few steps to watch whilst he opened it.

He read the note quickly and then studied the pin. Fastening it to his tie, he read the note once more, and then refolded it, placing it carefully in his coat pocket. "Thank you," he said to me, "but if it is so dear to you, you should no part with it."

"You have proven to be my closest friend," I replied, "and I am grateful for your many kindnesses. Who better to entrust with such a treasure?"

"It is very fine; I have never seen a pearl quite so large."

"Yes, it is old. I had it from my Father when I was a girl." I told him the story while we sipped at our milk. I was pleased that I did not cry as I often did when speaking of my dear Father. It would not be a good omen, I thought, to cry on my wedding day.

"Tell me about your own Father," I said finally.

Doctor Stewart grew quiet at this, and I waited until he answered. "He loved to fish, "my Da."

"The River Tweed ran through our property, and he would follow it on his day off from the mill, and fish for trout and salmon. He was a fly fisherman. Do you know what that is?"

"No," I answered, "I do not."

"Fly fishing is an art," he began, "and not merely sport. The cast requires a particular snap of the wrist at just the right moment, to play out the line. But before the fly hits the surface there is a beautiful loop that unfurls across the water. It's a lovely thing to watch. My Da had a number of casts that he developed, balancing the tension and speed needed to keep the fly afloat. He tried to teach all of us, but I had no the patience for it. All winter long he would tie flies in readiness for the season to come. I can see him yet sitting at a table in his office at the mill, with fine silk and horsehair and lovely coloured feathers piled before him. When he needed to think something through, he would distract himself by tying a fly. It was a disappointment to my Da, I think, that not one of his boys could really enjoy it with him."

The hour grew late; finally Doctor Stewart said to me that we should retire. He offered to carry the lamps, and I was pleased to have my hands free to manage my skirts on the staircase. He stopped outside my bedchamber, holding the lamp while I drew near. "I would like to bid you good night," he said, "but I don't know how best to do so. Would you prefer that we shake hands, or may I kiss you?"

"I do not know what is best proper," I replied, "nor how to address you when we are quite alone. Do you have a preference?"

"Decidedly," he grinned. "If I may choose, I will always choose a kiss from you over a handshake. And I would enjoy to hear my Christian name from your lips." He held the lamp close, trying to discern my reaction. I was uncomfortable and confused; his forth-rightness was making me uneasy.

"And you, Mrs. Stewart," he said, "what may I call you when we are quite alone?" He looked amused at this.

I decided to answer seriously. "Perhaps you would also use my given name. I am called Eleanor by most of my acquaintances at home in Ireland, and Ellie by those with whom I am most close."

"Then I should also call you Ellie," he said, leaning perilously close. "Rest well, Ellie. I will leave my door ajar should you require assistance with your fire in the night." He kissed my forehead light-ly, much as my Father had always done; I was overcome with the remembrance of this familiar rite. Doctor Stewart mistook my emo-tions I think, and looked at me most peculiar. He passed me the lamp then, and moved across the small gallery to his own suite.

Entering my room, I saw that a surprise had been placed upon my bed. John Clement must have carried it upstairs while we were in the parlour. A large box lay there. Opening it, I folded back the paper to see a cut velvet gown of the most brilliant deep green. It were a rich fabric and looked to be smartly cut and finely finished. The style was a daring one, with a deeply cut bodice. I saw at once that it would fit, as the back fastenings had been cleverly arranged to accommodate a difference in size. It was a handsome gift and had been chosen with great care and expense.

I deliberated trying it on but then was covered with confusion, wondering if the Doctor would expect me to parade before him in it, or if he would think me a foolish magpie fond of finery. If my Father had done such a kindness, I would fly to his room wearing it and twirl before him to demonstrate the fullness of the skirt. Thinking how best to thank him, I remembered Mrs. McLenaghan's shameful tuition and reached up to remove my hair combs. Unfolding my hair,

I moved to the mirror and brushed it out, counting the strokes until I reached one hundred. Then, nervously moving my lamp to the floor by the door, illuminating the gallery, I crossed the hall and stood outside the partly opened door. Knocking lightly, I called, "Are you within, Doctor Stewart? May I have speech with you?"

The door opened at once, and I saw a fire burning brightly in the cheery study. Books were piled upon every surface; it looked untidy, but inviting. My Husband stood before me without his coat, his shirt collar removed. He looked not displeased to see me and I felt strangely relieved by this.

"Robert," he said, smiling. "You have agreed to call me Robert."

"Robert," I began, "I have come to thank you—"

"No need," he interrupted. "Mrs. McLenaghan suggested before my last trip to Port Gibson that a lady always likes a new gown. I spoke to a seamstress there and she undertook to make it for you."

"It is exquisite. I don't know how to rightly thank you."

He smiled warmly at me. "Wear it in good health."

I curtseyed at this, colouring deeply, and was about to retreat when he placed his hand upon my arm. "Your hair is lovely in the firelight, Ellie."

I nodded, thanked him again, and then fled to my room, shutting the door behind me tightly. I had been too bold and found that I could scarcely draw breath. Mrs. McLenaghan had been correct. My loosened hair had caught his notice and made him tender.

I was not long back in the solitude of my room when I heard a din outside on the road. A loud group of men appeared to be shouting together and making a commotion. I wondered at the lateness of the hour, becoming alarmed by the increasing noise. A pounding commenced below stairs and I heard the rowdy group enter at our door. Doctor Stewart was quickly down the stairs; I followed after him, sure that the drunken party was bringing someone injured and needing the Doctor's attentions. I stood at the landing, and when they spied me they let out a loud yell and began to cheer mightily.

Puzzled by such merriment, I searched for a view of the Doctor among them to satisfy myself that he was safe. The men were carrying an assortment of pots and kitchen utensils and were beating these irregularly while Robert moved through the crowd. I saw him speaking to each man by turn, and they all clapped his back and made loud "Huzzah!" cheers in response. I recognized many men in our acquaintance and was puzzled greatly and not a little afeared by this strange gathering. Alex Hislop was there, and Harry McLenaghan and John Clement and Donald Nesbitt and Murty O'Brien and Miles Moore and many others besides. Wondering at the mystery of it all, I watched the scene with trepidation.

Robert seemed to be greatly amused by the clatter, I saw, and he looked up at me reassuringly. This greatly relieved me. He made his way through the small throng of men and climbed the stairs to join me on the landing. "Kiss her!" yelled Murty O'Brien, and the men began to pound a loud clattering racket, clamouring for a kiss. I was reddened by this and not a little frightened. Robert saw my discomfort and drew near, placing his arm protectively about my shoulder and standing close by. I felt him kiss the top of my head and the men below cheered greatly.

Robert then drew from his vest pocket a small purse and tossed some coin at the gang. "Be off with ye now," he said. "Have an ale to drink our health, and let us to bed!" The men cheered and pounded and yelled words of encouragement at this, but they picked up the coins and made their way solemnly out the front door and down along the roadway. Robert went down and secured the door after them.

"What in heaven's name was that? I have never seen the like of such a thing in my life."

"Were you much frightened, Ellie? They were only well-wishers. It is a country tradition called a chivaree and is a sign of their good will."

"Good will!" I exclaimed. "They very nearly frightened me."

"Very nearly, was it? That's all right then. Sometimes these things get carried away. If you were no really frightened, there was no harm done."

"Will they come again?" I asked him as we both of us climbed the stairs.

"No, Lass. They've had their fun. They'll use their coin for a pint or two and consider the whole thing a good night's work."

He stood at my chamber door and looked about awkwardly for a moment. Then, abruptly, he bowed and crossed the small gallery, retreating to his own suite of rooms.

In the morning, I rose early and went downstairs. I found that the reservoir in the range was already filled with hot water, and so I filled a jug easily and returned to my room to complete my morning toilette. I had slept but poorly the night before: the newness of the situation, the small, unfamiliar bed, and the sounds of a strange house, in addition to our uninvited guests, had made me uneasy. Dressing simply in my plain blue day gown, I looked longingly at the green velvet, anxious to feel it against my skin. Instead I pulled my hair back tightly, securing the combs and wetting down the loose strands with water.

I returned to the kitchen, determined to make myself of use by scratching a breakfast meal together. Cheese and bread were found in the pantry, and a jar of berry preserve on the sideboard. Having sliced the bread, I placed it in the range to toast whilst I set the small table with two places and made ready a pot of strong tea. These small tasks were now not entirely strange to me, as I had often watched Mrs. McLenaghan at work, and had, upon occasion, even assisted her.

I did not know where the Doctor was but did not want to intrude upon the privacy of his rooms. I was still in the kitchen when I heard the front door open and close. I rushed to greet him. "Good morning," I said. "Have you been walking?"

"Yes," he said, "a good brisk walk to the mill pond and back."

"Was it very cold?"

"Only if you stop awhile," he replied. "The cold can't creep in if you keep moving." At this, he removed his outer coat and laid it upon the stair rail.

"Come," I said, "there is some breakfast ready. May I pour you tea?"

Doctor Stewart obligingly followed me to the kitchen, where he complimented me on my domestic skills. We ate our little breakfast together and then he announced that he had calls to make and would be gone for most of the day. I was sorry to hear this, as I had wondered if we might have a holiday together, but he assured me that there were many cases of childhood measles in Tinkertown and that he was needed. "Have you had the measles, Ellie?"

"Yes, when I was only six or seven."

"I'm glad to hear it; I would not want to bring a disease back to the house that you have not had."

"But Kathleen? She has not had them."

He stood at this, and came forward to kiss me again on the brow. "We might perhaps ask the McLenaghans to keep her at the Inn until this outbreak is contained. Will you mind very much?"

"Yes," I answered, feeling tremulous. "I would not want her to think I had left for good."

"Only for a day or so. I think it safest for her." He then went into the Surgery, returned with his bag, and left the house.

Despondent, I walked to the Inn and asked Mrs. McLenaghan what she thought of the Doctor's recommendation; she agreed readily that she and Mary Ryan should take on Kathleen's care for a little longer. I ran upstairs to caress and kiss my Daughter briefly, but she was sleeping and I did not want to rouse her.

Once I had returned to the Doctor's house, I found nothing with which to occupy myself, and no one with whom to have a conversation. This was a desolate life, I thought while I walked through the empty rooms. I passed the day in lethargy, reading a little, sewing a little, and straightening the contents of my trunks.

At six o'clock, I heard the kitchen door open and went forward to greet the Doctor. "Stop!" he said to me sharply. "Do not come closer! I must undress and bathe lest my clothing carry contagion."

I was a little astonished by this but heard the gravity in his tone. "What can I do to assist you?" I asked.

"I'm accustomed to stripping off, bathing in my Surgery, and running back and forth for hot water. John sometimes helps me. But my clean clothes are yet upstairs and John is at the Inn this evening."

"Go to your Surgery," I said. "I will bring you some clean clothes, and I can draw a kettle of boiling water if you trust me."

"No, that would be too heavy. Let me bring the tub to the kitchen and bathe there. Then I can manage the lifting. If you would bring a clean change to me in the kitchen, I think we can manage."

I went upstairs to his rooms and found the closet and chest where his clothing was neatly folded and organized. Selecting what I hoped were the right pieces, I made a small pile and went back down, eager to be helpful. Pushing open the kitchen door, I saw at once my mistake. Doctor Stewart had wheeled the copper tub before the range and was just now stepping down into it when I entered. I backed out immediately, but I knew he had heard me.

"It is fine, Ellie. You can come in," he called to me. "I will have need of those clothes."

I hesitated but then moved back into the kitchen where he was scrubbing vigorously at himself with a brush. Fortunately the tub were a deep one and I could only see above his waist. Although I tried not to look, my eyes were drawn to him. He was very fit and I saw that there were well-formed muscles on his shoulders and arms. "Begging your pardon," I said. I was deeply coloured and could not make myself look at him in the face.

"This will likely happen again, Ellie," he said cheerfully. "The measles is an epidemic in Tinkertown and I will have to do this whenever I return home. There was much talk of contagion and sterilization at the conference I attended in Montreal last year. I must learn how to keep my instruments boiled and clean, and my clothing as well. It seems that there are growths we cannot see that poison and sicken. We will both of us need to become accustomed to such things."

I did not feel prepared for such intimacy, but at the same time I was relieved that my Husband was such a sensible man. All his ministrations were for our mutual safety. I withdrew to the parlour so that he could dress in privacy, and eventually he joined me there, looking flushed and warm from his efforts, his hair was sticking out all over. He had forgotten to comb it. "Is the epidemic very bad?" I asked.

"Yes, there is a baby come down with it that cannot nurse, its mouth and lips are so swollen with it. I saw eight children today and all of them had high fevers and signs of delirium."

"I am so sorry," I said, understanding the gravity of the circumstances and the seriousness with which he was taking this. "Shall I run to the Inn and bring back two plates of supper, so that you need not venture out again?"

"Yes, that would be welcome."

Glad of a diversion, I pulled on my cloak and made the short walk to the Inn, where Mrs. McLenaghan quickly prepared two plates and placed them in a basket. As she bustled about I checked on Kathleen, and then stepped quickly back to the house.

Doctor Stewart had removed the kitchen table and set it in the parlour with some cutlery and two glasses of claret. On the table stood a lit lamp, and the fire was blazing merrily. I produced our dinner; Doctor Stewart held my chair for me and then sat down across the table. Reaching for my hand, he bowed his head and gave thanks.

We ate quickly, both of us hungry. When we were done, he asked me how I would best like to spend our evening. "Do you wish some privacy," he asked, "or would you enjoy some part of the evening to be spent in shared company?"

"I've been alone most of the day, Sir. I should be glad of your company." He seemed pleased with this and we agreed to read together awhile.

Selecting last week's newspaper, he read aloud a few columns and then proposed that it was my turn. Taking the paper from him, I also read a few columns, and in this way we passed the evening agreeably enough. I tried very much to keep myself focused on the newspaper stories. I did not want to remember the look of him without his clothes on. It was a ridiculous event despite the handsome profile he made, and I coloured each time I recalled it. When we were done reading the paper, although it was still early, Doctor Stewart suggested that we retire. He banked the fire carefully as I blew out the candles. Then he walked me again to my door and kissed me on the brow before leaving.

I entered my room and saw that the fire had burned out. Placing some logs upon it and blowing at it hard, I thought again what a strange place I had come to. We had already advertised once for a housekeeper, but not one person had responded to our notice. Doctor Stewart had said that he would advertise in Port Gibson when he next went there for medicines. The fire caught, so I sat there for a minute, warming myself, then moved towards my bed as I took off my gown. On the pillow rested a tiny jeweller's box. I opened it and saw that a pair of earrings that matched my wedding band were cushioned within.

The earrings revived my longing, now irresistible, for the green velvet dress. I took it from its peg, but as I began to step into it, I saw that it was boned and would not fit over my corset. So I stopped, then, to remove both the corset and chemise before pulling up the gown. It fit perfectly, and was delicious against my skin. Moving to the glass, I could see that it was cut much lower than any dress I had ever worn: I would need to be careful when bending over, as there was a scarcity of material shielding my breasts. As before, I removed my hair combs and brushed my hair. Finally, I fastened the earrings and determined that the entire outfit fit together wonderfully. It was among the most elegant ensembles I had ever worn.

I crossed the gallery and saw that Robert's door stood wide open with a hot fire burning in the grate. He sat before the fire in a padded chair with his legs stretched out before him and a glass of whiskey. "Am I disturbing you?" I asked from the doorway.

He turned to look at me, and I was delighted to see the pleasure he took in my appearance. "You are the most beautiful woman I have ever seen," he said, standing quickly and walking towards me. "Come in." He took my hand, led me to his seat before the fire, and then stood before me for several moments, studying my appearance intently. It was disconcerting to be so ardently admired, and I tried to think of something that would redirect our interaction.

"I have had a pleasant evening, Robert," I began, "and wanted to thank you for your generous gift of the earrings, but should now retire."

"Stay awhile yet," he suggested.

I sat for a moment further but then stood up, gathering my luxurious skirt around me. "I should retire," I stated once again, this time more firmly.

"Yes," he said, "perhaps that would be best. Thank you for joining me." He came close to me, standing near, his chest lightly grazing my bosom, and then kissed my brow lightly. I smelled a little of the whiskey upon his breath. Looking down at me, he said again how lovely I looked. I returned hastily to my room then, and shut the door. We had entered upon a marriage of mutual convenience, I reminded myself, and were meant to live together as friends. I could not disrupt our arrangement by becoming sentimental and foolish. In the bright light of day he was a practical man and would not approve of such a change. I undressed and climbed quickly into bed.

The next morning I determined to visit the bank, and so I collected the money drafts from my Uncle and Father and dressed for the outside weather. Mr. Kershaw, the manager, greeted me cordially and then drew me into his office. I told him that I had two matters of business, the first being the deposit of the bank drafts. The second matter was that I wished Doctor Stewart to have ready access to my fortune. Mr. Kershaw obliged me on both matters and wrote the new total for me in the small ledger book I carried.

After my banking errands, I shopped for a selection of items that I thought might be useful until we were fortunate enough to hire a housekeeper. The clerk offered to have a boy deliver this order to the house late in the afternoon. Next I visited the Inn, where Mrs. McLenaghan embraced me tightly. Mary brought me Kathleen and I sat with her upon my lap, kissing her and whispering sweet words.

"Come, Lass, let's have a cup of tea and a good gab."

I was happy to have her company and found it easy to share in her satisfaction with my change in circumstances.

"And are things going well in *all* departments?" she asked me pointedly.

I coloured at this, but was able to assure her that *all* was well.

"I know'd it would be. I could see how it was between you."

"You could?" I asked her, astonished.

"Of course, the way he followed you around and made such a fuss over you. It were plain to see he was smitten at once."

"He was?"

"Of course he was! I never see'd a man fall so hard so fast."

"You haven't?"

"I hasn't."

I redirected the conversation to the subject of tonight's dinner menu, and she assured me that a nice stew and some fresh bread would be ready for me to collect at the appropriate time. I thanked her, and parted with Kathleen, before walking home slowly. I felt foolish. I was not in love with my Husband and could not consider desiring anything other than the friendship we had so comfortably established. And yet, if I were honest, I did find myself returning to the glimpse of his strong physique and wondering at the look of him. And I did enjoy his company. And last evening, I had enjoyed receiving his admiration. And more than once, I had felt a tension and excitement when he was near to me.

At five o'clock I heard the front door open, and Robert called out. "It is me, Ellie. I am needing to disinfect again. The epidemic is worse."

I went towards him to help remove his coat but he ordered me away. "I have put things ready in the kitchen," I said. "The water in the range has boiled already. I shall go to the Inn now for our dinner."

He thanked me, and I saw at once that he looked both troubled and weary.

"Is it very bad?"

"Yes, the baby died, and two or three of the other little ones will not last long. I visited the school and have quarantined it."

"I'm sorry. This must be terrible hard for the parents."

"That it is."

I went to the Inn where, good to her word, Mrs. McLenaghan had packed us a lovely supper in a hamper. I tucked it under my cloak and returned home quickly, eager to attend to Robert and ease his fatigue if I could.

We ate together in the kitchen. Our time was not so merry, for Robert was oppressed by the sickness and felt responsible for the death of the child despite his careful treatment. He told me about the disease and how quickly it was spread so that I would understand his shutting down the small school. Trying to lighten his mood, I pulled from my pocket my small ledger book and placed it upon the table before him.

"What is this?" he asked before picking it up.

"It is yours," I said.

He examined it, and then opened the pages to look at the entries. "There is a fortune accounted for here, Ellie. A sizeable fortune. Why have you given this to me?"

"Because it is yours now, Robert. I give it to you as my dowry."

"But it is yours, I will no take your fortune from you."

"You can and you must," I answered. "I have no need of it now. We are well situated and there is more there than I could ever spend on gowns or frippery."

"I had no idea that you were a woman of independent means."

"There is more, and you must help decide what is to happen to

Rosslare Hall. Uncle has leased it for now and we will receive that income quarterly, or we can try to sell it to my Cousin, and receive those monies instead."

"But it is your home, Ellie, and Kathy's. You must decide what you will. That is your decision entirely."

"But I desire your opinion."

"Well, let us think on it then. I am taken aback and will need some time to ponder."

I had set a banked fire in the kitchen, but while we talked it had gradually burned itself out. The room was growing cool around us.

"Let us retire, and set new fires upstairs."

I was disappointed to have our night's conversation ended so abruptly, but I understood his fatigue and agreed with him readily. We walked upstairs together and, once more, as was becoming our little ritual, he walked me to my door and kissed me upon the brow. I entered my room holding a lamp and saw that a large wooden crate had been placed upon the floor. I walked over to it; nestled atop a pile of rags was a sleeping beagle puppy. Its floppy ears were soft to the touch, and its tiny nose looked like a new leather button. I was instantly charmed and sat upon the floor to peer at him. Presently he opened his sleepy eyes and began to whimper. I picked him up and cuddled him close, inhaling his puppy smell and touching the pads on his sweet little paws. I discovered that his teeth were sharp as needles, as he quickly began chewing at my fingers.

I knew that my Husband was needing his rest, but I also suspected that he enjoyed our additional nightly visits. I needed to thank him. I would go, but I would not unfold my hair and thus tempt him in any way; I would not ruin our friendship by becoming sentimental. Resolved, I picked up the puppy and walked quickly across the dark hall. As expected, Robert's door stood open and a bright fire burned in the grate. Within, Robert sat reading a book, a small glass of whis-key once more upon his side table.

I set the puppy upon the floor and it scrabbled around smelling things. Robert looked up at this, and smiled to see him. He knelt quickly on the floor and allowed the small pup to climb upon him and nibble at his hands. I laughed to see him making himself so ridiculous. The puppy was delightful, and we both of us played with him by turns.

"Do you mind an additional companion?"

"Not I. My father always had dogs in the house. I love them."

"Finn Browne's bitch had a litter six weeks ago, and this little fel-low got my attention especially."

I picked up the puppy and nuzzled him, holding him close and kissing the top of his head. "But Robert, you must stop giving me extravagant gifts."

"I wanted the wee dog, and I enjoy doing such things."

His logic confounded me for a moment. "But you spoil me, Robert, and it is not necessary."

"I am no so much spoiling you as courting you," he corrected. "There was no time to linger at such things before we were married. I was wanting to marry quickly and thought it right to do so. But you are a girl yet and deserve to experience a man's attentions."

His candour left me without a response.

"What is it, Ellie?" he asked. "You are studying me. Did I speak too boldly?"

"No, I value your opinions and regard them highly."

"What is it then?"

"It is only that this all seems so strange to me. I am unaccustomed to such intimacy. You are now my best friend. I do not want to disappoint you, but I am not in love with you. You knew that when we married."

"Yes," he responded quietly, sipping his drink. "Yes, I knew that then."

"But I feel that things are changing between us, and I am worried."

"Things have not changed," he assured me. "My feelings are as they always were, and yours, you have just told me, have not changed either. So things are constant."

"But then why do I feel so?"

"What do you feel?" he enquired. "Can you tell me?"

"No," I said, reddening, "I could never tell you that." I was sorry that the conversation had taken this course. I did not wish for it to continue.

"If we are to remain friends, Ellie, you must speak plainly. There is nothing you can say that would startle me."

Shaking my head and colouring deeply, I crossed to the other side of the room. Was I becoming attached to him? I wondered. Was this love? My emotions stirred when we were alone together, and I truly missed his company when he was apart from me. I found myself eager to be with him and to have his conversation. But what of his feelings for me? Mrs. McLenaghan had said that he was "smitten," but I had no proof of this. He was always a gentleman. Was this how a Husband conducted himself? It was unsettling to be so unsure. With the exception of Mrs. McLenaghan's extraordinary advice, I had no training in such things and no Mother to explain them.

Robert left his chair and came to stand beside me, reaching for my hand. When I gave it to him, he turned it over and kissed the wrist. Then he moved up my arm, pushing aside the sleeve and brushing my skin softly with his lips. I closed my eyes and thought that I would faint from it. I sighed and then he let me loose. Bending to pick up the puppy, now contentedly asleep before the fire, I excused myself and left the room as quickly as I could manage.

At some point in the night, I heard a rapping at my door. I went to it and saw that Robert was fully dressed with his overcoat on and his medical bag in his hand. "Murty is at the door downstairs," he told me. "There are more sick at Tinkertown and I am called to see if I can offer relief. I did no want to leave the house without first telling you."

I woke early and spent a leisurely morning visiting with Kathleen and engaging in those small tasks that I thought might succour Robert at the end of his day. In the afternoon came a knocking at the door; I opened it to a young man who very politely removed his cap.

"Beg pardon, Mrs. Stewart, I have this from the Doctor." I took the note he offered, and thanked him.

"Wait here a minute." I ran quickly to my pocketbook to fetch him a penny. "Thank you for your trouble," I said, giving him the coin. He took the money, bowed, and then left. I closed the door and read the note quickly through.

> *Dear Ellie,*
>
> *I am detained and cannot join you for supper. Please do not wait upon my company this evening. The children are far worse.*
>
> *Yours,*
> *Robert*

Not having had such a note from him before, I studied it carefully. I was sorry to hear that the children were no better and sorry too that he would not be at home in the evening.

I fell asleep in a chair but was wakened by Robert's voice after midnight.

"Eleanor," he called, "you must go to bed. It is too late for you to be sitting here."

I rose directly, looked at him, and saw how tired he was. "It is you who should be in your bed," I said, "you who have been out all day and half the night."

"I have to disinfect, and then perhaps we can talk."

I had not left him alone long when he called out to me from the kitchen. "Ellie, are you near?"

"Yes, of course. Shall I come in?"

"Stay far back, but tell me, what do you see on my back?"

Opening the door slightly, I saw that he was again partially unclothed. His coat and shirt was removed and he stood with his bare back facing me: it were blotchy, with reddish areas, and these I described.

"Get out quickly, Eleanor. Listen to me. I am infected with the measles and must be quarantined. You must stay with Kathleen at the Inn. I will come for you when I am returned to health."

I tried to respond, but he was severe with me, raising his voice in anger, and so I ran quickly from the house, directly to the Inn. When I arrived I had to knock sharply to raise the McLenaghans, but they came finally. I explained the situation and they took me upstairs to an empty room and told me to sleep. "But who will look after the Doctor?" I asked Mrs. McLenaghan.

"We'll talk in the morning, Lass," she said.

I slept but fitfully. The bed and the room were unfamiliar to me and I had not brought a change of clothes or a night dress. I woke in the night worried also about the puppy. Rising early, I went downstairs; Mrs. McLenaghan was astonished to find me in the kitchen before her with the sookey already set to boil.

"You must tell me," I said, "how one looks after the measles. What will I need to do?"

"You, Lass? What do you know about nursing a man?"

"I have no experience of it but am about to learn. You must teach me."

"Are you sure, Lass? You could catch it yourself and be right ill. I think Doctor Stewart would not be happy about that."

"I am resolved. What do I need to know?"

"Well, first off," she began, "you must keep the fever down so he don't get delirium and spoil his head. You must cover him with cold wet sheets and sponge him when he's hot. Next, you must feed him hot beef broth to make him stronger. And you must rub his lips if they get cracked with some bacon fat. And you must not let him scratch. Cut his nails very short so that he cannot harm himself while he sleeps."

"That sounds like a manageable regime," I said. "Will you look after Kathleen? I will come for her when the Doctor is recovered."

She put her arms around me then and said, "You're a good lass. Be off with you to your man."

When I returned to the house I saw that a small card reading "QUARANTINE" had been pinned to the front door. I entered quietly, laying my coat aside and beginning to explore the rooms for our puppy. I found him asleep in his box, outside of my Husband's bed-chamber, with a bowl of water carefully nestled in the corner. Next I opened the door to my Husband's room and saw that he too was resting. The fire, though, had died down. I stood at the door, peeping at him from a distance, and then entered silently to check him for signs of fever. After touching his skin, just beneath the large protrusion of his brow, I drew my hand away moist. He was over-hot. I folded back one of his covers and went to raise the window sash. I was frightened while doing this lest I be the cause of his taking a chill.

Mrs. McLenaghan had encouraged me to cool him down to avoid delirium, and so I did as I thought best. I went to the kitchen and filled a bucket partway with cool water. Taking many small towels,

I wrapped these around the Doctor's wrists, hoping to cool him. I placed one also on his brow. His eyelids fluttered when I did so but he remained very still. Next I took the sponge and washed at his face and throat with it. His nightshirt stood partly open and I slipped the sponge inside, trying also to cool his chest. It worried me that these ministrations had not roused him at all.

I called his name softly to see if he could perhaps hear me, but this also passed without any notice from him. Becoming greatly panicked, I began to speak to both him and the puppy in desperate terms. I could see that his chest was moving evenly so I knew that he was yet living, but his silence was worrisome.

I left him briefly to find a meal for the puppy of some kitchen scraps. He reminded me a little of a gardener we once had at Rosslare Hall, always dashing from one thing to another and only ever sitting still long enough to eat a meal.

"You're just like Seamus, now, aren't you, boy?"

He wagged his little tail and looked up at me with the most adorable little face. "Do you like the name Seamus?" I asked him. Again I was rewarded with tail wagging. "Very well, you shall be called Seamus, after my old friend from away home."

I returned to my Husband's room, and removed the cloth from his brow: it had been warmed by his fever. Dipping it once more in the cool water, I replaced it upon him and began once more to wash at him with the sponge. I was glad for Seamus's company, and the sound of his nails scrabbling on the wooden floor along with his tiny snuffling noises.

Mrs. McLenaghan had also said that Robert's nails must be cut short. And so I collected my nail scissors and returned to execute my small task. Picking up his hand in mine own, I felt again its softness. These were strong hands, I thought. Capable of skilled work and tasks repulsive, but they were still lovely gentleman's hands. I began to trim the nails short and still he did not stir. Kissing the fingers lightly, I replaced his hand upon the bed and covered again his wrist with a cold cloth.

The Doctor stirred at this. "Ellie? Is that you?" he asked faintly, opening his eyes slowly and with difficulty.

"Yes, Robert, it is I."

"You should go," he said in a low voice. "Go now."

"No, I can't do that," I said, leaning in closer to him. "If I do there will be no one to look after you or the puppy."

"Go," he repeated.

"No, I am here now, Robert, and intend to bide with you. What can I get for you?" I asked in a voice more cheerful sounding than I felt.

"Thirsty," he whispered.

I ran down to the kitchen and filled a jug of fresh water. I took this upstairs and tried to hold a glass for him to drink with, but he was too low on the pillow and could not raise himself. We spilled more water on him than he actually drank. The spots were come out all over his face now, and I wondered if the washing had made them worse or if I had carried them from one place to another.

Down I went again, and looked in his Surgery for something to help him drink. In his black bag, I discovered a spoon with a half cover on it and a tiny metal tube that ran out at the bottom. Recognizing this as his medicine spoon, I took it quickly to the kitchen to pour boiling water over it as I had watched him do. The water took a few minutes to boil, and while I was waiting I found some sugar and mixed it in some hot water, along with a drop of milk. This was a mixture my Mother had prepared when we were unwell; I thought the sugar might be soothing. Then, taking the spoon and my sugar mixture upstairs, I tried again to deliver some liquid into him.

The spoon worked but slowly. He swallowed the liquid carefully as though it pained him. I continued to fill the spoon and tip the tube between his lips. He took in a full glass in this way and I felt pleased with my efforts.

He was tired after this, and drifted at once back to a feverish sleep. I once more changed the cloths and sponged him. Seamus entered the room and lay on the floor near my feet. I patted him absentmindedly, wondering if I would have to clean up puppy mess in addition to my nursing. Leaving the room, I found a small puddle and went downstairs for the mop. This was not the life I had been born to, I thought, but there was some joy to be had in labouring for those whom you hold dear.

Returning upstairs, I saw that Robert had been struggling; he had thrown off his covers and cold cloths and was half out of the bed. I rushed to him and put my arm around his shoulders. "What is it? What do you require?"

"My patients," he said in a weak voice. "I must see to my patients."

"No, Robert," I said, lifting his legs back upon the bed, "you must stay here awhile and rest. You are quarantined." I straightened the sheet over him, and once more covered his brow with a cloth.

"Measles," he said. "Contagious."

"Yes, Robert, we know that. Rest awhile quietly. I'll sit with you." Pulling a chair near to the bed, I picked up his hand and saw that it was yet unmarked by the red sores. Stroking it gently, I whispered nonsensical things to the puppy at my feet, and prayed that my Husband would recover.

I spent several hours in that position, until finally I heard knocking at the front door. Rushing downstairs, I was overjoyed to see Mr. Clement. "You mustn't come near," I said, "the measles are contagious."

"I know, Ma'am, but the McLenaghans are worried that you are in need of nourishment. They sent you this. There is a hot broth for the Doctor and a nursing cup in case you were without one. I'm to stay at the Inn unless you have need of me." He handed me a hamper filled with all manner of things, and I thanked him warmly.

"Is the Doctor very taken down?"

"Yes, I'm afraid so," I answered soberly. "He seems very hot and very weakened. I am afraid that I am not skilled enough to nurse him."

"You will be fine," he said. "Mrs. McLenaghan would come herself to stay with you but there are four new guests and she has to cook for them. If they go in the morning, she will come to you sure enough." He tipped his hat at me and then took his leave.

Returning upstairs, I entered the room cheerfully, determined to rouse the Doctor and get some real nourishment into him. He would not wake easily. He was very hot to the touch, so I ran back downstairs for more cool water, then sponged him as gently as I could, whispering to him all the while, trying to keep myself from panicking.

"When I was a girl at home," I began, "Mother and my Nursemaid would sit with me by turns, telling me fairy stories and singing me ballads. My Mother had the most lovely clear voice and she sang in Gaelic songs that she had learned from her Mother before her. I was very young when she died. She was consumptive, Father said. I do not know yet what that really means. I suppose you might tell me when you are again well."

I stopped my narrative and reached for the nursing cup filled with its nourishing broth. "I have something for you from Mrs. McLenaghan. She has instructed me in the way to take care of you, and you must drink this up or she will be cross with me." I placed one arm behind his pillow and tipped his head forward whilst holding the spout towards his lips. I dropped too much in at first and he sputtered and choked, waking entirely.

"Enough," he croaked.

"I'm sorry, I'm not very good at this." I tried again and was more careful. He swallowed small mouthfuls until finally he had finished it. I laid his head back down and he immediately closed his eyes again and went back to sleep.

I decided to continue my storytelling, as much to keep me awake as to stimulate him. "As I have told you, my home in Ireland is called Rosslare Hall. It is not a very grand estate as such things go, but the park is sizeable and leads directly to the sea on the one side. It was built in 1763 by my ancestor, the first Earl of Altamont. He was made a peer of Ireland several years later. It is not a very pretty house but it is filled with collections and artifacts. The staircase has two narwhal tusks as decoration, and the great hall is filled with Irish elk antlers, and tiger skins and weaponry."

The Doctor seemed oblivious to my story, but I carried on anyway. "You would like my Father's library, Robert. It is filled with lovely leather volumes and is the pleasantest room on earth. The upstairs rooms are named after all the places to which my ancestral family has travelled. We have Italy, Russia, Burmah, Muttra, and Sydney. There are eighteen such guest rooms in all, not including the nursery, of course. My Mother's room was France. It was a pale silver blue with lovely frescoes."

Although the Doctor was sleeping soundly and the puppy was off exploring his new domain, on I went. "Had I returned to Ireland I would have renamed one of the rooms Canada. I should have chosen the room for mine own and added a star in the atlas to show where I had travelled. My Father did not travel and had not entered any stars in the atlas. His work in Dublin kept him terrible busy. He was a Magistrate. I did tell you this before, I think. That is why, in part, I felt so compelled to follow my Cousin. I did not want two generations of

Courtowns to stay at home. It seemed against our blood."

I continued to narrate my story. "I intended to return home, of course. I thought to do so with Lily. I had planned our triumphant return and resolved to find something exotic for the great hall. I wanted to be able to add to the legacy of such things and to include my story with the rest.

"Father would have thought well of you, I know, Robert. He always had a great respect for medical men. He loved dogs also and would always have his setters by his side. Little Seamus would be delightful to him. We held the hunt at Rosslare Hall every August month. The park had many foxes. We had shooting parties too but these were in September month. Mostly partridge. As I told you, Lily used to ride in the hunt but I was not quite so skillful a rider as she, and I stayed close at home."

Robert was not responding to me at all, and I became quite desolate with worry. I could not fathom my future should something happen to him. Trying to shake myself from such dour thoughts, I went in search of Seamus and played with him upon the floor to pass some time and distract myself.

Presently I moved downstairs to the kitchen, where I sliced some of the fresh loaf and solemnly ate it with my ham dinner from the Inn. It was a good meal, and I was grateful for the loving heart that had thought to prepare it for me. It made me realize that I had, at home, never given a thought to those who cooked and washed and cleaned. They were simply a part of the house and I had taken them much for granted. They would be shocked, I realized, to know that I sat in an unfurnished house, eating a cold supper and giving thanks for it. It was a different life here, I realized, and it was changing the way I thought about all such things.

When I was done, I filled the nursing cup with more broth and returned to my patient. He seemed still unresponsive, and so I thought to rouse him to check on his mental state. "Robert, wake up, dear. Robert, I need to talk to you. Robert dear, please wake up and tell me how you are." There was no response and I felt panic rising in my throat.

I sat beside him, and reached down to hold his face in my hands. "Robert," I called, "please answer me. I need to know how you are." Still there was no response. His breathing was even, but he was feverish and did not seem able to talk to me. I wept a little then, and commenced bathing him yet again with cold water. Once done, I tried to raise him so that I could feed him more broth, but he fell limply to the side and I was not strong enough to both straighten him and feed him.

I was very frightened and stayed by his side, stroking his hands and talking softly to him. This was not a good sign I was sure.

I thought of Mrs. McLenaghan and her kindness. I was desperate to undertake some action that would be helpful but could not think what next to try. Deciding then that the room smelled stale, I opened the window wider yet. This made me cold, and so I went to my room to fetch a shawl. There I saw the green dress upon a peg, and was shocked to think it were not that long ago that I had worn it and had received Robert's attentions and compliments.

I heard a knocking at the door then, and went down to greet my caller. It was Mr. McLenaghan. "The guests are staying another night, lass," he said. "Mother must remain at the Inn. She has sent you this. She said as to tell you that Kathleen was well."

I took the hamper from him, swallowing my disappointment. "Thanking you both," I said. "The Doctor is not recovered," I continued. "I fear the worst."

"Ah, Lass, do not worry. He is a strong, healthy man with a young Wife. He'll come to all right, as sure as the Shannon."

I coloured to hear him speak this way, understanding what it was that he implied. "Please thank Mrs. McLenaghan," I said, handing him back the empty hamper from the day before.

"She'll come as soon as she can, Lass," he assured me, tipping his hat and taking his leave.

The spots were still a brilliant red upon Robert's chest and arms. I could not help but think, though, that the few sores on his face did not look quite so angry. His fever was hot and I noticed that his lips were now cracked and bleeding. Running downstairs to the kitchen, I searched out the small cup of bacon fat that Mrs. McLenaghan had sent me in one of the hampers. I found it quickly and returned upstairs. After placing my finger in the cup, I rubbed it gently over his lips, coating them with the fat. Without seeming to rouse, he licked his lips with his tongue when I did this but I saw that he had not entirely removed my work.

Robert continued to sleep. I went close to him very often, checking on his temperature and comfort. I fed him some more broth but did not trouble to eat myself. The afternoon passed quickly and silently, and soon the light had once more faded. I felt Robert's brow and discovered that it was not as hot as it had been. I removed the wet cloths at that, and decided that if the fever was breaking I should not let him become too cool, lest he catch a chill.

I went to his dressing room and found a clean nightshirt. This I took to him and then tried to puzzle out how to remove the sodden one. Pulling away the wet sheet, I raised up a wool blanket over his legs and other areas, and then pulled at the nightshirt until it were about his waist. Sitting beside him, I leaned him against me and lifted the wet shirt up and over his shoulders and head. I saw by this that the spots were much faded and becoming brown in colour; I rejoiced inwardly at our good fortune. Slipping the clean shirt over him, I struggled with his arms and had great difficulty forcing them into the sleeves. I was dreadful afraid of hurting him and proceeded as gently as I could. Eventually I guided his hands down through the sleeves, but this was not done without a great deal of pushing and pulling. He roused several times while I was thus manipulating him and I spoke softly to him, explaining my actions.

I was able to pull down his nightshirt so that it did not bunch under him and make him sore. This was the most uncomfortable and mortifying for me as I did not wish to glimpse his private areas, but I could not help but do so. His shaft, as Mrs. McLenaghan would call it, lay reasonably small and still between his legs. It did not look so menacing as I had imagined. Still, I was terribly abashed by this.

I banked the fire up and shut his window next. I had puzzled out that with the fever breaking I would need now to keep him warm. The room felt very hot to me, and I removed my shawl, resuming my post on the floor by his side, watching him carefully. He seemed comfortable, and so I relaxed and decided to take my own rest. Laying my head once more upon the bed, I closed my eyes and dozed.

Both of us slept through the night. When I woke next it was dawn, and as I raised my head I could see the lovely pink glow entering the sky. Looking at Robert, I saw that he was awake, and he reached his hand towards my head and caressed my hair. "You are a lovely sight," he said. I knew at once that he must now be past the worst of it and I threw my arms around his chest and embraced him.

"I am so glad. I am so glad you are recovering!"

He lay fairly still with me pressing against him, but his arms came up and he held me to him. I felt him kiss the top of my head but did not draw away. I rested there happily, giving thanks that he was to be well. "I was so worried," I told him. "You were feverish and slept and slept."

"You should no be here."

"But you needed someone to take care of you," I said. "You, who always look after others, needed some help."

"But you may become infected."

"I had it as a child," I answered. "It will not come to me again." I was still lying against him, and thought that I should sit up. I pulled away slightly but he kept his hands upon my back.

"Do no go far away," he said. "The feel of you does me good."

I lay back down against him and fitted myself closely. It was not repulsive to me to be so near to him and I felt happy and contented.

"You must be tired," he said.

"No," I replied, "I have had a good rest. The McLenaghans have been faithful friends and have daily looked in and prepared us hampers of foodstuffs. Shall I fetch you some of Mrs. McLenaghan's good broth?"

"Perhaps later," he said. "I will need to stay indoors and rest until these spots are entirely faded. It may be another week."

"I don't mind," I said happily, "as long as you are on the mend."

"Were you so very worried then?" he asked, rubbing his chin against the top of my head.

"I was," I answered him. "I thought for certain that you would die and that all of Orange Hill would hate me for killing you and that I would have to return home to Ireland a widow."

"I see," he said, "and which part of that would have made you the most unhappy?"

"Losing my best friend," I replied. I rose at this and excused myself so that he could rest. Then I went downstairs, drew a large kettle of boiling water from the range, carried it upstairs, and began to fill the small tub in his dressing room. I added cool water besides, not wanting to scald him. When all was prepared, I went to waken him. He rose at once when I spoke. I saw that he was quite weakened from several days of fever and with very little to eat or drink. We walked together to his dressing room and I turned my back discreetly while he removed his nightshirt and got into the tub. He sighed upon sitting in the water, but I saw how fatigued he was. I went to the closet and returned with some towelling which I handed to him from a distance. "Take this," I said, "to cover yourself."

He did so, and then I knelt beside the tub and took from him the sponge and bar of soap. "Let me help you," I said. "You are not yet well enough to do this on your own." Although he protested somewhat, he did allow that he was weak and I won out. It felt strange to me to perform this same task while he was awake. I thought of what I had done for him and reddened deeply at the recollection. It was evident to me that he was a well formed man.

His hair was needing a scrub, and while I did so I saw the whole ridge of his deformed brow. "What has caused this?"

"It were a casualty," he said. "A baby's skull is not yet hard. My Mother had a difficult time with my birth and somehow my skull became crushed. It hardened and grew that way."

When explained as such, it did not seem quite so monstrous. I stepped outside the room when he was ready to get out of the tub, and he called to me once he was dried and robed in a clean nightshirt. I meanwhile had stripped the bedding off his mattress only to discover that the mattress itself was soaked and damp. My many sponge baths had spilled so much water that the bed was not fit for sleeping in. "You must go to my room," I said. "The bed is clean enough, I think, and dry. You will catch a chill if you lie down upon such a sodden thing."

Nodding at my words, he crossed the gallery, noting the mass of newspapers and asking after the puppy. "His name is Seamus," I told him. "He put me in mind of a gardener at Rosslare Hall and he seemed to like the name, so it has stuck."

After a pause, he looked at me a little strangely. "I think I have dreamed of your home in Ireland," he said finally. "Was it close to the sea and with a library full of beautiful books? In my dream it seemed to have many rooms, and there were balls and hunting parties, too. I feel as though I have somehow seen this place myself."

I smiled at this while I led him to the bed, pulling back the covers for him and arranging the pillows. "I spoke to you of such things while you were with fever," I said. "I rambled on, not knowing if you heard me or not."

The fire received my attention next: in the little woodshed next to the kitchen I filled my apron with many logs and sticks of wood, which I carried quickly upstairs and dropped upon the floor whilst I made a fire. My small chores completed, I sat down, only to realize how wearied I had become. I was aware that I had not attended to my personal needs for some days and that I also felt unclean. Sighing deeply, I found an empty pail and carried this upstairs to the Doctor's bedchamber. I found the small spigot on the tub and let the filthy water drain into my bucket, then carried this down the stairs and emptied it. It took many trips up and down to empty the tub, and during this time I became aware that the sky was darkening with an approaching storm. It had already begun to rain, the drops freezing as soon as they touched any surface.

I heard the door being knocked upon and hurried back down the stairs. Seamus was barking at my guest and I laughed to see him so protective. Mrs. McLenaghan was there herself with yet another most welcome hamper of food. I took this with many words of appreciation, and then described Robert's condition. "The worst of the fever is broke again," I said proudly, and he has been awake and talking, but the spots are still present and his teeth are sometimes chattering."

She looked at me knowingly. "Do not be too secure on his recuperating just yet; if he remains chilled he may catch the pneumonia. Have you stoked the fire?"

"Yes," I said, "but the furnace may be not working correctly. I have shut the door to keep in the warmth. Is there naught anything else I can do to warm him?"

"Give him some brandy," she said, "and try to feed him. There are boiled eggs in the hamper and they should nourish him. If he continues to shake, you must remove your clothing and climb in beside him. Your body will warm him like nothing else, God love you. Look in the Surgery for a hot water bottle and fill it with boiling water to place by his feet. I will send Mr. Clement to tend the furnace."

Although I was shocked by her suggestions, I was grateful for some direction. We parted tearfully, she picking her steps carefully on the treacherous ice that was forming everywhere. The wind was howling and the sky had got darker yet. I went straight to the Surgery, found the hot water bottle, filled it in the kitchen, and carried it upstairs to tuck in by Robert's feet. My hand touched his foot; I was provoked to feel it ice cold despite the many covers. Quickly I went through to his room and found a thick woollen pair of socks which I took back to him and pulled on over his feet.

Feeling that I had done what I might for him for the present, I attended to my own needs. Returning to the kitchen, I carried the kettle with boiled water to the bath. The fire had caught and the room was comfortably warm. Two more such trips gave me enough water to bathe with. Removing my clothes, I knelt by the tub and scrubbed my hair first. When it was rinsed, I got into the tub and soaked in the warm water. I had worked hard these last few days and found that my arms ached from all the lifting.

After the water grew cool I stepped out from the tub and knelt before the fire to dry myself. Then, borrowing a comb from the Doctor's bureau, I straightened my hair and began to pull out some tangles. Satisfied with my ministrations, I suddenly remembered the brandy, and pulled on my wrapper to go in search of it. In his study, illuminated only by the fire, I found a decanter with the stuff and a crystal tumbler. These I took to him in my bedchamber and roused him gently. "Drink this," I said. "It will warm you." He continued to sleep. Placing them upon the floor, I drew close to him and placed my face next to his. "Robert, wake up," I encouraged. "I need you to drink some brandy."

He opened his eyes slowly and focused on me in the near dark. Although I was not properly dressed, I was not self-conscious as I knew the dark would mostly cover me. I went to hand him the tumbler but saw that his hand was shaking. I sat quickly down beside him on the bed and held the tumbler to his lips. His teeth chattered against the glass so that I thought they would break it. Still, I managed to pour some into him. He lay back down again then. "Did it warm you?" I asked.

He shook his head at me. "Are these all the covers?"

"I'm afraid they are, and the fire is most hot. Would some more brandy help warm you?"

He shook his head. "No, I don't think so."

"What can I do?"

"Nothing, Lass, you should get to sleep yourself, and perhaps this will pass."

"But Mrs. McLenaghan said you might get pneumonia if you were not warmed."

"Well, did she have a cure?" he asked, trying to smile at me weakly. "She is always full of advice and cautions."

"She did," I said, hesitating, "but it was not proper, I don't think."

"What was it?"

"She said I was to climb in with you and that my body would warm you." I was deeply mortified to explain this to him.

"It is a country practice," he said, "but perhaps does sometimes work. There is nowhere else to sleep anyway, I think. I have taken your bed."

"But I would be ashamed, it is not seemly."

"Ashamed? Of what? I am your Husband and I will not compromise you, Eleanor. You need your sleep; you have worked hard."

"You must turn around and promise not to look at me," I said.

"I will do my best." At this he turned on his side, facing away from me, and shifted to the far side of the bed, leaving me much room. Hesitating, I slowly sat down on the side of the bed, and then lay down and covered myself. I know that I slept so for several hours, aware of him breathing beside me, but both of us careful not to touch. When I woke very much later that night, Robert had risen to use the commode in the next room. The wind was blowing fiercely and the fire had died down, leaving the room's temperature cool. Before returning to bed, Robert stopped to add some logs to the fire, and I saw him bending before it looking strong and fit.

"You look as though you are feeling better," I said.

"Yes, Mrs. McLenaghan's cure has worked wonders. I have slept soundly and feel better than I have done for some days, I think." He walked towards the bed, and I saw, to my horror, that his shaft had grown and was standing out from his body.

He saw me looking at him, and smiled. "Would you like some brandy, Ellie? It is relaxing and will help you to sleep in this unfamiliar arrangement." When I nodded in agreement he came to my side of the bed and poured some liquid into the tumbler. I took it from him, swallowing it all at once. He placed the glass upon the floor and returned to his side of the bed, climbing in once more and presenting his back towards me. The brandy coursed through my veins immediately; I felt it warming my fingers and legs in an instant. I had not drunk spirits often and was surprised at how alert I suddenly felt.

"I have not had brandy before," I confessed. "Perhaps I should not have drunk so much."

"This is a night for new things, Ellie," he said. "There is a gale blowing outside and we would likely be iced in even if we weren't under quarantine. No one but us will ever know what passes here."

"You always say the right thing. How is it that you always know just what to say to me?"

"I only say what is in my heart."

"Is it medical school that has taught you to know all women so well, or is it only me that you understand so clearly?"

"Medical school teaches us how to diagnose and treat diseases of the body, Eleanor. Nothing more. What you and I are discussing is the coming together of two people. This is something that we must continue to learn about together. It is different for everybody."

"But do all friends come to such an understanding?" I probed. The subject interested me and the brandy had, I think, made me talkative.

"No, I don't think so," he replied. "Many couples marry in haste and in ignorance of their compatibility. Or at least, so I'm told."

"Why would that be?"

Turning onto his back, Robert smoothed the covers around him, pushing at them to ensure a fold of blanket between us. Putting his arms behind his head, he lay there a moment and said, "In my observation, many people marry for the wrong reasons. They marry because there is no one else suitable in their circle, or because they are drawn to one another, or because they wish to change their living situations. Very few couples, in my experience, take time to value one another before they marry."

"We married quickly, Robert. Or do we not count in this?"

"Of course we count, but we did no marry before we had taken each other's measure. We saw that our values and principles were similar. We enjoyed each other's company and enjoyed to talk openly with one another. And there was more, besides."

"Yes, that is true. I trusted and respected you, besides. And I admired you."

"Well, you are full of compliments, Mrs. Stewart. Perhaps I should more often become indisposed."

"No, don't you dare! I have been wretched with worry. What did you mean when you said, 'There was more, besides'?" I turned a little on my side to watch his face, careful to pull the covers around me so that I was not exposed.

"Perhaps we have spoken enough for one night, and should now get some rest."

"No, I have a desire to know such things."

"Well, I only meant that my feelings for you were always deeper than were your feelings for me. I knew that you were no in love with me but I hoped, in time, that you might perhaps feel differently. I, for my part, was prepared to take that risk. I have loved you since we first met."

If I had thought before speaking, I might perhaps have predicted such a declaration. But the brandy was working within me and I was tired and not thinking rightly in this strange intimacy. I knew that he had spoken from his heart, and I was moved by his words. I reached across and took his hand and pressed it to my lips.

"You are the dearest man I have ever known, but I have no experience of men and no experience of romantic love. I do not honestly know what it is that I feel for you now. Since you have been ill, I have worried and fretted and wondered how I could manage without you. I don't know if this is love, Robert."

"If it is no, it is more than enough for me, and far more than I deserve."

I turned to him at this, raised my arms around his neck, and rested my head against his chest. He was a fine man and I was aware of my good fortune to be joined with him. He returned my embrace. My breasts ached and my breathing grew faster. I said nothing to Robert but knew that he felt me quivering.

"What is it, Lass?" he asked softly. "Do you know what you want? Shall I try to satisfy you? Do you trust me to show you what Husbands do?"

"Yes, I think I would like to try."

Very gently, he arranged the covers so that they did not come between us. Then he kissed my lips, pushing into me with a long kiss. Moving from there, he kissed my ear, tickling me with his warm breath and tongue, all the while tracing his fingers lightly along my throat. He loosened my wrapper and pushed it down my arms and we were joined together as a Husband and Wife. I could not speak, for the pleasure had risen in my throat and taken away my words.

Smiling, Robert looked at me and said, "You are the most beautiful woman in the world."

Separating from him, I asked, "Was this safe to do when you are still so ill?"

He laughed and pulled me once more next to him, our bodies touching along their entire lengths. "I hope so," he said, "but if no, I shall die very contented."

We lay together and slept that way. When I woke I saw that the fire had been tended and that Seamus, who was now asleep before the fire, had been carried upstairs. My Husband had risen and dressed and was sitting nearby in a chair watching me.

"I wanted to be sure," he said, rising and coming towards me, "that this was no fevered dream. Are you sore, Ellie?"

Although I coloured deeply at these remarks, and was conscious of my undress, I smiled at him and shook my head by way of response. I was too shy to speak about what had transpired between us, or to rise unclothed before him.

"You are so beautiful," he said. "I have watched you slumber for an hour or more. Shall I make us some tea?"

"Are you well enough?"

"Yes," he said, "you have entirely healed me, I believe. In a day or two more, I shall resume my duties and see what has become of the others who were sickened."

He bent over to kiss my brow. "But no one will have had such a dedicated nurse as I have had," he said tenderly.

I waited in bed until he quit the room. I washed and dressed quickly, enjoying the feel of the cold water. When I sat before the glass to pin my hair, I was startled to see how pink my cheeks looked and how softened my face appeared. There had been such tension and worry for the past year, I realized, that I had long held myself in reserve. I felt as though something wonderful had just been released.

There was much for me to learn about being a Doctor's wife in those first weeks. Robert would rise early, exercise vigorously, and then pack his medical bag and prepare various remedies, all before his morning meal. He would often be away for the full day, returning early in the evening. When he joined me in our parlour of an evening, he was often weary. He would struggle to share a diverting story with me, or bring me some small news, and play briefly with Kathleen before her bedtime.

Most evenings, before he retired, he would go to his Surgery to record his calls and write out his accounts while I went upstairs. If perchance he had experienced an abbreviated day, we might visit the McLenaghans or the home of Alex Hislop for an evening's entertainment. Society during the winter months was much restricted.

One morning, while I was with Kathleen in the kitchen, Mrs. McLenaghan came to call. "I have a bit of news for you, Mrs Stewart," she began, coming to sit across from me at the table and smiling widely.

"I have heard of a young thing searching for work. She came here this morning to ask if I had anything for her. But you know we already have Rose-Marie for the laundering and Mary Ryan to wash up inside and the O'Brien boy to do the heavy carrying, so we really do not need another pair of hands, no matter how willing, but she was ever so polite. And I said to myself, 'Janet,' I said to myself, 'now don't you just wonder if this young thing might be just what the Stewarts are in need of?'

"And so I said to her, 'Irene, you look like a good girl as has been brought up to be honest and hard-working, and I will say that if you are in want of a situation, and not afraid to bend your back to it, then I might just know a good house that will be fair and generous with you, but you must not take advantage of them,' for that is what I fear for you, Mrs. Stewart, that your kind heart will be the ruin of you, for people will often view kindness as weakness, and so I said to Irene, 'You must give me your word that you are a good girl and I will send you to my good friends, to enquire for employment.'

"She said as she was raised to be a good girl and a God-fearing one at that and that she was honest and that the Reverend Elvey could speak to her character. And I was so persuaded that I fed her a hot bowl of soup and sent her to your house to try her fortunes with you and the good Doctor."

Mrs. McLenaghan finished the delivery of this news with a huge smile and slapped her hands down on her apron in great satisfaction. She was immensely proud to be the agent of such promising good fortune and I thanked her effusively. Shortly after her departure, there was yet another knock at the kitchen door.

"Good morning, Irene," I began as I opened the door to the girl who stood there. "Please come in."

"Thank you Ma'am," she replied after only a slight hesitation. She followed me inside. A glimpse of her boots revealed deep cracks; they would not provide much protection from bad weather. Her coat was sensibly cut, though it was quite thin. I saw that she was searching for a place to lay down her things.

"Let me take that from you," I said, reaching towards her. "Our furnishings will arrive shortly, and until then we are making do without." I laid her coat on a chair and gestured towards the table. I observed that her calico gown was clean, and that her hair was tidily pinned and arranged. Her hands, quiet at her sides, were likewise clean, with the nails trimmed short. I drew some hot water from the range and went to warm the teapot with it. Irene approached and stood by my side.

"Perhaps you would allow me to do that, Ma'am, if you will just tell me where to find things."

I stepped back and allowed her to take the teapot from my hand, gesturing towards the tea canister and the cups and saucers. Then I sat down and watched her finding her way about the kitchen with ease. She poured the tea and I produced the biscuit barrel with some store-bought biscuits which we nibbled at.

"This is a big kitchen, Ma'am; we all of us admired the house when it was being built."

"Yes," I agreed, "the Doctor spared no expense in the design. He was happy to give so many men work."

Irene listened to me carefully while I enumerated, in my best mistress-of-the-house voice, as many of the arrangements as I thought pertinent. I had not mentioned wages, as I did not know, with certainty, what to say. We did not wish to take advantage but neither did we wish to appear foolish by being too liberal. Mrs. McLenaghan had been very direct in her admonition that we not pay over-much and be the cause of a local controversy.

Irene nodded her head while I spoke. "Do you have any references?" I asked her when I was done speaking.

"No, Ma'am," she replied, looking at me earnestly. "I have not worked outside before, being needed at home, but the Reverend Elvey knows me and he can give you a character, if you wish."

"Thank you, Irene, I shall have Doctor Stewart speak to the Reverend, as you suggest."

She nodded shyly at this. "Yes Ma'am, that's fine then."

I walked Irene to the door, assuring her that we would send a message once Doctor Stewart had received her character from Reverend Elvey. We parted from one another with both of us smiling our satisfaction. I was pleased to think that my domestic trials might soon be ended, and eagerly anticipated my husband's return.

Robert and I would often talk long into the evening. We had each of us a lifetime to share and were eager that nothing in our histories should remain hidden from the other.

"Tell me about your brothers, Robert," I asked one night.

"Well now," he began, "there was nine of us, six boys and three girls: Donald, James, Archie, Margaret, Peter, Graham, me, Anne, and Chrissie. Mother had Macrae, the head gardener, plant a tree for each one of us when we were born. They stood as a sturdy line of oaks at the edge of the lawns. She called us her 'strong saplings.' Donald was the most active and worked closely with Da at our woollen mill. Da owned a large mill and employed many of the local men. We bought fleece from the sheep farmers around and about. In shearing season, we would go to the mill and help weigh it on the scales and move it to the warehouse. We'd be covered in lanolin and ticks for days after the work was done—but with the softest hands you can imagine. Donald was good at working with the men and could turn his hand to fixing machinery. James was not so hardy. He had a weak constitution; we were protective of him. He went off to the university but came home with tuberculosis and died. We were devastated, and Da closed the mill for a week. One night, after the burying, I found my father in the garden, hacking at James's tree with an axe. I stood there and watched him fell it in a rage but could not move to help him. It was his way, I suppose, of working out his grief. We never talked about it. Macrae must have cleaned up the brush, for the next day, when I dared to walk by, I saw that it was tidied and a fresh-cut stump was all that was left."

Robert grew quiet at this, but I urged him to continue.

"Archie was an adventurer. He encouraged Da to invest in tea and travelled to India to manage the investments. There were others going from Peebles at the time, older business men that were acquaintances of my family, and so in no time at all, it seems, we said 'God speed' and off he went. And then Margaret fell in love with David Cameron, and there was a great to do about when they could marry. The Camerons were beef farmers around Peebles. Black Angus. She and David were finally allowed to be married after her seventeenth birthday and they had a large family of their own, I suppose. She is too busy to write much, and letters from family do not come often, although I did have one from Graham a while back."

"A letter from family is always a welcome thing, Robert," I said. "I wonder at your not having mentioned it."

Robert looked discomforted at this and was silent for several minutes. Pouring himself a splash more of brandy, he settled again in his chair. "It was no news that would bring joy, Ellie, and I have no known how to begin."

"Robert?" I prompted, feeling strangely chilled. "Tell me."

He paused for a long moment. "When the Careys first came to Orange Hill," he began, "I treated your Cousin for an ailment. Broken ribs. It was a serious issue as she was already with child. There was danger of a rupture. She assured me that she had fallen from her horse."

"That *is* possible," I interjected.

"Yes," agreed Robert, "but a fall from a horse would no explain the marks I saw present. You well know, she was an expert horsewoman."

I was silent with the dark knowledge that was now being presented.

"Mr. Carey had made bold to share his connections in Arizona and spoke freely about his holdings in a copper mine. I wrote to Graham at once, and asked him to discover news of Jack Carey and to provide me with a character. I was in receipt of his return letter only recently. I have made a copy for the authorities and they will act accordingly."

"Robert," I said, "will you read it to me?" I was trembling with fear but knew that the contents of this letter must be shared with me. My Husband reached into his jacket pocket and slowly withdrew a much folded brief. He handed it to me and I record a section of it here.

Robert, I wonder at you knowing a man by such a name as Jack Carey. The coincidence seems uncanny. There was a Jackson Carey here, who owned a small copper holding adjacent to my own. He was a good soul, although a bit of a dandy, and given to drink. He was found shot dead sixteen months ago, and his employee, a

Charles Murdoch, is wanted for questioning. Murdoch disappeared before the discovery of Carey's body. When Carey's rooms were searched, it was noted that all his personal effects were stolen. In addition, Carey's fingers were crushed and it appears that several ornate rings were removed after his death. Murdoch is a tall, elegant man, but is known to have a foul temper. He has not been seen in these parts since the murder.

"How long have you known this?" I asked Robert.

"A fortnight only," he said. "No in time to have saved her. I engaged Mr. Clement to watch over her from the start and he did his best to safeguard her while he could."

We sat in silence for a long while, I feeling too spent to weep, and Robert too preoccupied with his own thoughts to offer any consolation.

Spring was approaching, and I found that I welcomed the change with eagerness. The days were lengthening, and the warm sunshine was melting the drifts of snow that had settled and hardened around us through the winter months. Although the air was still icy cold, the country all around seemed to be impatient for the turning of the season. The early rains came, and although the wind was raw and piercing and the rain cold and hard, the earth became visible through patches of snow and began to resemble once more the defined and happy patchwork of field and stone and bush.

Robert returned early from one of his morning walks to inform me that he had seen Loons in the marsh at Tinkertown. He had heard them calling, and walked further to investigate. He encouraged me to collect my wraps, and we walked together to the marsh, a long brisk walk, so that I could see them also. They were elegant birds, in black, with white spots and markings, and long pointed beaks.

They splashed and dove down in the water to fish, and called to one another playfully. They have a strange haunting cry that echoes along the water and remaining ice. It was a display well worth the walk, and I felt privileged to be there observing them in such quiet. A cold mist was yet rising from the marsh when we arrived, for the sun had not entirely risen, and Robert and I stood at the edge of it, holding hands and watching silently. Presently he remarked that Loons are migratory birds, and that they bracketed, for him, the change in seasons. It seemed a curious thing to say, but I was glad to have had such a glimpse of them.

As the last signs of winter began to recede, the local opportunities for socializing improved. A good friend of Robert's was the local town clerk, Alex Hislop. He, like Robert, was a Scot, and the two of them often enjoyed a pipe together of an evening. Mr. Hislop and his wife were in the habit of inviting friends and neighbours into their home for an evening's entertainment. In one such gathering, we were bidden together for the first of Alex's winter lectures. The subject of his discourse was the importance of sleep. It began:

> Sleep is that mysterious yet delightfully refreshing state of unconsciousness wherein all our mental powers are for a period suspended. It is no stranger in our world; all have felt her mysterious influence; all have drunk deep and often of her forgetful waters; all have loved; all have courted, and been accepted and have been down in her deliciously enrapturing embrace, from which they have arisen refreshed and strengthened for the labours and the duties of each successive day.

His oration was soothing to the ear, but I found that my thoughts wandered as he expounded on his theme.

After the lecture, we had small bowls of rum punch and currant cake. Annie Hislop was an agreeable woman who held her husband in very high regard. She was his greatest admirer. Robert also thought well of Mr. Hislop. Among his many fine qualities, I was told, is that he was an authority on the care of livestock. We suffered for want of a veterinarian in Orange Hill, but Alex Hislop, with his many recipes for influenza in horses and cures for choked cattle, was widely sought after.

Irene had not been long in employ with us, perhaps three weeks, when I suspected that Mr. Clement was becoming rather attached to her. On more than one occasion I noticed that he happened to be finishing his day's work just as Irene was leaving us to return to Tinkertown. I would see them walking off together. Irene looked a little timid, but John seemed animated and full of confidence. It would be many years, I thought, before he could provide for a Wife and family.

We were at our meal one evening when we heard someone knock. Irene had left us already, Robert insisting that she return to her own home once our meal was upon the table. He therefore excused himself and went to the door. I was dismayed by the interruption, having looked forward to my Husband's company all day and wanting to spend time with him in conversation.

Robert returned to the dining room with Hank Smiley beside him. "Hank has not eaten yet, Mrs. Stewart," said Robert matter-of-factly. "I told him you wouldn't mind sharing our meal before I go out."

"Of course not," I said, standing to collect cutlery and an extra plate from the sideboard, "we would be happy for some company, Mr. Smiley."

"Much obliged, Ma'am," answered our guest while pulling out a chair and sitting down at the table. "It was a wet ride," he offered. "The Doctor will need to cover himself before we set off again."

"What is the trouble?"

"Mrs. Smiley is still bleeding heavily," said Robert. "It should have stopped by now, what with the ergot in brandy I left for her."

"We used it all up, Doctor," said Mr. Smiley. "If you think all she needs is some more, you could just give it to me and stay at home with the Missus."

"I appreciate your consideration, Hank, but I would feel better if I checked on her progress myself. There may be something else I can do to offer her some comfort."

"Well, we'd surely be grateful for whatever you can do, Doctor."

I knew that Mrs. Smiley had been safely delivered of a son several days ago. Robert told me that he had needed to use his forceps to turn the baby and help draw it out. It seemed like a long time for her to still be bleeding.

"How is your baby?"

"As right as rain: he shrieks when he's hungry, and feeds like a little pig, rooting around until he finds her tit and latches on. Begging your pardon," he added.

I was becoming a little accustomed to such frank talk and did not colour as deeply as I once might have done. Still, I was discomforted to hear such things discussed so openly in mixed company, and looked down at my plate demurely.

"Shall I bring dessert?" I asked the gentlemen brightly.

"No, I think not," said Robert. "We must get ready for our ride." At this, the two of them stood and moved towards the Surgery, where I knew that Robert would ready his medical bag with fresh supplies.

I left the dining room as well, and went to the front hall where I found my husband's broad hat and oilskin, and laid them upon the stair rail. He joined me there moments later. "I am sorry to go out," he said quietly, "but do no wait up for me. I will likely no return for some hours."

I nodded at him, and followed him to the door where Mr. Smiley stood waiting.

"Ride carefully. I hope Mrs. Smiley recovers safely."

"Thanking you for supper, Ma'am," said Mr. Smiley, extending his hand to me in a hearty handshake before departing.

It was still such a strange place, I thought, when a carpenter feels free to dine with a doctor and shakes a lady by the hand although she be high born. The lack of propriety still shocked me from time to time.

When I went upstairs I took with me Seamus and an oil lamp. My room was not yet decorated and it seemed particularly dismal and uninviting that evening. I washed and readied myself for bed, brushing out my hair and slipping on a linen night dress from home. Alice, one of Rosslare's upstairs maids, was particularly good at cutwork, and she had embroidered and cut the linen with so much decoration that the overall effect was that of a heavily embroidered lace, with large panels on the skirt and bodice being entirely cut open by the pattern of work. Next, I loosened the lacing on the bodice so that it remained mostly open, and dusted myself liberally with talc. Locating a small bottle of scent, I applied some behind my ears, at my wrists, and behind my knees. I lit the fire and turned down the bed covers. Seamus settled happily by the fire, tucking himself into a tight little ball and in no time snoring softly. I knew that Robert would not return for some long hours, and so I climbed into his bed to wait for him. I must have fallen asleep waiting, because it was past midnight when I roused to hear the front door shutting, and Seamus barking excitedly.

I was about to get out of bed when I heard Robert upon the stairs. He came into his room at once, and smiled broadly to see me there. "You are lovely," he said, coming over to the bed and leaning down to kiss me. "But I told you not to wait up."

"I haven't waited up," I laughed. "I fell fast asleep and have only just roused. How are you?"

"I am well enough," he said, "but Mrs. Smiley, sadly, is not. I've given her more ergot in brandy, and now it's in the Almighty's hands, I'm afraid. She cannot sustain the loss of more blood. Her pulse is very weak."

"I'm so sorry. Is there nothing else we can do?"

"I would have done it, had I known," said Robert. "Let us get some sleep now, and I will check her again later."

"Shall I go to my room?" I asked, preparing to get out of bed. "So you can sleep more soundly?"

Robert placed his hands on my shoulders and pulled me gently towards him. "You canna be serious," he said. "How would you expect me to fare alone, when I've had a look at you in that?" He kissed me softly on the neck, and inserted his fingers through the cutwork of the fabric, "I'd prefer, Mrs. Stewart, that you stay right here." And so I did.

We spent the following morning at our leisure, bathing Kathleen together, reading the papers, and enjoying a quiet start to the day. Robert rode out in the afternoon to check on Mrs. Smiley and some other patients but came home early, proposing a visit to the Inn.

The McLenaghans were in good spirits when we arrived, and set places for us in the dining room at once. After dinner we adjourned to the parlour, where Mr. McLenaghan served us some fine claret. Robert, seated in his favourite armchair, stretched out his legs and smiled contentedly.

"Well, my boy," said Harry, "is there anything new in the world?"

"I don't rightly know, Sir," replied Robert. "There is nothing new that I have encountered this day. Although there is certainly a twist to the things I have experienced."

"Well, tell us all about it then," prompted our host.

"I heard from Wendall Carr that there was sickness at the Burke farm and so I rode out there this afternoon. When I arrived, I saw at once that Granny Hill's wagon was pulled up front."

"Oh, dear," exclaimed Mrs. McLenaghan, leaning forward in her eagerness to hear what next transpired. "Did you go in?"

"I thought to turn around directly," continued Robert, "hating as I do such nonsense, but could no bear to think that I had turned my back on someone who might need assistance. Resolved within myself to do the right thing, up to the door I marched, and rapped smartly to let them know I meant business. Bryan Burke came to the door at once and made as though to bar me from entering. 'Reverend Carr sent me, Bryan,' I said, 'to see if I could offer some comfort. Is it Mary that has burned herself?' Bryan moved aside to let me pass. Mary was in bed, with the little ones playing on the floor beside her, and Granny Hill was busy with something at the kitchen table. I went to Mary and saw at once that her arm was hurt. It was laid out straight beside her in the bed and was covered in a greasy weasel skin. I took the skin and threw it at once to the floor. Granny came to pick it up and made as though to replace it. 'Hold still,' I said to her, 'and let me examine this burn.'

"The entire hand and wrist and forearm were oozing with infection. The skin was reddened and melted away in the most appalling condition. And all of it was dotted with filth and would need to be cleaned and drained and dressed. 'Granny,' I said, 'you can help me do this properly and I will be glad of your assistance, or you can cover up this mess again with your filthy skin and potions and be responsible for the gangrene that kills her. Do you understand me?' To my astonishment, Granny nodded her head and stepped aside to let me prepare my instruments. I sent Bryan for a long walk with the children, and told him to get far from the house. Granny acted as assistant and we did the painful procedure together. Mary was brave although she fainted near the end from the pain. I had administered some morphine powder but was cautious in the amount. It was a good afternoon's work."

I was delighted to hear that Robert had made some inroads with Granny Hill. She was the local bush doctor and people went to her in ignorance, believing that her herbs and poultices would cure what ailed them. I had seen her driving through town, her long grey hair plaited like a girl's, her costume an assemblage of bright shawls and skirts and men's heavy boots. It was rumoured that she could brew a tea to dislodge an unwelcome pregnancy, and she sometimes concocted potions for good fortune and love. Her pumpkin seed tea was believed to heal stomach ailments and her carrot poultice was another well-known local cure-all.

We rounded out our evening with a quick rubber of whist. Robert winked at me after an hour of this and then remarked that we should be going home to check on Seamus. We had let him out before coming to the Inn, but I realized that Robert was eager to return home, and so we collected Kathleen and made leave to depart.

Seamus greeted us when we entered the house, running circles around our ankles while we removed our coats and outerwear. He was an excitable addition to our little family, and his obvious affinity for our company almost always made us smile. He had developed several attention-seeking antics which I knew we ought not to encourage, but his darling face was more than either of us could resist. Whenever Robert and I drew near to one another, Seamus would jump up on his short hind legs, inserting himself between us for a hug and an affectionate rub of his velvety ears. He had also discovered that if he crept under the table when we were dining at home, settled himself on Robert's feet, and whined ever so softly, Robert would reach down with some small tidbit for him from the table. I knew that these tricks were not to be encouraged in a well-trained animal, but they amused both of us and I am afraid we quite indulged him.

Mr. Clement was above stairs in his suite, and when he heard us arrive home he came downstairs and informed Robert that George Tait had been by to say that his Daughter was in the way of birthing and needed assistance. Robert moved to the Surgery at once to collect his bag, asking John to seek Mrs. McLenaghan's help. I stood aside and let the men rush around readying themselves. "How old is Mr. Tait's Daughter?" I asked Mr. Clement on one of his passes through the front hall. "Why has her Husband not come for the Doctor?"

"I don't know that there is a Husband in this," replied Mr. Clement, looking downward at his feet, and clearly discomforted. "She is only a young girl."

I was shocked to hear his response, and grew thoughtful at the news. Even in this society, I reasoned, certain morals were upheld and a girl with this history would have a bleak future.

Robert and Mr. Clement did not return until mid-morning. Both of them looked weary. Robert assured me that Amy Tait was safely delivered of a small son and that the Tait family would succour both Amy and the boy as was needful. "Is the Father not known?" I asked Robert. "Will the young man not be held to account for this?"

Robert, who was readying himself to go above stairs for some sleep, paused on the staircase. "We canna assume that the Father isna around. As like as no, things will work out, but it may be that the Father is someone who can no marry her. He may be married already or it may no be decent for him to do so."

"But Robert," I protested, "how can that possibly be?"

"Oftentimes, Ellie," he replied slowly, "oftentimes the Father knows perfectly well who is to blame." He bowed slightly at this, and moved upstairs to his chamber.

Mrs. Smiley did not survive her ailment, and all of Orange Hill turned out for the service and burial. It was now spring, and the ground was considered thawed enough for the men to hack at it with picks. A fresh grave stood open in the small cemetery while we all of us circled round to pay our respects. Robert was especially silent on this day. I knew that he felt responsible for her death, although he had done everything possible to fight the bleeding and shock that killed her. Mr. Smiley held his newborn son tightly in his arms throughout the proceedings. The sight of him weeping into the baby's blanket was grievous to watch. I felt his sorrow touch me as though it were a physical harm, bruising my heart.

Several days later, John Clement arrived at the door of my small morning room and presented me with a letter from Wexford. I took it from him with trembling hands, unsure as to the contents or the steadiness of my nerves to withstand news upsetting from home. I read the following:

Dear Cousin,

I do not lose a minute in answering your letter as I am so overcome to have news of you. How grieved we all were to hear the report of Lily's untimely death. It was a great comfort to all of us to know that you, who loved her as we all did, were with her at the end. She is with Rowland now and they will be united again. This is the one thought that brings us solace.

The news of your safe arrival was welcome to all of your beloved family. The servants at the Hall also make free to send their loves all round, for there were, as you might imagine, many kind and anxious enquiries. There are others, who also wait anxiously for your return.

The weather just now is propitious, and the country is green everywhere. I hope you have as much enjoyment of the nature where you are. I know how you also thrive in the outdoors. Are there good paths for walking, and rocks to climb upon for a view of the sea? Do you have a horse to equal those in the stable? Do you manage to ride daily? Have they hunts? You can know by my questioning that there is much we are eager to have news of.

How sorry we all were at the passing of your beloved Father, and my dear Uncle. Rest assured that everything was done for his comfort and that he is now peacefully at rest beside your sweet Mother.

By an exceptional favour of fortune, I have found happiness in a well-made marriage. My Wife is obliging in every regard and is proving to be the making of me. We are raising sheep at the Hall and you would be amused to see me taking such a keen interest in their care. The prodigious amount of oil that is secreted from their skin is extraordinary.

Margaret, my Wife, has instructed me to relate that we have taken Burmah and Russia for our own private use, leaving your Father's apartments, France, and your own rooms, as they always were. I have had the items you requested carefully crated and taken by wagon to the docks. Margaret has included a gift for you of fifteen yards each of good black and mauve silk for your mourning. I took the liberty of filling each crate with as many small pictures and carpets as I could insert. Margaret also took the liberty of selecting from your Family rooms some personal items that she thought would provide you much comfort.

I had word that Billy McCready, the son of Old Ned, was emigrating also to the Canadas. When I heard news of this, I rode out directly to enlist him in your service. I have paid his passage and his expenses, in return for which he is to personally deliver to you the ten large crates from the Hall. I am assured that by this method your goods stand a good chance to arrive. I have promised Billy a warm welcome from you when he delivers the crates.

To add to your satisfaction, I must tell you that my Father's good health continues, and that my Brother Denis is as objectionable and hale as ever, having passed several weeks imposing upon my hospitality and shooting woodcock and pheasant six days out of every seven.

I remain your affectionate Cousin and one among many who would take great pleasure in welcoming you safe home,

Henry Courtown

I have some plans to improve the estate by draining the small bog by the eastern border but will send you details of this in a future communication.

I read the letter over two or three times before settling back in my chair and pressing it to my heart. "It is all right, then," I thought. "There is no more amiss, and all is well with those that I love." I sighed happily to think of the rooms that Henry had mentioned: Burmah, and Russia and France, and I closed my eyes conjuring the look of each of them in turn. It was not known who had begun the naming of rooms at the Hall, but the tradition was a well-established one. There was a slate board in the kitchen that listed them, and a piece of chalk was used to fill in the names of family and guests who were in occupancy of each. The bells that connected to each of them were also labelled by these names, with gold script on a plain deal board, and I had loved, as a child, to watch them ring, swinging vigorously in their brackets as staff were summoned to various wings of the house.

Our own routines were becoming very nicely established. Irene would arrive early in the morning, usually before eight o'clock, and work steadily throughout the day, leaving for home once Robert and I were at supper, typically around seven o'clock. In this way I was rendered a great deal of assistance and comfort, and we were also assured of some privacy, which my Husband found necessary for his equanimity.

I had been in receipt of my letter from Henry for only a week when John Clement informed me that a wagon was outside with a Billy McCready asking to see me. I stood at once and followed John to the kitchen door.

"Billy," I cried, "you are a most welcome sight. Enter and welcome." I had nigh forgot myself in my excitement to see someone from home. Billy was taken aback by my effusive greeting and looked startled by it.

"Miss Courtown," he said soberly, doffing his cap and bowing.

"Please, Billy, come inside. But I am Mrs. Stewart now."

Stepping into the kitchen, Billy held his cap in his hands and looked at John and Irene who were standing together talking quietly. I introduced them to Billy and asked Irene to prepare him something to eat. I sent John to the Inn to secure accommodation for him for the evening.

"I have with me your furniture from the Hall," began Billy. "Mr. Henry paid my passage so as for me to bring it to you. There's three wagons outside, and drivers."

"Mr. Clement will take care of things when he returns. Please sit and give me news of home."

With my standing there watching him, Billy seemed unwilling to sit down to eat the eggs that Irene had quickly fried. Realizing his distress, I excused myself, promising to return shortly. I paced the front hall for a full ten minutes, wanting eagerly to return to Billy and hear what news he could give me. When I determined that enough time had elapsed, I re-entered the kitchen. I found Billy and John and Irene in conversation. It was evident that they had established a degree of comfort.

I asked John to attend to the wagon drivers and to have them bring their cartage into the house. The crates were over-large and would not fit through the kitchen door. In the end, the wagons were drawn to the front and were unloaded, by dint of much pulling and shoving and not a little cursing, onto the porch, and then in through the front doors. The small passageway to the Surgery was obstructed by this means and John was at pains to have the men shove the crates into the parlour, my morning room, and the dining room. Our house, which had so often seemed spacious, was now quickly filled.

When the men were done their heavy work, I gave them some coin and directed them to the Hotel. Billy I asked to join me in the Surgery. We sat upon two stiff chairs, both of us not a little uncomfortable with our surroundings and strange context.

"Tell me, Billy," I began, "how was your journey?"

"Well, it warn't as easy as you would wish," he said, pausing to stick out his tongue. "It war a bit rough."

Billy had a propensity to stick out his tongue, I remembered. The maids at home had often made fun of him when he was a little lad. Determining that he had now exhausted that topic, I prompted him again.

"Is there news from home, Billy?"

"Well," he began, sticking out his tongue once more, "your Pa died and Mr. Henry moved into the Hall with his new Missus. There's a mess o' sheep now. 'Bout a t'ousand or more. An' Hugh McAuley, the Gillie, were found dead in his bed like a stone, just a day or more after your Pa. An' t' Cook has wrenched her arm and canna be liftin' t' heavy pots no more."

"Well," I said, absorbing these abbreviated reports, "that is a lot of news. And is there word of Lord Driscoll?"

Billy hesitated before responding. "No, M'lady."

"Well, is the new Mrs. Courtown well thought of?"

"Yes, Ma'am, and dey all says as how she is handsome even dough she be tin as a whippet."

"I am glad. I would not wish Henry to be married to an ugly wife."

"No, Ma'am," agreed Billy. "For the young 'uns would be uglier still."

"Exactly right," I agreed, rising. "And did Mrs. Stevens return to the Hall in safety?"

"Yes, Ma'am, but she didna stay long. Only t' talk with your Pa an' off she wen' in a stew, or so was said."

"You have faithfully discharged your duty. You should go to the Inn and rest. The McLenaghans will treat you kindly."

"Tanking you, Ma'am," he said gravely, standing also.

I went to reach for my small purse, but seeing me do so made him flush. "Mr. Henry has looked after me, Ma'am."

I nodded at him and he took his leave. Although I was disappointed by the poverty of news, the presence of the crates excited me not a little. I left the Surgery to discover that John had readied some tools and was only waiting on my direction to begin work. He pried open the first of the crates and I was most eager to lean inside the top to have a look. It was a jumble of small wrapped objects and furniture legs and quilts and pictures. John reached in and pulled out a large, bulky package wrapped carefully in blankets and tied with cord. It was an oil painting by Catterson Smith, and I was partly sorry that my cousin had culled it from the portrait gallery where it had hung since my Mother was a bride. In it, my Mother was seated on a divan in the great hall surrounded by tall arrangements of flowers; she was smiling sweetly to herself, not looking at the portrait artist, and her cheeks were slightly flushed, accentuating her pale complexion. She wore a diamond pendant necklace with matching drop-shaped earrings. I had loved to watch her screw the backs tight on her earrings, adjusting small wisps of her hair, dabbing behind her ears with the crystal stopper from her perfume bottle. And I had loved to catch the look on my Father's face when she made her entrance and he first caught sight of her. It conveyed such pride and love blended together in the briefest of flashes, and then his sense of reserve would quickly take over and he would compose his face so none could see how moved he was.

For the next few days, I spent my time divided between Seamus and Kathleen and the unpacking of the Irish crates. Among the many items that Henry had sent was my Mother's Celtic harp, a very old instrument that had been passed down through the Kavanaughs for generations. I had learned to play when very young, standing beside my Mother while she knelt upon the floor beside me. The harp was carved from a single piece of bogwood, shining almost black, with some decoration along the neck.

I discovered, plucking at the strings, that the sound of it enthralled Kathleen. As a result I often laid her on the rug whilst I sat near to her with the instrument. "This harp will be yours one day, Kathleen," I began, "and it is important that you know it is a Kavanaugh harp and has been in my family for generations. My Mother was a Kavanaugh and she sang lovely Irish melodies when she played. I am not a song-stress but I can play well enough to begin your instruction."

Kathleen looked at me intently and I knew that she was listening. I continued to pluck the strings softly, as the sound seemed to enchant her.

The next day, Robert joined me for tea before riding out on his calls. He sat down beside me upon the floor and wrapped his arms about me, settling comfortably. He had not spoken much more about his family, and I was suddenly moved to ask him a question: "Were your parents pleased that you became a Doctor?"

"They never said directly. It was always understood that whatever we did we had to do well. My Da said that the most important thing in life was to make a contribution. I hold that to be true and have tried to do so."

"Tell me about your parents, Robert."

"Well, my Da died five year or more ago and my mother no long after. I had a letter from Donald telling me. He took over the mill."

"I'm sorry."

"Ach, they both of them had a good life. You canna wish more than that."

Robert and I talked until late in the afternoon. My crates from Ireland had made us contemplative and stirred memories of home. We shared our stories with one another and drew closer yet.

I continued to tell Kathleen stories, too. "The first harp in Ireland was owned by an Irish Chieftain," I began one evening. "It was carved from magical bogwood by the little people. And the music he made was so beautiful that he could bring about a change in seasons. Some say harps were used in battle to make the opposing armies sleep, and so they were vanquished. Later, the harpists in Ireland were nationalists who fought to keep their independence. The Queen of England had them killed, and their harps burned, to fight the insurgence.

"So you see," I said, stroking Kathleen's little fingers, "that when you learn to play, my little one, you will become an important part of Irish history." I felt a greater equanimity and peace after playing my harp, and speaking with Kathleen, than I had done in some weeks. Kathleen had dozed off and was sleeping lightly on the rug. I reached for my embroidery basket, sat beside her on a chair, and began to work a new strawberry on my silk. Wednesday was fast approaching and I was conscious of the need to prepare materials for my sewing group. I had postponed my classes when word reached us of Lily's injuries, and then again when there was her funeral to plan. Although I was still in mourning, I did not wish to further prolong the pleasure of the girls' company. I was particularly eager to introduce them to Kathleen.

Saturday evening was set for the Hislops' grand fête—an annual event, I was told, where various of the townspeople were asked to perform. There was much excitement in town as many of us prepared for the roles we had been assigned. I practised my harp daily until my fingertips grew tender, determined to respectably reproduce a tune. I played for Robert one evening, before retiring, and was gratified to see that he was deeply moved. He gave me a great many assurances that I would be the star feature of the evening, and that I was not to fret about any small mistakes I may make, as "none will have heard better. "

We arrived at the Hislops' carrying Kathleen, my harp, and a plate of ginger cakes that Irene had prepared. Robert took charge of Kathleen, keeping her with him as he joined the men in Mr. Hislop's study. I saw that Mrs. Hislop had been hard at work with her preparations. The furniture had been removed from their dining room and the doors opened to the adjoining drawing room, creating a large space with many chairs lined up in rows. Curtains had been hung on a series of poles at one end to contrive a formal stage. I placed my harp in a corner and went to join the ladies who had congregated around the refreshments in the small parlour.

At eight o'clock a large gong sounded, and Mr. Hislop summoned us to the newly devised theatre. I spied Robert in the small crowd, and waited for him so that we could be seated together. As Kathleen had fallen asleep, he very carefully turned an armchair to the wall, laying her down upon the seat of it. Mrs. Hislop had placed a large number of lamps on tables at the front of the room, producing a warm ambience there and leaving the rest of the theatre in darkness.

Mrs. Hislop stood up first and welcomed us to her humble Celebration of Spring. She then introduced her Husband, who walked to the improvised stage and ceremoniously withdrew from his vest a sheaf of papers which he unfolded. Placing his spectacles on, he began to read:

To A Chipmunk
I love it, I love it, and who shall dare
To chide me for loving what I did prepare
O' a wee bit speech to chipmunk rare
I met in the bush one day.

What gars ye rin, wee timid beastie skirlin' sae frae fun or fear
It isna in my heart to harm yee, I'm vext ye think an enemy's near.

O' wad ye but e'en now approach me wi' nimble feet and trustfu' e'e;
Whirlin', skirlin', as tho' ye'd dout me, syne a' at ance got on my knee.
I'd draw my hand sae sleekly ower ye, thy pantin' heart nae illmight dree;
Syne gently to my bosom hug ye, and bless ye for sic trust in me.

The poem was far longer, but this is the extent to which I can recall it. The applause was enthusiastic; Mr. Hislop bowed repeatedly and seemed much moved by the audience's endorsement. Mrs. Hislop then introduced a Spring Tableau to be performed by the Reverend and Mrs. Carr. After some prolonged bumping, and furtive arrangements taking place behind the fabric, Mr. and Mrs. Hislop were finally able to pull back the draperies.

We seemed, all of us, to draw our breath in a collective gasp. Revealed was a tableau taken from Botticelli's *Primavera*. Mrs. Carr, presumably in homage to the arts, had chosen to abandon her fine silks and carefully dressed hair in favour of a rather transparent chemise with a casually draped red shawl. Her grey locks hung down loose upon her shoulders and back. It was a rather intimate, if not scandalous, portrayal of Venus. She stood in a fixed pose with her hand pointing slightly towards Reverend Carr, who had been persuaded, ill advisedly, to dress as Cupid. Cupid was clad only in slippers and a carefully positioned rug which he had belted about the middle. His thin white appendages were evident, and I'm afraid that

I recoiled with considerable distaste.

Robert, who sat beside me, was convulsed with mirth and saved us all from the embarrassing scene by laughing and applauding loudly. "Bravo," he called. "Allegory of Spring!"

The others joined in applause and nodded to one another, saying such things as "Oh, yes, Allegory of Spring," and "Of course, Botticelli," as though naming the painting somehow removed the mortification. I was utterly reddened by the display and wished to excuse myself. I looked at Robert imploringly, but he was enjoying himself and made no indication that he wished to be elsewhere. Mercifully, the Hislops soon pulled the draperies and we were spared further glimpses of the unclothed Carrs.

Our third performer for the evening was Mr. Dickie. I had limited my interactions with him since his unfortunate visit at the McLenaghans' prior to Christmas. Any correspondence that was needful regarding my sewing group I had conducted by way of written note. Although my wishes had been carried out, and the girls given my messages, he had declined the opportunity of a return correspondence. I was assured by this that he felt in some way aggrieved by my behaviour and that he wished to cut me.

After a generous and prolonged introduction by Mrs. Hislop, Mr. Dickie rose from his seat and proceeded to the stage. He was fully clothed. I saw this as a positive sign and relaxed somewhat. His selection for the evening was Wordsworth's "I Wandered Lonely as a Cloud." This seemed a harmless choice and I smiled to myself, thinking how gladdened Mr. McLenaghan would be that the poem was not in Latin.

Mr. Dickie cleared his throat, struck a theatrical pose with his legs parted in a solid stance and his arms raised high above his head, and began:

I wandered lonely as a cloud
That floats on high o'er vales and hills,
When all at once I saw a crowd,
A host, of golden daffodils;
Beside the lake, beneath the trees,
Fluttering and dancing in the breeze.

He paused there, and looking upwards, presumably at the clouds, began to float around the room, holding his right hand to his brow and searching for something in the distance. Suddenly he stopped, resumed his stance, and began again:

Continuous as the stars that shine
And twinkle on the milky way,
They stretched in never-ending line
Along the margin of a bay;
Ten thousand saw I at a glance,
Tossing their heads in sprightly dance.

The waves beside them danced; but they
Out-did the sparkling waves in glee:
A poet could not but be gay,
In such a jocund company:
I gazed—and gazed—but little thought
What wealth the show to me had brought:

At this, Mr. Dickie lowered his arms and began to wave them around, simulating, I featured, the sea. He then skipped across the front of the small stage before stopping dramatically to resume his pose and his recitation.

For oft, when on my couch I lie

In vacant or in pensive mood,
They flash upon that inward eye
Which is the bliss of solitude;
And then my heart with pleasure fills,
And dances with the daffodils.

Mr. Dickie had clearly saved the finest for the last. He began to dance an awkward and silent homage to Wordsworth, which involved much head bobbing and jerking of limbs. Then he retrieved from behind the draperies a basket filled with paper daffodils. These he tossed to the audience while he skipped from the room.

The applause was thunderous. Robert was choking with laughter, and in trying to control himself made several loud sputters and some very strange sounds. Fortunately the room was still in a loud uproar and I do not think anyone attended to Robert's noises in particular. It was wrong of him to laugh, and I looked at him sternly in a silent rebuke. Seeing such displeasure further amused the Doctor and he positively shook with merriment, wiping tears from his eyes and taking large breaths to steady himself.

I was to be the fourth and final entertainment prior to Intermission. Mrs. Hislop introduced me as "Mrs. Robert Stewart, an accomplished harpist, recently from Ireland."

I proceeded slowly to the front of the room, conscious that I was now the object of study. Kneeling upon the floor, I drew my harp to my shoulder and positioned my fingers above the strings. Without further introduction I began to play, plucking with surety. And while I played, I remembered my own tuition on the instrument and the feel of my Mother's hands correcting mine own; and also the curious and intent look of Kathleen studying me while I practised of late; and then the remembrance of Lily, at school in Dublin, playing this same tune with an intensity that made us weep to hear her; and all of these thoughts filled me and poured into my playing of "The Battle of the Boyne" that evening. I do not consider myself to be a particularly good songstress, but the words of this ballad are haunting, and I sang easily:

A kingly host upon a stream, a monarch camped around,
Its southern upland far and wide their white pavilions crowned;
Not long ago that sky unclouded showed, nor beneath the ray,
That gentle stream in silver flowed to meet the new-born day.

Peals the loud gun—its thunders boom the echoing vales along,
While curtained in its sulphurous boom moves on the gallant throng,
And Foot and Horse in mingled mass, regardless all of life,
With furious ardor onward pass to join the deadly strife.

Nor strange that with such ardent flame each glowing heart beats high,
Their battle-word was William's name and "Death and Liberty!"
Then Ouldbridge, then thy peaceful bowers with sounds unwonted rang,
And Tredagh, mid thy distant towers, was heard the mighty clang.

The silver stream is crimsoned wide and clogged with many a corpse,
As floating down its gentle tide come mingled man and horse;
Now fiercer grows the battle's rage, the guarded stream is crossed,
And furious, hand-to-hand, engage each bold contending host.

He falls—the veteran hero falls, renowned along the Rhine—
And he whose name, while Derry's walls endure, shall brightly shine;
Oh! Would to heaven that churchman bold, his arms with triumph blest,
The soldier spirit had controlled that fired his pious breast.

And he, the chief of yonder brave and persecuted band,
Who foremost rushed amid the wave and gained the hostile strand,
He bleeds, brave Caillemonte—he bleeds—'tis closed, his bright career,
Yet still that band to glorious deeds his dying accents cheer.

And now that well-contested strand successive columns gain,
While backward James' yielding band are borne across the plain;
In vain the sword green Erin draws, and life away doth fling—
Oh! Worthy of a better cause and of a bolder king.

In vain thy bearing bold is shown upon that blood-stained ground;
Thy towering hopes are overthrown, thy choicest fall around;
Nor, shamed abandon thou the fray, nor blush though conquered there,
A power against thee fights today no mortal arm may dare.

Hurrah! Hurrah! For Liberty, for her sword we draw,
And dared the battle while on high our Orange banners flew.
Woe worth the hour—woe worth the state, when men shall cease to join
With grateful hearts to celebrate the glories of the Boyne!

When the piece was completed I continued to play an improvisation of the last two lines, unwilling to break the spell. I am not an accomplished musician, but my playing on this one evening was inspired and I knew that I had acquitted myself with distinction.

The assembly stayed silent for a long while, waiting for the last of the strings to complete its vibration. There was a hush in the room before the clapping commenced. I stood and curtseyed, while looking downward, not willing to face the crowd. It felt suddenly as though I was too early in company and that the excitement of the evening was proving more than I could manage.

Mrs. Hislop introduced the Intermission and I went quickly to Robert. He had been moved by my playing I saw, for his cheeks were wet with tears. He smiled to see me and placed his arm about me protectively. I whispered to him that I was wearied and he nodded at me, understanding. Steering me through the room, he picked up Kathleen and navigated our passage through to the front doors. Then he left me there briefly as he collected my harp and made our excuses to the Hislops.

We were silent on our short walk home, and I was grateful for the quiet. Inside the house, Robert settled Kathleen in her small crib and rejoined me in my dressing room. "Mr. Dickie," he began, "has many talents." I'm confident that he intended to say more, but the image of Mr. Dickie dancing so amused him that he began, once more, to laugh.

I smiled at the recollection but could not do anything other than watch my Husband's merriment. He was fully engaged in the endeavour. I had begun to remove the pins and unfold my hair when Robert picked up my brush from the table and very gently lifted my hair and slid it through his hands. Standing behind me, he began the brushing, being careful not to tug or move too quickly. I closed my eyes to enjoy the feel of it.

Robert suggested after supper one evening that we pay a visit to the Inn to check on the newly begun progress of combing. Collecting Kathleen, we walked the short distance and arrived to find the front door open and the Mewhinneys at work. All the woodwork had been painted a pale yellow, and the men were now at work with feathers and sponges and broken bits of comb, streaking a newly applied coat of brown varnish. Mr. Mewhinney the senior, by using the feather as a paintbrush in the wet varnish, was fashioning an artful representation of wood grain. It was meticulous work, and I could see he was very skilled at it.

"Come in, come in," beckoned Mrs. McLenaghan. "You've brought my Sweetheart to see me, and admire the work that is being done. Is it not an elegant job?" She reached her arms out for Kathleen and I transferred my small burden to her welcoming embrace. "I have been at sixes and sevens all day," she remarked while bussing Kathleen repeatedly, "and I don't know where Harry has gone to; he keeps disappearing on me. Come to the kitchen for tea," she added, "and then you can admire the papering upstairs."

Robert and I followed her to the kitchen and sat down. "I can't decide," she continued, "whether we should have a grand reopening of the Inn or if we should host a party. We need something to celebrate for a party, though, and I can't think what that could be. Wasn't the Hislops' fête a wonderful evening? I don't know when I have had so much fun."

"Yes," said Robert, smiling at her, "I especially enjoyed Mr. Dickie's performance."

"You are a naughty boy," she said, swatting at him lightly. "Just imagine, he actually thought he stood a chance with our Miss Courtown, God love him."

I coloured at this, but mercifully neither she nor Robert commented upon my discomfort. "Do you know what I think?" continued Mrs. McLenaghan. "I think that John and Irene have formed an attachment."

"But she is just a child," I protested.

"Well, she's a child then who has formed an attachment," replied Mrs. McLenaghan, nodding her head at me. "I can tell these things, you know. Why, I was the first one that saw how it was between the two of you. I puzzled it out before you even know'd it. Isn't that so?"

Robert was considering this thoughtfully. "Irene is young," he said, "but no so young as some."

Harry McLenaghan entered the kitchen just then and joined us at the table. "Hello, Mother," he greeted his WVife. "How is your work progressing?"

"Harry McLenaghan," she began, "where have you been hiding today? I called and called for you not one hour ago and you were not to be found. You could have been laid out dead somewhere for all I knew."

Mr. McLenaghan had the good grace to look slightly ashamed at this, but he winked at me naughtily before replying, "I am ne' dead yet, Janet, but if ye keep workin' me so hard, there's a good chance of it happening sooner rather than later."

"Workin' you to death!" she roared. "And what about me, scrubbing and papering and getting all this work organized and feeding everyone besides, and you slinking off to hide somewheres while I have the work to do with only the help of God?"

"Slinking off, is it?" he retorted. "As if a man can't be free in his own house to do as he pleases."

Several days later, John requested an audience with Robert. He told him that he wished to marry and required direction on how best to accomplish the desires of his heart. Robert came to me with a surprising recommendation. The Carey farm had been left unattended these long months, its deed remaining in Rowland's name only. The cattle Robert had sold off directly after Lily's death, but nothing else had been done. I myself had not ridden out and did not wish to see the place where Lily had suffered. Although I might choose to haze it in its entirety, Robert said that we ought to offer it to John, on easy terms, so that he and Irene could marry.

"Robert," I said, "I will gladly do as you suggest, but I do not understand the need for such expediency. Irene is yet a child. It will not harm them to know their minds one year for her to finish growing."

"I will no stand by and see them separated," he said. "There have been enough young people separated by obstacles who have ruined their chance of happiness as a result." There was a passion to his words, and much anger in his tone.

I looked at him wonderingly. Robert then strode from the room, banging the door violently as he left. I sat down, not a little astonished by his outburst. I heard him proceed to his Surgery, and after several minutes, I followed him there.

He looked abashed to see me enter, and bade me sit. "There was a girl," he began, "an Irish girl from Mayo. I was twenty-two and she was but fifteen. We were in love." He stopped briefly to move his chair close to mine, and then resumed his tale. "Her Father was a botanist and I had studied with him briefly in Edinburgh. When I finished my training and was casting about for an occupation, he offered me employment as an assistant. I was to help him compile a catalogue of his research. It was not engaging work, and I was soon longing to find an opportunity more suited to the practice of medicine. In my every spare moment I would steal away so that I could meet his Daughter and have time alone with her. I was entirely fascinated, and in the throes of young love, I did no act honourably.

"When her Father discovered us, I was dismissed and took immediate work on a convict ship. Eighteen months later, when I returned, I learned that she had given birth to a still-born child and was sent to live with family in London. Dr. Stevens would no give me her address, nor the name of those she resided with. I am still sorely troubled by the harm I did to her."

The name Stevens had caught my notice. The account was a devastating one, but it was a long time ago, and I could not fault him now for his part in the sad story. I wondered if "my" Mrs. Stevens, the gentlewoman who served as companion on my ocean voyage, was the girl he had left behind. There could not be so many Scots surgeons, I thought, who set sail for Australia. If so, perhaps her Father had manufactured Robert's "death by pestilence" in a further effort to separate them, and had not allowed Robert to correct his misstep.

It pleased Robert to think that we might provide the means for John and Irene's ready happiness. He felt, I think, that by this act he would redeem his misdeed against the Irish girl of so long ago. I gave my consent, of course—Robert was not to be dissuaded from his generous scheme—but I did not rest easily with it. I am not, by nature, fanciful, but I did wonder if perchance any evil lingered in the place, or if its unhappy history would adversely affect them. There was at least some comfort in knowing that a place so desolate would become the means of happiness for so deserving a pair.

My days are filled now with the running of our small household and Surgery. Kathleen is asleep still, beside me on this verge, where I have come to finish my story. I have studiously applied myself to it since Christmas, when Robert gave me my beautiful journal. I am happy to have recorded this story for my Daughter, for I would have her know the whole of it when she is of age, and to appreciate the legacy of love which has framed all of her life.

One day, I will have speech with the menfolk who, while negotiat- ing dowries and land claims and titles, shirked their responsibility to my Cousin and left her friendless in a foreign country. They should hear the cry of the Banshee and know what it was to die solitary and without family near. I would shame the McDonoughs yet for their part in Lily's story.

I will take Kathleen to Rosslare Hall and to Lowry Castle, as I have promised, and I will introduce her to the Courtowns and to the McDonoughs and the Kavanaughs. And she and I together will mark Orange Hill with a small red star in the family atlas. And I will tell her stories of her beautiful Mother and her happy youth. And we will ride across the county, and I will show her the lough, and the strand, and take her to court in Dublin.

And when I am sure she has seen these places, we will return to the Hall and explore the park and the gardens and the rooms together. And we will ride and shoot woodcock and pheasants. And we will attend the horse racing. And I will have a saddle made for her in Dublin. And we will go to London and take the train to see the Crystal Palace, and undertake a short tour there while I call upon family and see the sights.

But before winter comes, I will return to Orange Hill and to my beloved Doctor, and to all our friends and acquaintances. And though it break my heart, I will leave Kathleen in Ireland with her family, so that she can know the taste and feel of her homeland, and learn to value her connections and her blood. Come the spring, my Darling will need to make her own choice and return to us in Orange Hill or remain in Ireland. But I will not venture so far afield again. I will stay with Robert, and savour the time we have been given to try, as we best can, to make a difference in the lives of those around us.

ACKNOWLEDGEMENTS

Many thanks to Seraphim Editions, and especially to Maureen Whyte, Publisher, to Rolf Busch typographer and cover design artist, and to Richard Van Holst, copy-editor, for their belief in this story and for their collective efforts to guide me through this process.

My deepest gratitude to Donna Morrissey, who is my mentor, editor, champion and beloved friend.

I am especially grateful to Karen Alliston for her careful and expert editing of the manuscript.

I am indebted also to Paul Butler for his skillful editing suggestions.

With thanks also to Antanas Sileika and David Bezmozgis for their leadership at the Humber College School of Writing and for all that they do to develop and support writing in Canada.

With appreciation also to Wendy Bentley for her friendship and her many hours of clerical work on early drafts of this manuscript. To Marianne Froelich, an early reader and avid supporter of this fictional history, I extend my gratitude. And also to dear friends, Joy Barratt, Marilyn Black, Kandis Thompson, Susan and Llewellyn Jones, and Mary Graniero who have encouraged my story-telling.

With thanks also to my son, Andrew, who has listened to this story in its many incarnations for several years, and who has always been indulgent and encouraging about my writing projects.

With love and appreciation to my sisters, Janny, Lia and Joan and also to my brother, John.

I must also acknowledge the late Mrs. Marion Hodge of Cartwright Township for her weekly phone calls about the wind, and her many narratives about growing up in Cartwright.

I am particularly indebted to Marjorie and Don Green for lovely visits in their kitchen, and especially for Don's true story of "a poisoning down the road" which was the beginning of this tale.

Although this is a work of fiction, I must mark my indebtedness to these works:

For lectures, readings and poetry:

Hislop, A. "The Unpublished Diary of A. Hislop, 1855-1862." Sunnidale Township, Ontario, 1862. The Diary is the property of Dr. Michael J.B. Black and was written by his ancestor. I have quoted Mr. Hislop directly in the novel.

Ovid, *Metamorphoses.* http://www.thelatinlibrary.com/ovid/ovid. met1.shtml

Perkins, D., ed., *English Romantic Writers.* New York: Harcourt Brace Jovanovich, Harvard UP, 1967.

The Holy Bible, KJV. New York: The World Publishing Company, no date.

The Book of Common Prayer, Toronto: T.H. Best Printing
Company, 1962.

Regarding crossing the Atlantic:

"The Ocean Steamer: Crossing the Atlantic in Early Steamships."
Harper's New Monthly Magazine, vol. 41, no. 242, August
1870, pp. 185-198. Gjenvik-Gjønvick Archives.
URL: www.gjenvick.com/SteamshipArticles/1870-08-The-
OceanSteamer-HarpersMagazine... Accessed 26 June 2010.

Herring, Rev. A. Styleman. "1870 Voyage of the Clerkenwell
Emigration Society on the *Peruvian.*" *Immigrants to Canada.*
URL: retirees.uwaterloo.ca/. ~marj/genealogy/voyages/
clerkenwell.html . Accessed 26 June, 2010.

Swain, John Gwynn. "Voyage on the SS St. George, 1867." Immigrants to Canada: Sessional Papers/Parliamentary Papers.
URL: retirees.uwaterloo.ca/~marj/genealogy/voyages/swain.
html. Accessed 1 July 2010.

Mageean, Deirdre M. "Emigration From Irish Ports." *Journal of
American Ethnic History,* vol. 13, no. 1, Fall 1993, pp.6-30. JS-
TOR. URL: http://www.jstor.org/pss/27501112. Accessed 26
June, 2010.

Early Medicine:

Bliss, Michael. *William Osler: A Life in Medicine.* Toronto: University
of Toronto Press, 1999.

Duffin, Jacalyn. *Langstaff: A Nineteenth-Century Medical Life.*
Toronto: University of Toronto Press, 1993.

Harvard University Library, Open Collections Program.
"Contagion: Historical Views of diseases and Epidemics,

Robert Koch, 1843-1910." URL: http://ocp.hul.harvard.edu/
contagion/koch.html. Accessed 13 March 2010.

Architecture:

Cruikshanks, Tom, and John deVisser. *Old Ontario Houses:
Traditions in Local Architecture*. Willowdale: Firefly Books,
2000.

Massingberd, Hugh Montgomery, and Christopher Simon Sykes.
Great Houses of Ireland. New York: Rizzoli International, 1999.

Irish History:

Akenson, Donald Harman. *The Irish in Ontario: A Study in Rural
History*. Kingston: McGill-Queen's University Press, 1984.

Akenson, Don. *An Irish History of Civilization, Volume One*. Kingston: McGill-Queen's University Press, 2005.

"The Battle of the Boyne." *Folk and Traditional Song Lyrics*. URL:
http://www.traditionalmusic.co.uk/folk-song-lyrics/Battle_
of_the_Boyne.htm Accessed 4 June 2017. This is only one of
many different versions of this ballad with small but interesting
variations in the text.

Broderick, Marian. *Wild Irish Women*. Dublin: The O'Brien Press,
2001.

Cregier, D.M. *The Irish RMs: The Resident Magistrates in the British
Administration of Ireland*." *Canadian Journal of History*, vol.
33, no. 3, December 1998.

Debrett, John. *The Peerage of the United Kingdom of Great Britain
and Ireland*. London: David Barbicon, 1809.

MacManus, Seumas. *The Story of the Irish Race: A Popular History
of Ireland*. Old Greenwich, Conn.: Devin-Adair, 1992.

Newman, Peter R. *Companion to Irish History: From the Submission of Tyrone to Partition 1603-1921.* Oxford: Facts on File Limited, 1991.

Ladies' Fashion:

"Tidbits: Victorian sidesaddle riding habit 1, and The Comical Crinoline. "*Corsets and crinolines, unique vintage clothing and antique fashion.* URL: http://www.corsetsand crinolines.com/ tidbits.php?index=3. Accessed 28 February 2000.

Peterson's Magazine. 1970. URL: http://www.festiveattyre.com/ victorian/p70/index.html. Accessed 28 February 2000.

Ontario History:

Anyan, Kevin W., and Charles D. Taws, eds. *Bowmanville: 150 Years – 150 Stories.* Bowmanville, ON: Bowmanville Sesquicentennial Committee, 2008.

Carr, Mrs. Ross N. *The Rolling Hill: Manvers Township Centennial Project.* Victoria County: Manvers Township Council, 1984.

Galbraith, John K.*The Scotch.* Toronto: Macmillan, 1985.

Heriot, George. *Travels through the Canadas, 1807.* Vols. 1 and 2. Toronto: Coles Publishing Company, 1971. Facsimile Reprint of 1807 edition.

Johnson, Leo A. *History of the County of Ontario, 1615-1875.* Whitby, ON: The Corporation of the County of Ontario, 1973.

Leetooze, Sherrell Branton. *Along the Gravel Road, A Brief History of Cartwright Township.* Bowmanville, ON: Lynn Michael-John Associates, 1996.

Mika, Nick, and Helma Mika. *Places in Ontario: Their Name Origins and History, Part I.* Belleville, ON: Mika Publishing Company, 1977.

Peterman, Michael, and Charlotte Gray. *Sisters in Two Worlds: A Visual Biography of Susanna Moodie and Catharine Parr Traill.* New York: Doubleday, 2007.

VanCamp, Doreen. *Cartwright Revisited, 1983.* Port Perry, ON: Scugog Township Council, 1983

Miscellaneous:

"The Bogwood Story." *Celtic Roots Studio.* URL: http://store.celtic-roots.com/handraftstory.html. Accessed 15 June 2010.

The Canadian Almanac and Directory 1856-1867, pp.262, 295, URL:http://ia800307.us.archive.org/33/items/canada18565700unknuoft/canada18565700unknuoft.pdft. Accessed 28 February 2000.

Cust, Lionel Henry. "Stephen Catterson Smith." In *Dictionary of National Biography, 1885-1900,* vol. 53, ed. Leslie Stephen. London: Smith, Elder & Co., 1882. Pp. 118-19.

Durnford, Megan and Joyce Glasner. *Christmas in Canada: Heartwarming Legends, Tales and Traditions.* [Canmore, Alberta]: Altitude Publishing, 2004.

Girouard, Mark. *The Victorian Country House.* New Haven: Yale University Press, 1985.

Hale, Mrs. Sarah J. and L.A. Godey, eds. *Godey's Lady's Book,* vol. 74, no. 444, June 1867.

The Osler Library. "Tour of Osler's Montreal 1870-1885." URL: http://osler.library.mcgill.ca/exhibits/tour/tour.html. Accessed 1 January 2002.

The Victoria & Albert archives. "Oppitz Jewellers, About 1840, Museum number AAD/1984/2/1 Pendant designs for necklaces." URL: http://www.vam.ac.uk/images/image/19947-popup. html. Accessed 28 February 2000.